PUZZLE PIECES

OTHER COVENANT BOOKS AND AUDIO BOOKS BY
BETSY BRANNON GREEN:

KENNEDY KILLINGSWORTH MYSTERIES

Murder by the Book

Murder by Design

Murder by the Way

HAGGERTY MYSTERIES

Hearts in Hiding

Until Proven Guilty

Above Suspicion

Silenced

Copycat

Poison

Double Cross

Backtrack

HAZARDOUS DUTY

Hazardous Duty

Above and Beyond

Code of Honor

Proceed with Caution

Danger Ahead

OTHER NOVELS

Never Look Back

Don't Cross Your Eyes

Foul Play

PUZZLE PIECES

BETSY BRANNON GREEN

Covenant Communications, Inc.

Cover image *Hand Holding Puzzle Card* © Hong Li, iStockphotography.com

Published by Covenant Communications, Inc.
American Fork, Utah

Printed in the United States of America
First Printing: October 2015

20 19 18 17 16 15 10 9 8 7 6 5 4 3 2 1

ISBN 978-1-68047-865-5

To my grandson Banx Robert Green—
who has a pure heart, a gentle spirit, and strong faith.
He is destined to be a force for good on the earth!

ACKNOWLEDGMENTS

It's hard to believe that this is my twentieth LDS fiction novel! Time really does fly when you're having fun! Thanks first and foremost to my husband, Butch, who is still and forever will be my romantic interest. I am also grateful for my children—who are so close to perfect that I almost never have to worry about them—and for my grandchildren, who are completely perfect. A special thanks to my sister, Dr. Julie B. Brown, for her information regarding simulation mannequins. Thanks also to my editor, Stacey Owen, and the other great people at Covenant Communications who help to make my books the best they can be. And finally a huge thank you to all my readers who encourage and inspire me through each new adventure!

PROLOGUE

Presley DeGraff was curled on her side in the hospital bed, staring at the slightly blurred urban landscape through the safety glass, when Dr. Khan came in. Based on the circles of fatigue around his eyes and the wrinkled condition of his lab coat, Presley guessed that he had been on duty for too long, as usual. Dr. Khan took human suffering personally and refused to accept that he couldn't relieve it all.

"You need rest," she whispered as he approached her.

"I'll rest when I'm dead. Until then, I'll work." He adjusted the gauze bandage that covered her face. Then, lowering his voice, he added, "All is ready. Moon will come for you soon."

She nodded slightly. "I'll be watching for him. Thank you for everything."

Dr. Khan gave her a weary smile. "Good luck, Miss DeGraff." Then he turned and left the room.

Presley was surprised by the sadness she felt as she watched him go. For months her mind had been consumed with plans to leave Dr. Khan and the hospital. But he had been good to her, and she would miss him. Assuming she was able to escape. There was still much that could go wrong.

A few minutes later, the bell rang for shift change. Presley rolled onto her back and pulled the sheet up to her chin. Keeping her eyes closed, she waited for Moon. He wouldn't come until the confusion caused by the transfer of responsibilities had reached its peak. They needed the distraction in order for their plan to work, so the delay was necessary—but it was also excruciating.

Finally the door swung open, and Moon's large, round face loomed above her. "Here we go," he whispered.

He unhooked the various monitors and wheeled her hospital bed into the hallway. Presley concentrated on staying relaxed and keeping her eyes from reacting to the brighter light.

"Where are you going with Miss DeGraff?" a woman demanded.

Presley recognized the voice of the dayshift charge nurse, Ms. Renata, and wondered if their escape plan was over before it really began.

"Dr. Khan is having her moved to the student section," Moon replied. His tone was the perfect mixture of professional and indifferent. "He's gonna be responsible for her care from now on."

"He's always been *responsible*." Presley heard a shuffle of papers as Ms. Renata checked Dr. Khan's written orders. "But how can we monitor her vitals if she's in the student section?"

"The kids will monitor her vitals, but an alarm will go off here if they drop below normal levels," Moon said. "Dr. Khan will administer meds. The students will do all the routine stuff—changing sheets and feeding tubes and diapers."

This reminder that the transfer would mean less work for her nursing staff seemed to sell Ms. Renata on the idea. "It's most unusual, but as you pointed out, Dr. Khan is responsible."

"He said since the patient's got to be sedated all the time now, she'll be like a live simulation mannequin for the students to practice on," Moon explained further.

"Is that legal?" Ms. Renata asked.

Presley resisted the urge to cringe. Ms. Renata had already accepted the transfer and was well on her way to forgetting that Presley even existed. Moon needed to stop talking and push the bed.

But he persisted. "Dr. Khan's going to waive Miss DeGraff's hospital charges, so her lawyer agreed."

"I'm sure he did," the nurse murmured with obvious disapproval. Then Presley felt a hand rest gently on her shoulder. "It's such a shame. Miss DeGraff seemed to be making good progress. And now look at her."

"Yeah, it's a real shame," Moon agreed.

Presley felt a slight pressure on her midsection as Ms. Renata placed the medical chart there. "Okay, well, since that's what the doctor has approved, take her on."

And they were rolling again. Presley marked their progress by the various smells along the way. Just past the elevators, they turned sharply to the left, and the light filtering through her closed eyelids dimmed. Moon pulled the bed to a sudden stop and whispered, "We're here, and we've gotta hurry."

Presley threw back the sheet and slid to the ground beside the door to a storage room. Moon was facing away from her, eating a candy bar so that it looked like he was taking an unauthorized break. Actually he was using his considerable bulk to shield her from the security camera and any hospital personnel who might pass by while she opened the storage room door and slipped inside.

She walked straight to the back of the room, where a female simulation mannequin was stretched out on a cot against the wall. Presley removed a roll of gauze from her pocket and wound it neatly around the mannequin's head and face. Once she was satisfied that she had replicated the bandage on her own head, she grabbed the fake woman by the artificial arms and hauled it through the door.

The mannequin weighed almost eighty pounds, and Presley was sweating by the time she had it settled on the hospital bed. She covered it up to the chin with the sheet and smoothed the plastic blonde hair below the gauze. It was like looking at herself—small, hurt, helpless.

She heard the candy wrapper crinkle, and Moon asked, "Is she ready to go?"

"Yes." Presley stepped back into the storage room and closed the door. Pressing her ear against cool wood, she listened as her bed rolled down the hall. Then she climbed on to the cot against the wall and pulled the mannequin's sheet up until it touched her nose. It smelled damp and dank like the storage room. She took a deep, savoring breath. To her it was the smell of freedom.

* * *

It was nearly an hour before Moon returned, but when he stepped into the storage room, he was all smiles.

"The mannequin is in place?" she asked.

His grin broadened. "It looks so real it's freaky. She's breathing and has a heart rate and blood pressure and everything—just like a real patient. Your name is on the door to her room, and he's put up a sign up saying there's danger of MRSA exposure. He figures that will keep any curiosity seekers away."

Presley nodded. "That should do it."

"He's told the students that their final grade depends on how long they can keep anyone from guessing that their patient is a simulation mannequin instead of a real person. So they are taking it very seriously."

Presley felt a wave of tenderness toward Dr. Khan. He was doing his best for her. "Realistically, though, how long do I have before someone figures it out?"

He shrugged. "It could be a few hours, or it could be months. Plan for the worst, and hope for the best."

It had been a long time since she'd felt hopeful about anything, so planning for the worst was easy.

"But don't worry about that now," Moon advised. "Worry about getting out of the hospital first."

She stretched back out on the cot and pulled the sheet up so it covered her face. Then she concentrated on keeping her breathing shallow as Moon wheeled the cot into the hall. One of Moon's fellow orderlies rode down the elevator with them.

"You got a dead one?" he asked.

"Naw," Moon replied. "This is Simu-Lady, a mannequin they use to train nurses. The hospital bought a new one so this old girl is being donated to a poor teaching hospital."

The other orderly whooped in laughter. "There's a teaching hospital poorer than *ours*?"

Moon chuckled, playing along. "I guess there is."

The elevator door opened, and the men exchanged good-byes. Then Moon pushed her down a long hall. When the bed finally came to a stop, Presley pulled the sheet down a little and opened her eyes.

Moon pointed to the door of a family restroom. "There's a Walmart sack in the bottom of the garbage can. Lift out the plastic liner, and you'll see it. I got you a change of clothes and some shoes. There's a little cash and your driver's license too, but I wouldn't show it to anyone unless you have to."

Presley nodded. Moon thought it was dangerous to use her real name and had offered to provide her with a fake license, but there were risks associated with using a false name too, so she had decided to ignore his advice.

"Put the hospital gown in the garbage can. I'll come back and get it later. When you're ready to go, use the side exit." He pointed to a sign down the hallway. "There's a bus stop at the corner."

"Thank you, Moon."

He waved her gratitude aside. "Just hurry. I'll meet you outside the Flying J at the Jeffersonville exit with the rest of the stuff."

"I'll be there as soon as I can."

He looked anxious. "Or we could just skip the bus, and I'll drive you wherever you're going."

Presley shook her head. "No one can see us together. You go on. I'll be fine."

After giving her one last doubtful look, he stood tall to shield her while she climbed off the cot and hurried into the bathroom. Once the door was closed, she heard the bed rattle off down the hall.

There was no time to waste; Presley removed the Walmart sack from the garbage can and yanked off her hospital gown. Then she unwound the gauze from her head. The incisions had been healed for weeks, but Dr. Khan had kept the bandages in place to facilitate her escape plan. Turning to the mirror, she looked at her new face for the first time. The transformation was so shocking that she gasped and pressed her fingers along her jawline to be sure it was real.

Still shaken but conscious of the danger posed by each moment of delay, she slipped on the stiff blue jeans and the oversized T-shirt Moon had left her. There was a baseball hat that she put on her head, and she carefully tucked her pale blonde hair under it. Socks and a pair of tennis shoes completed her ensemble. Once she was dressed in normal clothes for the first time in months, she studied herself critically.

She was average height—and average was good when you didn't want to be noticed. Her weight was a little below average, through strict avoidance of carbohydrates. Hopefully the oversized shirt would hide that fact. Her pale blue eyes were unique and hard to disguise. In fact, her entire face worked against her like a traitor. The plastic surgeon had it called his "masterpiece." But right now she would much prefer to be plain—since plain, like average, was unmemorable.

Turning away from the mirror, she reached back into the Walmart sack and removed her driver's license and two twenty-dollar bills. She put both into the pocket of her new jeans and tossed the hospital gown in the garbage can as Moon had instructed. Then she cracked open the restroom door and peeked out into the hall. The coast appeared to be clear, so she slipped out of the restroom and walked to the side exit.

When she reached the door, she put her hands on the push-bar and pressed against it. The door swung open and no alarms sounded. Presley took a deep breath of fresh air and stepped out into the beautiful spring evening. As she walked to the bus stop, she tried not to worry that her future was now in the hands of an exhausted and overworked doctor, an orderly with a criminal record, and a handful of nursing students.

CHAPTER ONE

EUGENIA ATKINS ADJUSTED THE TEMPERATURE on the stove, where she had eggs boiling in a large pot. The Iverson children were coming over the next morning to dye them for Easter, and she wanted to make sure there were no cracks in the shells.

Her sister, Annabelle, was watching this process from Eugenia's kitchen table. "Nobody dyes real eggs anymore," she said. "Why can't you just buy some cute plastic ones like everyone else?"

Eugenia waved the steam away from the top of the pot. "I have wonderful memories of dying eggs as a child, and I want Emily and Charles to experience the same. Besides, if you buy plastic eggs, you don't have an excuse to make deviled eggs on Easter afternoon."

Annabelle wrinkled her nose. "I could never make myself eat deviled Easter eggs because some of the dye always seeped through and stained the whites."

Eugenia shook her head. "You always were too finicky. Mother's deviled eggs were one of the best things about Easter. That and chocolate bunnies."

"You make pretty good deviled eggs too," Annabelle bestowed a rare compliment. "Not quite as good as Mother's, but close."

This remark pleased Eugenia, and she considered holding back some eggs from the dyeing process so she could make Annabelle a few color-free deviled eggs. Then she remembered how annoying her sister was and discarded this idea.

She was startled from these thoughts by a knock on the back door. Eugenia's little dog, Lady, sat up and barked in surprise.

"You expecting anyone?" Annabelle asked. "Besides me?"

"I wasn't expecting you, and I'm certainly not expecting anyone else." Eugenia glanced at the clock. It was almost nine. That was too late to drop in and stay within the bounds of Southern etiquette, which meant her visitor was either mannerless or the bearer of bad news. Her eyes met Annabelle's, and they shared a moment of silent dread.

There was another knock, more insistent this time.

"You're just delaying the inevitable," Annabelle said.

With a nod of resignation, Eugenia dried her hands on the threadbare apron that had belonged to her mother. "I hope nobody died. I'm not dressed for the funeral home." She walked reluctantly toward the door with Lady at her heels. Taking a deep breath, she pulled open the door to find Winston Jones and George Ann Simmons on her back porch. Eugenia blinked twice to be sure she wasn't hallucinating. But both times when she opened her eyes, the pair was still there.

"Hey, Miss Eugenia," Winston said.

George Ann just stood there silently.

"What a surprise to see the two of you here . . . together . . . at this hour."

Winston was Haggerty's police chief, not brilliant but kind at heart. George Ann was an elderly snob with no heart who thought she was better than everyone else. Their joint appearance made no sense.

"We're here on official business," Winston informed her.

That sounded fishy. "Official business at this time of night?"

"May we come inside, please?" He gave Eugenia a pleading look, so she stepped aside—not exactly welcoming them in but allowing them to pass.

Winston led George Ann into the kitchen and waited while Eugenia and Annabelle cleared off chairs so they could sit. Winston seemed distracted. George Ann seemed lost.

Once they were all seated, Eugenia addressed the police chief. "What's going on here?"

He cleared his throat. "Well, Miss George Ann was at the Piggly Wiggly tonight," he began. Then he paused.

"And," Annabelle prompted.

"She started opening cartons of large eggs and removing ones she thought were too small to qualify as *large*." Winston sighed.

Eugenia glanced at George Ann, who was staring at the dark window. Then she looked back at Winston. "Why?"

George Ann took an interest in the conversation for the first time. "I felt certain that the manager, that unpleasant young man . . ." She turned to Winston. "What is his name?"

"Brewster. Brewster Hoage."

George Ann nodded. "Yes, well, I was standing in the dairy section at the Piggly Wiggly, and all of a sudden I was quite sure that Mr. Hoage had switched medium eggs into large-egg cartons so he could sell them for more money."

"I wouldn't put that past Brewster," Eugenia murmured.

"That's certainly possible," Annabelle agreed.

Winston cleared his throat again. "It doesn't matter whether Brewster switched the eggs or not. What matters is that Miss George Ann was taking the eggs out of the large cartons and piling them in the dairy section of the Piggly Wiggly. She had more than a hundred eggs on the floor—and most of them broken—before the produce manager stopped her. It was a huge mess, and Brewster was furious."

"I was sure the eggs were in the wrong cartons," George Ann defended.

Eugenia was starting to be alarmed. "But why did you think you should fix it?"

George Ann shook her head in obvious confusion. "I don't know. It seemed very important at the time—vital even. Did I ever work at the Piggy Wiggly?"

Eugenia and Annabelle shared a look of panic with Winston. George Ann considered it beneath her to *walk into* a grocery store. The idea of her actually *working* at the Piggly Wiggly, or anywhere, was laughable. But no one laughed. George Ann was completely sincere. She really didn't know.

"Uh, no," Eugenia said as calmly as she could. "You never worked at the Piggly Wiggly."

George Ann shrugged. "Then I don't know why I did it. I'm sorry, and I'll pay for the eggs that got broken." The confused look was replaced by fear. "If I have any money." She reached across the table to clasp one of Eugenia's hands in hers. "Do I?"

Eugenia nodded slowly. George Ann was a millionaire several times over. "I'm sure you have enough money to cover the eggs."

Now Annabelle looked like she was about to cry.

Winston leaned his elbows on the table and lowered his voice. "Brewster wanted to press charges."

"Against George Ann!" Eugenia whispered back in dismay. "The very idea! He knows she'll pay for the damage."

"Apparently there have been other incidents recently," Winston replied with a quick glance at George Ann. "He says he's caught her shoplifting several times."

Eugenia waved this aside. "She just forgot to pay."

Winston rubbed the back of his neck. "Yeah, well, the only way I talked him out of an outright arrest was to promise I'd take her away and make sure she never sets foot in there again."

Eugenia frowned. "And how do you plan to make sure of that?"

Winston shrugged. "I'm not worried about Brewster. I can handle him. But I am worried about her." He gestured toward George Ann. "Something's wrong. I thought about taking her to the emergency room, but she's not in pain or a danger to herself. She's just confused, and I was afraid all the commotion at the hospital would make her worse."

"But why did you bring her *here*?"

"I thought she could stay with you," he said. "Just for the night, until we can get her to the doctor tomorrow."

Eugenia was not pleased at the prospect of babysitting George Ann, but Winston was right. The emergency room was not the place for her, and she certainly couldn't stay alone in this confused state. "Okay, but just until she can see her doctor in the morning."

"Thank you!" Winston looked immensely relieved. He stood and hurried toward the back door, as if he were afraid she might change her mind.

"I'll call the police station as soon as I can set up an appointment for George Ann," Eugenia reiterated.

"Yes, ma'am." He put his hat on and stepped outside.

As Eugenia closed the door behind him, she heard thunder in the distance. Lady looked up at the sky and whimpered. Eugenia sighed. "Yes, girl, it looks like there's a storm coming our way."

CHAPTER TWO

It was three hours and several transfers later when Presley stepped off the bus at her final destination—an industrial section of Columbus, Ohio. She was careful to keep her eyes down and the brim of her baseball cap pulled low as she turned onto the dark, deserted street. It had been more than a year since she'd visited the area, but it still looked familiar and almost dear—despite the dead leaves mixed with litter that blew around her feet and the garish graffiti sprayed on the weathered brick walls.

The air was cold, and the heavy clouds above her spit snow in spurts. Anxious to be gone before conditions deteriorated further, Presley increased her pace. Finally she reached the storage facility—several long rows of units surrounded by a ten-foot chain-link fence. Tears stung her eyes, and her hands trembled as she put in the code at the gate.

Once she was inside the enclosure, the sound of her shoes striking the concrete echoed through the empty space, bouncing off the cinderblock walls and metal, garage-style doors. At the fourth row, she turned into the gaping darkness. Her mouth was dry; her neck ached with stress. Finally she reached number 417.

Presley entered another combination on the lock's keypad. As she waited for the lock to respond, she was startled by a noise from across the large lot. It sounded like someone had dropped a heavy, metal object, maybe a crowbar. Her hands started to tremble again. But she had come so far, too far, to give up now.

She looked back at the keypad and saw a green light flashing in approval. She grasped the door handle and jerked upward. The mechanism squealed in resistance, but slowly, the door rose. She turned on her flashlight and stepped inside, closing the door behind her.

The unit contained only one item. Centered in the middle, facing the door, and covered with a dusty canvas tarp was her father's Aston Martin coupe. Purchased just a year before his death, it was, in her mother's opinion, a futile effort to stay the hands of time. According to her father, it was the fulfillment of a well-deserved dream. He had rented this storage unit, conveniently located halfway between the mechanic's shop and his office, as a temporary holding spot. Whenever the Aston needed maintenance, he dropped it off here. The mechanic picked it up and put it back when he was finished. The car had been trapped in this limbo for almost a year. Like the loss of her parents, the car was something she hadn't been able to face. But she was more than facing the car now. She was going to drive out of this storage room, away from Ohio, and into a new life.

Presley pulled off the canvas and coughed as dust billowed in the small space. She heard an engine start somewhere nearby followed by the sound of people talking. Boxes scraped against the concrete floor of a neighboring unit. She had chosen to retrieve the Aston in the middle of the night, thinking she would be the only customer at the storage facility. The fact that she wasn't alone was a little unnerving.

With an effort she controlled her anxiety. No one knew she was there. She wasn't in any danger. But she decided to quicken her pace as a precaution.

Presley located the spare key hidden in the magnetic box by the license plate. She pushed the unlock button, and the interior lights gave an anemic flash, indicating that the battery was weak after a year of inactivity. She removed a portable battery charger from her father's emergency kit in the trunk and hooked it up. Then she opened the driver's door and slipped behind the wheel.

There wasn't time to think about her father or how much he had loved this car. Sentimentality was a luxury she couldn't afford. She had to work quickly if the new life she'd planned was to become a reality.

Once the key was in the ignition, she turned it, and the engine roared to life. A wave of relief washed over her. But she couldn't celebrate yet. Presley opened the glove compartment and removed the .38 caliber pistol her father kept there. She didn't like guns, but he'd made sure she knew how to use one. After checking that it was loaded, she reset the safety, put the gun in her pocket, and climbed out of the car. She unhooked the battery charger before closing the Aston's sleek hood. She reopened the door to the storage unit, causing a jarring metallic rattle. Then she got back in the car and drove out into the space that separated the rows of storage buildings.

Presley didn't want to waste time closing the door of unit 417 but knew she had to do it. An open door would draw attention—which she couldn't afford. So she left the car and hurried back to the storage unit. As she replaced the combination lock, she sensed a presence. Someone had stepped between her and the starlit sky, casting a vague shadow. In her peripheral vision, she saw a large man standing a few yards away. And right between them was the Aston, the engine purring.

"Nice car." His voice was soft and forced, like a stage whisper.

She knew that the flashy sports car might be targeted by thieves, but she hadn't expected it to be a problem so soon. She also knew she should be glad if all the man wanted was the Aston. But without transportation she had no way to carry out her desperate escape plan. She could accept defeat, but she'd found that accepting defeat was easy; *living* with defeat was not. So instead she put her hand into the pocket of her jeans and pulled out the gun. Then she turned around to face the threat.

She had hoped that when the man saw the gun he'd step back. All she needed was a couple of feet so she could jump into the car before he had a chance to intercept her. But instead of backing up, he moved forward.

"Now why you wanna go and pull a gun on me, Calamity Jane?" Moonlight glinted off the shaved head of Roger "Moon" Smith. The pale skin that had earned him his nickname fairly glowed in the dimness.

"Moon?" She felt weak with relief. "What are you doing here?"

"Been following you," he admitted without remorse.

Her relief evaporated. Moon was a career criminal. So although she had helped his lawyer get an acquittal, the one—and probably only—time he had been falsely accused of a crime, Presley knew she couldn't trust him. Especially not out here in the dark. Not when he'd just admitted to following her. And not when possession of a very expensive car hung in the balance. Her fingers tightened around the gun. "You were supposed to meet me at the Jeffersonville exit."

"You should have had that gun in your hand *before* you got out of the car," he said.

She acknowledged her foolishness with a little shrug. "It was a rookie mistake."

He gave her a crooked-toothed grin. "Now you can put it away. You wouldn't shoot me."

He was wrong. She didn't want to shoot him, but she would if she had to. "Step away from the car, Moon. I've got to go."

He didn't move. "But I've got all kinds of stuff to give you."

"You can give it to me at the Flying J like we planned."

"You don't trust me?" His tone was aggrieved.

"I don't trust anyone."

"Good girl. That's the way to stay safe." He moved back several paces.

"Why did you follow me?" she asked, keeping the gun pointed at his chest.

"This is a dangerous part of town. I couldn't let you come here alone."

Presley was offended. "I could have handled it. I have a gun."

Moon laughed derisively. "Yeah, if I wanted to, I'd have you, the fancy car, and your gun. So put it away. You're as likely to shoot yourself as me."

Presley couldn't dispute this possibility, so she decided to trust him. She put the gun back in her pocket. "I really need to get out of here."

"First I gotta put some new license plates on your car."

"How did you know I was picking up a car?"

"Dr. Khan told me." Moon pulled a little tool from his shirt pocket. "I'll just use my lock-pick."

Presley rolled her eyes. "You might want to throw that lock-pick away, Moon. I'm leaving town, so if you get in trouble with the law again, I won't be here to help you."

He grinned. "Lock-picking ain't my specialty anyway."

She hated to imagine what he considered his specialty to be, so she didn't respond.

He continued, "A friend of mine hooked us up with these plates. If anybody checks they'll find an Aston Martin registered to Dr. Khan. That way nobody can trace the car back to you or your father."

Presley had to admit it was wise and probably necessary, but she hated for Dr. Khan to become more involved in her problems.

Moon finished with the license plates and pulled an envelope from inside his jacket. "Here's some other stuff you'll need. There's more money and a letter saying you have permission to drive the doctor's car. I got you a disposable phone so I can warn you if trouble's on the way. My number's already programmed in. Feel free to call me if you need something."

She stared at the envelope for a few seconds, feeling unpleasantly obligated to both Moon and Dr. Khan. Finally she reached for it. "There is no way I can ever adequately thank either of you."

"Hey, I owe you," Moon claimed. "You believed in me when nobody else did."

Researching his case had been mostly a way to escape boredom, so she didn't deserve his loyalty. But she needed it, so she nodded. "I've got to go."

Moon walked along beside her and watched as she slid in under the wheel of the Aston.

"So you're just going to run away from the past." It wasn't a question.

Presley nodded. "If I stay here, I'll still be *in* the past."

"Dr. Khan says we can fight it . . ." he tried.

"I can't put Dr. Khan or the hospital at risk. I will fight it—from a distance. If I can straighten things out, maybe I'll come back."

Presley was never coming back to Columbus, and Moon must have known that, but he didn't contradict her.

"Don't follow me," she added. "I'm on my own from this point forward."

Moon feigned indignation. "You think I ain't got better things to do than follow you around?"

Presley was familiar with this evasive tactic. She used it often herself. "Moon."

"I won't follow you," he muttered.

"Thank you again, for everything," she told him, "but this is good-bye."

Moon smiled and gave her a little salute. "Off you go into the wild blue yonder!"

She shook her head as she closed the door and put the car in gear. Moments later she was driving down the dark streets of Columbus, leaving the storage facility and Moon and the past behind her.

CHAPTER THREE

WHEN EUGENIA WOKE UP ON Tuesday morning, she was in a good mood. The Iverson children were coming over to dye Easter eggs. Then she had a meeting of the Haggerty Civic Club, where they would plan the town's annual Fourth of July parade. After that, she and Annabelle would go out to lunch at Haggerty Station. Then they would ride to Cecelia's Salon, where Annabelle would get her hair cut and Eugenia would work a jigsaw puzzle with her old friend Violet Newberry. It would be a full day but a pleasant one.

Then she remembered that George Ann Simmons was in her guest room. Instantly her optimistic mood was replaced by gloom. Now her whole day would have to be rearranged—and spent with George Ann.

Without enthusiasm, she climbed out of bed. Once she was dressed, Eugenia looked in the guestroom and found George Ann still sleeping soundly. She closed the door and went downstairs with Lady right behind her.

Lady's outside break was abbreviated because of a steady rain. When they came back in, Eugenia measured out some of the expensive dog food recommended by the vet and poured it into Lady's dish. Then while Lady ate, she called George Ann's doctor in Albany.

She explained the situation to a sympathetic nurse who worked in an appointment for George Ann at 11:00. That meant Eugenia would miss the patriotic parade meeting, but she could keep the rest of her day intact.

Next Eugenia made breakfast—scrambled eggs, grits, bacon, and canned biscuits. Then she went upstairs to wake her guest.

George Ann was the same as she'd been the night before, confused but docile. Eugenia showed her guest to the bathroom and handed her the clothes she'd worn the previous day. "Put these back on," Eugenia instructed. "Then come downstairs for breakfast."

George Ann nodded, but Eugenia wasn't confident the woman knew what to do. After the bathroom door was closed, she leaned down and addressed the little dog. "When Miss George Ann is dressed, you make sure she comes to the kitchen."

The little dog barked in apparent understanding and took up sentry duty beside the bathroom door. Eugenia hurried back to the kitchen to check on her biscuits. She had time to clear off the table and set two plates before George Ann came wandering in, followed closely by Lady.

Eugenia gave the little dog a pat. "Good job."

George Ann looked around the room like she'd never seen it before. Her blouse was misbuttoned and her hair mussed.

Eugenia felt a lump form in her throat. There was no dignity in growing old. "Have a seat. I've made breakfast."

George Ann sat in the nearest chair and picked up a fork. She ate a couple of bites before saying, "My mind feels clearer today than yesterday."

"That's good," Eugenia said.

"I know that I live in Haggerty," George Ann continued. "But all the details are fuzzy." She glanced at the window. "I don't think I could find my way home, but I know it's green with black shutters."

"Your house *is* green with black shutters, and I know exactly how to get there. We'll go in a little while so you can change clothes before your doctor's appointment at eleven." Eugenia hoped her positive tone inspired confidence.

George Ann nodded vaguely. Then she asked, "What's your dog's name?"

"Lady."

"She's cute," George Ann said.

Lady cocked her head to the side in confusion.

"You don't like dogs," Eugenia said softly. "Especially not Lady."

"Why not?"

"I don't know," Eugenia replied. "Maybe you'll remember when the doctor gives you some medicine to help your memory."

Another nod from George Ann.

"Of course, if you get your memory back, you won't like Lady anymore," Eugenia tried to keep her tone light. "So maybe we should skip the medicine."

George Ann frowned. "You don't want me to take the medicine for my memory?"

"It was a joke," Eugenia said, regretting her attempt at humor.

"Oh." George Ann returned her attention to the food on her plate.

There was a knock on the door, followed almost immediately by the sound of running feet. "Miss Eugenia!" Emily Iverson called out. "I'm here!"

"Me too!" her brother Charles added. "Here I am!"

Eugenia smiled and turned to greet them with enthusiastic hugs. Emily's long blonde hair was damp from the rain. Charles's dark brown hair was plastered to his forehead.

"I'm sure your mother told you to come straight over here," Eugenia said sternly. "But it looks like you dawdled."

"What does that mean?" Charles asked.

"It means you stopped to play in the rain."

Emily hung her head. "We did."

Charles grinned. "We jumped in a puddle too!" He held up a sodden shoe as evidence.

Trying not to smile, Eugenia got a couple of towels and helped them dry off. As she put their wet shoes in the dryer, she thought about how much the children meant to her. When her husband died, Eugenia thought her life was over. Then Kate and Mark moved in next door, and life had meaning once again.

"Mom said thank you for letting us dye Easter eggs with you like you did in the olden days," Emily said as she pulled a chair up to the counter, where four dozen hard-boiled eggs were waiting for them.

"And Daddy says he's glad it's your house that will be stinky with egg smells instead of ours," Charles added honestly.

Eugenia helped Charles into his chair. "You can tell them both they are welcome."

Emily noticed George Ann, who was mechanically spooning grits into her mouth. "Oh, hey, Miss George Ann!" she greeted.

The older woman looked up blankly. "Hello." Then she turned to Eugenia. "Do I know them?"

"Yes, but as far as you're concerned, children are in the same category as dogs. You don't like them either, so you probably wouldn't remember their names even if you weren't having trouble with your memory," Eugenia murmured. She waited until George Ann continued eating and then returned her attention to the children.

They were now staring at George Ann with concern.

"It's okay," she told them. "Miss George Ann just isn't feeling very well. Now, let's get started on these Easter eggs."

The children were easily distracted. They dissolved colored tablets in vinegar water and began dyeing the eggs. Soon they had forgotten all about George Ann's memory problems. When the eggs were decorated to their satisfaction, the children returned home, each wearing dry shoes and carrying two cartons of eggs. Eugenia watched them go with a feeling of complete contentment.

Then she remembered that George Ann was still sitting at the kitchen table.

She walked to her wall-mounted phone—which Annabelle said should be in a museum—and called the Haggerty Police Station. The call was answered by Arnold, the youngest officer on the small force.

"Arnold," Eugenia said in a commanding tone. "I need to speak to Winston."

"He's not here, Miss Eugenia," Arnold replied with a slightly nervous stammer. "Do you have an emergency or something?"

She glanced at George Ann. "You could say that. The chief promised to take Miss George Ann and me into Albany this morning. He knows why. Tell him I don't care if he takes us personally or assigns someone else, but I don't drive in the city, and I have to be there at eleven."

"Yes, ma'am. Someone will be at your house to take you and Miss George Ann to Albany," Arnold promised.

As Eugenia hung up the phone, George Ann looked up expectantly. The fork was still clutched in her hand even though all her food was gone. Eugenia walked over and gently removed the utensil. She placed it on the table and said, "I guess it's time to take you home."

During the drive George Ann was anxious. She looked out the windows and seemed startled by everything. Eugenia wondered if it might be amnesia or dementia or Alzheimer's. At their age anything was possible.

"We went to school together," she told the other woman as they drove by the Haggerty town square, hoping to jog her memory. "First grade all the way through high school."

"I remember that I went to school, but I can't think of any details. I don't have any specific memories."

Eugenia stared at the road in front of her with dismay. Losing her mind was her biggest fear.

They arrived at the house, and after ushering George Ann inside, Eugenia stood by the door and watched as she walked around, touching various items. Eugenia thought it might help the woman remember, so she described the things George Ann picked up.

"Those ribbons are from spelling bees in elementary school," she said. "You were a very good speller. And that's a certificate you received as a sophomore in high school from the Future Homemakers of America. Those are the trophies you won as a soloist in the show choir our senior year." Eugenia didn't mention that George Ann was tone deaf, and the trophies were purchased by her father.

"Why do I have all this stuff displayed in my living room?"

Eugenia was taken aback by the question. "I guess because these things are important to you."

"But they happened so long ago."

"Yes," Eugenia agreed carefully.

"So what do I do now?"

"Well, let's see, you attend meetings. A *lot* of meetings. You belong to several clubs, and you sit on boards and committees. You volunteer at the library. And you talk to lawyers and accountants about all your money and property."

George Ann was still frowning.

"You play bridge!" Eugenia added a little desperately. Making George Ann's life sound fulfilling was beyond difficult.

"That's all?"

Eugenia looked around for a sign of something important. Finally her eyes settled on an old picture of the groundbreaking ceremony for the Haggerty Baptist Church. George Ann's grandfather was shoveling a little mound of dirt. "Your grandfather donated the land the Baptist church is built on!"

"Did *I* do anything to help build the church?"

Eugenia had to shake her head in the negative.

George Ann shrugged and turned away from the picture.

For a few seconds Eugenia found it difficult to breathe. George Ann had always been inordinately proud of the fact that her family had provided the property for the Baptist Church. Now she not only didn't remember, she didn't care in the least.

George Ann touched the piano. "Do I play?"

"No, not really," Eugenia was forced to admit. For years she'd wanted to point out to George Ann just how meaningless and self-centered her life was. But now that the other woman was coming to this conclusion herself, Eugenia found no satisfaction in it. Then she thought of one good thing about George Ann. "You make a delicious key lime pie!"

This perked her up a little. "I do?"

"The best I've ever tasted! You're basically famous for them."

George Ann gave her a tentative smile. "I'd like to try and make one. Will you help me?"

"Maybe after your doctor's appointment." Eugenia was confident that George Ann would forget by the time they got back. "Now you'd better change your clothes."

George Ann stood in the middle of the room, and finally Eugenia realized she needed help finding her bedroom. She led the way down the hall to the room George Ann had inhabited since childhood.

It was pretty, if a little dated, and overly full of antique furniture. There was more self-important memorabilia scattered around the bedroom, but George Ann didn't seem to notice. She allowed Eugenia to help her change as if she were eight instead of eighty-three.

When they arrived back at Eugenia's house, Kate Iverson and Polly Kirby were waiting on the back steps. Polly was a year younger than Eugenia and George Ann, overweight, with curly hair and florid cheeks. She was wearing her signature floral-print dress with a lace hankie tucked in the neckline. She removed the latter to dab droplets of rain that had collected on her forehead during the short walk to Eugenia's house.

"Emily said George Ann spent the night with you!" Polly cried out. "Why did you invite George Ann and not me?"

"It wasn't a slumber party," Eugenia muttered with flagging patience. "George Ann isn't feeling well, so Winston brought her over because he didn't think she should be alone." Eugenia widened her eyes, trying to convey the need for tact.

The subtlety was lost on Polly. "What's wrong with her? She looks fine to me!"

Eugenia glanced at George Ann before responding. "It's her memory." She gave Polly another wide-eyed look. "Now why don't we go inside out of the rain?"

Eugenia stepped back and allowed both Polly and George Ann to precede her into the kitchen. Then she spoke quietly to Kate. "She forgot that she makes the best key lime pies in Haggerty and that her grandfather donated the land for the Baptist Church."

"Oh no," Kate whispered.

"She was taking eggs out of the cartons at the Piggly Wiggly. That's why Winston brought her here. Brewster Hoage was threatening to have her arrested."

Kate looked horrified.

"She asked me if she used to work there—and then she didn't know if she had enough money to pay for the eggs she broke."

Kate shook her head. "What are you going to do?"

"I'm taking her to the doctor this morning. Maybe it's something simple like dehydration."

"I hope so," Kate replied, but she didn't sound optimistic.

Polly stuck her head out of the kitchen door. "George Ann just asked me my name. That's more than a little trouble with her memory! I think it's serious. Is she going to have to move to the retirement home?"

"I declare, Polly, keep your voice down!" Eugenia commanded. "And for heaven's sake, don't mention the retirement home again!" It was a worse fate than the cemetery as far as Eugenia was concerned.

Polly dabbed her eyes with her damp hankie. "I'm sorry. It's just such a shock. George Ann has gone down so fast. I saw her just a few days ago, and she was fine. Well, I mean she was crabby and critical, but at least she knew my name!"

"And hopefully she'll be back to her crabby self soon," Eugenia said. "Now go sit down at the table." She turned back to Kate. "Would you like to come in for some lemonade?"

Kate shook her head. "No, thank you. I'd better get back to my kids. Because of the rain, they're hiding your real Easter eggs inside the house. I'm trying to keep track of each hiding spot because if one gets hidden *too* well, we may have to move. Mark can't deal with the smell of boiled eggs; I know he won't be able to handle rotten ones."

Eugenia watched Kate hurry off, wishing she could go with her. Then with a sigh, she walked into her kitchen, where George Ann and Polly were settled in uneasy silence around the table.

"Can I get you all some lemonade?" she offered.

"No iced tea?" Polly asked with a suspicious look at George Ann, who was sitting quietly, staring at her hands.

"No," Eugenia tried to sound apologetic. "I'm not sure I could make a decent pitcher of tea anymore."

Polly pursed her lips. "You're spending so much time with Kate you're starting to act like a Mormon."

"There are a lot of people who don't drink tea, not just Mormons." Eugenia prayed for patience.

Polly sighed. "I don't really care for lemonade, but if you can't remember how to make tea, I guess I'll have some."

"How about you, George Ann?" Eugenia asked. "Would you like some lemonade?"

"No, thank you," George Ann declined.

Polly tucked her handkerchief back under the neckline of her dress. Then she put her nose in the air and sniffed. "Did you make deviled eggs?"

Eugenia put a glass of lemonade in front of Polly. "No. I did boil some eggs. Then Emily and Charles dyed them and took them all home."

Polly frowned. "Well, that's a shame. You can devil an egg almost as well as your mother, and she was a master."

Eugenia was unaccountably pleased by this remark—her second deviled-egg compliment in as many days. And she determined that once she got George Ann settled she'd make some—as a tribute to her mother.

"Do you have any cookies?" Polly asked. "Or pound cake?"

"I appreciate you stopping by, and I hate to rush you, Polly," Eugenia said untruthfully. "But we don't have time for cake and cookies. Winston will be here soon to take us to George Ann's doctor appointment." She opened the refrigerator and removed a pecan pie. "But you can take this with you."

Polly accepted the pie. "I could go along with you to the doctor. In case you need help." She cut her eyes over to George Ann. Polly was not an unkind person, but she was a consummate busybody. So her offer probably came more from a desire to get the inside scoop than to be of any real assistance. And the less she knew about George Ann's situation, the less it would be discussed all over Haggerty.

"Thanks anyway, but I don't want to get you out in this bad weather," Eugenia said. "Just go on home and enjoy your pie."

The choice between George Ann and pecan pie was really no choice at all. Polly hurried off happily, the pie plate clutched to her ample chest.

Eugenia and George Ann were waiting on the back porch when Winston came to pick them up. He had an umbrella and walked the ladies to the police car one at a time. George Ann was quiet all the way to Albany, and Winston was concerned.

"It's just not like her," he said softly.

"No," Eugenia agreed.

Winston dropped them off at the doctor's office and told Eugenia he had business at the courthouse. She was to call his cell phone when they were ready to be picked up. They had to wait for quite a while in the doctor's waiting room, but George Ann didn't complain a single time—which should have been a good thing, but it wasn't.

Finally they were taken to an exam room, and a few minutes later the doctor rushed in, followed by a frazzled-looking nurse. He did a quick, superficial examination and asked George Ann some questions. Then he turned to Eugenia.

"I think we need to run some tests," he said in the aggressively positive tone that Eugenia associated with bad news. "Let's admit her to the hospital for a day or two. We want to rule things out—like diet and fatigue. Then we can look into other possibilities."

Eugenia nodded, relieved that the doctor was taking control and she wouldn't be responsible for George Ann anymore.

The doctor was still making notes on his chart. "It will be best if she doesn't have visitors while she's there. When people are confused, it can make things worse if they have a lot of people around them."

"I will get that word out."

"You can call my office in the morning to get an update." He looked at George Ann and gave her a bright smile. "My nurse will take you across to the hospital in a wheelchair. I'll see you there in a little while."

Eugenia walked alongside George Ann's wheelchair as she was transferred to the hospital. Then she waited during the admissions process, although her presence seemed totally unnecessary. When they were ready to take George Ann up to her room, Eugenia leaned down and said good-bye.

"You're going to spend the night in the hospital," she explained. "They'll take good care of you, and I'll check on you tomorrow."

George Ann nodded, not upset in the least.

"Be glad she's like this," the nurse whispered. "It's much worse when they're afraid or anxious."

Eugenia found it impossible to be glad about George Ann's condition, but she stepped back while the nurse rolled the patient into the elevator. Then she called Winston and gave him the news.

"I sure hope they can help her," he said.

"I can't believe I'm saying this, but I'd like to have the old, insulting, bragging George Ann back."

"Me too. I'll be there in a few minutes to pick you up."

While Eugenia waited for Winston, she called Annabelle and reported on George Ann. Then she suggested that since she was in Albany, they could eat at Annabelle's house.

"I don't have anything to eat here," Annabelle replied.

"Your husband is a gourmet cook!"

"My gourmet cook husband is out of town—that's why I'm willing to spend the afternoon with you."

Eugenia sighed. "I'll have Winston run me by the Taco Truck for a couple of guacamole salads. I should be there in thirty minutes."

"Good," Annabelle muttered. "That will give me just enough time to find some antacids."

* * *

After Winston dropped her off at Annabelle's, the two women sat at the enormous marble island in the ostentatious kitchen, eating their salads. In between bites Eugenia told her sister that she felt guilty for leaving George Ann at the hospital alone.

"Do you think I should go back up there?"

"No," Annabelle said impatiently. "The doctor told you to leave her. Just do what he says."

"It seems wrong for her to be up there without anyone."

"Why do you care? You can't stand George Ann."

Eugenia considered this. "Partly it's just that I feel a Christian duty. But George Ann isn't nearly as annoying now that she can't remember how to be herself."

They ate in silence for a few minutes, and then Eugenia put down her fork. "To be honest, I'm scared," she admitted. "It could be you or me lying in that hospital, confused and lost."

"We have each other," Annabelle said softly.

Eugenia frowned. "Sometimes I don't like you any better than I do George Ann."

"But we're still sisters, and we'll take care of each other."

"Unless we get senile at the same time."

Annabelle laughed. "That's why we have to stay on good terms with young folks like Kate and Mark."

Eugenia felt a little better. There were a lot of benefits to being nice to the people around you. That way, unlike George Ann, you actually had friends.

"No matter what the doctor said, you need to tell Brother Patrick about George Ann," Annabelle warned. "If she comes to herself and finds out he didn't visit her in the hospital, she'll cut off her contributions to the church."

"George Ann is so stingy the church probably won't even miss her contributions."

"But she can cause trouble for him. And he's new and young and trying to establish himself. So call him."

Eugenia made the call, and Brother Patrick promised to drop in on George Ann whether she remembered him or not.

After she hung up, Annabelle said, "How's that going with Patrick Wentworth as the preacher at Haggerty Baptist?"

"Now how in the world would I know that? I'm a Methodist."

"And you attend church with the Mormons," Annabelle said with a dismissive wave. "But you know everything that happens in Haggerty, and I heard it caused a minor scandal when the church hired him since he doesn't have a wife. I heard they just did it as a courtesy since his great-great-grandparents were some of the first people to live in the area."

"He's related to the Armstrongs—DuPont and Blanche," Eugenia said. "And there was a little fuss at first because he's not married, but now he's the town's most eligible bachelor. All the mothers want their daughters to marry him, poor boy."

Annabelle stood and cleared away the remains of their lunch. Then she checked her watch. "Time to go get my hair done."

"After all the rain we've had?" Eugenia cried in dismay. "It's just going to frizz right up. Why don't you cancel?"

"Because I have a standing appointment, that's why. I can't cancel on Cecelia at the last minute. She has few enough customers as it is."

Eugenia rolls her eyes. “And plenty of money.”

“It’s the principle,” Annabelle claimed. “I’ll drop you off at your house if you don’t want to go with me.”

“I want to go, but drop me off at my house anyway.” Eugenia forced her stiff old bones into a standing position. “I want to have my own transportation so I can leave Violet’s whenever I’m ready.”

CHAPTER FOUR

PRESLEY PEERED THROUGH THE SMALL windshield of the Aston Martin coupe and tried not to worry about the travel grit that now marred the car's previously pristine exterior. She also kept her eyes averted from the odometer. The Aston had been driven more miles that day than it had in the previous two years. And based on the associated devaluation, each mile was a crime.

The trip to Georgia was the longest distance she had ever driven by herself, and she'd been surprised by how easy it had been. She'd taken a circuitous route to confuse anyone who might try to follow her—including well-meaning friends. She knew it would be suspicious if she arrived at her aunt's house empty-handed, so just south of Atlanta, she had stopped at a thrift store, where she purchased some clothes and a couple of old suitcases. At a drug store near Macon, she bought toiletries and a supply of protein powder.

Based on her map, she had now arrived at her destination, but all she'd seen so far was a Dollar General and a fireworks stand. She took a leap of faith and turned between the two establishments. A few yards down the road, she passed a Kwik Mart and a Pizza Palace. It amused her that the latter was situated in a very unpalatial mobile home.

There was a smallish house behind the pizza trailer, with a man in the front yard. He was facing away from her, arranging large plastic Easter Bunnies in a wide semicircle across the overgrown lawn. His head was covered with a battered baseball cap, and a fringe of longish gray hair protruded from underneath. His sleeveless T-shirt hung loosely on his thin frame, and his camouflage cargo pants were baggy as well. She wasn't accustomed to approaching strangers, but he looked harmless. She decided to ask him for directions.

As she pulled the Aston onto the gravel shoulder, the man turned to stare; his eyes squinted against the setting sun. Presley climbed out of the car, started across the yard toward him, and tried not to think about the damage being inflicted on her leather shoes by the long damp grass.

Once she was close enough to converse without yelling, she pushed her drug store sunglasses up onto her head and said, "Hello! Can you help me with some directions?"

"Depends on where you're headed," he replied without dislodging the cigarette clamped in the corner of his mouth.

"Can you tell me if I'm in the town of Haggerty?"

"You're close," he said. The long ash-collection on the end of his cigarette quivered, poised to fall at any moment. "This is Dougherty County but outside the Haggerty city limits." He pointed back toward the Dollar General. "Go out that way and turn right. About a mile down the road, you'll come to a four-way stop. Take a left, and you'll be in downtown Haggerty."

"Thank you! I'm sorry I interrupted your decorating."

"Aw, that's okay." He nudged one of the sun-bleached, mildew-stained giant bunnies with the toe of his shoe. "I don't know why my wife wants to put out these old things anyway. The kids are grown. Heck, even our grandkids are grown! But Miss Kitty wants them put out, so here I am. You know what they say about a happy wife."

Presley had no idea, and apparently her expression conveyed this.

"Happy wife, happy life!" he enlightened her.

She nodded. "Oh, yes, I see."

"I'm Hollis Cleckler."

"It's nice to meet you, Mr. Cleckler. I'm Presley DeGraff."

"Presley," he repeated. "Like Elvis Presley?"

"Exactly like that." She took a step toward her car. "Thanks again for the directions."

He was studying her closely now. "Where you from?"

"Columbus."

"It's real pretty over that way." He shoved his baseball cap up so that the brim was pointing toward the sky. "I got some cousins in Auburn just across the Alabama line. We visit sometimes during football season and drive right through Columbus."

"I'm from Columbus, *Ohio*," she corrected.

He stared at her as if she'd claimed to be from Mars. "Oh, well, I guess that's why you talk so funny."

Since his accent was somewhere between Hee-Haw and the Beverly Hillbillies, she decided this comment didn't deserve a reply. She kept walking and murmured over her shoulder, "Thanks again."

Not discouraged in the least, Mr. Cleckler followed her down the hill and right up to her car. "Whooee!" he exclaimed. "Is this a race car?"

"No, it's an Aston Martin. They're made in England." She was regretting her decision to stop here for directions. If only she'd driven on a little farther, she'd have found Haggerty without assistance. She climbed into her car.

"If you need anything else, just come right back!" Mr. Cleckler invited. "I know how to get almost everywhere around here."

"That's very kind." After she pulled onto the road, she glanced into her rearview mirror and saw him standing on the gravel shoulder, watching her departure.

* * *

She followed Mr. Cleckler's directions, and soon she was in Haggerty. It was lovely, exactly what she'd expected a Southern town to look like. There was a charming town square with rose-covered arbors at each corner. Well-maintained businesses lined each side of the square. She circled around twice, looking for her aunt's law office but finally accepted that it wasn't there. The third time she passed the Haggerty Pharmacy, a man sweeping the sidewalk in front waved her over and asked if she was lost.

She told him she was looking for the law offices of Violet Newberry, and he directed her back out of Haggerty to the Dollar General. When she passed Mr. Cleckler again, he had all the big bunnies arranged and was hanging pastel plastic eggs from the limbs of a sagging oak tree.

He saw her and hollered, "You didn't find Haggerty?"

She slowed to an idle and rolled down her window. "I did, but I was looking for Violet Newberry's law offices.

"Well, her office ain't in Haggerty."

She sighed heavily. "So I learned." She didn't add that since Violet had a Haggerty address her mistake was understandable.

He pointed past his house. "Just keep on down this road. You'll go around a little curve, and then if you don't watch out, you'll run right into it."

"I'll be careful not to do that."

He pulled off his baseball cap and scratched his head. "If you would have told me in the first place, you could have saved a lot of time."

Presley had no response for this, so she just nodded and rolled up her window. She put the Aston in gear and made it about a hundred yards down the road before the car stalled out. She maneuvered it toward the shoulder and got it mostly off the road before it came to a complete stop. Despite repeated attempts, she couldn't get it to start again. She hooked up the portable battery starter, but still nothing happened.

Fighting frustration and a little bit of panic, she got back into the car and stared out the dirty windshield. She was in a strange town, in a car that wouldn't start, and everything she owned was in the trunk. Yet somehow she had to come up with a way to salvage her plan.

Mr. Cleckler had said Aunt Violet's house was nearby, so she could probably walk there. But she couldn't leave an expensive car on the side of the road—even in a relatively safe area like Haggerty, Georgia.

The car would have to be towed to Aunt Violet's house. She pulled out the prepaid phone Moon had given her and was in the process of trying to find the number for the closest towing company when a knock on her window startled a little scream from her throat. She looked over to see Mr. Cleckler's face inches from her own, separated only by the window glass.

"Car won't start?" he asked, even though this was perfectly obvious.

She tried to roll the window down, but it didn't budge. So the battery was dead—permanently deceased. Still that was an easy enough fix, so she tried to remain positive. She pushed open the door.

"My car won't start, so I'm going to have it towed to Aunt Violet's house. I was just looking up the number for a tow company."

"Don't need to look up that number," Mr. Cleckler said. "There's only one tow truck around here, McIntyre Towing. I've got the number on a refrigerator magnet up at the house. I can call him if you want."

"Thanks. I would appreciate that." She was doubly grateful since calling the tow truck would require him to go away.

"You want to come wait inside?" he offered. "Miss Kitty would be real pleased if she was the first lady in town to meet you."

"No thanks. I'd better stay with my car."

He nodded and hurried up the hill toward his house.

She waited for what seemed like a very long time. Finally a police car pulled up, and she felt her anxiety level rise.

The policeman rolled down his window. "Hello, ma'am. Do you need help?"

He was just concerned about her car situation—nothing more. She took several deep breaths to relieve her anxiety. Then, since she couldn't roll her window down, she had to get out of the car again in order to answer him. "I'm Presley DeGraff, Violet Newberry's niece. My car won't start, and Mr. Cleckler has called McIntyre Towing to come get me."

The policeman got out of his car too, as if to put himself on equal footing. He was tall and, though not really fat, his uniform was too tight, so it gave that impression. He took off his hat to expose sandy blond hair and a receding hairline. "My name is Winston Jones. I'm the police chief here in Haggerty. I'll wait with you until Mac gets here."

She tried to dissuade him by saying, "That won't be necessary."

But he was determined. "I can't leave a damsel in distress." His neck turned red, and she realized he was flirting with her.

Great. And she had thought this situation couldn't get any worse. She flexed her fingers several times, utilizing a relaxation exercise her therapist had taught her. Then she tried again. "Really, Chief Jones, I'll be fine until the tow truck gets here. I hate for you to waste your valuable time."

He smiled. "I insist. And my time isn't all that valuable."

He had a pleasant face and a friendly demeanor. Someone who had the slightest interest in romance might even find him attractive. But Presley was not that someone.

She abandoned her attempt to relax through finger exercises and decided she was just going to get back into her car and ignore the police chief until the tow truck arrived. But then the Clecklers came down the hill.

Mr. Cleckler's first order of business was to report on his assignment. "Tow truck is on the way!" Next he introduced his wife, Miss Kitty, a barrel-chested woman with stick thin legs that seemed totally insufficient for the job of keeping her upright. Presley could barely take her eyes off the woman, expecting that at any moment she was going to topple over.

Miss Kitty teetered up to the car and presented Presley with a ziplock bag. "These are fruitcake cookies left over from Christmas," she explained. "They've been in the freezer, so they're still good."

Presley eyed the filmy plastic bag and dreamed of the moment when she could throw it away.

Miss Kitty then began to talk. She talked about the weather and the condition of the county roads and the ant hills in their backyard and what she wanted for her birthday this year. It didn't seem to matter what she said, as long as she filled the empty minutes with chatter. Presley found the woman mildly fascinating, but the police chief became more and more agitated until finally he broke in right during Miss Kitty's discourse on why they had to buy a new lawn mower.

"I'm sorry, but I've got to go." He looked at Presley with sincere apology. "I'm really sorry, but I've just got to." Apparently even in Haggerty, chivalry had its limits.

"I understand completely," she assured him. "You're a busy man, and I have the Clecklers to protect me until the tow truck arrives."

"Protect you from what?" Mr. Cleckler squinted at her.

"It's just a figure of speech," Presley told him.

He stared back blankly.

The police chief left with one last apologetic look in her direction. Presley had no interest in the man and didn't want to give him any other impression. But she did like him a little more after watching him suffer through Miss Kitty's diatribe on her behalf.

Finally, as the sun set, she saw headlights approaching.

"It's Mac!" Mr. Cleckler announced.

She nodded as a truck drew closer and drew to a stop a few feet in front of her car. In the dim light, she could see "McIntyre Towing" emblazoned on the side.

She had hoped the Clecklers would leave once the tow truck arrived, but it was clear now that this had been wishful thinking. The tow guy was just someone else the Clecklers could talk to.

A man wearing a T-shirt with the same "McIntyre Towing" logo swung down from the truck and closed the door with a slam. Then he started toward them, pushing his longish auburn hair from his blue eyes.

"Hey, Mac!" Mr. Cleckler greeted.

"Mr. Hollis, Miss Kitty." He was polite without encouraging conversation. Obviously he'd dealt with the Clecklers before. Then he turned to Presley. "Prissy DeGrass?"

"Presley," she corrected mildly. "DeGraff."

He referred to the scrap of paper in his hand and said, "Sorry. Can't read my own handwriting."

"No problem," she assured him.

He circled the Aston once. "Aston Martin Vantage coupe 2010?"

"It's a 2012."

"Nice car." He studied it more carefully. "So it just stopped on you?"

She nodded. "It's been parked for a while, until today. I jumped it using this portable battery charger." She lifted the device for him to see. "And I didn't have any trouble with it all the way from Columbus—"

"Ohio," Mr. Cleckler inserted. "Not Georgia."

"That is an important distinction," Mr. McIntyre said.

Presley wanted Mr. Cleckler and his chatty wife to disappear. She was considering the gun in her pocket when the tow guy seemed to sense that she had reached her Cleckler limit.

"Thanks for waiting with Miss . . ." he referred to the paper again, "DeGraff, but I'll take care of her now so you folks can go on inside."

Mr. Cleckler looked aggrieved. "I thought I'd stay in case you need a hand."

"Oh, I can't let you do that," Mr. McIntyre said with a firm shake of his head. "It's against my insurance coverage."

"You don't say?" Mr. Cleckler seemed astonished but not suspicious.

"We can't mess up Mac's insurance, Hollis, honey," Miss Kitty said. "Come on in. It's time for dinner anyway."

Presley and Mr. McIntyre watched together as Miss Kitty teetered up the hill on her skinny little legs, followed closely by her skinny little husband.

Once the couple had disappeared inside the house, Mac returned his gaze to her.

She raised her eyebrows. "Insurance coverage?"

He gave her a half smile. "I figured you'd suffered enough of Miss Kitty for one day. Are the keys in the car?"

"They are."

He slid under the wheel and turned the key. Nothing happened. "It's got gas?"

She tried not to be insulted by this question. "Of course."

He grinned. "You'd be surprised how often that's the problem."

"I wish that was my problem," she said. "I probably need a new engine."

"I hope not. A new engine for a car like this probably costs a fortune."

"Replacing anything on this car costs a fortune," she muttered.

He popped the hood and propped it open. As he peered at the inner workings of the Aston, she studied him. His T-shirt, which doubled as an advertisement, fit snug across his chest. Well-developed biceps flexed impressively as he checked the oil and battery cables. Finally he stood and rubbed his hands on his jeans. "It's nothing obvious, and there's no point in trying to figure out what's wrong here in the dark. I'll tow it to my dad's shop and have a look at it tomorrow."

"You're a mechanic too?" she asked.

"Not really." He pushed at his hair again. Either it was a nervous habit or he needed a haircut. "Unless it's something very simple, I won't be able to fix it, and we'll have to take it somewhere else."

"You'll be careful with it?" she asked.

He nodded. "I really will put my insurance coverage at risk if I have to make a claim on this. After I get your car loaded up, I can drop you off at home."

"I would appreciate that, Mr. McIntyre."

"Call me Mac," he requested.

"Mac McIntyre?"

He shrugged. "I didn't pick the nickname, but I'm stuck with it."

She stood back out of his way and watched as he lowered the ramp, pulled the car up onto the back of his truck, and then raised the ramp.

"I have two suitcases in the trunk," she remembered belatedly. It was going to take some time to get used to having possessions—however meager—again.

"I'll unload them once we get to your place." He walked over to the passenger door of his truck and opened it. "We're ready to go."

And then it started to rain, hard.

She made a dash for the truck but was drenched anyway by the time she reached it. Mac McIntyre grabbed her around the waist and basically threw her inside. She clutched her sopping wet handbag and prayed it wasn't ruined. It was a tattered Dooney and Bourke—possibly counterfeit, but definitely her most prized thrift store purchase.

By the time he swung in under the wheel and slammed the door, he was soaked as well. His hair looked dark now that it was wet and slicked back from his forehead. At least he wouldn't need to swipe it out of his eyes for a while. He had a sprinkle of freckles across his nose, and his teeth were very white.

He turned to her with rain dripping off his nose. "So where do you live?"

"Up the street," she pointed out the windshield. "I'm not sure of the exact address."

"You don't know your address?"

"I just moved here."

"From Columbus, Ohio," he supplied.

"I live with Violet Newberry. Or I'm going to," she corrected and then realized she shouldn't have. "I mean, I've only been here for an hour. So I haven't lived there yet."

His eyebrows shot up.

She sighed. "I don't know why I'm so flustered. I sound just like Miss Kitty."

"No, you didn't even come close. You're an amateur compared to Miss Kitty. It takes years of practice to get that good at babbling."

For some reason she found this thought very comforting.

"So let me get this straight. You want to go to Miss Violet's house. You haven't ever lived there before, but you will from now on."

"It's amazing that you could make any sense at all out of what I said."

He waived her praise aside modestly. "And why are you going to be living with Miss Violet? If you don't mind me asking."

"I don't mind. She's invited me to join her law practice."

His eyes widened. "You're Miss Violet's niece?"

She nodded.

"The one she's been expecting for a year?"

"I'm a little late," she acknowledged.

"But you're so young!"

"I'm her *grand*-niece. Sort of. Actually we're only related by marriage. Her sister married my grandmother's brother." She glanced up at him. "Miss Kitty could have said it better."

"The 'grand' part is key. That's why you're young."

Presley felt a hundred years old, at least, but she didn't share this with Mac.

"Anyway, I know where Miss Violet lives." He gave her a sympathetic look. "And your luck is worse than mine. Your car quit on you just a few yards from your destination."

"Actually, that is an improvement from my usual luck," she confided.

He smiled, and she smiled back.

In that moment Presley decided to let Mac be her friend. He was pleasant but didn't flirt. And since she was driving the temperamental Aston, it made sense to be on good terms with the local tow guy.

CHAPTER FIVE

MAC PULLED HIS TRUCK TO a stop in front of a large structure that had probably been a single family home at one time. The middle section was two stories with two shorter wings on each side.

The house had since been divided into three store fronts so that it resembled a mini–strip mall. The law office was in the middle, with First Video Rentals on one side and Cecelia's Beauty Salon on the other. The sign over the door to the law office was old and faded: *Violet Newberry, Attorney at Law—Specialties: Divorces and Wills*. All three establishments had CLOSED signs posted in their respective windows. However there were still lights on in the beauty salon and several cars parked in the small lot that ran the length of the building.

The blinds spanning the plate glass window of the video rental store were hanging askew, and Presley could see that the shelves were mostly empty. Leaves were piled up against the door as if it hadn't been opened for some time. Based on the neglected look—and the fact that no one rented videos anymore—Presley guessed that the shop was more than closed. It was out of business.

The beauty shop looked a little more vibrant, and she knew Aunt Violet was still practicing law on at least a limited basis.

Mac opened his door and encouraged her to slide across so she wouldn't have to walk in the rain. Once he had her under the minimal protection of the overhang, he climbed up on the back of his tow truck and retrieved her suitcases from the Aston's trunk. By the time he joined her, he was dripping wet and so was her thrift-store luggage.

He led the way to the entrance of the law office and set the suitcases down briefly. "It sticks," he explained as he put his shoulder to the door and shoved it while turning the knob. He smiled and waved toward the interior. "Ladies first."

She narrowed her eyes. "Do I look like someone who can't open a door?"

He laughed. "I was raised as a Southern gentleman."

"Then I'll let it pass, just this once. But I was raised as an independent woman, so don't get in the habit of opening doors for me."

"I'll let you get the next one," he promised. "Unless it's this one—since it sticks."

She stepped through the door into what had once been an entry hall but was now a tiny waiting room. "I'll talk to my aunt about getting the sticking door fixed." She flipped on the lights.

He followed her inside, still carrying the suitcases. "Miss Violet just leaves it propped open—except when it rains."

That explained the assortment of dry leaves that had accumulated under a couple of metal folding chairs against the wall. Her eyes skimmed everything from the cobwebs on the water-stained ceiling to the wooden floors, scarred and gouged by years of rough treatment.

Mac McIntyre followed the direction of her gaze and apparently felt compelled to defend Aunt Violet. "She cares about people, not things."

Presley nodded. "If you can only care about one or the other, people are definitely more important." Then she frowned as she noticed the discoloration around his eye for the first time in the improved light. "Are you hurt?"

He seemed surprised by the question. Then he smiled. "Oh, my eye. No, just an occupational hazard."

"You should be more careful," she advised as he moved farther into the house.

"I'll keep that in mind," he said with a wink. Then he called out, "Miss Violet?" There was no answer.

"Maybe she's not home."

"Her car's in the carport. She's probably next door at Cecelia's."

Presley crossed the lobby and walked into Aunt Violet's office. She turned on the light to reveal a desk that was too large for the space. Heavy brocade curtains layered with dust covered the window. Three more metal folding chairs were lined up in front of the desk. Behind it was a large swivel chair.

Boxes were stacked four or five high against all the walls. The desk was piled with books, papers, and manila folders. Even the three chairs in front of the desk were overflowing.

Mac cleared his throat. "Your aunt is a unique person. She has her own way of doing things, but she can always find anything she needs." He waved his hand around the incredibly cluttered room. "I've seen her do it many times."

Presley surveyed the confusion. A tornado site probably wouldn't look much worse.

"But now that you're here, you can help her rearrange things into a little more traditional filing system."

"I want to help Aunt Violet, and I want to learn from her," Presley said carefully. "But I don't want to overhaul her whole system, especially if it's working. I don't plan to be here forever."

Mac looked surprised. "I thought she was going to turn the practice over to you."

Presley didn't owe him any explanations, so she was purposely vague. "I haven't made any definite decisions yet."

They walked across the grim entryway and into a smallish living room. The dusty drapes there were identical to the ones in the office. Presley imagined that during the day they would exclude light from the room with terrible efficiency. The furniture was mismatched but comfortable looking. A large television seemed to be the focal point of the room.

They continued into a small hallway with three doors and a set of stairs leading to the upper floor. Presley turned on more lights and opened each door. The one on the right led into a fairly large bedroom. A king-size bed and two dressers filled most of the space.

Across the hall was the bathroom. The fixtures and tiles were a jarring mixture of turquoise and pink. But worst of all, it seemed to be the only bathroom on this floor.

"My aunt has to share her bathroom with her clients?"

He shrugged. "That's something else that doesn't bother Miss Violet."

He walked through the third door. "This is the kitchen."

The kitchen was surprisingly nice. It was not modern, by any means, but it seemed less neglected, and it was definitely less cluttered. The linoleum floor was worn and the pink laminate countertops were stained. But there were plenty of cabinets, and all the appliances appeared to be in working order. It smelled like cinnamon and bacon.

There was a jigsaw puzzle spread out on the kitchen table. From the pieces already assembled, it looked like a close-up of Big Ben.

Mac said, "Make yourself at home. I'm going next door to see if Miss Violet is there."

Presley nodded and sat at the kitchen table. She picked up a puzzle piece and tried to place it. The rain pounded on the roof with increased intensity. She was just hoping that the roof didn't leak when the lights flickered and went out.

Abandoning the puzzle, she leaned back in her chair and waited for Mac to return. Lightning flashed, and in the temporary brightness, Presley saw an apparition standing by the back door. The specter, with long, flowing white hair, was wearing an oversized cotton dress and no shoes.

Startled, Presley screamed.

The specter laughed—proving it was alive if not completely harmless.

Presley was not amused. She put a hand to her chest and scowled at the old woman. "Who are you, and what are you doing in my aunt's house?"

The specter came closer. "My name is Loralee, and I'm here because Violet's my lawyer. She said you're going to work with her, so I guess you're my lawyer now too. She's coming, your aunt." Loralee pointed vaguely over her shoulder. "They just aren't as quick as me."

Presley glanced down at the woman's feet. "Why are you barefoot?"

"I hate shoes," she said, as if this was all the reason she needed. "I rode here with Versie. While she's getting her hair trimmed, I do puzzles with Violet." She pointed at Big Ben on the table. "Because of the rain we all stayed together at Cecelia's tonight. But then Mac came and said you were here."

It was a very complete, if not totally sensible, explanation.

"I'm sorry I scared you," she added. "I can't help how I look."

It was true that there wasn't much Loralee could have done to alter her appearance. With her long, wild hair, wrinkled skin, stooped posture, and claw-like hands, it was possible that she might actually look worse in the light.

"You should wear shoes outside at least. Otherwise you might hurt your feet."

"I've been walking around barefoot my whole life and never hurt my feet yet."

Presley decided to give up on the whole shoe issue. She glanced toward the back door, anxious for the others to arrive.

Loralee said, "It takes your aunt a while because of that oxygen tank."

"Is she okay?"

Loralee shrugged. "As long as she has her oxygen." She crossed the dark room to the kitchen cupboards and took down a box of Swiss Miss. "Cecelia's got doughnuts, and I'm going to make some hot chocolate to go with them."

"But the electricity is off."

"This is instant, and the water in the pipes is still hot."

Finally the others arrived with flashlight beams bouncing light off the walls.

A painfully thin woman with steel-gray hair pulled back into a severe ponytail moved forward as quickly as her rolling oxygen tank would allow. "Presley?"

"Hello, Aunt Violet."

Her aunt put loving arms around Presley and hugged her tightly. "I can't believe you're here—that you decided to come."

"It was kind of a last minute decision," Presley hedged. "I should have called, but I thought it would be fun to surprise you."

"It's a wonderful surprise, but if I'd known I would have picked up the house."

Presley assumed this was Southern for "cleaned." "I didn't want you to go to any special trouble for me."

"Oh, she went to trouble all right," a tall, elderly woman wearing a NASCAR T-shirt and holding a barking little dog stepped in through the back door with a damp magazine over her white-gray hair. "When Violet thought you were coming last summer, she renovated the whole upstairs to make you a bedroom with an attached bathroom."

"En suite," a smaller woman who bore a family resemblance to the NASCAR lady joined them. "I'm Annabelle, and this is my sister, Eugenia Atkins. The yapping dog is Lady. And Violet enjoyed preparing her house to accommodate you."

Presley felt guilty and pleased at the same time.

"I can speak for myself," the sister said. Then she leaned down and put the dog on the floor.

Annabelle rolled her eyes. "Unfortunately, that is completely true."

"It's nice to meet you, Annabelle," Presley said. "And Mrs. Atkins."

"Call me Miss Eugenia," the larger sister invited. "Everyone does."

Loralee giggled as Mac ushered two more women into the dark kitchen. One was a small African-American woman with very short, very white hair. The other was probably in her late twenties and looked like Heidi Klum except better. She had managed to stay mostly dry by holding two boxes of doughnuts above her like an umbrella.

"I'm Versie," the white-haired woman said. "Welcome to Haggerty."

"And I'm Cecelia," the gorgeous woman added, studying Presley with speculative eyes. "So this is what Mac dragged in to town."

Presley smoothed her damp hair, self-conscious to be meeting so many new people in her current bedraggled condition.

"This is Presley," Mac confirmed as he took a seat at the table. "And for the record, Cecelia, her car is nicer than yours. It's an Aston Martin."

The beautician laughed. "I may just own a shabby old Porsche, but at least my car runs!"

"You've got me there," Presley muttered.

Cecelia popped open the lid of the doughnut box. "Care for a Krispy Kreme? They were fresh this morning."

Presley shook her head. "No thanks. I limit my carbs."

"Probably how you stay so slim," said Cecelia, whose body was model-perfect.

Aunt Violet took a doughnut and sat beside Presley. "I see you've met Loralee."

She glanced at the old woman who was across the room making semi-hot chocolate. "I have."

"I scared her," Loralee said. "But I apologized."

"Loralee is our backdoor neighbor, by country standards anyway," Aunt Violet said. "Barely a mile separates the houses, but if you follow the roads, it's nearly three miles."

Loralee put a mug of hot chocolate in front of Mac. "I used to walk over here every day before folks got so nervous about me falling. Now I only come when I can get a ride."

"We just don't want you to get hurt," Aunt Violet said. "You're too old to be walking across those fields alone."

"I'm too old to worry about getting hurt!" Loralee returned smartly.

"I'd like to see one of you come up with an argument for that," Cecelia said as she placed the doughnut boxes in the middle of the table. Then she waved a hand at Versie. "Well, we've met Presley. Now let's go back and finish sculpting your hair."

As the back door closed behind them, Presley asked, "How can she cut hair without electricity?"

"Scissors and a candle?" Mac hypothesized.

Loralee laughed. "Goodness, in my day we did everything without electricity!"

"Really?" Presley mentally tried to calculate how long ago that must have been.

Loralee seemed to know exactly what she was thinking. "I'll be a hundred years old on my birthday. I don't know for sure when it is. I never knew my mother, and by the time I thought to ask my daddy, he couldn't remember. So I always celebrate it on June 1. It seems like as good a time as any."

"I guess so," Presley agreed.

Loralee continued passing out mugs of hot chocolate. "'Course everyone around here wanted to make a big deal out of it this year since I'm a whole century old, but I told them no. I did let them send my name in to the *Today Show*, although seeing them read it won't be as fun without Willard Scott. It's a shame when the man who reads the old folks' birthdays gets too old to do it."

Mac laughed at this.

"We're all very proud to have Loralee with us," Annabelle said as Loralee handed her a mug.

Aunt Violet added, "Making it to a hundred years is very impressive."

Loralee shrugged as she sat at the table. "The Lord decides how long we stay here, and there's still a chance I won't make it to my birthday. In fact, I might not wake up tomorrow."

"There's a chance none of us will," Miss Eugenia said.

Loralee giggled again. The pounding rain slowed and then stopped. A few seconds later the lights flickered briefly and came back on.

"Wouldn't you know it," Miss Eugenia muttered. "It stops raining right *after* we walked over here and got soaking wet."

"Just be glad the power's back on," Annabelle advised.

The sisters got towels from Aunt Violet's semi-public bathroom and dispersed them. Aunt Violet wrapped one around Presley's shoulders and offered another to Mac, but he declined.

"I won't melt," he claimed with a smile.

Loralee ruffled his wet hair. "I don't know about that. You're sweet enough."

Presley used her damp towel to mop water from the floor. Aunt Violet pointed at a spot where the linoleum was completely worn through. "Watch out. Those boards are rotted. I've been meaning to have Hollis come over and fix them, but I keep forgetting."

"I'll do it," Mac offered. "I'm cheaper than Mr. Hollis and a lot faster."

"Hollis is slow," Annabelle concurred.

"He's an old man," Miss Eugenia pointed out. "Of course he's slow."

Loralee sighed. "I remember when Hollis was born."

"Me too," Miss Eugenia nodded. "He was the cutest baby with all that curly hair."

Presley found it impossible to think of Hollis as cute.

"The worst thing about dealing with Hollis is Miss Kitty," Mac said. "Not everyone can put up with all that babbling." He winked at Presley, and she smiled back.

Mac extended the nearly empty doughnut box toward her. "You sure you don't want one before I finish them off?"

"I'm sure." She couldn't help but notice the multitude of cuts and scratches on his hands. Some looked deep and might have benefited from stitches. Pulling her eyes away from his damaged hands, she watched as he ate the last doughnuts in two bites each.

"We're glad to have you here, Presley," Miss Eugenia said. "Although I understand that the circumstances that brought you are sad ones."

Presley stared at the other woman, frozen by anxiety. Her fresh start was over already.

"Eugenia!" Annabelle scolded. "The death of her parents is still a recent and painful memory. Why did you bring that up?"

Miss Eugenia scowled at her sister. "I just wanted her to know that she can talk about it with us."

Presley wouldn't have thought the day could ever come when she'd be glad to talk about her dead parents. But now there were other subjects much more painful. "It's been almost a year. I still miss them terribly, and Columbus just doesn't seem like home anymore."

"I'm sorry," Mac said.

Presley nodded. "I am too."

"I hated to miss the funeral," Aunt Violet told her, "but this oxygen tank is so limiting."

"I got your card inviting me to come here and join your practice," Presley said. "I'm sorry it took me so long to respond. Things have been, well, difficult."

Aunt Violet reached over and patted her hand. "You're here now."

"And I have two lawyers instead of just one," Loralee said proudly. "Violet has my power of attorney. She makes sure my social security checks get deposited and pays my bills. She even gets my groceries and has Mac deliver them." She pulled a piece of paper from a pocket of her dress and pushed it across the table. "But now that you're here, you can do it. Here's my list."

Aunt Violet started to object, but Presley spoke first. "I'll be happy to pick up your groceries for you—as soon as Mac gets my car fixed."

"You can use mine in the meantime," Aunt Violet offered. "I don't drive much anymore."

"And I'd like to add Presley to my power of attorney," Loralee said. "No offense, Violet, but you aren't getting any younger, and if you die, I want someone else ready to take care of my business."

Aunt Violet nodded. "That sounds like a good idea to me. We'll get you to sign another power of attorney that includes both our names."

Loralee stood. "I'm going to get my file so Presley can be looking it over. I want her prepared when we have our first business meeting."

Based on the constant references to business, Presley assumed Loralee was the world's oldest tycoon and felt obligated to follow her into Aunt Violet's office. And based on the condition of the office, she expected it to take a long time to find the file, but Loralee walked straight to it.

Loralee seemed to glean her thoughts again. "My file has been on the right-hand corner of Violet's desk for years now. She keeps it there so she can always find it when I come to visit."

Presley accepted the file, and taking a quick glance through it, she found the power of attorney and a neat ledger sheet showing where bills had been paid. There was a stack of bank statements since the first of the year. Based on this information, Loralee was definitely not a tycoon. She received a modest monthly annuity payment and an even more modest amount from social security.

"Are your legal fees going to be the same as Violet's?" she asked. "Because I can't afford any fancy city prices."

That was true, which was probably why there was no fee for legal services listed on the ledger. Frowning, Presley did some quick mental arithmetic. Then she sighed. Loralee didn't have enough monthly income to cover her bills. Not only was there no charge for legal services, being Loralee's attorney was actually *costing* Aunt Violet money.

"There won't be a change in the fee schedule," she promised.

Loralee grinned. "Good."

When they returned to the kitchen, they found Annabelle digging desserts out of the freezer at Aunt Violet's request.

Presley surveyed the carrot cake and the lemon icebox pie lined up on the counter. "What is all this?"

"We're making preparations for the company we'll be receiving tomorrow," Aunt Violet explained.

"I have a pound cake I can contribute to your cause," Eugenia said.

"I'd give you something too," Annabelle said. "But I'm leaving tomorrow to join my husband in Charlotte. He's giving a genealogy seminar there."

"Why are we going to be having company?" Presley tried to hide her dread.

"When people find out you're here, they'll want meet you," Aunt Violet explained.

"I'm not very good with crowds," Presley said.

Mac gave her a sympathetic look. "My advice is to greet anyone who comes by and visit for a minute or so. Then go hide and let your aunt deal with them until they get bored and leave. It always worked when I was a kid."

"Mac!" Miss Eugenia seemed scandalized. "The people who come will want to get to know Presley. They already know Violet."

"I stand by my original statement. It's every man for himself when it comes to awkward social situations." He smiled at Presley. "Hide!"

"They're sharks," Annabelle inserted. "They'll ask you all kinds of personal questions, so be prepared. Every girl is entitled to a few secrets."

Presley barely controlled a shudder. "Maybe all of you could stop the visits by announcing that I'm too busy with the law practice to socialize."

"I doubt if there's enough legal work in the entire town of Haggerty to take up all your waking hours," Miss Eugenia murmured. "An announcement like that would get twice as many people over here twice as fast."

"You're doomed," Annabelle said morosely.

Aunt Violet patted Presley's hand. "I'll be here, dear."

"I'll get Versie to help me make an Italian cream cake," Loralee offered.

"I love your Italian cream cake," Aunt Violet said.

Loralee waved the praise aside. "Mine's passable, but nobody can make one like Miss Blanche could. She made the finest Italian cream cake. Mr. DuPont used to tease her about it because her people were from Ireland, not Italy."

Presley rubbed the headache forming at her temples. "Who are Blanche and DuPont? More sharks?"

"Oh no! Blanche and DuPont Armstrong have been dead for decades," Loralee explained. "They helped to build up this area."

That was not much of an accomplishment in Presley's opinion.

"I'll show you their house tomorrow when you bring my groceries."

"Loralee is an expert on local history," Miss Eugenia said.

"That comes with being a hundred years old," Loralee replied. "And I'm really only an expert on the Armstrong family." Loralee's tone became a little dreamy. "Mr. DuPont was a great man, and Miss Blanche was the finest woman that ever walked God's green earth." She pulled a picture from a dress pocket that apparently contained a little of everything and handed it to Presley. "That's her."

Presley accepted the picture, which was faded with age.

"Isn't she beautiful?" Loralee asked.

The young woman in the picture was pleasant looking in a pale, plain sort of way. Presley would not have described her as beautiful, but she smiled as she handed the picture back. "Very nice."

"I'll tell you more about her tomorrow." Loralee scooted her chair closer to Presley's. "So what made you decide to move to Haggerty after all this time? I mean since your parents have been dead for a year."

Presley could see that the others were shocked by the blunt question but curious to hear her answer. "I tried to build a new life in Ohio but finally decided it was just too hard to be there without my parents. I needed a fresh start, and Aunt Violet had offered me a job. So I came."

"It's more just a place to live than a job," Miss Eugenia said. "Most of Violet's clients are charity cases."

Presley was careful to keep her eyes lowered. "A place to live is all I need for now."

"Don't you have a husband or children?" Loralee asked.

Mac stepped in at this point. "I thought the sharks weren't supposed to get here until tomorrow. And didn't we just agree that girls were entitled to a few secrets?"

Loralee nodded. "I'm sorry. I let my curiosity get the best of me."

"Your surprise arrival is kind of mysterious," Annabelle said. "In fairness to Loralee and her shark-ish personal questions."

"I wasn't offended," Presley told them. "But there's really nothing to tell."

Loralee gave her a mind-probing look, and Presley was terrified about what the next question might be. But Loralee just said, "I hope you'll like it here."

Relief washed over Presley, and she smiled. "Thank you."

Loralee waved a hand at Big Ben spread out on the table. "Now, let's work on this puzzle."

"I'd rather have bamboo shoots put up my fingernails," Annabelle claimed.

Presley asked, "You don't like puzzles?"

"Puzzles are the world's biggest waste of time," Annabelle replied. "A picture, cut into pieces, and then put back together. Does that make sense?"

No one answered.

"And to make it worse, Miss Violet and Loralee and Eugenia do the same puzzles over and over. They finish one, break it apart, and put it back together."

"Not right away," Aunt Violet interjected. "They're all on a casual rotation system so we have time to forget where the pieces go before they come around again."

"We write the dates we finish them on the box so we remember," Loralee said. "Some of them have ten or fifteen dates."

"Pointless!" Annabelle proclaimed as Versie and Cecelia walked back in.

Mac's eyes seemed drawn to Cecelia. Presley watched them, looking for signs of romance.

"What's pointless?" Cecelia asked.

"Puzzles," Presley told her. "Annabelle hates them."

"Poor Big Ben," Cecelia said. Then she pointed at Versie. "Doesn't her hair look great?"

"Better than great," Mac complimented. "Now can I take you ladies home?" He caught Presley's gaze briefly and winked. "This is a big group for a little kitchen."

She realized he was trying to reduce the crowd for her, and she winked back. "Thanks."

Versie seemed unsure. "My son Clifton was planning to come get us."

"Call and tell him I'm going to be your chauffeur tonight," Mac suggested.

Versie smiled. "Clifton does like to limit the miles he drives. His suburban is a gas-guzzler."

"It's settled then," Mac said. "Let's go, ladies."

Annabelle stood. "I guess I'll go too. I have to be at the airport at the crack of dawn tomorrow."

Cecelia yawned. "I've got an early cut and color in the morning, so I should go too."

Presley wondered if the young woman was timing her departure to match up with Mac's on purpose. Not that she cared, really. They opened the back door so Cecelia could go lock up her salon, and in the process, Lady escaped.

"I'll get her," Mac offered.

"It's okay," Miss Eugenia said. "Now that the rain has stopped she can have a bathroom break."

So Mac waved good-bye and closed the door. The house seemed quiet once they were gone.

Miss Eugenia and Violet started talking about a mutual friend who had died recently. Presley put a few pieces of Big Ben in place, biding her time until she could politely excuse herself.

Then Miss Eugenia stood and said she needed to go. “Let me collect Lady, and I’ll be on my way.”

Presley followed her to the back door and out onto the patio. There were so many cracks in the old flagstones that it qualified more as flagstone gravel.

“I’m sorry you got here before we finished planting the garden,” Miss Eugenia said. “Violet’s yard usually looks much better than this.”

Presley surveyed the sloped lawn surrounded by overgrown shrubs. Apparently Miss Eugenia was in a generous mood.

“Violet always has a garden,” Miss Eugenia was continuing, “but this year she wanted a big one, so Mac brought in a backhoe and dug that spot.” She pointed to an area in the far-right corner of the large lot. “Since then we’ve had almost a week of rain, so we had to put the project on hold. As soon as it dries out, we’ll finish.”

“I really appreciate your help,” Aunt Violet told her from the doorway. “And Mac’s.”

“I’d hoped to have it done this weekend,” Miss Eugenia said. “It’s best to plant on Good Friday. But we have a long growing season in Georgia, so next week will be fine.”

“Presley might want to help with the garden,” Aunt Violet suggested.

Presley’s mother had loved to grow things, so she wasn’t opposed to this idea. “I’d like to help, but I don’t know anything about plants or vegetables or gardens.”

“Eugenia can teach you,” Aunt Violet said. “She knows everything about gardens.”

“Loralee’s very knowledgeable too,” Miss Eugenia added. “She’s almost a flower-whisperer. I’ve never seen a plant she couldn’t save.”

They heard Lady barking from near the garden site. Miss Eugenia called, but the dog didn’t come. “Hmmm,” Miss Eugenia said with a frown. “That’s not like Lady. She’s usually very obedient.”

Presley stepped off into the wet grass. “I’ll go get her.”

“You’ll ruin your shoes,” Miss Eugenia said. Then she raised her voice and hollered, “Lady!”

Still the dog didn't come.

"Well, I declare," Miss Eugenia said. "I guess we have no choice but to go after her."

Then Aunt Violet said, "There she is!"

They followed the direction of her pointing finger and saw Lady climbing out of the hole Mac had made with the backhoe.

"What in the world?" Miss Eugenia said. "It looks like she's trying to drag something."

They all kept moving.

Presley peered into the darkness. "It looks like a bone."

Miss Eugenia put out an arm to stop them from going any closer. "I think it might be human."

CHAPTER SIX

At this announcement, Aunt Violet started having a wheezing fit. Presley rushed her inside while Miss Eugenia captured Lady.

Presley settled her aunt on the couch in the living room. She put pillows under Aunt Violet's head and got a blanket from the bedroom. Then she watched anxiously as her aunt huffed on an inhaler.

Finally, when her breathing was under control, Aunt Violet gasped, "It's emphysema. I never smoked a day in my life. It doesn't seem fair."

"No," Presley agreed.

Miss Eugenia returned with the dog in her arms and called the Haggerty Police Department. When she reported that they had found a body in Aunt Violet's backyard, Presley's hands began to shake.

"They're on their way," Miss Eugenia reported grimly after ending the call. "Winston said to stay in the house until he gets here."

It was only a matter of minutes before they heard sirens. Presley opened the heavy drapes that covered the living room window to watch the vehicles approach.

"The sheriff's department is here too," Eugenia said. "Winston probably called them since Violet lives right outside the city limits."

Two vehicles pulled up at the same time and parked beside each other in front of the vacant video store. Winston Jones climbed out of the police car, and a tall, dark-haired man got out of the sheriff's department car.

After instructing Aunt Violet to lie still, Miss Eugenia led Presley to the front door. The pair worked together to get the stuck door open and then walked outside.

"Everybody okay here?" the deputy asked. His badge identified him as Deputy Burrell.

"We're fine," Miss Eugenia assured him.

"Where's the body?" Chief Jones wanted to know.

"Well, it's not a body exactly but a skeleton—or part of one," Presley explained. "It's in the backyard."

She led the men around the building and into the backyard, with Miss Eugenia following behind at a slightly slower pace. At first Presley tried to avoid the worst puddles but finally decided her leather shoes were a total loss and stopped caring where she stepped. When they reached the edge of the hole, Presley pointed down. "It's in there."

Winston pulled out his flashlight and shone it down. The light found the bone Lady had been tugging at. Then, after a little more searching, he illuminated the top of a human skull.

Presley closed her eyes briefly.

"It's not nearly as bad as I expected," Winston said. "The way Miss Eugenia sounded on the phone I expected blood and gore."

"When we were on the phone, I didn't know what we were dealing with." Miss Eugenia stepped up beside them and defended herself. "For all I knew there *was* blood and gore. Lady just dragged up a bone."

"Stand back, please, ladies," Winston requested.

"Oh, stop trying to sound all official," Miss Eugenia complained. "We were here first." But she did take a step back, so Presley did the same.

"Yeah, this is manageable," Deputy Burrell sounded encouraged. "We can handle a skeleton. I just wish it wasn't so wet and dark."

"I'm going to call the county coroner," Winston said. "The sooner we get this out of the ground the better." He made his call and then reported, "Coroner is out of town, visiting his family for Easter. The operator suggested we call the funeral director to extract the body."

"I should have known it wasn't going to be easy," the deputy muttered.

Winston Jones called the Haggerty Mortuary and after a short conversation told the deputy that the funeral director was on his way.

Then Deputy Burrell said, "I'd better call Sheriff Bonham and let him know what is going on."

It wasn't long before a white van with roses painted on the side pulled into Aunt Violet's yard. A tall, thin man with a solemn expression climbed out first, followed by a younger version of himself. They unloaded a variety of shovels, bright blue tarps, and clear plastic tubs. Then they walked up to the hole, dragging their equipment behind them.

"Darnell Mobley," the older man introduced himself to Presley. "And this is my boy, Junior."

It seemed inappropriate to say she was happy to meet them under the circumstances, so Presley just nodded at both men.

"Darnell," Miss Eugenia said. "Junior."

"I can't say I'm surprised to see you here," Mr. Mobley told her. "Whenever there's a body, it seems like you're always nearby."

She sighed. "I do have a talent for solving crimes."

Mr. Mobley's smile seemed sinister in his solemn face. "It's a real opportunity to get a chance to work on a murder case like this."

"We're not sure it's murder," Winston told him quickly. "Let's not jump to any conclusions."

Darnell Mobley continued as if the police chief hadn't spoken. "My son, Junior, will be assisting me as I document the crime scene. He just completed a forensic course at Woodrow Wilson Junior College, so he has the expertise and credentials required."

Winston blinked once and then shook his head. "Okay, well let me show you what we've got." He pointed his flashlight at the hole in Aunt Violet's yard.

Darnell Mobley squatted down to examine the skeleton; then he whistled. "What do you know about that?"

Junior Mobley pulled out an iPad and started taking pictures.

His father said, "Junior has a special app that can penetrate the earth a couple of inches, almost like a dirt X-ray. That helps us get accurate pictures of the body's position, depth, etc."

Presley was mildly impressed, and she could tell that Winston was too.

The chief said, "Well, good. Take a lot of pictures and X-rays or whatever. Then we've got to get this skeleton out of here."

"What else do you need to dig it up?" Deputy Burrell asked.

"We'll need more light," Darnell said. "And more manpower. Bones may have shifted since burial and could be several feet or even yards from the skull and arm bone."

Winton took off his uniform hat and pulled at his thinning hair in obvious frustration. "I wish we had night equipment like bigger towns, but we'll just have to work with what we've got. We'll pull our cars around and shine the headlights on the hole. And Burrell, will you see if you can get some more people over here? I'm short-staffed at the police station tonight."

Deputy Burrell made a phone call requesting additional deputies. Then both men spent several minutes trying to get their cars across the muddy grass in the backyard. They had just completed this task and had their headlights illuminating the area when the sheriff arrived. He was a tall African-American man with a no-nonsense expression.

The sheriff held a little conference with his deputy and Chief Jones beside the gaping hole. The car headlights cast garish shadows all around them. From what Presley could overhear, there was some question about jurisdiction, but unlike on TV, they weren't fighting *for* the case. They were each trying to give it to the other. Finally they agreed, with obvious mutual reluctance, to share the case.

"Containment is key," the sheriff said. "If this gets out before we know what we've got here . . ." He let his voice trail off. The sheriff turned back to the funeral director. "Take pictures as you go, and when you start collecting bones, make sure you get a lot of the dirt around each one since there might be something there we can use to identify the remains—buttons, jewelry, fillings from teeth."

"Yes, sir!" Darnell replied. "We know exactly how to do it. My son has a degree in forensics from Woodrow Wilson."

The sheriff glanced at Junior but didn't comment on his credentials. "Do you have a sterile tub to pack it all in?"

"Yes, sir," the funeral director replied. "I wiped all these tubs down with bleach, and then Junior rinsed them three times with distilled water."

The sheriff nodded. "Once it's packed up, I want you to take it to the morgue in Albany. I'll tell them to be expecting it, and I'll send a car to follow you."

"To protect the chain of evidence," Junior said in a conspiratorial tone.

The sheriff glared at him. "To be sure you don't get lost."

Junior stepped back, and the sheriff turned stern eyes to Presley and Miss Eugenia. He scowled down at them from his superior height. Lesser women might have been intimidated. Presley and Miss Eugenia just stared back.

"Who are you?" he asked Presley.

"My name is Presley DeGraff. I'm Violet Newberry's niece. I just arrived in Haggerty a couple of hours ago."

He turned to Miss Eugenia. "And what do you know about this?"

"Not much," she replied. "Violet wanted to plant a big garden this year, so Mac and I have been helping her."

"Mac McIntyre?" the sheriff confirmed.

Miss Eugenia nodded. "He used a backhoe." She waved vaguely at the hole. "I guess we disturbed the grave, and then rain finished the process of exposing the skeleton."

"I'll need you both to write down a statement about how you found it. No rush. Anytime over the next few days will be fine."

Both women nodded.

Then, without any expression of appreciation for the time this would take, the sheriff moved back to where the Mobleys were working on the skeleton. They had spread out a tarp and were putting bones on it like a puzzle in the basic shape of a person.

"This way we'll know we've got them all," Junior said importantly.

Presley felt a little queasy, but she couldn't look away from the person-puzzle.

More sheriff deputies arrived, and soon the backyard was crowded with vehicles and law enforcement personnel. The sheriff assigned some of them to cordon off the area with police crime tape while others assisted with the digging.

The wet ground was scored with shovels approximately four feet around the existing hole. Then the diggers slowly enlarged it. Soggy soil samples were placed in ziplock bags, and then the bags were stored in the clear tubs. Any bones they found were added to the ones on the tarp.

Deputy Burrell's cell phone kept buzzing, and each time the sheriff told him not to answer it. Finally the sheriff said, "If your wife and a Channel 3 News crew show up here, you're fired."

"Yes, sir," Deputy Burrell acknowledged and kept digging.

"Cade's wife is a reporter," Miss Eugenia whispered.

"That seems like kind of a conflict of interest," Presley replied.

"It can be," Miss Eugenia agreed, "but you love who you love."

It was a long, sweaty process in the moist evening air, but finally they had four tubs of dirt and what looked like a complete skeleton arranged on the bright blue tarp.

"We're still missing a few phalanges from the feet," the funeral director said as they looked at the skeleton.

"Three distal and two intermediate," Junior provided with authority.

His father beamed proudly, but everyone else ignored him.

"Could they be crushed in the dirt?" the sheriff asked, pointing to the tubs filled with soil samples.

"Possibly," Mr. Mobley acknowledged. "If so, the morgue folks will find traces."

"Or they might have been dragged off by animals," Junior contributed, "which means we'll never find them."

The sheriff squatted down beside the funeral director and stared at the tarp. Then he asked, "Based on this, what can you tell me?"

"It's a woman," the funeral director said.

Deputy Burrell cursed under his breath.

"You're sure?" Winston confirmed.

"Pretty sure," Mr. Mobley qualified his comments.

Junior inserted himself into the conversation again. "Based on overall size, jawbone, and pelvic cavity, I agree that this skeleton belongs to a woman. And she was probably fairly young when she died."

The sheriff scowled. "Great."

Junior continued, "Since there's just a skeleton left—no skin or hair or clothes—she's probably been here awhile."

"How long is a while?" Winston asked. "Weeks?"

"At least a few months, maybe a year or more," Junior provided. "Though because of the heat and humidity, a body buried in Georgia without embalming and protection from the elements can decompose pretty fast."

"What about fabric? How fast does it decompose?" Chief Jones asked.

"It takes longer," Mr. Mobley said.

"But there's no guarantee the body was wearing clothes when it was buried," Junior pointed out.

Deputy Burrell cursed some more.

"The morgue in Albany can probably give you an age range and an idea of how long she's been here, but you'll need a forensic autopsy to confirm all that," Junior continued knowledgably. Then he pointed to the back of the skull and the pieces of bone he had placed near it. "Especially since the back of her skull is caved in."

"A result of decomposition?" the sheriff asked hopefully.

Junior shook his head. "I believe we have a murder on our hands. There could be more bodies." He waved to encompass Aunt Violet's entire yard. "This could be the burial ground for a serial killer."

Presley was trying to process this information, filtering it with Junior's lack of maturity, experience, and bona fide qualifications, when a strident voice cried out from behind her.

"Murder! A *serial killer?*"

Presley turned to see Miss Kitty Cleckler standing on Aunt Violet's muddy grass. How she had managed to get past all the law enforcement personnel was as much of a mystery as the skeleton on the blue tarp. Miss Kitty took in the bones spread out by the gaping hole for a split second, and then she started screaming.

"Chief," the sheriff said in a warning voice.

Chief Jones stepped toward Miss Kitty with his hands stretched out in a pleading gesture. "We don't know anything for sure yet! Please just remain calm."

But it was too late. Miss Kitty already had her cell phone up to her ear. "Hollis!" she yelled into the phone. "There's a serial killer murdering people in Haggerty! He's buried a bunch of bodies in Miss Violet's backyard! Call the neighbors, and tell them to keep their doors locked!"

Chief Jones's shoulders slumped in defeat, and Deputy Burrell took up cursing again.

"So much for containment," Sheriff Bonham muttered.

"Oh, this is going to be a real mess," Junior Mobley agreed with unabashed glee.

CHAPTER SEVEN

CHIEF JONES USHERED A SOBBING Miss Kitty toward the house and requested that Presley and Miss Eugenia follow him. He took Miss Kitty into the living room and sat her in a chair near Aunt Violet. They all tried to console the distraught woman, but this proved to be impossible.

"There's a skeleton in your yard!" Miss Kitty wailed.

Aunt Violet nodded. "I know."

"And Junior Mobley said there are a lot more bodies!"

"He said there *could* be more bodies," Miss Eugenia corrected, but Miss Kitty wasn't listening.

"Oh, this is such a terrible day!" Miss Kitty pulled several tissues from a box on the lamp table and pressed them to her lips. Every few seconds she moaned.

It was beyond annoying, and Presley was glad when Hollis arrived to collect his wife. After the Clecklers left, the remaining three women enjoyed a few moments of peace. Then the neighbors started to arrive in droves, followed closely by two news crews from Albany.

Aunt Violet and Miss Eugenia stood at the front window, looking out as the police and sheriff's deputies tried to control the growing crowd.

"If they hurry, they can get something on the ten o'clock news," Miss Eugenia muttered as the camera crews set up.

Presley walked back to the kitchen and watched as the Mobleys took more pictures of the skeleton arranged on the tarp. Then they loaded it into a tub identical to the ones filled with dirt samples. Finally they put all the tubs in the back of the funeral home van.

Miss Eugenia walked up beside her. "Are you okay?"

Presley nodded. "It just bothers me that everyone is interested in her because they think it means there's been a murder or might be a serial killer. No one cares that she was a person."

"The sensationalism will die down eventually, and the focus will shift to the victim. But in the meantime, I'm sure she appreciates your acknowledgment of her as an individual."

Presley looked at the older woman in surprise. "You think that dead people still appreciate things?"

"Of course. They're still people and still have feelings. Don't you believe in heaven?"

Presley turned her eyes back to the window and watched as a sheriff's department vehicle escorted the van out of the yard, slipping and sliding in the wet grass. "I don't know. I'm not sure."

"Well until you are, you can trust in what I know. When people die, they still exist. I've felt the presence of my deceased husband many times."

"I don't feel my parents," Presley said.

"Maybe you just haven't learned to recognize their presence yet," Miss Eugenia said thoughtfully.

Their conversation was interrupted by Aunt Violet calling from the front of the house. "Presley! Eugenia!"

They both hurried into the living room and found Aunt Violet pointing at the television set. "Look!" she managed in a strangled tone.

Miss Kitty's tear-stained face filled the screen. "I saw bones everywhere!" she cried. "No telling how many bodies are buried out there. Everyone needs to keep their doors locked and their guns handy until the police apprehend this psycho murderer!"

Presley was offended. "She is making that up!"

"She's exaggerating," Miss Eugenia corrected.

"She's scared," Aunt Violet added. Then she looked at Presley. "I hope you aren't sorry you came."

Presley gave her a wan smile. "Not at all. I feel kind of a connection to that girl." She pointed vaguely toward the backyard.

"Since I got here the same night she was found. I'd like to make sure she gets laid to rest correctly this time."

Aunt Violet patted her arm. "I think that's very sweet, dear."

There was a sharp knock on the back door, and they heard Winston Jones call out. "Miss Violet!"

"We're in here," she replied.

A few seconds later, the sheriff and Chief Jones came into the small living room. The sheriff spoke to them as a group. "No one goes out into the backyard tonight. That hole is dangerous. Someone might fall in and get hurt. Or someone might destroy evidence that we can't see in the dark. We're leaving some men to protect the area and keep the press away. Hopefully this whole disaster will blow over quickly." He glared at Presley as if this was all her fault.

She glared back. If anyone in Haggerty was innocent, it was her.

Chief Jones said, "We'll come back in the morning to do a little more digging and see what else we can find." He glanced toward the backyard. "Look for more skeletons."

Then with one last sigh, the sheriff walked outside with Chief Jones right beside him.

"I'd better get going too," Miss Eugenia said. "There's no telling how long it will take me to get my car out with all these police vehicles everywhere, and it's almost Lady's bedtime."

* * *

After Miss Eugenia left, Presley and Aunt Violet moved to the kitchen.

"We missed dinner," Aunt Violet pointed out. "I'm going to heat up some soup. Would you like some?"

Presley shook her head. "I'm not hungry."

While Violet heated the soup, Presley put the empty doughnut boxes into the garbage and wiped down the counters. When she was finished, she sat by her aunt at the table. "You don't seem overly concerned about the skeleton."

"I'm sure there is a logical explanation." Aunt Violet paused to blow on a spoonful of soup. "Years ago people buried family members behind their homes. Finding a skeleton or even several isn't such an unusual occurrence."

"I hope that's what it is," Presley said, although she had her doubts. She couldn't forget the hole in the back of the skull.

Aunt Violet put down her spoon and smiled. "I just want to tell you again how happy I am to have you here."

Presley took a deep breath. "I owe you an explanation for my sudden arrival."

"You don't have to tell me anything."

Presley knew the comment was sincere and appreciated that, but it was time to share at least a little of her burden. "After my parents died, I was so lonely and lost. Your invitation meant a lot to me, and I really did consider it. But there had been so much change already and more just seemed . . . too much. I went through the motions every day and hoped things would get better. For a while it seemed like they were, but then suddenly, well, things got worse. I had what some people would call a nervous breakdown. I spent some time in a mental hospital. I'm much better but still taking it one day at a time."

Aunt Violet reached over and patted her hand. "You're not alone anymore. You're here with me, and we'll take each day one at a time together."

"I don't know if I even want to practice law anymore," she admitted. "And if I do, I'll have to pass the Georgia bar and get licensed here. All that may take a long time."

"There's no rush." Aunt Violet's tone was soothing. "You can be my assistant for now, learn about my practice. Then decide. No pressure. No obligations. You're a young woman with a whole life ahead of you. I never want you to feel trapped in my life. Stay as long as you want—and not a minute longer."

Presley smiled. "I wish I had come sooner. Maybe if I had, things wouldn't have gotten so bad in Columbus."

"There's no point in second-guessing yourself now. What's past is past." Her aunt stood. "I know you're exhausted, so I'll show you to your room." She led the way to the stairs, where Presley's damp suitcases were waiting.

"Because of this," she tugged on the oxygen tank, "I can't climb the stairs, so the upper floor hasn't been used for years. When I wanted to make room for you, I hired Hollis to renovate it. Since he never gets in a hurry about anything, it's probably good you didn't come right away."

Presley smiled.

"I'm sure it's a little dusty. I have a lady come in and clean every so often, but it's been a while."

"A little dust won't hurt me." Presley hefted her suitcases and put her foot on the first stair.

"There are clean sheets and towels in the closet by the bathroom," Aunt Violet said. "Open the windows to let in some fresh air. There's one of those wall-mounted air conditioners with a remote to turn it on. I don't know how to do it, but Mac can show you when he comes tomorrow."

"I'm so tired I could sleep on a bed of nails," Presley assured her aunt, continuing up the stairs. Then a thought made her stop and turn back. "Speaking of Mac, does he box?"

Aunt Violet stared up at her blankly.

"I mean I know he's not a *professional* fighter, but he's got a black eye and his hands are all cut up, so I thought he might do amateur matches to make some extra money."

Aunt Violet shook her head. "I don't think so."

Presley was relieved. "Good. I hate violent sports, and well, I just didn't want him to be a boxer. I guess it would be easy to bump into things and get bruises in his line of work. He should probably wear gloves when he's towing cars."

"I wish he would take a little better care of himself," Aunt Violet said. "Mention it to him. Maybe he'll listen to you."

Presley smiled. "I doubt that." Then she turned and climbed the rest of the stairs.

* * *

The second floor of Aunt Violet's house was surprisingly nice. Presley was almost certain that the original footprint of the space had been altered, even though she couldn't spot any patchwork in the refinished hardwood floors. But regardless of how the area had been previously divided, there was now a sitting area, a large bedroom with a spacious walk-in closet, and a private, if not particularly luxurious, bathroom.

It was all new, unquestionably expensive, and all for her. That guilty/pleased feeling washed over her again. It had been a while since someone had shown such consideration for her.

Presley opened all the windows and got a cross breeze going to air out the musty rooms. It was cool enough outside to do without the air conditioner, so she didn't even try to figure it out.

She was past exhaustion, and once she climbed into the bed, she thought she'd fall straight to sleep. Instead she stared at the ceiling as thoughts of Tate came unbidden to her weary mind. She was too tired to fight them, so she closed her eyes and gave in to the memory.

* * *

On the day she met Tate, she'd been working at the law firm of Sorenson and Lowe for almost two years. During that entire time, she'd been tucked back in an office doing research and writing arguments for more charismatic lawyers to present. But since she hated the limelight, she didn't mind.

Meeting new people and developing relationships had always been difficult. The patience required to move past the superficial small talk to an actual friendship seemed overwhelming. As a result she'd never had many childhood friends. Her parents had been the only social group she needed. With them she felt comfortable and confident. She had never felt that way with anyone else until the day Tate Sheridan had walked into her office.

With Tate there was none of the initial awkwardness. No jokes about her name, no boring small talk. He'd looked her straight in the eyes and said, "Hey, you must be Presley DeGraff. I like that suit. I've heard pink is this year's power color."

It was the perfect thing to say. No insincere compliments, just statements of fact. Normally an attractive man in her office would have sent her into a panic attack, but with Tate she was surprisingly at ease.

He said he'd been assigned to work with her on a case. Fresh out of law school, he was happy for the opportunity. He'd been told she was the best researcher in the firm. She suspected he was in over his head and needed her help desperately. So even though she was sure he had ulterior motives, at least he was being nice.

They went over the case, and when it was lunchtime, he asked if she wanted to get something to eat. She had declined. She never ate with anyone, certainly not lawyers in the firm. But he didn't accept no for an answer. He cajoled and begged and teased until finally she accepted just to make him stop.

For the first time since he'd walked into her tiny office, she'd felt anxiety. The thought of going into a restaurant and ordering and talking and arguing over the check . . . It was just too much. She was about to back out when he said they'd order in. He suggested her favorite local deli and picked up a pen off her desk. He wrote his order on the palm of his hand and then asked for hers. It was a funny thing to do, and she laughed, relaxing.

When their order arrived, Tate paid for it, and she cleared off her desk. While they ate Reuben sandwiches with German potato salad, he regaled her with funny stories from his youth. His pleasant company made the food taste even better than usual. She had blinked back tears when she realized she hadn't laughed that much since her parents died.

They finished their meal with brownies for dessert. Then they worked all through the afternoon and into the early evening. He didn't seem anxious to get away. He didn't check his watch every few minutes and mention that a date was waiting, hoping she'd offer to finish up alone the way many others had done.

When they were finally ready to go, he had walked her to her car, but before she could get in, he suggested that they grab a pizza. He said he'd invite her to his place, but his roommates were slobs. So she invited him to her house. She prepared him in advance—about the guard at the gate and the butler. He seemed impressed but not judgmental. Before she'd eaten a bite of pizza, she was already halfway in love with him.

Tears seeped out of Presley's eyes, and she knew she had to stop. She needed rest. She couldn't think about Tate or her parents or the fact that there was a grave in her aunt's backyard. So she started counting and made it to 295 before she drifted off into a troubled sleep.

CHAPTER EIGHT

EUGENIA WAS AWAKENED AT SIX o'clock the next morning by a call from her sister.

"Is there really a serial killer in Haggerty?" Annabelle demanded without so much as hello. "And if so why didn't you tell me about it last night?"

Eugenia forced herself into a semi-sitting position. "I tried to tell you last night, but you wouldn't answer the phone."

"That's because you were calling so late and you never call about anything important," Annabelle replied. "So it's true then?"

"No." Eugenia stifled a yawn. "Lady just found a skeleton. One."

"Kitty Cleckler said there were bodies buried all over the yard."

"Kitty Cleckler also said she was Miss Haggerty High School, and we both know that's not true."

There was a brief pause while Annabelle considered this. Then she said, "Well, you'd better get up and turn on the TV to be sure something hasn't changed overnight."

Eugenia swung her legs over the side of the bed. "I'm getting up."

"My plane is about to board," Annabelle's voice continued. "I'll buy you a ticket on the next flight to Charlotte, and you can pick it up at the Delta counter."

"Why would I want to do that?" Eugenia was truly bewildered.

"So you don't get murdered in your sleep!"

Eugenia laughed. "I'm not scared!"

"Well, maybe you should be." Then Annabelle hung up abruptly.

Eugenia put the phone down and looked at Lady, who was watching from her little dog bed.

"Well, girl, it looks like we've got to get up even though we're still tired." Eugenia forced herself to stand and then stepped gingerly for a few feet until her stiff muscles had a chance to loosen.

When she got downstairs, she fed Lady and then turned on the little television set she kept on her kitchen counter. The mayor of Haggerty was being interviewed by Cade Burrell's cute little reporter wife, Hannah-Leigh.

Mayor Witherspoon, looking harried yet serious, was saying, "I was informed at approximately ten o'clock last night by our police chief that human remains had been found just outside the Haggerty city limits. Because the safety of the town was at risk, I called the governor immediately. He has promised support from the state police and is requesting that the FBI send in some of their top agents from Atlanta. Our local guys do a great job on the regular stuff, but for a potential serial killer, we need to bring in the big guns."

Eugenia groaned, imagining how Winston and Mark Iverson and Sheriff Bonham felt about this backhanded insult.

The camera zoomed in on Hannah-Leigh's face. "Additionally, we have information from a knowledgeable inside source that the skeleton was that of a young female."

Eugenia glanced at Lady. "That source will be Junior Mobley."

Hannah-Leigh continued, "And an eyewitness reported that Violet Newberry's backyard was, and I quote, 'covered with hundreds of bones,' unquote."

"That witness will be Kitty Cleckler," Eugenia muttered. "Hundreds of bones, the very idea."

The phone rang, and she reached for the receiver without taking her eyes off the television screen. "Hello?"

It was Annabelle. "Well?"

"When I left Violet's house last night, there was one skeleton—not even a whole body. Certainly not hundreds of bones. And Junior Mobley determined it was a young female based on a forensic course at Woodrow Wilson Junior College."

"So why does Mayor Witherspoon think he needs the state police and better FBI agents than Mark?"

Eugenia was stumped on this one. "I don't know."

"Any number of things might have happened after you left Violet's house last night. Maybe they found more skeletons!" Annabelle said. "Maybe a serial killer *has* been using Miss Violet's backyard for his burial ground!"

"Don't you think Violet would have noticed if her yard was constantly being dug up for new graves?"

"Maybe not. You know she doesn't do much gardening," Annabelle answered sharply. "You need to come to Charlotte."

"I'm not coming to Charlotte."

"I don't have the time or the energy to plan your funeral right now. Please talk to Violet before you make a final decision about coming to Charlotte," Annabelle pled.

"I can't talk to anyone if you don't quit calling me." Eugenia hung up on her sister, mildly alarmed. Maybe there were murdered women buried all over Violet's backyard. It was time she found out for sure.

She dialed Violet's number and got a busy signal. Frowning she wished she had thought to get a cell number for the niece. She hit redial on her phone for the next several minutes while watching the mayor on a different local station. He called the situation a "crisis," even though he admitted he hadn't even visited the scene of the crime yet.

Finally she gave up on Violet and tried the Haggerty Police Department and the county sheriff's office. The lines in both places were also busy.

She turned her television back to Channel 3, where they were now showing live footage of Violet's house taken from down the road. The police tape they used to rope off the area makes it look almost as serious as the mayor had indicated.

She turned to Lady. "It's a good thing neither Violet nor Cecelia have much business anymore because after this no one will want to go near the place except at Halloween."

Lady barked in agreement.

Then there was a knock on the back door. Since the sun hadn't risen yet, it was too early for polite company. But at least the back door indicated a friend rather than foe or reporter, if there's a difference. Unless it was a serial killer.

Just in case, Eugenia took a butcher knife with her and called through the door, "Who's there?"

"Me, Winston," the police chief's tired voice replied.

She put down the knife and opened the door. Winston was standing on the steps. Based on the wrinkled condition of his uniform and his bloodshot, dark-circled eyes, she guessed that he'd been up all night.

"Oh, Miss Eugenia," he said. "This is a nightmare."

* * *

Eugenia brought Winston into the kitchen and made him some instant hot chocolate.

"Is this the strongest thing you've got?" he asked when she set the mug in front of him.

"Sorry, yes. I don't drink coffee anymore. Lost my taste for it."

Winston took a sip and made a face. "I have the Mormons to thank for this."

"Hot chocolate tastes good once you get used to it." She got some marshmallows out of the cupboard and tossed a handful into his mug. "There. Now what in the world is going on?"

"I've never seen anything like it," he told her. "And having lived in Haggerty all my life, I know how a story can take on a life of its own."

She nodded in complete understanding.

"But this," he waved toward the television, where the governor was looking earnestly into the camera and gesturing as he spoke. The volume was turned down so Eugenia couldn't hear what he was saying, but she could guess. "Hannah-Leigh is calling it the Skeleton Murders."

Eugenia believed in giving credit where it was due. "You've got to admit that's catchy." She sat down across from him. "So there's not a serial killer in Haggerty?"

"No!" Winston said in exasperation. "Nothing has changed since last night. We've got one skeleton. Junior Mobley went all around the yard with his X-ray app and didn't find evidence of any more. The FBI's sending some forensic guys over this morning to check officially, but there's absolutely no reason for all the uproar and panic." He ran his hands through his thinning hair.

"You're going to be bald as an egg if you keep doing that," Eugenia scolded mildly.

He ignored this. "We've got the governor sending in the state police and more FBI agents, and he's even threatened to enforce a curfew!"

"And all of that might be completely necessary," Eugenia pointed out. "We did find the remains of a body last night, and Darnell said it may have been buried for only a few months, which could add up to a murderer in Haggerty."

"Darnell Mobley," Winston said in disgust, "is fueling part of the runaway rumors—him and that son who thinks he's a forensic expert because he has a two-year degree from the junior college, which it took him three years to get, by the way!"

Eugenia stifled a laugh. "I guess it would be hard for a small town mortician to resist a moment of fame. The Mobleys probably never felt so important. What are they saying to fuel the rumors?"

"Just vague stuff like they aren't sure how many bodies are in Miss Violet's backyard or that they can't give out details since they are part of the investigation but there is evidence of foul play. Stupid stuff like that."

"Dangerous stuff like that," Eugenia murmured.

"Yeah, Mark's already packed his family up and sent them to Utah, just in case."

And in that moment it all became personal. Eugenia couldn't control a little whimper as she hurried to her back porch and looked out to the driveway she shared with her neighbors. Sure enough, the Iversons' van was gone.

She trudged back into the kitchen. "You may have multiple murders on your hands after all," she muttered, "because I may kill Darnell and his silly son for taking Emily and Charles away at Easter."

"If you're going to do it, make it soon," Winston requested without a trace of humor. "Before they star in another phony TV interview."

The phone rang, and Eugenia answered it.

"Eugenia!" Polly Kirby's excited voice came piercingly through the phone line. "Have you heard? There's a murderer in Haggerty! I haven't slept a wink all night!"

"You can't believe everything you hear on television," Eugenia tried to calm her.

"If I only believe a tenth of what I've heard on TV, I'd still be terrified," Polly replied. "I've called my friend Lucy. You know, the one who lives right across the Florida state line? I figure it's safe at her house. I asked her if I could stay for a few days. She's sending her son to pick me up." Polly made a noise that was something between a wail and a giggle. "I'm sure she'd let you come too."

"Thanks, Polly, but I have to stay in Haggerty."

"You're so brave!" Polly proclaimed. "I need to hang up so I can finish packing. If you're smart, you'll at least go to Annabelle's house and stay there until this mass-murderer is in custody."

"There is no mass-murderer in Haggerty," Eugenia said, but Polly had already hung up.

"See what I mean?" Winston moaned. "Facts have absolutely no effect."

"You're right. It's an insane state of affairs, even for Haggerty."

He drained the last of his hot chocolate. "Well, I've got to go. I just wanted to tell you it was mostly hysterical nonsense and ask you to try and set the record straight—if you can get anyone to listen."

"It's times like this when I really wish Brother Patrick was married," she said. "People listen to a preacher's wife, someone who provides a calming feminine influence."

"It's not a bad idea to tell Brother Patrick, though," Winston said. "He may not be feminine, but maybe he can still have a calming influence. It can't hurt anyway."

"I'll call him," Eugenia promised. And she did, right after she locked the door behind Winston, just in case. But she got his answering machine and could only leave a message. She had just put the phone down when it rang again. Assuming it was Annabelle, she answered curtly, "Hello?"

It was George Ann's doctor, and Eugenia felt ashamed. In all that had happened over the past few hours, she'd forgotten that George Ann was in the hospital with amnesia or dementia or a combination of the two.

"I just wanted to let you know that I've finished my morning rounds and reviewed Miss Simmons's test results. She is still a little confused, and I've prescribed some medication that will hopefully help, but there's no medical reason to keep her in the hospital. You will need to make a decision about whether to hire someone to care for Miss Simmons at home or put her in a retirement home—whatever you think is best."

"Whatever I think is best?" Eugenia repeated, dumbfounded.

"Since she's given you power of attorney," he explained. "And named you both the executor of her estate and her major beneficiary."

"I'm what?" Eugenia was shocked. "There must be some mistake."

"Unless she's changed her will in the past month, there isn't," the doctor continued calmly. "She brought me a copy to put in her file a few weeks ago."

Eugenia shook her head, trying to make sense of it. She and George Ann were not close friends. She didn't want or need George Ann's money. Finally she said, "I don't know what she was thinking, but I'll get it changed immediately." Surely it was possible to refuse power of attorney and to opt out of an unwanted inheritance.

"There probably is a legal procedure, but that will be complicated now because of Miss Simmons's mental state," the doctor pointed out. "A lawyer named Violet Newberry prepared the power of attorney and the will. You can talk to her about changing things. In the meantime, I'm afraid Miss Simmons is your responsibility."

And then understanding dawned. George Ann must have known that her memory, and possibly her sanity, was slipping. She didn't have any relatives, and she certainly didn't have any close friends since she'd been an unpleasant person all her life. So she went to Violet and made up a new will giving Eugenia legal responsibility for her estate. She knew that would obligate Eugenia to take care of her when she could no longer take care of herself. It was just like George Ann to do such a thing instead of asking for help.

"Mrs. Atkins?" the doctor was saying. "Are you still there?"

Eugenia realized she'd been lost in thought for too long. "Oh, yes. I'll come get George Ann," she promised with extreme reluctance. *And then we will drive straight over to Violet Newberry's office,* she thought to herself. *And I will have my name removed from George Ann's will even if I have to fight my way through a line of policemen to get inside.*

"Good," the doctor sounded relieved, and she wondered how legal her obligation to George Ann really was. Maybe if she had refused to pick her up, the doctor would have been stuck with the responsibility. "I'll tell the nurses to have her ready."

Eugenia hung up the phone and looked at Lady. "Well, I guess that means I've got to rearrange another entire day because of George Ann. I'll have to cancel a dental appointment and miss the baby shower for Moira Linsley's granddaughter."

Lady barked twice.

Eugenia sighed. "You're right, I don't mind postponing the dentist, and I'm getting too old for baby showers. But I don't like it that George Ann is running my life. I guess there's no way around it, at least until I talk to Violet and find out how to disavow or abdicate or whatever I need to do to remove myself from George Ann's will."

As Eugenia trudged upstairs to dress for the day, she realized that there was one bright spot to this whole thing. At least she'd have a good excuse to find out firsthand just what was going on in Violet's backyard.

* * *

When Presley woke up, she wondered if the whole skeleton episode had been a dream. But when she looked out the bedroom window and saw the police tape cordoning off the huge hole in her aunt's backyard, she knew it had been a real-life nightmare. However, even a nightmare was an improvement over what her life had been like for the past year, so she got up to face the day with something approaching optimism.

After a shower, she looked through her "new" clothes and picked out a pair of black pants and a blue silk shirt. Both were baggy, and the shirt had puffy sleeves that hadn't been in style for decades. But the outfit was much better than a hospital gown.

While pulling her hair back into a ponytail, Presley surveyed the drug store bag full of cosmetics. She'd never put makeup on this face before and felt oddly intimidated by the prospect. She finally decided to skip that step all together.

Downstairs she found Aunt Violet and the beautician, Cecelia, sitting at the kitchen table. Her aunt was talking into the receiver of a landline phone, and Cecelia had a cell phone pressed to her ear.

Aunt Violet ended her call and greeted Presley cheerfully. "Good morning!"

The phone started ringing again. Presley stared at it. "Why are you getting so many phone calls?"

"People want to know if any more bodies have been found in the backyard."

"And have they?" Presley asked. "Found more bodies, I mean?"

"Not so far." It was Cecelia who answered. She had just ended her call. She reached over Aunt Violet and answered the landline. "Hello."

Presley looked out the kitchen window and then back to her aunt. "So what's been happening?"

"The funeral director's son brought his iPad over this morning and scanned the yard again. He didn't find any more skeletons, so it looks like we don't have a serial killer. But the FBI is sending over a guy with a much stronger machine to double-check later."

"It will be nice to rule that out," Presley murmured.

Aunt Violet pointed at a box of Krispy Kremes on the counter. "Cecelia brought doughnuts for breakfast."

Presley held up a canister of protein powder. "I'm about to make myself a shake."

Aunt Violet wrinkled her nose. "That doesn't sound very substantial or delicious."

It was Presley's turn to smile. "It isn't, but it gives me what I need to get through until lunch." She mixed her shake and drank it quickly. When she was finished, she pointed at the desserts lined up on the counter. "No visitors yet?"

"We've had several, but the policemen wouldn't let anyone in."

"I hate to feel glad about a dead person in your backyard, but that news is so good I almost do."

Aunt Violet smiled again. "The people who live in Haggerty are mostly well-meaning. It won't be that terrible to meet them."

"I'd rather meet them gradually, instead of all at once."

Presley noticed that Cecelia was answering both phones alternately, making a brief statement to the effect that there were no new bodies and then hanging up.

"Do you want me to take a turn with the phones?" Presley offered. "Or one of them at least?"

Cecelia sighed. "I say we just turn them off. It's mostly reporters anyway, and they don't want to hear the truth."

Aunt Violet nodded. "We could except that Mac might get a call."

Presley was surprised by this. "You take messages for Mac?"

Aunt Violet nodded. "Just the tow requests called in through the 1-800 number."

Presley controlled a groan. No doubt her aunt provided this service for free as well.

"We could turn the ringers off and let people leave messages," Cecelia suggested. "Then we can get Mac's from voicemail."

"Let's do that for a little while anyway," Aunt Violet agreed. "We need a break." Once both ringers were off, the trio enjoyed the silence for a few seconds.

Then Presley asked, "Do you have any appointments you want me to sit in on this morning?"

"I did, but Sheriff Bonham made me reschedule," Aunt Violet replied.

"Me too," Cecelia added.

Presley frowned. "Hopefully your appointments weren't critical."

"Mine was a color touch-up for a woman with terrible gray roots, so it might qualify for the critical category," Cecelia said. "I'll probably have to make a house call later today."

Aunt Violet smiled. "Mine was just a divorce consultation."

Presley raised her eyebrow at her aunt's casual tone.

"Nothing urgent. And since I only charge $25 for consultation visits, I'm not even losing much money."

Presley was stunned. "Do you undercharge everyone?"

"Maybe not everyone," her aunt hedged.

"I don't undercharge, in case you're interested," Cecelia said. "But I don't have many customers, so fortunately I'm independently wealthy."

Presley wasn't sure how to respond to this. She finally settled on, "That's good, I guess."

Cecelia laughed. "Don't you want to know how someone like me got rich? Especially since I don't have any clients?"

"Cecelia," Aunt Violet said in a mildly reproving tone.

"She's going to hear the story eventually," Cecelia insisted. "I'd rather tell it myself. That way at least I know she's getting the truth."

Presley was thoroughly intrigued now but didn't want to seem overly curious. So she remained quiet.

"It's your story," Aunt Violet conceded. "Tell it if you want to."

Cecelia turned in her chair to face Presley. There was challenge in her eyes, and Presley felt like this story was a test of some kind.

"I went to cosmetology school in Albany, and when I finished, I took a job at a salon in a fancy retirement home there. The pay wasn't great, but the hours were good. I didn't love it, but I didn't hate it. Then one day a nice elderly gentleman came in for a haircut." Cecelia's voice trembled a little, but she pressed on. "His name was Edison Moore, and he was a new resident. He told me he was having trouble adjusting to the retirement home. He was lonely and didn't like being on someone else's schedule. He invited me to come up to his room after work, and I accepted."

"Even though fraternizing with residents specifically violated the terms of your employment," Aunt Violet mentioned.

"Yes, in spite of that. I went up to his room every day. I only stayed about an hour, and nothing inappropriate happened. Then someone turned me in, and I got fired. Those snobs who ran the retirement home thought that would be the end of it, but Edison showed them. He *hired* me to come visit him every afternoon. It turned out he was obscenely rich, so I was making more money by visiting him for an hour a day than I did working all week at the salon!" Cecelia smiled fondly. "Oh, how the administrators hated that. But they couldn't stop me from visiting since I wasn't an employee anymore."

"They did have the authority to kick Edison out of the retirement home, though," Aunt Violet moved the story along.

"And that was the best thing that ever happened to either of us," Cecelia said. "When he got word that he was being evicted, he asked me to marry him. He presented it as a business arrangement. With a spouse to supervise his care, he could move back into his palatial home and live out his final years in familiar surroundings. When he died, I would get some of his money. So that's what we did."

"Let me guess, his heirs weren't happy about this arrangement?" Presley had seen it many times.

"No," Cecelia confirmed. "They still got plenty—millions—but they wanted it *all*. They couldn't break his will, but they tried. They took me to court and called me all kinds of horrible things. I was on the news every day for weeks. The court ruled in my favor, but people in this town believe everything they hear on TV. I've been a pariah since Edison died. Rich, but still a pariah."

"Why don't you move?" Presley asked. This seemed like the obvious solution.

"I've thought about it," Cecelia said. "And eventually that's probably what I'll do. But I hate to let the gossipers around here think they won."

Presley frowned. "You can't live in misery just to prove a point."

"I'm not miserable," Cecelia claimed. "I have a few friends, the non-judgmental people like your aunt."

The two women shared a smile.

"And I really enjoy doing hair," she added.

"Cecelia has many friends besides me, and Haggerty would miss her if she moved, whether anyone realizes it or not," Aunt Violet said. "She anonymously donates a lot of money to local charities."

"If I could find the right cause, I'd give it all away," Cecelia said. "Being rich isn't as fun as it sounds."

Presley laughed at this. "Thanks for telling me your story. I'm glad I heard it from you first, but I wouldn't have believed it if anyone had called you a gold digger. I've done a lot of estate law, so I know the kind of people who marry only for money. I can tell by the way you talk about your husband that you cared for him very much."

"I did," Cecelia said softly. Then she smiled at Aunt Violet. "I think I'm going to like your niece!"

Presley was enjoying the moment.

Then Cecelia said, "Now that I've bared my soul, will you answer one question for me?"

Presley felt cold all over. Anxiety made her vision blur, but she forced herself to nod. She waited, expecting the worst.

Cecelia leaned close and asked earnestly, "Is your hair color natural? Because if it's not, I want the name of your stylist in Ohio. I've never seen a more pure platinum-blonde."

Presley laughed more from relief than humor. "Sorry, it's natural."

"Darn!" Cecelia was obviously disappointed. "If I could give the women in this town your hair color, they might accept me despite my dark past."

Presley laughed again, but Aunt Violet shook her head. "I wish you wouldn't say things like that, Cecelia."

"It's just a joke," Cecelia claimed. But Presley got the feeling that Cecelia didn't find it funny either.

* * *

They turned the phones back on and took turns answering calls for a while. Presley kept checking *her* cell phone, hoping Mac McIntyre would call with a report on her car. When her aunt noticed, she asked if Presley was expecting an important call.

"I'm just anxious to find out what's wrong with my car," she said.

Aunt Violet hit the heel of her hand against her forehead. "Oh, I forgot to tell you he called earlier! He's going to stop by later to talk to you about it."

Cecelia shook her head. "That sounds bad. If it was fixed, he would have told your aunt. It's the bad news everyone thinks they have to deliver in person."

Presley's heart sank. "You're probably right."

The phone rang, and Cecelia reached for it. She listened for a few seconds and then grabbed a little message notepad and started writing.

Aunt Violet lowered her voice to keep from disturbing Cecelia's message-taking. "Don't forget about Loralee's groceries. I really appreciate you assuming responsibility for that job. It's difficult for me to shop with this thing." She motioned toward the oxygen tank.

"Yet you didn't tell her you couldn't do it."

"How could I say that to sweet Loralee?"

Cecelia finished taking the message and stood. "I'm going to take a break from the phones and go order my supplies for the week." She held up the message she'd taken. "This is for Mac; he needs to pick up a boat this afternoon. Where do you want me to put it?"

"I put Mac's messages on my desk," Aunt Violet said.

"Then I guess I'll take the long way around to my shop." Cecelia started toward the front.

"I'll take care of that." Presley stood and reached for the message. "I need to stretch my legs a little."

So Cecelia went out the back door toward her salon, and Presley walked up to the front of the house. She went into the office and put the message neatly in the middle of Aunt Violet's desk.

As she was leaving the office, she saw a black Mercedes pull to a stop near the police tape. A tall man climbed out, talking on his phone. Presley noted his expensive suit and reddish-blond hair.

She assumed he was trying to visit the lovely Cecelia and that he wouldn't be allowed past the barricade. She was wrong on both counts. The police officer in charge lifted the tape for him to pass, and then he walked straight up to the door of Aunt Violet's law offices. He had obviously been there before, since he twisted the handle and shoved with his shoulder at the same time.

He saw her as he stepped inside the lobby and bestowed a dazzling smile.

This didn't have the desired effect since Presley was immune to charm. "May I help you?"

"I'm Wyatt Abernathy." He extended his hand. "You look like a Scandinavian ice-princess, but we don't get many of those around here. So I think you must actually be Miss Violet's grand-niece, Presley."

"I am." She took his outstretched hand and shook it one time firmly. "The niece, not the princess."

He gave her another grin. "Any relation to Elvis?"

"How original," she murmured. "But no."

"I had to ask." He shrugged. "I mean, how cool would that be?"

She gave him an impatient look. "I don't know."

Realizing that his tactics were not working, he shifted gears. He cleared his throat and said, "I'm a lawyer too."

That explained the suit. "So you're Aunt Violet's competition?"

"Oh, no. I work for a firm in Albany. We handle big cases for big clients. Your aunt's practice is limited to small, dull, unprofitable cases."

Presley thought about the faded sign outside. "Wills and divorces."

He nodded. "Right.

"Somebody's got to do the small stuff."

"But a city girl like you is bound to get bored with it fast. And when you do, just give me a call and we can go out to dinner." He was more than just a flirt, he was a confident flirt.

"I like small towns," she told him. "And I'll be too busy learning about my aunt's practice to have a social life for the foreseeable future. But thank you for the offer."

He raised an eyebrow. "It shouldn't take you more than an hour to get a handle on your aunt's practice."

"I like to be thorough."

He pursed his lips. "I just don't see it keeping your interest."

"You don't even know me."

"I know you're from Columbus, Ohio, and that your previous firm handled all kinds of big cases."

Presley wanted to move away from that subject as quickly as possible. "How did you get past the police?"

"I told them I was here on legal business." He grinned. "It works every time."

It was the genuine amusement that made her see the resemblance—and notice his bright blue eyes. Wyatt Abernathy looked a lot like Mac McIntyre. "Do you have a brother?" she asked.

"Nope, but I have a couple of cousins—Justifus and Patrick."

"Does Justifus go by Mac?"

The grin again. "He does."

That explained Mac's willingness to go by the odd nickname. "I met him last night. He had to tow my car."

"See, you've only been here one day, and you've already started having bad luck. You need to get out of Haggerty fast, at least long enough for a nice dinner."

She shook her head. "Don't you ever give up?"

"Never," he promised.

"Let's go see Aunt Violet since you're supposed to be here on *legal* business." She led him into the kitchen, where her aunt was still sitting at the kitchen table. Presley was surprised when Aunt Violet seemed pleased to see him.

"You'd better not be trying to convince Presley to come work at your fancy firm in Albany."

"So far I've only been trying to convince her to go out to dinner with me." He looked over at Presley. "I've been begging Miss Violet to fold up shop for some time. My firm would like to open a satellite office out here and has offered to buy this place for more than it's worth. She could retire and live out her golden years in luxury."

"Your firm isn't offering me *that* much," Aunt Violet countered. "And the people around here can't afford the fees your firm charges. Who would handle all the nickel and dime stuff if I retire?"

He shrugged. "You can't take care of everyone forever."

"No, but I can do it for a while longer. Besides, Presley might want to take over my practice."

Presley kept her face expressionless.

Wyatt seemed to sense her reluctance, and the calculating smile returned to his handsome face. "It's more of a charity than a practice."

There was a commotion at the front of the house, and a few seconds later Miss Eugenia walked in accompanied by her little bone-finding dog, a tall woman with a long neck, and a harried-looking police officer.

"I declare! It takes an act of Congress to get in to see you!" Miss Eugenia exclaimed with obvious displeasure.

"Sheriff Bonham is going to write me up for this," the young deputy looked terrified. "But she said she had an emergency, and then she just started walking past the tape. I couldn't exactly tackle two old ladies and a dog."

"Did you just call me old?" Miss Eugenia demanded. "I'm going to file a complaint with the sheriff's office. There's got to be a rule against that! Age discrimination or something!"

Aunt Violet addressed the deputy. "No complaints will be filed, and I will personally make sure Sheriff Bonham doesn't hold this forced entry against you. No one is a match for Miss Eugenia."

This comment seemed to mollify both parties. The deputy returned to his post, and Miss Eugenia sat down at the kitchen table. She put Lady on the floor and told the other woman to sit beside her.

"Presley, this is Miss George Ann Simmons," Aunt Violet introduced them. "She's a client of mine."

Miss Simmons nodded vaguely then stared at the puzzle.

"Is she okay?" Presley whispered.

Miss Eugenia shrugged. "We aren't really sure. That's one of the reasons I'm here. Your aunt drew up George Ann's most recent will, and for some reason I'm named as the executor and beneficiary. And she gave me power of attorney!"

Wyatt Abernathy stood. "Well, it sounds like this is about to become a privileged conversation, so I'll say my good-byes."

"Don't rush off, Wyatt," Aunt Violet said with a twinkle in her eye. "Miss Eugenia might need some free legal advice."

"That's your department, not mine." He handed Presley a business card. "Nice to meet you. My offer for dinner is a standing one. My social calendar stays pretty full, but I will gladly make room if you change your mind." After a polite nod in the general direction of the other ladies, Wyatt moved to the back door. "I think I'll go over and flirt with Cecelia for a while. She likes me."

Once he was gone, Aunt Violet shook her head. "That boy."

Presley stifled a laugh. "That boy is a grown man, and he's pushy."

"Wyatt's okay," Miss Eugenia said. "Just a little too slick for my comfort." She looked out the kitchen window. "Any more skeletons?"

"Not yet," Aunt Violet reported. "We're expecting the FBI to come X-ray my yard any minute."

Miss Eugenia spotted Cecelia's Krispy Kremes. "I'm starving. Can I have a doughnut?" she asked. "George Ann might want one too."

Presley got the box and put it on the table between them. Then she distributed napkins and glasses of milk at her aunt's request. She noted that a doughnut had to be placed on a napkin directly in front of Miss George Ann before she would eat it.

"So what did the doctor say?" Aunt Violet asked.

"There's nothing they can do for her in the hospital," Miss Eugenia replied. "They've started her on some new medication that might help with her memory and confusion. Time will tell, but so far I don't see any improvement."

Aunt Violet's expression was solemn.

Miss George Ann was staring at the Big Ben puzzle.

Presley picked up a piece of the puzzle and handed it to the woman. Then she pointed at the spot where it was supposed to go. It took Miss George Ann a few tries, but finally she got it to fit. Then she looked up at Presley and smiled. Presley handed her another piece.

Miss Eugenia narrowed her eyes. "You've been trying to distract me with doughnuts and small talk, but it won't work, Violet Newberry. I am going to discuss the will."

Aunt Violet looked down at her lap in a rare show of embarrassment. "I'm sorry, Eugenia. I know you're not happy about it, but George Ann really had no one else."

"What's going on?" Presley asked.

"Your aunt tricked me into taking responsibility for her." Miss Eugenia pointed at the other woman.

"George Ann has no relatives," Aunt Violet reiterated. "She knew her mind was failing, and she didn't want her future to be determined by the state. She decided it was best to give you power of attorney and make you her executor and beneficiary."

"Why didn't she just tell me about her problem and ask for help?"

"I suggested that. She was afraid you'd say no."

"I probably would have," Miss Eugenia admitted. "It's too much to ask! I'm an old woman myself. Why couldn't she put this off on a lawyer or a banker, someone like Wyatt?"

"I'm her lawyer, and I'm in worse health than she is," Violet pointed out. "And she didn't want her fate to be in the hands of a stranger. She trusts you to do what's best for her. That may be the greatest compliment anyone has ever given you—except maybe when Geneva Mackey bequeathed you Lady."

Presley didn't understand everything, but she was getting the basic gist, so she didn't slow down the conversation with questions.

"But what can I do with her?" Miss Eugenia asked. "Is it my Christian duty to take her into my home and spend the rest of my life caring for her?"

Aunt Violet shook her head. "No one would expect that! Not George Ann and not even the Lord. Your duty is to decide whether she can stay at home with sitters or if a nursing home is the best option. And when she dies, you'll make sure her money goes to a good cause."

Miss Eugenia glanced at Miss George Ann, who was alternately taking small bites of doughnut and placing puzzle pieces at Presley's direction. "You're sure that's all she expects of me?"

"That's exactly what she told me," Aunt Violet confirmed.

"I hate the thought of going to a nursing home myself; it's my worst nightmare," Miss Eugenia told them. "And to think that I might have to condemn someone else to that fate . . ."

Aunt Violet laughed. "You won't be condemning her! You'll pick a nice place with an attentive staff. You'll visit her, and so will many other good Christians from Haggerty. She'll be comfortable and well-cared for." Aunt Violet lowered her voice. "And honestly, she probably won't even know where she is."

Miss Eugenia nodded. "We've been to her house twice now, and she doesn't seem to enjoy being there. She's not connected to her things anymore. They confuse her."

"She'll probably be better off in a more impersonal setting, where everything she sees doesn't challenge her to remember something she's forgotten."

"Okay, then." Miss Eugenia sounded unhappy but determined. "I won't protest the will, and I'll take care of George Ann."

Aunt Violet smiled. "You don't have to make any final decisions now. Her confusion could be temporary."

"True," Miss Eugenia agreed.

"And given more time, the new medication might help," Aunt Violet added. "So we don't want to do anything too drastic. Not yet."

"She can stay with me for a few days," Miss Eugenia continued. "It's not fair and I know she wouldn't do the same for me, but I'll rearrange my life to accommodate her."

Aunt Violet laughed. "You don't have to rearrange your whole life. George Ann can stay here during the day. I have Loralee most of the time anyway. They can be buddies."

Miss Eugenia was obviously relieved by this. "That would make the whole thing less painful. I had to cancel a dentist appointment this morning, and I'm missing a baby shower this afternoon. I know it doesn't sound like much, but it's my life and I'm not ready to give it up."

"I understand completely," Aunt Violet told her. "Why don't you go on to the baby shower? George Ann will be fine with me."

"I would feel terrible about saddling you with her," Miss Eugenia said. "Except that you let her sneak me into her will."

Aunt Violet laughed again. "You're right—I deserve it!"

* * *

After Miss Eugenia left, Presley continued to guide Miss George Ann through the puzzle process. "Will Loralee be upset if we have this puzzle finished the next time she comes?"

"She'll understand," Aunt Violet predicted. "And we have plenty more."

"You may have to set up two puzzles so the buddies won't fight."

"I have an old card table in the basement. We can bring it up for a second puzzle if a problem arises, but Loralee's usually pretty good about sharing."

A deputy came in and said that Hollis Cleckler was there claiming he'd been hired to fix the front door. Aunt Violet confirmed this, so Hollis was allowed to cross the police line. Unfortunately Miss Kitty was with him.

She gave Presley a foil pan that she said contained a ham casserole. Presley put it on the counter, knowing it was destined to the same fate as the fruitcake cookies.

While Hollis and Aunt Violet consulted about the front door, Miss Kitty took up a position near the kitchen window. From there she had a good view of the backyard. Presley suspected that Miss Kitty's presence was mostly an attempt to get something else to say on television.

Hollis warned Aunt Violet that he was probably going to have to chisel some wood off the top of her door in order to make it shut properly, and she gave her permission. Then he took his toolbox to the front of the house and went to work. Presley suggested that they all go into the living room and watch, mostly to get Miss Kitty away from the kitchen window.

As they stood to follow Mr. Clecker, Presley leaned close to Aunt Violet. "Will Miss George Ann be okay without a puzzle?"

Aunt Violet nodded. "I think so, but if she gets fidgety, I'll take her back to the kitchen."

The ladies settled in the living room and watched as Hollis Cleckler used one of the rickety folding chairs as a ladder and began chiseling, slowly. Presley hoped Hollis didn't fall, and she really hoped he would hurry since she couldn't take much more of Miss Kitty's constant chatter.

A few minutes later Sheriff Bonham walked through the open door. He surveyed the area, and when his eyes landed on Miss Kitty, his displeasure was obvious. "How did she get in here?" he asked the deputy on the sidewalk.

"She was with the repair guy. She said she was his assistant."

The sheriff glanced back inside where Miss Kitty was sitting comfortably on the couch. "Keep an eye on her," he instructed the deputy. Then he told Aunt Violet that the FBI had arrived. "They will be working in the backyard for the next hour or so. No one is to set a foot out there." He gave Miss Kitty a hard look.

"We'll all sit right here," Aunt Violet promised.

After the sheriff left, Miss Kitty wrung her hands. "This is the worst thing I've ever been a part of. A mass murderer in Haggerty!"

"As far as we know there's only one skeleton," Presley tried. "And it's probably been there awhile since everything had decomposed except the bones."

"I saw on *America's Most Wanted* that a body can decompose in a matter of weeks if the soil conditions are just right," Miss Kitty informed them. "This one man buried a girl, and less than a month later, all that was left was her teeth. Did your skeleton have teeth?"

Presley didn't want ownership of the bones. "It's not *my* skeleton, and I don't remember about the teeth. Honestly I was trying not to look."

"Well, of course not!" Kitty shuddered. "If this is not a fine way to welcome you to the community. Skeletons in your backyard."

"Just one," Aunt Violet reiterated for all the good it did.

Anxious to get away from Kitty, Presley moved over by the door. She watched Hollis shave the wood for a few minutes. And then, as her bad luck would have it, Miss Kitty joined them.

"Did you get your little sports car fixed?" she asked.

"It's in the shop. I'm waiting to hear from Mac about it."

Miss Kitty shook her head. "God love him."

Presley waited for her to explain why God should love Mac particularly, but for once Miss Kitty didn't expound.

Soon the sheriff escorted the subject of their conversation into Aunt Violet's living room. Today Mac was wearing another T-shirt advertising his towing business. This one was white and looked crisp against his tanned skin. As before, the longish auburn hair was falling onto his forehead above his blue eyes.

"We asked you to keep visitors to a minimum so we can do our job instead of being an escort service," the sheriff said tersely.

Presley knew the sheriff hadn't had much sleep, if any, and that he was under a great deal of pressure, so she tried not to take his remarks personally. "Just imagine how many people would have come if we weren't trying to keep visitors to a minimum," she replied.

The sheriff gave her a narrowed look and then stalked back outside.

"I didn't mean to cause a big problem," Mac said as he walked in.

"You didn't," Presley assured him. "He's just stressed."

"Well, look who's here!" Miss Kitty greeted Mac, as if she hadn't just been talking about him behind his back.

"Miss Kitty, Hollis," he replied. He nodded at Miss George Ann; his eyes settled on Aunt Violet. "Usually people keep skeletons in the closet, but apparently you like yours in the backyard."

Aunt Violet smiled. "You've got to admit that a skeleton in the backyard is more exciting! It might even get me a visit from the governor."

Mac shook his head. "Don't count on that. From what I heard, the governor is only coming if they find *more* skeletons in your backyard. One dead person doesn't have enough political impact to warrant a visit."

"I don't really want to meet the governor. I'm ready for all this excitement to be over so we can settle down to regular life."

"I'd love to meet the governor," Miss Kitty inserted herself into the conversation. "If I get my picture with him, the ladies in my Sunday School will be so jealous!"

Mac ignored Miss Kitty completely. "I guess it was in the hole we dug up for the vegetable garden?"

Presley nodded, but before she could answer, Miss Kitty interrupted again. "I saw the bones," she confided in a conspiratorial whisper. "Darnell from the funeral home had them all laid out on a tarp like a big puzzle."

"I saw you describing your eyewitness experience on TV," Mac said. "Unbelievable."

Presley hid a smile.

Miss Kitty didn't catch the implied insult. "There were so many bones, I don't think it could be just one person. And Mary Beth Pettigrew over at the gas station said it was definitely a murder."

Mac raised an eyebrow. "And Mary Beth knows this because . . . ?"

"Her cousin works at the morgue in Albany, and he overheard the coroner say it."

"They don't know for sure." Presley tried to keep Miss Kitty in check. "They have to run tests."

"Well, that's what Mary Beth told me," Miss Kitty said, as if quoting an expert witness. "Her cousin heard it at the morgue."

"We should let the sheriff worry about that," Mac said with barely concealed impatience. Then he took Presley by the arm. "Can I speak to you for a minute?"

She allowed him to lead her into her aunt's office and watched as he closed the door, pretty much right in Miss Kitty's face. Once they had some privacy, he said, "Are things really okay here?"

"Yes. Don't believe everything you see on TV, and believe nothing Miss Kitty tells you."

He nodded. "I learned that a long time ago."

She leaned against the desk, bracing herself for the worst. "Now what about my car?"

"It's not the battery."

"Of course it isn't." She let out a breath. "That would be too simple."

"Like I told you, I'm not a mechanic." His voice was sympathetic. "You need to have the service department at a dealership look at it, and the closest one is in Atlanta."

Presley felt ill. Just the towing fee would be more than she could afford, let alone the cost of repairing the Aston. She was trying to figure out how to explain this without humiliating herself when he continued.

"Or you could just leave it in my parents' garage and drive your aunt's car. They're in Honduras on a mission trip right now, but they'll be back in a month. My dad's an amateur mechanic. He can look at it and then advise you better than I can."

A month would give her time to make some decisions about the future. And with the Aston secluded in a garage, it couldn't provide anyone with a clue to her location. So she nodded. "That's what we'll do then." It felt good to make a decision—especially since it didn't require her to take action immediately. "And I still owe you for the tow last night."

"Don't worry about it," he said. "It was only a few feet."

She narrowed her eyes at him. "Is that what you'd tell anyone?"

"Anyone who was Miss Violet's niece," he returned.

Her aunt did plenty for everyone, including Mac, so she decided this was acceptable. She pushed away from the desk. "I'd better go break the news to Aunt Violet that she's losing her car, at least temporarily. I need to get Loralee's groceries, and I'd better do it before dark in case they go through with the curfew." She pointed at the desk. "You have a message."

"Thanks." He picked up the slip and read it. Then he put it in his pocket. "Why don't I just take you to get Loralee's groceries? I've got some time this afternoon, and it might be better if you aren't driving around alone—just in case there is a murderer in Haggerty."

Taking a car she wasn't familiar with to buy groceries for an old woman she didn't know and then delivering them to a place she'd never seen would have been stressful even without the possibility of a serial killer. So she was grateful for Mac's offer. "I'd appreciate that."

"Of course, if we leave, that means we'll have to disturb the sheriff again," he teased.

"He doesn't scare me," Presley lied.

Mac laughed. "He scares *me*!"

"One of the first things I learned in law school was never show fear." She moved toward the door. "Let me make sure Aunt Violet can handle things here while I'm gone."

They left the office and joined the others in the living room. Presley told her aunt that her car repairs were on hold for a month and that Mac had offered to help her buy and deliver Loralee's groceries.

"But I'm concerned about leaving you here with all"—she looked around the room and out the window—"this."

"You go on with Mac and do Loralee's shopping," Aunt Violet insisted. "Hollis and the FBI can take care of themselves, and Kitty can help me with George Ann."

This remark had the effect Aunt Violet undoubtedly intended on Miss Kitty.

"Oh, I'd love to help you," the woman said. "But I've got so much to do this afternoon." She turned to her husband. "Come on, Hollis."

Hollis looked startled. "I'm not quite through with the door."

Miss Kitty dismissed this. "I'm sure it will do."

Hollis climbed down from his folding chair and tried the door. There was no noticeable improvement. "It still sticks a little," he said.

"You can chisel it some more another time," Aunt Violet told him kindly.

Miss Kitty grabbed his arm and hauled him toward the door. "Come on. This place is giving me the creeps. And we need to be at the mayor's office in case the governor comes."

After they were gone, Presley looked at her aunt. "Are you sure you'll be okay?"

Aunt Violet nodded. "Miss Eugenia will be back soon. Don't worry about me."

Presley hooked her bag over her shoulder and turned to Mac. "Then I guess I'm ready."

CHAPTER NINE

The sheriff was standing in the parking lot when they stepped outside. He watched their progress across the sidewalk with a stern expression.

"It's an emergency!" Presley was purposely a little dramatic. "A hundred-year-old lady might starve if we don't go!"

The sheriff turned to Mac.

"Loralee needs groceries."

The sheriff nodded. "Go on."

Since he seemed to be in a relatively good mood, Presley risked a question. "Do you know how much longer you'll be here?"

"That depends on what the FBI finds," Sheriff Bonham replied. "If the backyard is clean, I expect everyone will be cleared out by dark. But if they come up with something—anything—then we'll probably have the state police and the governor here. Your aunt may never get her house back. I'm sorry," he added a little grudgingly. "It's out of my control."

"We understand," Presley assured him. "I've seen the television reports on the Skeleton Murders."

Sheriff Bonham rolled his eyes. "I hate news reporters."

Presley tried to imagine the stern sheriff actually *liking* anyone as they ducked under the crime-scene tape and walked to the tow truck. Mac opened the passenger door and gave her a hand up.

As they drove past the Cleckler's house, he said, "Seriously, even though you've been taught not to show fear, I'm surprised you didn't change your mind about Haggerty after last night."

She couldn't tell him how limited her options were, so she said, "I'll give Haggerty another chance, but one more skeleton and I'm gone."

He shifted gears, and she stole a glance at his right hand to check for evidence of new cuts. His hand looked as bad as it did the day before but no worse. She turned slightly in her seat so she could face his profile. "I met your cousin today."

He shifted into a higher gear. "Which one?"

"Wyatt."

He smiled. "Let me guess, he asked you out?"

"Several times," she confirmed. "He even offered to clear a spot on his busy social calendar."

"He always works hard at being a ladies' man."

"But you don't?" She regretted the question immediately, but it was too late to recall it.

"I did my share of flirting before I got married," he said. "But Wyatt has turned it into an art form."

Presley stared back, horrified. It never occurred to her that she was taking him away from his family. "You're *married*?"

He winced. "Well, I used to be. I'm in the process of getting a divorce now."

"I'm sorry."

"Yeah," he said. "Me too. But it's been over for a while. She's already with someone else, and they have a kid."

Presley stared out the windshield, dumbfounded. It was hard to imagine Mac married and even harder to imagine a woman who would let him go.

He pulled into the parking lot of a grocery store called the Piggly Wiggly. Presley looked up at the big smiling pig's head in awe. "I didn't know these stores existed anymore. It's like something from the past."

"The entire town of Haggerty is something from the past." He climbed out and waved for her to slide across. Then he took her hand and helped her down. "We have a nice Walmart Supercenter out on Highway 11, but Loralee insists on buying her groceries here even though the prices are higher. She likes to support local businesses."

"People like Loralee will save the Piggly Wigglys of the world."

He raised an eyebrow. "And that's a good thing?"

Before she could answer, his phone rang. He looked at the screen and grimaced. "I have to take this. You want to wait for me?"

"I'll go ahead and get started. Catch up when you finish your call."

The store was small, cramped, and a little smelly but surprisingly pleasant. She went up and down every aisle searching for the items Loralee had requested. It was a good list, complete with little notes like "real butter not that healthy stuff."

By the time Mac joined her, she was almost done.

"Sorry," he said.

"Don't be. Just double-check the things in my basket and make sure it's what Loralee wants."

He looked through everything and only switched out the milk. "Loralee supports local dairies too, so you can't buy the store brand."

She nodded. "I'll remember that."

"Well, Mac!" the cashier said when they were ready to pay. "How are you, honey?"

"I'm good, Miss Raye."

"The football team is starting spring practice this week," she said. "You gonna go by and offer any advice?"

"Probably not." Mac pulled out some cash and paid for the groceries.

"If you want tickets to the inter-squad game next Friday, my daughter, Carla, is selling 'em. Just five bucks a piece!"

Mac put the last bag into the cart. "Thanks, but I'm done with football."

She patted him on the arm. "Bless your heart."

As they walked outside, Presley whispered, "You played football?"

"Just about every boy in Haggerty played football at some point. It was a big part of my life when I was growing up."

"I hate all contact sports, especially football." She took his hand, and he propelled her into the truck.

He passed the grocery bags up, and she arranged them at her feet.

"It's just a game."

"It's very dangerous," she said. "Do you know how many children get hurt every year playing football?" Assuming he didn't have that statistic memorized, she didn't wait for him to respond. "And it has psychological and emotional effects as well. Studies show that it encourages violent tendencies, promotes bullying, and damages self-esteem."

He swung up into the driver's seat. "Football promotes exercise, teamwork, and is a lot of fun. You can take anything too far, but I can't agree that football is inherently bad."

"Google it," Presley said. "You'll see."

He smiled. "Have you ever been to a football game?"

She shook her head. "Why would I help support something I'm morally opposed to?"

He raised an eyebrow. "I didn't know it was possible to be morally opposed to football."

She smirked. "I'm living proof."

"You should go to a game sometime. It might change your opinion."

She hoped her face expressed how much she doubted this.

He started the truck. "If you stay in Haggerty, you might not have a choice about that. But in the meantime, on Friday nights in the fall, we can go to the movies and have the theater all to ourselves."

She felt a little quivery inside. It was nice to think about sitting in a movie theater with Mac, but she didn't know if she would still be in Haggerty in the fall.

"Football's a part of my past," he continued. "So can we be friends? Or are there more qualifications?"

She laughed. "You've met all my criteria. We are officially friends."

They rode by the high school, and Mac pointed out the players on the football field. "Spring practice. Are you sure you don't want to stop and watch?"

She cut her eyes over at him. "I'm sure."

They passed the Dollar General and the Pizza Palace. "That place is pretty good," he said. "Probably worth the carbs if you ever get in the mood for pizza."

"I'll keep that in mind," she said, although she doubted that particular mood would ever strike. But the mention of food reminded her that Mac had paid for Loralee's groceries. "Are you supposed to give me the receipt for Loralee's groceries so Aunt Violet can reimburse you?"

"Loralee doesn't have enough in her account to cover all her expenses, so we take turns paying for her groceries. That way it's not too much for anyone."

She nodded. "Sounds sensible. Who is 'we'?"

"My cousins and me."

"Wyatt Abernathy pays for Loralee's groceries?"

"Once a month," Mac confirmed. "And he pays her annual property taxes. That's one of the reasons he came to your aunt's office today. I'm sure he wanted to ask you out too," he was quick to add, "but the taxes will be due soon."

Presley frowned. "I didn't see him give my aunt any money."

"But I'll guarantee you he did. Ask your aunt when you get home."

"If that's true, I'm going to have to rethink my entire opinion of your cousin."

"He's not completely vain and self-centered. He does have a little touch of humanity."

As she considered this, Presley noticed that the road seemed to get smaller and the trees seemed to get closer. Finally Mac pulled the truck to a stop. "Loralee's house is right through there." He pointed to a gap in the trees. "I've got a tow job, so if you'll take the perishables with you, I'll bring the rest when I come back."

She stared at him in unhappy astonishment. "You're going to leave me here? In the middle of the woods?"

He laughed. "It's not the middle of the woods. If you look close, you can see her gate from here."

"But you're going to leave me," she confirmed. "With Loralee."

"You'll be fine. She may talk your ear off, but that won't hurt you. And I know you don't want to go with me while I repossess a fishing boat."

"Repossess?" She hadn't realized that was part of what he did. "Like the people on TV?"

"Not nearly that exciting, but it's steady money. I'd postpone this one if I could, but if I don't do it now, I'll lose it."

She sighed. "I don't want you to lose your opportunity, and I guess I'd rather be here with Loralee than repossessing a boat. But just barely." She consolidated the perishable food into three bags.

"I'll be back soon," he promised.

With a nod she hefted the grocery bags and trudged toward the woods.

"Presley!" He called out.

She turned.

"Let's not mention the skeleton in Miss Violet's backyard to Loralee. She'll hear about it eventually, but . . ."

She nodded and then walked on to the gap in the trees.

Loralee's house was more of a cottage, small and picturesque. Hansel and Gretel came to mind. It was surrounded by a picket fence that had been painted white but was peeling so a lot of weathered wood was exposed. The fence was lined with slightly overgrown shrubs, as if they were being allowed to look natural without overstepping their bounds.

An arched arbor covered with tiny budding rose blossoms curved above the gate. Presley pushed the gate, and it swung open. As she followed the brick walkway up to the cottage, she noticed that the flowerbeds surrounding the house were beginning to bloom and would be spectacular in the summer. There were small rosebushes, fragrant gardenias, lacy hydrangeas, and dramatic hyacinth. Honeysuckle vines tangled with wild blackberry bushes grew along the back fence. It was like a little paradise carved out of the forest.

She knocked on the door, and Versie answered.

"I'm delivering groceries for Loralee."

"Come on in," Versie invited.

"Do you stay here all the time with Loralee?"

"No, just a few hours every day. Mac wanted me to spend the night, but she won't hear of it."

Presley turned her attention to the cottage. She could see a small bedroom to the right through an open door. The room was dominated by an iron bed covered with what looked like an antique patchwork quilt.

The main room was small but beautiful in a rustic, unpretentious way. There were photographs all over the walls. Some were brittle with age and held in place with yellowed tape. Some were nailed directly to the wood planks. A few were in actual frames. There were flowers everywhere—in pots, in vases, in buckets. Some were dried, some cut, and some alive. It was almost as if the outside had continued indoors.

Versie waved toward the kitchen as she settled into a recliner near the fireplace. "You go on in there. I'll sit here and work on my crocheting. I've got a great-grandbaby coming next month, and I'm trying to get a blanket ready."

Presley carried the groceries around the corner to a kitchen that was predictably quaint but surprisingly spacious. She gestured to the photos on the wall. "You have an impressive picture gallery here."

Loralee glanced at them. "I probably should put them in a book or something—to protect them. But they're so old and brittle, I'm afraid they'll disintegrate if I try to move them. I'll be dead soon, and whoever moves into this place can just pull them off, I guess. Thank you for getting my groceries."

"I just brought in the perishables," Presley told her. "Mac had to go repossess a boat. He'll bring the rest when he's through."

Loralee shook her head. "I wish that boy wouldn't do such dangerous work."

And then it clicked. The black eye and the cuts on his hands didn't come from towing cars. They were injuries sustained while trying to repossess things. That's what Aunt Violet had meant about hazards of his profession. Presley put the groceries on the table, feeling a little stunned and foolish.

Loralee searched through each bag until she found the butter. "I need this for the pecan pies I'm making for our Easter dinner. Violet always does the dressing, so she can teach you how. It's a wonderful recipe that should be passed down in your family."

Presley assumed this was a backhanded invitation to the holiday meal and was about to decline when Loralee continued. "Everyone will start arriving right after church, but Violet always serves the meal around one o'clock."

"The dinner is at Aunt Violet's house?"

She nodded. "Well, of course. I'm sure Violet has mentioned it."

Presley was sure she hadn't but kept this fact to herself. She was horrified at the thought of having to be polite and make small talk with strangers on Easter since holidays were particularly difficult.

It was as if Loralee read her mind. "It will be mostly people you've met—Cecelia and Mac and Wyatt. Sometimes Winston Jones comes, depending on his girlfriend situation at the time. Eugenia and George Ann will probably come this year since the Iversons are out of town."

"I don't cook," Presley said. "I'll be no help to Aunt Violet at all."

Loralee laughed. "Tell her to let you start by learning how to make cornbread! Once you master that, you can move on to dressing. By Christmas you should be ready."

Christmas. There was no telling where she would be then.

Again Loralee voiced her thoughts. "Of course, I probably won't live until Christmas. Now come sit down and eat a piece of Italian cream cake."

"I don't eat dessert."

"You need to put a little fat on those bones," Loralee said. "If you don't watch it, you'll be a skeleton."

Presley was startled by the choice of words, but there was no guile in Loralee's expression.

"If you won't eat cake, how about a little biscuit with some of my homemade blackberry jelly. You do eat jelly, don't you?"

"Sometimes," Presley murmured.

"Miss Blanche taught me how to make jelly, and blackberry was her favorite."

Loralee obviously wanted to tell her about the Armstrongs, but Presley just couldn't make herself care about them. So she didn't ask any leading questions, hoping the subject would change.

Loralee went right on anyway. "And you should have tasted Miss Blanche's biscuits. They were so light you almost had to hold them down to keep them from floating in the air."

Presley raised an eyebrow.

Loralee did not amend her statement. "Would you like a tour of their house? It's just a little ways away, and Mac can pick you up there when he's through collecting the boat."

"Sure, I guess," Presley said without enthusiasm.

"You're going to love it!" Loralee promised. She headed for the door. When they passed Versie, she said, "I'm going to give Presley a tour of the old place. When Mac gets here, will you tell him he can pick her up there?"

"You be careful," Versie admonished. She looked at Presley. "That place is an accident waiting to happen. Don't fall through any rotten floorboards or get knocked in the head by falling rafters."

"I'll be on the lookout for both," Presley promised. Then she followed Loralee outside.

They walked out the front door of the little cottage and up the brick walkway to the gate. It was a lovely spring day—bright sunshine and still a little cool after the rain from the day before. Instead of walking to the road, the way Presley had come in, they turned to the left and entered the woods along a well-worn path. The trees above them grew together, creating a roof of sorts. Parked by a stately old oak was a modern scooter chair.

"I don't really need this," Loralee said as she settled herself into the seat, "but I promised the boys I would use it, and I try not to lie."

Presley almost smiled. Loralee was odd, but her honesty was refreshing. "The boys, you mean Mac and Wyatt and Patrick?"

"Yes. Have you met them all?"

"Not Patrick."

She smiled. "Then you have a treat in store! All the boys are wonderful, but Patrick, now he's special."

And then Loralee buzzed off down the path on her scooter. Presley had to walk briskly to keep up. She was out of breath when finally they emerged from the woods into a large clearing with a little creek on one side and a house in the middle.

The house was almost completely covered by flowering vines. There were holes in the roof, and grass grew through the rotted boards on the porch. Most of the glass in the window panes was broken. Some shutters hung askew; others had fallen to the ground.

Presley turned to look at the creek.

"It's a cove," Loralee told her with delight. "There are several along the creek, but this is the biggest one."

Presley nodded, her eyes moving around the property. There were a few outbuildings along the perimeter, and all were falling in on themselves.

Based on Loralee's glowing descriptions, Presley had pictured something much different. She thought the house would be nicely preserved, cared for. It made Presley sad to see it, and she didn't even know Blanche and DuPont Armstrong. Once this had been a thriving place, a farm and a home. Now it was a ruin. "It's in terrible condition. Can it be fixed?" she asked.

Loralee looked up in surprise. "To me it just looks like Miss Blanche's garden is protecting the house. Mac is going to restore it, but he can only work in his spare time, and his ex-wife makes sure he doesn't have much of that. She gets a percentage of his income." Loralee looked down.

"Divorces can be very difficult," Presley said. "I've never handled them."

"I'm glad. It would be a sad line of work." She parked the scooter. "Let's go inside, and I'll show you around."

Presley was hesitant. "Is it safe?"

"I've walked on these old floorboards a thousand times and never fallen through!" Loralee said. "But we'll go in through the back, since the front porch is in the worst shape."

She led the way to the back door and turned the knob. Loralee's voice quivered a little as she said, "Every time I step through this door I get a feeling of peace and love. I believe Miss Blanche's spirit is still here. That's the only explanation for it."

Presley followed the old woman inside, hoping the place wasn't haunted. They crossed a closed-in porch. An ancient wash tub occupied one corner, and a scrub board took up the other. Both were covered with dust and cobwebs. The next room was a large kitchen. Presley looked at the wooden table and chairs, the old fashioned appliances, dishes, pots, and pans with awe.

"This stuff is valuable!" she said. "It should be in a museum or sold to an antique dealer. They're being ruined by exposure to the elements and bugs and probably rats."

Loralee shook her head. "We could never sell Miss Blanche's things. Her spirit might leave if we did."

Realizing that Loralee might not be as sane as she had previously thought, Presley stepped over a broken mason jar and followed the older woman into a wide hallway. To one side was a dining room, where a hole in the roof had already done considerable damage. The surface of the table was warped, and the chairs were overturned. The china cabinet was intact, but the dishes inside were broken and shining in the sunlight, fragments of a former time.

On the other side of the hallway were two bedrooms and a bathroom. The last room was a large open area. Loralee called it a sleeping porch. Frames of old cots, with scraps of canvas hanging off them leaned against the walls. Screens that had kept insects out and let a cool breeze in were gone except for a few stray wires.

"The upstairs is divided into two rooms as well," Loralee explained. "It was an addition, done the same time as the new kitchen." She waved a hand to encompass the whole ruin. "Now this all belongs to the boys."

Presley looked around. It seemed hopeless to her. "What is Mac going to do first?"

"He's going to shore up the foundation. Then he'll start on the back porch and work his way forward."

They walked back outside and sat on a fallen log by the road to wait for Mac.

"To pass the time I could tell you about Miss Blanche and how she came here."

Obviously Loralee was determined, and they had nothing else to talk about, so Presley nodded.

Loralee smiled, rearranging the many wrinkles that lined her face. Her dress was tucked around her legs more like a child than a nearly hundred-year-old woman.

"All this land used to belong to my father. Then he became a drunkard, and Mr. DuPont bought it for the back taxes."

"And you didn't mind that DuPont bought your land?"

Loralee shrugged. "Somebody was going to get it, so it might as well be Mr. DuPont. I thought we'd have to leave, and we didn't have anywhere to go. But Mr. DuPont let us move into the cottage, and I've been there ever since." Loralee paused for a dreamy smile and then continued. "Mr. DuPont came on weekends with some of his college friends to fix up the place. I watched from the trees. After they'd leave, I'd collect the beer bottles they left behind. Old Mr. Pardee at the general store gave me a dollar for them."

"The actual deposit was probably more than what he gave you."

Loralee didn't hold a grudge. "I was thankful to get the dollar."

"You have the strangest way of looking at things."

She smiled. "Mr. DuPont said I'm an optimist."

And then some, Presley thought to herself.

"Since the money came from Mr. DuPont indirectly, I started working in the yard around the house to repay him. I cleared away weeds and transplanted wildflowers. About a week later they came back. Mr. DuPont walked around the house looking at the flowers I'd planted, scratching his head like he was trying to figure out how they could have grown while he was gone." Loralee paused for a flurry of giggles. "This time they stayed for nearly a week. They put on a new roof and built an outhouse and a smokehouse.

"Then they used the leftover wood to build long benches and tables. At first I thought it was furniture for the house. But when they lined everything up in the yard, I realized they were meant to stay outside. And meant to feed a lot of people." She stood up and demonstrated the placement of the tables.

"Again when the work was finished, the men celebrated with beer and then left. I collected the bottles and turned them in to Mr. Pardee."

"And got another dollar?"

Loralee nodded. "I was rich!"

"When did DuPont come again?"

"A week later he arrived with three boats full of linens and dishes and furniture—fine things with carved legs and shiny polished surfaces, even a small piano. And so much food! There were barrels of flour and sugar, smoked hams and some chickens for fresh eggs. But he didn't have any friends with him this time. Just people to drive the boats and a German immigrant couple he'd hired and their children, Peter and Irma."

"I know you were disappointed there wouldn't be a beer-drinking party to benefit your stash of dollars," Presley teased.

"I was at first," Loralee admitted. "But the furniture and food meant he would soon be moving in, and I figured that meant more parties in the future."

"You *are* an optimist."

She was too wrapped up in her story to comment on this. "Mr. DuPont looked at the flowers that were flourishing in the beds and then looked straight at the tree where I was sitting and tipped his hat. At the end of that weekend, Mr. DuPont left, but the Heinrichs stayed. They started building themselves a place to live"—she pointed in the direction of Aunt Violet's property—"and worked around here. After everything inside the house was set up, they started roasting meat on a spit, making stew in a big black pot, and baking pies.

"Then Mr. DuPont returned with his boat and his beer-loving friends, but they were all sober this time. And they had some young ladies with them wearing lacy white dresses. They looked like angels as the boys carried them from the boat to the shore.

"Back in those days, it was considered improper for young ladies to be in the company of young men without chaperones. So Miss Blanche's mama came along to supervise. Some of the girls got in the water, splashing and falling down. She looked on with disapproval. But Mr. DuPont was so handsome and charming he teased her into a good mood."

Presley looked out at the sparkling water and tried to imagine it full of boisterous youth. "He was handsome and charming?"

"Oh, yes," Loralee said. "His great-great-grandsons are a lot like him in different ways. Wyatt has red hair, Mac's got his charm, and Patrick is irresistible."

"Just like DuPont?"

Loralee nodded. "First the ladies went inside to freshen up. Then they all sat at the long tables for lunch. The Heinrichs' daughter, Irma, helped serve. She was a pretty girl, and the ladies claimed her as a pet. One of them had an extra dress that they let Irma put on. Then they fixed her hair so she looked just like one of them. Irma loved it, but I thought it was cruel, letting her pretend to be something she wasn't."

There was a little edge to her voice, and Presley suspected that Loralee didn't like Irma. Or maybe she had been jealous that the girl had been included in the party.

"After the meal some of the ladies took off their shoes, rolled up their stockings, and waded into the creek. Old Mrs. Monroe took her chaperone duties seriously and kept her eyes right on them. Mr. DuPont turned this to his advantage and took Miss Blanche to a spot down the creek bank a little ways where white orchids grow. I followed them, climbing from tree to tree.

"Miss Blanche said she'd never seen orchids growing wild. He picked one and put it behind her ear. He told her she was a rare beauty, like the flower. They were the prettiest words I had ever heard. And they were true. Miss Blanche was beautiful inside and out. Then he kissed her cheek."

It was very romantic, and Presley's heart started to hurt a little.

"She used the broach on her blouse to pin the flower over her heart, and it was plain to see that they loved each other. From that day forward, I never saw Miss Blanche without a flower pinned to her chest, even the last time I saw her, when she was lying in her coffin."

Tears welled up in Presley's eyes, and she felt foolish. These were people she didn't even know, but Loralee made them seem so real. And the thought of Blanche wearing a token of her love for DuPont every day of her life was beyond sweet. She couldn't imagine loving or being loved so much.

Loralee continued, "This time when they left, there were no beer bottles, which was a disappointment, but there was a box of food on the porch. That's when I knew for sure that Mr. DuPont did see me up in the tree. Because it wasn't just scraps; it was pulled pork and stew and pie, all neatly wrapped up and waiting for me."

"He was thanking you for the improvements you'd made around his house."

She nodded. "And I figured the food was an invitation to keep coming back. So I came every day and watered the flowers. Then I edged the little flowerbed with some smooth pebbles from the creek.

"The parties continued all through the summer. I kept working on the yard when the house was unoccupied and hid in the trees when Mr. DuPont and his guests were there. Each time they left, there was a box of food waiting for me on the porch. Toward the end of October, I was sitting on the steps, going through the box they'd left, when Mr. DuPont stepped out of the woods right over there." She pointed to a spot where the trees parted.

"He just pretended to leave and then circled back and caught you?" Presley guessed.

Loralee nodded. "He told me there wouldn't be any more parties during the winter, and he wanted to make sure I'd be okay until spring. He said he'd bring supplies when he could, but it was a long, lonely winter."

"In the spring he came back?"

She nodded. "His boat pulled up while I was transplanting some of the wild orchids to a flowerbed right by the porch. He was upset when he saw what I was doing. He said that orchids were very delicate and wouldn't be able to survive the move to a new location. I told him I'd transferred all kinds of flowers and never killed a one of them. And I said that orchids were stronger than they look and promised him that they'd still be growing there long after he was dead." Her eyes drifted back toward the house. "And it's true."

Presley stared at the little patch of wild orchids growing near the front porch. They had been there for almost a hundred years.

"He didn't look convinced about the orchids, but he didn't mention them again. Instead he told me that soon Miss Blanche would be coming back, this time as his bride, and that she might need a girl to help around the house."

"And you became that girl?"

"I did," Loralee confirmed. "Miss Blanche arrived the second week in June. She'd had a beautiful church wedding and a honeymoon at Myrtle Beach. That's in South Carolina." Loralee's lips parted, and she said reverently, "I always hoped I'd see it before I died."

"Maybe you could still go?" Presley said hopefully.

Loralee shook her head. "I'll never leave here."

"I'm sorry." It seemed so sad that Loralee had been dreaming about a place all her life and would never see it.

"Don't feel bad for me," Loralee said with a smile. "I've been blessed to live my life in the best place on earth. There's nowhere I'd rather be than here at Orchid Cove—not even Myrtle Beach."

Presley smiled back. "So Blanche arrived as a new bride, and they lived happily ever after?"

"They were happy, but life wasn't always easy," Loralee replied. "Old Mrs. Monroe was here for almost a month. She showed me how to cook and clean and run a proper house. She planted an herb garden and taught me how to treat illnesses with plants. But finally it was time for her to go home. She called me aside just before she left and told me that Miss Blanche had weak lungs. It was asthma, but they didn't know the name for it then. She asked me to watch out for her and keep her from working too hard. I caught Miss Blanche crying after her mother left. She asked me not to tell Mr. DuPont. She said it wasn't that she didn't want to be his wife. She just missed her mother. I certainly knew how that felt. I'd missed my mother my whole life."

"My mother died a year ago." The words were out before Presley could stop them. "I still miss her so much."

Loralee reached over and patted her hand. "You'll always miss her, but time does help a little."

Presley cleared her throat. "So Miss Blanche adjusted to life without her mother?"

"Oh, yes, she did fine for several weeks. Then, for no reason, she had a bad spell. I didn't leave the house until she got her strength back. While I sat by her bed, she taught me to read using the Bible. When she got well, we canned vegetables and visited sick folks together. I even helped her deliver a baby. Then the summer ended, and they started packing up. I never dreamed that they had another, much bigger, nicer house in town, but they did. This was just a summer place. I watched them leave and thought my heart would break."

"Once again everything was quiet and lonely here."

"Yes. But now it was worse. I knew them better, loved them more, and so I missed them terribly. They sent supplies during the winter like before and came back when the weather got warm. That's how it went for the next few years. The winters were dark and lonely, but I always knew that summer was just around the corner."

They heard the rumble of a truck in the distance.

"That will be Mac," Loralee predicted. A few seconds later, the tow truck appeared over the hill.

Presley watched the tow truck approach with an odd combination of emotions. When Loralee started the story, Presley was just enduring it, but by the end, she didn't want it to be over. Mac parked and jumped down from his truck.

As they walked over to greet him, the old woman looked tired. It seemed that sharing the story had sapped her strength.

Mac greeted Loralee warmly. She pointed at the nice boat on the back. "It's a shame that whoever bought that couldn't pay for it."

"Yeah, he wasn't happy about it either."

Presley noticed a new cut near his lip that was swollen and oozing blood. He caught her eye and shook his head slightly. She knew he didn't want her to draw attention to it in front of Loralee.

"We've been talking about DuPont and Blanche," Presley said.

"Oh, then you've been well entertained."

Loralee looked back at the house. "It's always hard for me to leave them, you know."

"I know. Why don't I help you up into the truck?" he suggested. "We'll put your scooter in back, and I'll drive you home."

She shook her head. "Thank you, but I'd rather stay with Miss Blanche for a while longer."

Mac didn't argue. "Just don't stay out here too long. You know Miss Versie worries."

Mac helped Presley into the truck and they drove away. Presley turned in her seat so that she could see the lone figure sitting on the steps of the dilapidated house for as long as possible.

"Do you think she'll be okay?" Presley asked as Loralee disappeared from view.

He frowned. "I hope so, but if she dies there at Blanche's house . . . Well, she'll be in heaven before her heart stops beating."

CHAPTER TEN

Mac got a phone call and answered it with an apologetic look in her direction. She hoped it wasn't another repossession job.

When he ended the call, she asked, "What happened to your mouth?"

"Oh, it's nothing."

In addition to the swelling and blood she'd noticed earlier, it was now beginning to bruise. "It doesn't look like nothing."

"The man with the boat didn't appreciate me taking it away from him."

She frowned. "Can't you sneak up on these people and take their stuff when they're asleep or something."

He laughed. "Maybe, but if it gives them a little bit of satisfaction to hit me . . ."

She was aghast. "You let them hit you on purpose."

"No, but if they throw a punch and it happens to connect, I figure I have it coming. Repo guys are the lowest form of life around here—worse than lawyers." He grinned and then winced.

"So why are you doing it?"

"I have to," he said. "My ex-wife gets a percentage of my earnings. It doesn't matter how much I make, just that I work a reasonable number of hours each week. That way she can't go back to court and claim that I'm lazing around to cheat her out of money."

Presley nodded. "Employing a little passive resistance."

"I guess. It's complicated."

"It always is." She stared out the window for a minute. Then she had to ask, "Why did that Miss Raye woman at the Piggly Wiggly say 'Bless your heart'?"

He looked a little startled by the question but then said, "It's a Southern thing—like saying, 'Have a good day,' in Ohio."

She nodded although she wasn't sure his translation was accurate. Blessing somebody's heart seemed to indicate sympathy at least on some level.

"I thought you were a boxer," she admitted as they turned past Dollar General. "Because of your black eye and the cuts on your hand."

He laughed. "No, I'm just the world's worst repo man."

"Anything's better than being a boxer," she said.

* * *

When they turned the curve near her aunt's house, Presley peered into the distance and observed, "No press, only one police car, and they've taken down the tape that was blocking the parking lot. Those are all good signs."

Mac pointed to a dark-haired man standing by the door. "Yes, it looks like your luck is changing. That's my cousin, the preacher. I guess this is what you might call divine intervention because he's holding a homemade pie."

"I'm tired of meeting new people, and I don't eat pie," she muttered.

"Come on. You'll love Patrick," he encouraged as he parked. "Everybody does."

Reluctantly Presley got out of the truck, and together they approached Mac's other cousin.

The preacher looked to be about Mac's age, late twenties. He had unruly, dark hair that may have been combed earlier in the day but was now a mass of ebony curls. He wasn't tall like Wyatt, and he wasn't muscular like Mac. His blue eyes matched his cousins' exactly. However instead of being friendly or flirtatious, the preacher's eyes were sincere. He wasn't classically beautiful, but there was something almost hypnotically attractive about him as he gave her a straight-toothed smile. "Welcome to Haggerty!" he said. "I'm Patrick."

"I'm Presley," she replied.

"I feel obligated to warn you," Mac said from behind her. "There's not a woman on this earth from one to one hundred that can resist Brother Patrick. So guard your heart carefully."

Patrick retained his pleasant expression, but his tone was reproving. "Please excuse Mac. He loves to tease."

"I've noticed," she replied.

"What kind of pie you got there?" Mac asked.

"It's a peach pie," Patrick replied. "And it's for Presley not you."

"Presley doesn't eat pie." Mac held out his hands.

Brother Patrick looked to Presley for confirmation.

Reluctantly she nodded. "It's true. I do appreciate the thought, though."

Brother Patrick let Mac take the pie. "What do you eat?" he asked. "I'll bring the right thing next time."

"She doesn't eat carbs, so next time bring her steaks or pork chops," Mac suggested.

Presley gave Mac an exasperated look and then asked the preacher, "Would you like to come in and see Aunt Violet?"

"No," he declined. "I won't impose. I just wanted to welcome you to Haggerty and invite you to the Baptist church on Sunday." He gave her another one of his heavenly smiles.

"I'm not very religious," Presley said.

"Apparently for Presley, church is in the same category with carbs," Mac told his cousin. "She avoids it. So you struck out all around."

Presley sighed. "Please stop teasing, Mac."

Brother Patrick persevered. "I wish you'd come just once. I put a lot of extra time and effort into my Easter sermon."

"I'm sure it's very good. Thank you for the invitation." She was careful not to say anything that could be interpreted as a commitment.

He handed her a card. "Here are the numbers where I can be reached. Please call if you need anything."

She didn't feel that she could say thank you again without feeling like a babbling idiot. So she just nodded.

At that moment Cecelia walked out of her hair salon. Her honey-blonde mane was tumbling down her back. Black leather pants fit her like a glove. A sheer black shirt hung off one shoulder and exposed a leopard-print tank top below. Stilettos and black pearl ankle bracelets completed the ensemble. No one else could have carried the look off, but on Cecelia it was spectacular.

"Hey, Presley," she greeted when she saw them.

"Hi," Presley replied.

Cecelia turned to the men. "Well, Mac. I see you've been in another fight."

Mac shrugged. "It goes with the territory."

"It seems like with all this experience your fighting skills would improve." She moved her catlike eyes to Patrick. "Hello, Preacher Pat."

Brother Patrick's posture was suddenly very stiff and formal. "Good evening, Mrs. Moore."

Presley didn't know if he used that tone with all married women or if he was one of the people in Haggerty who judged Cecelia harshly. It was a disappointing thought.

"Patrick made Presley a pie," Mac told her. "But since she doesn't eat carbs, I inherited it."

"Bad choice of words, Mac," Cecelia said. "As an accused gold digger, I'm sensitive about words like *inherited.* Since you've offended me, you'll have to give me the pie." She took it straight out of his hands. Then she walked toward her Porsche—which was sleek and lovely just like her. "Good-bye, Presley. Fellas."

Everyone stood staring after her until her car was out of sight.

"I can't believe she took my pie," Mac said finally.

Brother Patrick said, "Yeah, you have terrible luck with women."

Mac scowled. "Preachers are supposed to make people feel better, not worse."

Brother Patrick smiled, but Cecelia's appearance had taken the fun out of him. "Come back to my place, and I'll doctor your latest battle scar."

"Do you have another pie there?" Mac asked.

Brother Patrick shook his head. "No, but I can probably scrounge up some Oreos."

Mac stared back at the road where Cecelia's car had disappeared. "I *really* can't believe I let her take my pie!"

Brother Patrick turned to wave at Presley. "I hope to see you Sunday."

She waved back. Then she unlocked the door and pushed with her shoulder several times before she got it to open. Remembering that Mac had said Aunt Violet usually left the door open, she didn't close it all the way.

She found Aunt Violet in the kitchen with Miss George Ann. Her aunt was going through a stack of mail. Miss George Ann was still working on the puzzle of Big Ben.

Presley got a glass of water. "It feels funny to pull up and not see police cars everywhere."

"It feels wonderful to me. There's still an officer in the back to protect the crime scene and to keep people from wandering into the hole. But otherwise we're back to normal."

Presley looked out the window. "I'll be glad when they fill that hole up. It's unnerving to have an open grave in the backyard. So I'm guessing the FBI didn't find any more bodies."

"No," her aunt confirmed. "And since they estimate that the skeleton we found has been dead for about a hundred years, there's no reason to suspect that Haggerty is harboring a murderer, let alone a serial killer. The governor's not coming, and the request for help from the state police has been canceled."

"A lot of people must be disappointed about that," Presley murmured.

"Oh, yes. No more free publicity for Mayor Witherspoon, and Kitty Cleckler has lost her chance to impress her Sunday School class," Aunt Violet said with a smile. "So how was your visit with Loralee?"

"She told me all about Blanche and DuPont."

Aunt Violet nodded. "Of course she did."

"I didn't hate it as much as I thought I would."

"Loralee is a good storyteller, and she loved them very much."

"When we got back here, we found Brother Patrick on the sidewalk. So now I've met all the cousins."

Aunt Violet looked toward the front of the house. "Patrick didn't come in?"

"No, he was just stopping by to welcome me. He baked me a pie, but Cecelia stole it."

Aunt Violet smiled. "We've got plenty of desserts."

Presley frowned. "I don't think he likes Cecelia very much."

"Who?"

"Brother Patrick."

Aunt Violet seemed surprised. "I thought he liked everyone."

"He just acted kind of cold toward her. Maybe it was my imagination."

"Maybe."

Presley added, "Mac got beat up again when he repossessed a boat."

"How badly?"

"Just a split lip, but I wish he'd find a less dangerous profession."

Her aunt nodded. "We all do."

* * *

On the way back to Violet's to pick up George Ann, Eugenia called her sister and explained the whole will situation.

Annabelle screamed with delight. "You're going to be rich!"

"I'm not going to be rich," Eugenia corrected. "I can't keep the money. I have to give it to charity."

"Why?" Annabelle asked. "Is that stipulated in the will?"

"I don't know. Why do you have to be so annoying? I called hoping for a little sympathy."

"I don't see why you need sympathy. One of the wealthiest women in southern Georgia has decided to leave you the bulk of her estate. That's cause for celebration."

Eugenia clutched the steering wheel of her old Buick. "The very idea. It was just a trick, a way to make me responsible for her in her declining years."

"So find her a nice nursing home and stop worrying about it."

Eugenia sighed. "I can't talk to you."

"Then don't call me."

They hung up on each other simultaneously.

* * *

When Eugenia arrived at Violet's house, she noted that there was no police presence. Presumably the murder crisis was over before it really began.

Violet's front door was propped open a few inches, so Eugenia carried Lady inside without knocking. When she called out, announcing her presence, she heard Violet respond with an invitation to join them in the kitchen.

"Good afternoon," Eugenia said breathlessly.

Violet and Presley returned the greeting. George Ann looked up from the nearly completed Big Ben puzzle but didn't comment.

"So how has she been?" Eugenia tipped her head toward George Ann.

"Perfect all day," Violet said. "No bother at all."

They exchanged worried looks.

"That's not like her," Eugenia said with false cheerfulness.

"No," Violet agreed.

Eugenia sighed. "We'll give it a few more days and then decide on a more permanent solution."

Lady yelped, so Eugenia put her on the floor. The little dog ran straight to the back door and started scratching to be let out.

"No, ma'am," Eugenia told her firmly. "I know you think you've discovered the bone mother lode, but there will be no more digging in Miss Violet's backyard."

Lady looked disappointed. She stopped scratching but laid down right by the door so if it opened she'd have an opportunity to run out before anyone could stop her.

Eugenia helped herself to a slightly stale doughnut and sat at the table.

"How was the baby shower?" Violet asked.

"Fine," Eugenia replied. "But sort of exhausting. I watched that girl open all those gifts—modern contraptions the young people all think you need to raise a baby these days—and it made me feel old and tired."

"Everything makes me feel old and tired," Violet responded with a smile. "And speaking of old, Presley spent part of the afternoon with Loralee."

Eugenia turned. "How did that go?"

"Okay," Presley replied. "She's obsessed with DuPont and Blanche Armstrong, but talking about it makes her happy, so what's the harm? She showed me their old house."

"That pile of rubble!" Eugenia scoffed. "It was never what I'd call a fine home, just a summer house for casual living. But it was livable, and maybe it will be again once Mac restores it."

"It will take a long time and a lot of money," Violet said.

"But it will be worth it," Presley expressed her opinion with feeling.

Despite her doubts, Eugenia was impressed. "It's nice to see a young person who appreciates old things and understands that the journey is as important as the destination. Most want everything now and don't realize that the process can be very satisfying."

"I hadn't really thought of it that way," Presley said. "But I agree."

"No wonder you and Mac get along so well."

"Do we?" Presley asked. "We barely know each other."

"It sure seems to me like you've hit it off," Eugenia said.

Presley's laugh seemed a little nervous. "Well, we do share a dislike for football."

"Poor Mac," Aunt Violet said.

"Bless his heart," Eugenia agreed.

"Why does everyone keep doing that?" Presley demanded.

Up to this point the young woman hadn't shown much animation, and Eugenia was a little startled. "Doing what?"

"Blessing his heart and saying 'God love him,'" Presley explained. "It seems like every time his name is mentioned those phrases come up. Is there something wrong with him?"

Eugenia laughed. "He's had his share of problems, but there's nothing *wrong* with him. And he can't hate football! He was the best player ever in Haggerty High School history. They even won the state championship his senior year."

Presley's shock was obvious.

"The cousins were all on the team," Violet said. "Wyatt was the quarterback, and Mac was the kicker. I can't remember what Brother Patrick did."

"It was something to do with the ball; he either ran it or caught it," Eugenia said.

"But Mac was the best?" Presley verified.

Eugenia nodded. "He got a scholarship to the University of Georgia and then went to the NFL. The Miami Dolphins signed him."

"He had a contract and promotional deals worth millions," Violet put in.

Eugenia took up the narrative. "He played with them for two years. He lived the high-life, married a floozy, made it to the Super Bowl, and missed three field goals."

"That cost them the game," Violet said mournfully. "So they fired him."

"He lost his fancy house and his fancy cars and even his fancy wife," Eugenia summed up Mac's dismal football career. "So he came back to Haggerty and bought a tow truck."

"People feel sorry for him because he ruined his big chance," Violet said.

All this obviously came as a surprise to Presley, who just stared at them in dismay. "I hate football even more now," she said finally.

Eugenia shook her head. "You can't blame the game. Mac certainly doesn't. He blames himself."

"Mac made some mistakes, but that's all in the past now," Violet said. "He needs to move on and so does the town."

"Speaking of moving on . . ." Eugenia took another doughnut. "Since the police and news reporters are gone, I'm assuming the FBI didn't find any more graves?"

Violet put a hand to her heart. "No, thank goodness. And they think that the girl died almost a hundred years ago."

"Which means if it *was* murder, the killer is probably dead by now," Eugenia said thoughtfully.

Violet nodded. "Since it happened so long ago, the news reporters—and even the police—don't really care about the details anymore."

Presley seemed to pull herself out of deep thought. "I care. Just because the people involved are dead doesn't mean the crime shouldn't be investigated. If the police aren't going to try to solve it, I'll do what I can on my own. I'm a good researcher."

Eugenia was pleased by this. "I have a little experience solving crimes. I'd be glad to help you."

"Eugenia is actually a murder expert," Violet said with obvious good intentions.

"Not exactly a title of distinction," Eugenia murmured. "Thank goodness Annabelle isn't here; she'd have a heyday with that."

Violet blushed. "I meant that in the most complimentary way."

Eugenia nodded. "I know you did."

"It would be great if the two of you could solve the mystery of the Skeleton Murders," Violet said with a little smile. "Then maybe Deputy Burrell's wife will want to interview you."

"Heaven forbid," Eugenia said.

"Kitty Cleckler would die of envy!" Aunt Violet teased.

"Seriously, though, I wish we had a more accurate death date." Eugenia was already thinking of the investigation ahead.

"But Haggerty is a small town," Presley pointed out. "How many young girls could have died from a head wound here a hundred years ago?"

"Information is going to be the problem," Eugenia said. "All deaths didn't get reported to the authorities—especially in poor rural communities."

George Ann put the final piece in the Big Ben puzzle. "Finished!" she said proudly. "Is it time to go now?"

The puzzle had kept George Ann busy all day, and now, right when Eugenia needed to concentrate, the other woman wanted to leave. Exasperated, Eugenia reached over and dislodged several pieces from a corner of the puzzle. "There. Do that part again, and then we'll go."

"Eugenia!" Violet scolded.

"What? She enjoyed it the first time! And I'm trying to solve a murder here."

George Ann went straight back to work on Big Ben, like a puzzle robot. Violet still looked annoyed, but she refrained from further comment.

Eugenia turned her attention back to Presley. "Our best source of information on anything that happened a hundred years ago will be Loralee."

Presley nodded. "That's true. I'll ask her about it."

Eugenia stood. "Or we could go visit her together. I'll be in touch." She took George Ann by the arm and pulled her gently. "Let's go."

George Ann stood and looked down at the puzzle. "But it's not finished."

"We want Violet to think twice before she puts me in someone's will again, so I'll bring you back tomorrow during my March of Dimes meeting," Eugenia told her with a sly look at Violet. "You can finish it then."

Violet laughed. "I don't mind George Ann's company at all."

They walked to the front door as a group. When they got there, Eugenia murmured, "I don't think it's wise to leave your door open since there might be a murderer in Haggerty."

"We've established that whoever killed our skeleton is dead by now," Violet replied.

"Your house has been the center of attention for the past couple of days," Eugenia insisted. "Your door needs to stay closed for a while—to keep out reporters if nothing else."

Violet nodded. "I guess you're right, but it's so hard to open."

"We may have to hire someone to fix it," Presley told her aunt. "I'm not sure Mr. Cleckler is up to the challenge."

"He can fix it," Eugenia said. "Whether he can get it done before the turn of the next century is the question." She led George Ann outside and helped her into the car. Then she secured the docile woman's seatbelt before walking around to the driver's side. She waved to Violet and Presley, who were standing in the doorway. "I can't wait to go pick Loralee's old brain and solve our mystery."

Presley nodded. "We'd better hope either Blanche or DuPont Armstrong is the murderer because they're the only people Loralee seems to know about."

Eugenia laughed. "You have a point there. Maybe we'll get lucky and find out that Miss Blanche had a homicidal streak."

Violet gasped. "I know the two of you are just kidding, but we shouldn't speak ill of the dead, especially someone like Miss Blanche. If Haggerty had a patron saint, it would be her."

"I know Blanche Armstrong didn't murder anyone," Eugenia assured Violet.

Violet looked somewhat mollified. "Since the Iversons are out of town, you should come eat Easter dinner with us on Sunday. You can go to church with us, too, and hear Brother Patrick preach."

Eugenia liked this idea. "Won't *that* confuse all the gossips in town who object to me attending church with the Mormons!"

"So you'll come?"

"If you'll let me bring something." She glanced into the car, where George Ann was sitting patiently. "Besides George Ann."

"Maybe you could bring some of your famous deviled eggs."

"We'll be there," Eugenia promised.

She climbed into her old Buick and headed home with a smile. She had a new mystery—even if it was a hundred years old—and an invitation to Easter dinner. Suddenly life was looking up.

* * *

After their company left, Presley led the way back to the kitchen, turning on lights as she went to dispel the late-afternoon gloom. Violet came behind her, the oxygen tank rolling along the floor.

"Loralee told me about this big dinner you're hosting on Sunday."

Aunt Violet frowned. "I'm surprised she would call it a big dinner. She knows it's just a few close friends."

"I guess I added the 'big' part," Presley admitted. "Anything more than two guests seems large to me."

"I hope you won't be uncomfortable." Now her aunt looked worried. "It's mostly people you've already met, and I'd cancel it, but, well, it's a tradition, and I don't want my guests to miss Easter dinner."

"I don't want you to cancel it," Presley assured her.

Aunt Violet patted her arm. "If you don't enjoy it, you can take Mac's advice and hide in your room."

Presley smiled. "That will be my backup plan."

"Loralee always brings the most delicious Italian cream cake. Maybe you can forget about carbs for one day and eat a piece."

"Maybe," Presley replied. "She also said that you need to teach me how to make cornbread so I can help with the dressing—which apparently you make at every holiday gathering. She said it's a secret family recipe that should be passed down to me."

"The recipe is secret and delicious," Aunt Violet confirmed. "I'll show you how to make cornbread right now, and we can eat it with dinner."

"Pure carbs, I'm guessing?"

She nodded. "That's what makes it good."

So Presley made her first batch of cornbread. She had never felt completely confident in the kitchen, but Aunt Violet was patient and specific. She told Presley to combine whole buttermilk, a dozen eggs, and real butter in a large bowl—definitely not healthy stuff. She measured out the corn meal and stirred it in. There was something so satisfying about creating this rich and delicious batter.

Once Aunt Violet determined that the batter was ready, she instructed Presley to pour it into a hot cast-iron skillet. As Presley put the skillet into the oven, she felt a kinship with Loralee and Blanche Armstrong and all the Southern women of old.

"Perfect," Aunt Violet praised as Presley began the cleanup process. "I've never seen anyone learn a recipe so quickly!"

Presley knew her aunt was being generous with her praise, but she was pleased just the same.

Aunt Violet was a Southern woman too, and she undoubtedly had worthwhile stories and experiences to share. Presley pulled out a chair at the kitchen table and sat down. "While the cornbread cooks, why don't you tell me about your childhood?"

Aunt Violet blushed with pleasure and then started talking.

* * *

Aunt Violet had just finished describing her years in the Girl Scouts, and Presley was beginning to regret her impulsive decision to learn more about the past when there was a knock on the front door.

Grateful for the reprieve, Presley walked through the living room and forced the door open. On the sidewalk outside was an attractive blonde woman Presley recognized from TV. A man with a large camera on his shoulder was standing behind her.

"Hello," the woman said. "I'm Hannah-Leigh Burrell, a reporter for Channel 3 in Albany."

"You're Deputy Burrell's wife," Presley said.

Hannah-Leigh ignored this comment and shoved a microphone in Presley's face. "Is it true that a murder was committed in your backyard?"

Presley kept her face carefully blank as she responded. "You'll have to discuss that with the sheriff." Then she closed the door. The reporter knocked again, but Presley ignored it.

Finally the knocking stopped. Presley walked back into the kitchen, assuming that the news crew had given up. But she had underestimated the resourceful Hannah-Leigh. The blonde head bobbed passed the kitchen window with her faithful cameraman right behind.

"Apparently there are a few reporters desperate enough to cover a hundred-year-old murder!" Presley told her aunt. Then she cracked the kitchen door so they could hear the exchange.

The deputy who had been assigned to guard the hole came to attention immediately and held up a hand. "You aren't allowed back here!"

Aunt Violet dragged her oxygen tank over to the door and stood beside Presley.

"So this is a crime scene?" Hannah-Leigh demanded.

"That has not been confirmed."

The reporter persisted. "But a body was found here?"

"I have no comment on that," the deputy replied.

Hannah-Leigh turned to her cameraman. "Did you get plenty of footage, including the deputy and the grave?"

"Yes, ma'am," he replied.

The reporter flashed the deputy a smile. "Thanks! That's enough for the ten o'clock news!"

"Hannah-Leigh!" the deputy yelled. "You're gonna get Cade fired!"

"There's such a thing as freedom of the press," Hannah-Leigh informed him.

Aunt Violet pushed the door open a little farther. "There's also such a thing as private property. Now get out of here and don't come back, or I'll have you arrested."

Presley wasn't sure if her aunt was serious, but Hannah-Leigh must have thought so because she and the cameraman scurried off.

"Poor Cade," Aunt Violet muttered. Then she waved to the deputy and pulled the door closed.

CHAPTER ELEVEN

THEIR DINNER CONSISTED OF SALAD with cornbread on the side. Presley only ate a few bites of the bread—it was delicious—but she felt guilty afterward.

"I need to get some exercise," she told her aunt as they washed the dishes. "Once we're through here, I think I'll go for a run."

Aunt Violet looked alarmed. "You can't run alone in the dark! We might have a murderer in Haggerty!"

Presley laughed. "If the person who murdered our skeleton is still alive, I think I can outrun them."

"Still, I wish you wouldn't go alone," her aunt fretted. "I could call Mac."

"Do not call Mac." Presley was firm. "I'll just run up the road a couple miles. It won't take long. And I have a gun."

"If you must run, I'm going to have to insist that you go to the track at the high school." Aunt Violet could be firm too. "It's lighted until midnight, and there's a road that runs by it, so you won't be completely alone."

Presley decided to accept these terms rather than fight with her aunt. "Tell me how to get there."

* * *

After Presley changed into sweats and her running shoes, Aunt Violet gave her the keys to the Honda. "It's parked under a carport on Cecelia's end of the building."

"Thanks," Presley said as she hurried outside.

She spent a few minutes familiarizing herself with the Honda and then drove to the high school. It wasn't far, and she found the well-lit football stadium without any problem. She jogged out to the track that circled the field and did a few stretches. Then she took off running at a steady pace.

She took deep breaths of moist, fragrant air. Her legs felt strong, and she pushed a little harder. After two circuits she heard footsteps coming up behind her, fast.

Presley reached into the pocket of her sweatpants and wrapped her fingers around her gun. Then she spun around. Mac McIntyre was trotting toward her. His gait was long and easy, like someone who ran regularly.

"Evening," he said as he pulled even with her. His longish auburn hair was hanging over his eyes, and he pushed it back with his hand.

She scowled and kept pace beside him. "Aunt Violet called and asked you to come?"

"Actually I called her to check for messages," he said. "During the course of our conversation, she mentioned that you were foolishly running all alone in a town that might be harboring a murderer. I volunteered to come protect you, as any good Southern gentleman would."

"Forgive me if I don't swoon." She rolled her eyes. "And be glad I didn't shoot you."

He laughed and picked up the pace a little. They ran in silence for a while. By the time he slowed to a cooldown trot, her lungs were burning. He came to a stop and leaned on the fence for a few minutes.

Presley forced herself to stay upright just to prove a point. When their breathing had returned to normal, he said, "Have you ever been on a football field before?"

She shook her head. "Of course not. I told you I hate football."

He walked a few feet to a gate and opened it. Then he beckoned her to join him.

"I don't want to go out there."

"Please, just for a minute."

She felt obligated since he had run with her to give Aunt Violet peace of mind. So she walked over to the gate, thinking mean thoughts about Aunt Violet with each step.

He walked to the end zone and wrapped his arms around the base of the goal posts. "Do you feel it?"

She frowned. "Feel what?"

"The energy in this place?" he whispered. "It's like an electric charge running through me."

"I don't feel anything except mosquitoes." She swatted at one of the large flying predators.

"I can hear the band playing and the crowd cheering. I can smell the hot dogs cooking on the grill and the popcorn and even the huge dill pickles."

"I can't hear or smell anything either."

He turned his head up toward the floodlights. "This was a magical place on Friday nights in the fall when those lights were shining down on me."

"Aunt Violet told me you played professionally," she said. "It seems like you could have mentioned that earlier when we were discussing the subject."

He sat down and rested his back against the goalpost, staring out at the field. She sat beside him, facing the stands. Their shoulders were close but not touching.

"I was afraid if I admitted my involvement in a sport you are morally opposed to, you'd say we couldn't be friends. And I could use a friend, especially someone who isn't from Haggerty."

"I'll make an exception to my no-football-player-friends rule just for you. And be glad I don't have a rule against liars." Out of the corner of her eye, she saw him smile.

"Do you want to hear about it?"

"Only if you want to tell me," she said.

He was quiet for a few minutes, and she wondered if he'd decided that he didn't want to discuss his ill-fated football career. But finally he began, "So for years, football was my life. On this field, I was a hero, a king. Everyone loved me just because I could kick a ball with incredible accuracy. I never missed."

"But then in the Super Bowl, you did miss."

"I missed three kicks," he corrected. "I lost the game for my team."

"I don't know that much about football," she began, "since I hate it. But I think the only reason a team would kick a field goal is if they can't score a touchdown. Isn't that right?"

He turned to face her. "What are you saying?"

"You didn't *lose* that game. You didn't help the team win," she conceded. "But if they had scored touchdowns, they wouldn't have needed you to kick field goals."

He smiled. "That doesn't make me feel any better, but it was a nice thing to say."

"Don't you get tired of people holding a mistake you made in a *game* against you?"

"Yes, but I understand. I was born with talent and then given an opportunity that almost nobody gets—the chance to play in the pros. I wasted it. I blew it. And that's what some people can't forgive."

"Everybody makes mistakes," she countered. "Even extremely talented people."

"It's worse than that," he admitted. "A mistake would be hard to forgive, but the general consensus is that I threw the game. And that's impossible to forgive."

Presley's eyes widened. "You wouldn't do something like that."

"It's hard to say what a person would or wouldn't do under the right set of circumstances," he hedged. "But I didn't throw the game."

"Still you lost everything."

"I lost that life," he said.

"And your wife?"

He shrugged. "She was more attached to the life than she was to me."

"That's why she wants a portion of your earnings," Presley realized. "Because she thinks you'll go back to football and make a lot of money."

He nodded. "She won't finalize the divorce until I sign a paper saying I won't ever play football again. It's her insurance against me making millions that I don't have to share with her."

"Doesn't she want to marry the baby's father?"

He shrugged. "I don't know. We don't talk personally anymore. Everything is handled through lawyers."

"Do you plan to play football again?"

"Naw." He tossed his hair back from his face. "But I don't like being forced to give up that option. And if I agree to a portion of future earnings, she'll have a say in everything I do employment-wise. Either way she controls me."

Presley could certainly understand his reluctance to accept either option, and she was trying to think of an appropriate response when someone yelled at them from the track.

"Hey, get off the field!"

Presley turned to see a man wearing athletic shorts and a T-Shirt with *Haggerty High* printed across the front in bold letters.

"You'll kill the grass!" he added. Then he pointed toward the gate. "Out!" He watched with a scowl as Mac helped Presley to her feet and then led the way off the field.

"Evening, Phil," Mac said as they passed the man.

The man just stared.

Once they were standing between the tow truck and Aunt Violet's car, Presley whispered, "You know him?"

"Sure," he returned. "He was my high school football coach."

* * *

When Presley was alone in her bedroom, she pulled the disposable cell phone out of her purse and called Moon.

"So, are you all settled . . . somewhere?" he asked.

She wondered, not for the first time, if the phone gave him the ability to track her. "Please don't try and figure out where I am," she begged. "I'm trusting you with my life."

He was quiet for a few seconds. Then he said, "Nobody's ever trusted me before. So I won't try to find you—*if* you promise me that you're safe."

She felt weak with relief. "I'm safe."

"And you'll tell me if something changes?"

"Yes," she promised. "Has anything happened with, well, you know?"

"Dr. Khan called your lawyer today," he said softly.

Presley's heart tightened painfully.

"He told him you'd been moved to the teaching wing and that he wouldn't be receiving any more bills for your care. Dr. Khan mentioned the possibility that you'd been exposed to MRSA, just to keep him away."

"And he didn't seem suspicious?"

"No," Moon replied. "Dr. Khan told me all the lawyer said was to make sure the nursing students knew that you were under a do-not-resuscitate order."

Presley couldn't control a small gasp. Even based on what she knew about the depths of Tate's cruelty, this was a shock.

"He's a real piece of work, that lawyer of yours."

"Yes, he is," she agreed softly. "I'll be in touch, but call if anything happens."

After turning off the phone, Presley crawled under the covers, stared at the ceiling of her new room, and cried.

* * *

The next morning Presley woke up feeling a little stiff from her run but surprising optimistic. She loved running and was determined to make it a regular part of her daily routine, which should limit future soreness. And since Tate thought she was unconscious at the hospital, she might be able to stay in Haggerty for an extended length of time. Both thoughts made her happy.

When Presley arrived downstairs, she found Loralee sitting at the kitchen table, working on a new puzzle.

"The Eiffel Tower?" Presley observed, looking over Loralee's shoulder.

"Good morning!" the old woman greeted. "Versie had a doctor's appointment, so her son Clifton dropped me off. I brought breakfast—buttermilk biscuits just like Miss Blanche used to make!"

Presley's eyes followed the direction of Loralee's pointing finger. "I'm surprised they aren't floating off the plate."

Loralee seemed to think this was funny. "I don't quite have Miss Blanche's touch," she said around giggles. "I also brought real butter and homemade jelly."

"Wasn't it nice of Loralee?" Aunt Violet prompted with minimal subtlety.

"It was nice," Presley agreed. "Thanks. But biscuits are full of carbs, and jelly is even worse."

"Just eat half a biscuit then," Loralee suggested as if this eliminated the problem. She stood and got a small plate down from the cupboard. After carefully slicing a biscuit in half, she put one part on the plate and slathered it with jelly. "Eat it quick before it gets cold."

Presley took a bite of biscuit and had to admit it was heavenly. "I've never tasted anything like it."

Loralee clapped her hands in pleasure. "I knew you'd like it!"

"I love it." Presley finished her biscuit and was contemplating the other half when there was a knock on the door. "I'll get it," she said. She walked up to the front of the house and, with effort, pulled the door open.

Junior Mobley was standing on the front sidewalk. He blushed crimson when he saw her.

"Can I help you?" she asked in confusion. The police were gone, the hole in the back was filled in, and the governor had canceled his visit. She could not imagine the circumstances that would have brought the funeral director's son to their front door.

"I just wanted to check on you, ma'am," Junior said, his blush deepening. "I felt real bad that you found that body in your backyard on your first day here in Haggerty."

Presley had no idea how to respond to this. So she remained silent.

"I know how hard it can be to get used to a new place, and I thought I could show you around town." His face was now an alarming shade of burgundy.

Presley opened her mouth to speak, but no words came out.

Then a familiar voice broke the awkward silence. "Hey, Junior," Miss Eugenia said as she charged up the sidewalk carrying Lady in a basket. Miss George Ann was trailing behind. "What brings you out so early this morning?"

"I was just offering to take Presley around town, show her where things are," Junior stammered.

Presley turned to Miss Eugenia with wide, desperate eyes.

Miss Eugenia stepped between them, effectively shielding Presley. "Well, Junior, that is very nice and polite of you," she told him. "But Presley is dating Mac McIntyre, so if she needs to be shown around town, Mac will take care of it."

Presley was relieved and horrified in equal measure.

Junior took a step back. "Oh, I wasn't trying to move in on Mac."

"Of course you weren't." Miss Eugenia patted his arm. "You were just being neighborly. But now that you know Presley is already taken, you can head on back to the funeral home. And tell your daddy I said hello."

Left with no option, Junior Mobley turned and walked quickly to the Haggerty Mortuary van that was parked near the road.

Presley stepped aside so Miss Eugenia and her entourage could enter the house. Once the door was shoved closed, she gave the older woman a grateful smile. "Thanks for your help with Junior. I didn't know what to say."

"That was obvious."

"Of course, now I've got to figure out how to explain our 'dating' to Mac."

"You *should* date Mac. A girl could do worse."

Presley had no intention of listing all the reasons she could and would not date Mac McIntyre—beginning with the fact that he was still married—so she just turned and walked back to the kitchen, where Aunt Violet and Loralee were sitting.

Miss George Ann seemed to light up when she saw the new puzzle. She sat down beside Loralee and picked up an edge piece. Loralee kindly assisted her with its placement and then handed her another piece.

Miss Eugenia shook her head. "If there isn't such a thing as puzzle therapy, then there should be. The only time George Ann doesn't seem anxious or confused is when she's working on a puzzle."

"I'm glad it calms her," Aunt Violet said.

"And thank you so much for George Ann–sitting for me again. My March of Dimes meeting would be very boring for George

Ann, and well, honestly I don't trust her to behave. So far she's been docile, but if that changes, I don't want it to be in front of a bunch of strangers in Albany."

"She'll be fine here," Aunt Violet assured her. "We've got a whole closet full of puzzles and Loralee to help."

Miss Eugenia looked relieved. "I won't be gone too long," she promised. Then she rushed out with Lady still in the basket on her arm.

* * *

After Miss Eugenia left, Presley asked about the agenda for the day.

"I only have one appointment, and that's at two o'clock this afternoon," Aunt Violet said. "This morning I need to mail out some billing statements."

Presley raised an eyebrow. "For the clients you actually charge?"

Her aunt smiled as Cecelia walked in the back door carrying the customary box of doughnuts. "Morning, ladies!" She plopped the box down on the table, careful to avoid the Eiffel Tower. Then she turned to Presley. "I hear you and Mac are dating."

Aunt Violet's eyebrows shot up, and Presley groaned. "We're not dating," Presley assured her. "Miss Eugenia just made that up to discourage Junior Mobley, who was here to 'show me around town.'"

"Junior Mobley." Cecelia shuddered. "Desperate times do call for desperate measures. But it's part of the Haggerty gossip mill now, so there's no calling it back. By lunchtime they'll probably have y'all engaged."

Presley felt a little ill. "Oh, gosh."

Cecelia laughed. "Don't worry about it. Right after lunch they'll remember what a trashy gold digger I am, and that story will be back on top of the gossip list."

Presley gave her a weak smile. She was more concerned about what Mac was going to think than the Haggerty gossipers.

"You should come up with some ready replies so when you get unwanted attention from men you can take care of it," Cecelia continued. "I know Junior won't be the last—not the way you look."

Presley put a hand to her ponytail self-consciously.

"And don't think that Clark Kent disguise is working."

Aunt Violet's eyebrows went higher. "Clark Kent?"

Loralee giggled. "I don't think Presley looks anything like Clark Kent."

"I mean how she pulls her hair back in that severe ponytail, wears hideous clothes, and doesn't put on makeup. She's trying to hide her beauty the way Superman hid his powers. He put on a pair of ugly glasses and called himself Clark Kent. A disguise like that doesn't work in the real world. It just makes people wonder how great you would look if you really tried." She spoke directly to Presley. "So you might as well just accept your beauty and go with it. Let me style your hair and do your makeup. You're like the most perfect blank canvas."

Presley smiled nervously. "Thank you. I guess I do try to discourage men by keeping my appearance plain. I'm not very comfortable with my looks."

Cecelia nodded. "There are worse problems than being pretty, and I'd say it's time for you to get used to your own face. You should leave your hair down and keep it about shoulder length. And wear a little makeup—nothing garish with that porcelain skin. Give it a try and see if it doesn't help. Men like Junior Mobley will be too intimidated to even approach you, and the braver souls, like Wyatt—well, you're going to have to deal with them either way."

Presley nodded. "I'll consider your advice."

Cecelia turned back to the door. "Okay, well, I'll get back to my salon and share beauty secrets with paying customers for a while. Have a good day, girls!" And then she was gone like a tall, beautiful tornado.

"I hope you won't take any of that personally," Aunt Violet said after Cecelia was gone. "She means well."

"She didn't hurt my feelings," Presley assured her.

They had a few peaceful, puzzle-working moments, and then a woman named Sue Perkins and her brother, Stan, came by to get advice from Aunt Violet with a property line issue. They appeared to be in their forties and, based on their style of dress, were simple folks, probably farmers, who didn't get into town much.

Aunt Violet introduced them to everyone and then had them sit down at the far end of the kitchen table, away from the puzzle. She offered them each a doughnut, which they both declined. Then she asked them to explain the problem.

"You know we inherited the old home place when our parents died," Sue began.

"Out on Rural Route 57?" Aunt Violet verified.

Sue and Stan nodded in unison.

Sue said, "We haven't decided what to do with it yet. It's in bad repair, and we both have our own homes. But we don't want to sell it since it's been in our family for so long."

"We've rented the farmland, and that gives us a little income at least," Stan inserted.

"So what's the problem?" Aunt Violet prompted.

"The mayor is trying to push us around," Stan said in an aggrieved tone.

"He owns a hundred acres that border the back of our land," Sue explained. "He wants to sell it to a real estate developer, but he doesn't have road access and apparently there's no deal without it."

"We only have fifteen acres, but we have road access," Stan said.

"So he's pressuring us to sell him four acres by the road."

"Then he'll turn around and sell his land for millions, and we'll have a huge housing development right next to the farmhouse," Stan finished.

This offended Presley's basic sense of right and wrong. "Of course you don't have to sell."

Stan's head bobbed. "That's what I thought. This is America, land of the free. Mayor Witherspoon can't make us do anything. But I was wrong. Since we wouldn't sell, he's arranged for the city to claim imminent domain, and then he can buy it from them."

"We still lose the four acres *and* won't get paid for them," Sue said dejectedly.

"That was shrewd, if not ethical," Presley said. "But he hasn't won yet."

"He's pretty much the government in Haggerty. He has everyone on his side one way or another because he owns a lot of property and several businesses around here."

Presley started to say something, but Aunt Violet gave her a warning look, so she remained quiet.

"I'll check into it and give you a call when I have some advice," Aunt Violet said.

After a few minutes of small talk, she escorted Stan and Sue out the front door.

When her aunt came back, Presley said, "I'm shocked that the mayor is using his position and money to push people around."

"Why are you shocked?" Aunt Violet asked. "It happens all the time. I'm sure you must have seen it in Ohio."

"Well, yes, big corporations and things like that. But to see one individual trying to take advantage of the very people he's been elected to protect." Presley shook her head. "It just seems so personal."

Aunt Violet smiled. "Everything's personal when it affects you."

"So what are you going to do?"

"I'll call around a little and see what I can find out about options. I'll start with Wyatt. Since he's used to handling big cases, he'll probably have some valuable insight."

Presley smiled, and Loralee giggled again.

Her aunt put her cell phone on speaker and placed the call to Wyatt. She explained the situation, and then they waited to hear his response. Presley expected that even someone like Wyatt, a cold-blooded corporate lawyer, would side with the Perkins in this case. But she was wrong.

Through the phone Wyatt's voice said, "I've found that it's important to pick your battles wisely and be cautious about the enemies you make because some fights are pointless. If Witherspoon wants those four acres of land, then he's going to get them. He's the mayor. So instead of letting the county take it from them and getting nothing, the Perkins siblings should sell it for a good price."

Presley was incensed. "I think we should fight the imminent domain. If there's no benefit to the city as a whole and no logical reason to seize the property—except to profit the mayor—we have a good chance of winning. I have some contacts who can advise us—"

"Your contacts are in Ohio, and that's not going to do you a lot of good here. Trust me," Wyatt implored. "Make a deal with the mayor. Get your clients some money. Don't try to fight city hall. It never works—well, it rarely works. And sometimes even winning can be losing."

Aunt Violet thanked him for his advice and ended the call. Then she turned to Presley. "Well?"

"I'd still like to try to fight it. Will you let me do some research and see what I can come up with?"

Aunt Violet nodded. "See what you can find out."

"Then if you'll excuse me, I have some phone calls to make." Presley went into her aunt's office and worked for an hour. She called a few people and did some Internet searches. Finally she felt like she had put out enough feelers for the moment and went back to the kitchen.

"Case solved?" Aunt Violet asked.

"Not yet, but I've made a good start."

"Excellent," Aunt Violet said. "Now do you mind watching our guests while I try to generate some income?"

"I'll be happy to do anything that will help you generate income," Presley teased.

Laughing, Aunt Violet dragged her oxygen tank into the office.

Presley watched Miss George Ann and Loralee work the puzzle for a few minutes. Then finally she said, "Okay, Loralee, I'm ready to hear more about Blanche and DuPont."

Loralee grinned. "Where did we leave off yesterday?"

"They were married, and old Mrs. Monroe had just left."

Loralee closed her eyes for a few seconds, like she was searching for this particular spot in the story. Then she opened her eyes and began again. "Just after I turned fourteen, we found out that Miss Blanche was going to have a baby. It was the most exciting day of my life. But she didn't bloom like most women do. The pregnancy aggravated her asthma, and she had to go to a special doctor in Albany, who insisted that she spend the last few months in bed. She fretted and cried a lot. She was afraid her asthma would make delivery difficult, if not impossible.

"It was a hard time. She wasn't herself. I learned how to deal with her mood swings, but Mr. DuPont wasn't able to handle it very well. I caught him drinking beer behind the barn on several occasions. I understood that he was under a big strain, so I didn't let him know I saw. I just collected the beer bottles, turned them in to Mr. Pardee at the general store, and watched my nest egg grow."

Presley laughed. "Ever resourceful!"

Miss George Ann placed a puzzle piece and reached for another one.

Loralee continued, "When it was time for the baby to be born, Miss Blanche's doctor wanted her to come to the hospital in Albany, which was very unusual in those days. It was run by nuns—which scared the folks around here since they were all Protestant. But Mr. DuPont wanted the baby to be delivered by the specialist, so she went. She came home a couple of weeks later with the most precious little baby girl I'd ever seen. They named her Eloise."

"Eloise," Presley repeated. "What a beautiful name."

Miss George Ann looked up from the puzzle. "I knew Eloise," she said. "She was a lovely girl. She would sing in church sometimes."

Presley wanted to encourage this moment of mental clarity. "Was she your age?"

Miss George Ann's eyes clouded again. "I don't know." She looked back down at the puzzle.

Presley shrugged and turned to Loralee. "Back to your story."

"Miss Blanche had a slow recovery from childbirth, so they asked old Mrs. Monroe to come nurse her back to health. That left me to take care of Eloise. She was the sweetest baby with the best nature. She slept through the night almost from the first. Miss Blanche gradually got her strength back and took over her mothering responsibilities, but Eloise always felt like she was partly mine."

"Your real-live baby doll?"

Loralee nodded. "The only dark spot on this wonderful time was that the doctor said Miss Blanche couldn't have any more children because it put too much stress on her lungs. She cried and cried about that.

"When it was time for them to move back to town for the winter, they wanted me to go with them. Miss Blanche said she couldn't manage the baby without me, so I went. I'd never been to Albany, and I didn't much like it. So much noise, and the neighbors were right on top of us. There were no woods or places to fish. I could tell Mr. DuPont didn't like it either. Sometimes I would see him staring out the window, and I knew exactly what he was wishing."

"That he was back at Orchid Cove?"

"Yes, and that's where I wanted to be too. But spring came, and we headed home. Mr. DuPont decided that the house was too small with the new baby, so he hired some men to come and add an upstairs and a proper kitchen. Miss Blanche was so excited. The entire summer we had extra people there working on the house. When we left in the fall, it was all finished and looked pretty much the way it does now."

"Except that it wasn't falling down," Presley contributed.

"Except for that," Loralee agreed.

"So you went with them back to Albany for the winter even though you hated it the year before?"

"Miss Blanche needed me," Loralee said simply.

"And spring came soon enough?"

"It never came soon enough," Loralee corrected with a smile. "But it came. And so did the Depression. Miss Blanche insisted that Mr. DuPont get her more chickens, some pigs, and a milk cow. You should have seen us on that flatboat trying to keep the animals from falling off and drowning—and trying to keep that huge cow from turning the whole boat over! But we finally made it.

"Mr. DuPont set the Heinrichs to work making pens for all those animals, and Miss Blanche told me we were going to double the size of our vegetable garden, so we started weeding. It was a good summer, full of hard work and bountiful harvest and chasing chickens. Little Eloise loved to hear them screech. When the weather changed, I kept waiting for them to say it was time to pack up, but they never did. Finally I asked Miss Blanche. She said with the bad economy, they had decided to rent out their home in town to save money, and we were going to stay at Orchid Cove for the winter. It was the first time I remember crying with happiness."

The past was safe and enticing. Presley wished she could stay there forever. "So it was your first winter here with the family."

"It was wonderful!" Loralee whispered. "Mr. DuPont had to go into town a couple of days a week to see patients. And Blanche had no shortage of patients herself—since poor people couldn't afford to pay a doctor and almost everyone was poor. She usually took me with her; she said I was a natural." Loralee blushed with pleasure at the memory. "She said my knowledge of plants had prepared me."

"So while most of the country was suffering through the Depression, the folks at Orchid Cove were doing fine?"

She nodded. "Our garden produced more than we could eat or can, so we shared the extra with neighbors or drifters who passed through looking for work. Miss Blanche provided free medical care to those who needed it. The holidays were coming, and we were all excited about celebrating at Orchid Cove. Life was perfect. And then my father got sick."

Loralee hadn't mentioned him in a while, and Presley had assumed he was already dead by this point in the story.

"He couldn't stay alone, so I had to leave the family to take care of him."

Presley felt sorry for the young Loralee. There had been so much injustice in her life already; although, she didn't seem to feel sorry for herself. It wasn't fair that she was required to leave the family she loved right at Christmas and take care of the man who hadn't done the same for her. "That must have been hard."

"It was my duty, but you're right. Being away from the family was hard, and being with my father was even harder. He was mean anyway, and the sickness just made it worse. Mr. DuPont came every few days to check on us. There wasn't much he could do except give my father something for the pain. The medicine made him sleep, and that made things easier for me."

"You must have missed your life at Orchid Cove."

"Of course I did. I missed Miss Blanche and Eloise and even nursing poor sick folks. Just after Christmas my father died. Mr. DuPont arranged for the funeral and even paid the cost. Miss Blanche didn't want me to stay at the old cabin alone at night. She was scared for me and thought it wasn't proper. She offered to let me move into the big house. She said Mr. DuPont would make a room for me upstairs. But I didn't want to give up my own home."

"It seems perfectly reasonable that you would want to keep your independence," Presley said.

"It was more that I didn't want to forget I wasn't really one of them," she said softly. "I loved them and they loved me, but I was a Puckett. I was afraid if I moved into their house, I wouldn't remember that."

She looked tired again, and Presley felt instant guilt. "I've worn you out. I shouldn't have asked so many questions."

"No, I love talking about the past, but it does take a lot out of me sometimes."

Aunt Violet walked in, followed closely by Miss Eugenia.

"You'll be happy to know I've finished with the monthly statements," Aunt Violet told Presley. "Have you girls had a good visit?"

Presley nodded. "Loralee's been telling me some more about Blanche and DuPont." She turned to Miss Eugenia. "And Miss George Ann remembered their daughter, Eloise."

Miss Eugenia's eyes widened. "She did?"

"Just for a second." Presley tried to limit expectations. "But she said she remembered Eloise and that she was a lovely girl who used to sing at church."

Miss Eugenia considered this. "Well, that is all true. Maybe George Ann is just going through a spell and will snap out of it soon."

"Or maybe the medicine the doctor gave her is helping?" Aunt Violet suggested.

Presley looked at Miss George Ann, methodically trying to fit a puzzle piece into each available spot. Her heart sank. It didn't look like a passing spell to her. She was afraid that Miss George Ann would never again be the person she once was.

"It's convenient that Loralee is here since we need to get her ideas about the skeleton," Miss Eugenia said.

Loralee looked up. "Skeleton?"

"I've worn Loralee out talking about Miss Blanche," Presley said. "Maybe she'd rather wait until another time."

"Oh, no," Loralee said. "I want to hear it now."

They took turns explaining about the skeleton in the backyard and how it had come to be uncovered.

Then Miss Eugenia said, "The forensic people in Albany think she's been dead a hundred years, give or take a few. She would have been a teenager when she died. If the dating is correct, that would have been about the time you were born, so you may not have known the girl personally, but we're wondering if you heard about a girl who died and was buried out here." She pointed toward the backyard.

"There is a hole in the back of her skull, so she was probably murdered," Presley added.

Loralee sat very still for a few seconds, and then she said, "I only know of one teenage girl who died around here. It happened when I was sixteen though, so it would have been about eighty-four years ago not a hundred."

"The hundred-year figure was an estimate," Presley said. "Who died eighty-four years ago?"

"Irma Heinrich," she said, "the daughter of the couple Mr. DuPont hired to help run Orchid Cove. They had a house on the far corner of the property." Her eyes strayed to the kitchen window. "Which I guess would have been just right out here."

"What do you remember about Irma's death?"

"Nothing really," Loralee said. "Peter told us she got sick and died. She was buried before we knew anything about it."

"Maybe the skeleton wasn't Irma," Miss Eugenia said. "The hole in the back of the skull indicates that she was a murder victim not someone who died of natural causes."

"Did the skeleton have two toes missing?" Loralee asked.

They all turned to her.

"Yes," Presley said. "The funeral director thought the missing bones might have been carried off by animals."

Loralee shook her head. "Irma lost two toes when she was thirteen. She was chopping wood and dropped an axe on her foot."

"Well, it was Irma then," Miss Eugenia said.

Presley nodded. "And she didn't die of a sickness."

Aunt Violet shook her head. "If she was hurt, even if they were pretty sure she was already dead, surely they would have tried to save her. It doesn't make sense that they didn't call Blanche or DuPont over to see about her."

"Yes, it does," Loralee said quietly. "Miss Blanche was going to have another baby, and this time her pregnancy was even worse than before. She had Liam just a few days before Irma died. Miss Blanche couldn't come, and Mr. DuPont wouldn't have left her—even to save a girl's life."

Miss Eugenia nodded. "Okay, so that's why they didn't ask the Armstrongs for help, but why did Peter tell you his sister died from a sickness when she obviously didn't?"

"I hate to speak ill of the dead," Loralee prefaced her remarks, "but Irma was not a good person. She was vain and silly and lazy. And those weren't even her bad qualities. She was also a liar and a thief, and well, she didn't have morals. Everybody liked Peter and his parents. But not Irma."

Aunt Violet frowned. "Did anyone dislike her enough to kill her?"

"I don't know. There were a lot of rumors, but I didn't know whether to believe them and Miss Blanche absolutely would not discuss it."

"What rumors did you hear?" Miss Eugenia asked.

"That she would dress up skimpy and go to bars in Albany on weekends. Could be one of the fellows she dated got mad at her. Or . . ."

"Or?" Presley prompted.

"Her daddy might have gotten sick of her trashy behavior."

Presley tried to hide her shock. "You think her father might have *killed* her?"

"Maybe," Loralee said thoughtfully. "Back then a girl acting the way she did wasn't something people overlooked. It could have cost her parents their jobs and their home."

"Very serious, especially for German immigrants during the Depression," Miss Eugenia murmured.

"And there was always the risk of pregnancy," Presley said.

Aunt Violet nodded. "The community wouldn't have been able to accept an unwed mother and her baby living here. No matter how Christian Blanche was, she wouldn't have had much choice but to fire the Heinrichs—which would have left them homeless and destitute."

"So the situation could have been very desperate." Presley was bonding with this idea. "If she told her parents she was pregnant, the father might have been enraged, fueled by fear and frustration. He might have hit her or pushed her or somehow caused that fatal wound on the back of her head."

"*If* that's true," Aunt Violet stressed. "We're getting very far afield from the facts."

"We can ask the forensic people in Atlanta to look through the soil they collected for evidence of an unborn baby," Miss Eugenia suggested.

Aunt Violet frowned. "It's unlikely they'll be able to find anything. The bones of a fetus in the early weeks would be tiny, and after eighty-four years, it's hard to imagine there would be anything left."

"It's worth a try," Miss Eugenia insisted. "I'll ask Mark."

Presley turned to Loralee. "You knew the Heinrichs. Did the father seem like the kind of man who could get so mad at his daughter that he might kill her, even by mistake?"

Loralee considered this carefully. "I rarely saw Mr. Heinrich lose his temper. But Irma had a way about her—sassy and disrespectful. If her parents were trying to correct her about anything, even just the company she kept, I can see her refusing to listen. And I can see how that might have pushed her father to violence."

"It might not have been her father. We have to look for other suspects, and we have to find some facts," Aunt Violet urged them.

"How will we find facts?" Miss Eugenia asked. "Loralee's the only person who was living then, and this is all she knows."

"What about records?" Presley asked. "Newspaper records? Church records? Police records?"

"I can check around," Miss Eugenia said. "But I don't hold out much hope. Back then newspapers didn't sensationalize everything the way they do now. There may have been a short obituary in the paper, but it wouldn't have any details. Since she was buried out here, in what must have been the Heinrich's backyard, there wouldn't be any cemetery records. Or church records, either, if there was no funeral."

Presley nodded. "It's certainly going to be a challenge, but maybe we can think of another way to find out information about Irma and her death."

Loralee reached over and put her hand on Presley's arm. "I'm sorry to interrupt your investigation, but I really am feeling tired now. Would you take me home?"

"Of course," Presley promised anxiously. "That is if Aunt Violet will let me use her car again?"

Aunt Violet nodded. "Consider that car yours until you get your own back."

All the way out to the Honda, Presley was chastising herself. They shouldn't have involved Loralee in the unpleasant topic of Irma and her death—not when the old woman was already tired.

Loralee was quiet all the way home. As they walked slowly up the brick pathway toward the little cottage, Presley felt that an apology was in order. "I'm sorry for all that talk about Irma," she said. "She was a real person to you, and we should have realized it would be hard for you to talk about something so sad."

"Irma's death doesn't make me sad," she said. "I told you I didn't even like her. I just get tired easy."

Presley was thankful when Versie opened the door. At least she wouldn't have to leave Loralee there alone.

"We wore her out talking about the past," Presley told the sitter.

"She'll be good as new after she rests awhile," Versie said. "Don't you worry about Miss Loralee."

* * *

On the way back through town, Presley passed the Haggerty police station and decided to go in. She wanted to talk to Chief Jones about Stan and Sue Perkins and their property disagreement with Mayor Witherspoon.

She walked into the dingy, cinderblock building and up to the desk where the receptionist was sitting. Then she asked to speak to Chief Jones.

The receptionist had on garish makeup, including long, fake eyelashes. Her features were so exaggerated that Presley felt like she was looking at a caricature instead of a real person.

"And you are?" the woman demanded impatiently.

"Presley DeGraff. I'm Violet Newberry's niece . . ."

"Oh my gosh!" The woman stood abruptly, overturning her chair in the process. Then she punched a button on the phone console. "Chief! They found more bodies at Miss Violet's house!"

"No," Presley corrected. "I came about something else."

The receptionist batted her fake eyelashes. "What?"

But Chief Jones was already trotting down the hall. "More bodies?" he gasped. His eyes were filled with something very much like terror.

"No!" Presley insisted. "We didn't find any more skeletons."

He sagged against the wall. "Thank goodness. Because I'm quitting if the governor threatens to come here again."

Presley smiled. "I'm sorry I upset you. There was a little . . . misunderstanding." She shot the receptionist an annoyed look.

"So what can I do for you?" Winston's voice sounded stronger, but he was still pale.

"Could I speak to you privately for just a minute?" Presley asked.

He nodded and led the way down the hall to a small office with glass windows on two sides. He pointed to a chair in front of the desk, and Presley sat down. Then she told him about the Perkins siblings and her plan to fight the imminent domain threat made by the mayor.

He listened closely, and when she was finished, he advised her against it. "You don't want to take on Mayor Witherspoon," he said. "The mayor is used to getting his way, and he can make real trouble for you and your aunt if you step between him and this little strip of property he wants so bad."

"You're saying these people have to sell him part of their land even though they don't want to? Just because a rich man says so?

That goes against everything I believe about law and justice and the American way.'"

Winston smiled ruefully. "You're young and idealistic. After you've been practicing law here a little while, you'll see it doesn't have that much to do with justice. And rich people getting what they want at the poor man's expense has always been the American way."

She stood. "I disagree with you, Chief."

"Now that's one good thing about our system of government. You are entitled to disagree with me." He sat up straight in his chair. "My advice is for you to work out some kind of compromise that makes everyone happy."

"And just what would make them both happy when they want opposite things?"

Winston shrugged. "That's your job to figure out. Put all those years of law school to good use."

She left the police station feeling annoyed and disillusioned. Apparently she could expect no help from Chief Jones.

Distracted by her concerns for Loralee and her disappointment with Winston Jones, Presley didn't notice that her aunt's Honda had overheated until the engine shut itself off to prevent irreparable damage. For a few seconds she was paralyzed. She stared at the dashboard's flashing red lights and dire warnings without comprehension. Finally common sense kicked in, and she guided the car off the road and onto the shoulder.

She rested her forearms on the steering wheel and marveled at this catastrophic turn of events. Surely, even by her standards, this was too much bad luck in a short period of time. After investing a few minutes in self-pity, she climbed out of the car and propped the hood—her signal for "every car I drive breaks down."

She considered leaving the car and walking back to Aunt Violet's, but the Honda was too close to the road for comfort, and a wrecked car was worse than one that wouldn't start. It occurred to her that the time she'd spent on the side of the road may have allowed the engine to cool, thus enabling her to start it and at least get home. With this hope, she turned the key in the ignition. Nothing.

So, left with no recourse yet again, she called her aunt and asked her to have Mac come tow the car.

CHAPTER TWELVE

When Eugenia took Lady out for a bathroom break right after lunch, she looked over at the Iversons' house and was surprised to see their van parked in the driveway. Her heart pounding with happiness, she hurried to their back door as fast as her old legs would carry her.

After several minutes of insistent knocking, the door finally opened. Mark stood there in his pajamas with mused hair. He blinked bleary eyes and then said, "I hope there's a fire somewhere."

She laughed, so happy to see him she wouldn't have taken offense to anything he might have said. "No fire. I'm just here to welcome you all home."

He pulled the door open so she and Lady could come inside. "Sorry, but it's just me."

Her good mood evaporated. "You left Kate and the kids in Utah?"

He ran a hand over his eyes. "Yeah. Since they were already there, I didn't see any point in making them rush home. Besides, Kate's mom would have killed me. So, yeah, I came back by myself."

"It never occurred to me that you might be asleep at this time of day." Eugenia's tone, like her mood, was now subdued.

"My plane just got in a few hours ago. I haven't slept in two days, so I was trying to catch up a little."

This made Eugenia feel terrible. "I'm sorry. Go back to sleep, and I won't bother you again."

He smiled. "I needed to get up anyway. Do you have something I could eat at your house? Our cupboards are bare."

Eugenia was relieved to be able to make things up to Mark. "Go put some clothes on and then come over. I'll have a nice meal waiting for you."

* * *

By the time Mark arrived, Eugenia had pork chops, cream potatoes, black-eyed peas, and cornbread arranged on her kitchen table. While he ate, they discussed all that had gone on in Haggerty during his absence.

"I'm sorry the mayor insulted you on TV," she said with real compassion. "The very idea of saying he needed 'top FBI agents from Atlanta' because the case was too big for the *local guys*."

Mark waved his cornbread dismissively. "I don't have the highest opinion of Witherspoon either, so it didn't bother me. Besides, if there really had been a serial killer in Haggerty, he'd have been right. I would have needed a lot of help from people with skills and knowledge that I'm glad I don't have."

"We do still have one murder that needs to be investigated. Do you think the FBI will want to look into Irma Heinrich's death?" she asked.

He shook his head. "It's a local matter, so it would be up to Winston or Sheriff Bonham. In my opinion it doesn't make sense for anyone to invest resources and man hours into trying to solve it. Irma Heinrich died too long ago. There's no real evidence, and everyone involved is dead."

"Poor Irma," Eugenia said. "It just seems like someone should care about what happened to her."

"I didn't say I don't care," Mark corrected. "I just said the FBI isn't going to open an investigation, and I wouldn't advise anyone else to either."

"Presley DeGraff, Violet Newberry's niece, wants to do an amateur investigation. I told her I'd help."

He nodded. "I have no objection to that. Since it's not being investigated officially by anyone, you won't be getting in the way. And since all the principles are dead, I don't see how it can be dangerous."

She smiled. "It's nice to have your approval for once."

He took a big sip of lemonade. "And I'll be glad to help if I can."

Eugenia was pleased by this offer. "Maybe you can run it through your database," she suggested, "the names, dates, and so on, and see what you come up with."

He nodded. "I'll do that when I get to the office. Now do you have any dessert?"

* * *

Presley was sitting in her aunt's car, waiting for Mac. The hot Southern sunshine beat down, and combined with the near 100 percent humidity, she was sweating like she never had before. Her entire blouse was damp, and her hair was stuck to her head by the time he arrived. A quick glance in the rearview mirror confirmed that her face was pink and shiny with a film of perspiration.

She climbed out of the car as he pulled his tow truck in front of Aunt Violet's Honda. He was grinning when he swung down from the driver's door and trotted toward her. "Do the cars you drive always breakdown, or is this something new?" he teased.

"My luck hasn't been good for a while now," she told him. "But since I arrived in Haggerty . . . I've been on a seriously bad streak."

He laughed. "Yeah, I knew that when I heard through the grapevine that we were dating. No girl's luck could get worse than me."

She groaned. "Oh, Mac, I'm so sorry! It's Miss Eugenia's fault, although she was just trying to help. I guess it's really Junior Mobley's fault for asking me out." Her eyes dropped to the ground. "Or mine for being a jinx."

"It's okay," he assured her. "That's probably the best thing anyone in Haggerty has had to say about me for a while."

She stood back while he loaded her aunt's Honda up on the back of his tow truck. Once he had it secured, he opened his door. She climbed in and slid over into the passenger seat while he swung under the wheel.

"Let me get some air conditioning going." He adjusted the dials on the dash until cold air was hitting her with pleasant force.

"Oh, this feels good." She lifted her ponytail so the cool air could reach her neck.

He pointed at a white sack on the seat between them. "I just picked up some chili dogs if you're hungry. And there are bottles of cold water in that cooler." He gestured toward the Igloo on the floorboard.

She was starving, so she took a chili dog out of the bag. "I'm pretty sure chili dogs don't have any nutritional value whatsoever."

"But they're low carb if you don't eat the bun."

"I'm too discouraged to care about carbs." She took a big bite, bun and all. It didn't taste as bad as she'd expected. So she took another one.

He laughed again. Apparently he found her bad fortune and disregard for nutrition hilarious.

"I guess I'm going to have to give up on cars," she said, swallowing her second bite. "Maybe I should get a horse."

He shook his head and pulled the tow truck out onto the road. "Then you'll have a dead animal on your hands instead of a broken car."

"You've got a point there—unquestionably whatever I drive will die." They sat in comfortable silence while she polished off the chili dog and drank an entire bottle of water without stopping for a breath. Then she collapsed against the seat of the truck. "I'm probably going to get fat since every food choice in Haggerty is full of carbs!"

He took his eyes off the road long enough to grin at her. "Not if you run every night—several miles of fast laps around the track at the football stadium."

"I guess that might save me from obesity. Just as long as we stay off the grass so that crabby coach doesn't yell at us again."

"He'll probably find a reason to yell even if we stay off the grass," Mac said. This time there was no humor in his voice. "He resents me more than the rest of the folks here. I was his big success story, and well, my failure reflects on him."

"He needs to get over that and find himself a new success story," Presley said. "I mean, I know you were the best that ever lived and all that, but surely in the hundreds of kids he's coached since you there have been a few with potential?"

Mac laughed. "You have the funniest way of twisting things around."

"That's the second thing I learned in law school," she muttered. "And the coach can't keep us from running there, right?"

"Right."

"Then let him yell." She was feeling better about life, having made the decision to stand up against the grudge-holding football coach—until she saw the big glob of chili sauce on her shirt.

"Oh gosh!" She searched through the white sack for napkins. There was only one, and it was tissue-thin. She rubbed it on her shirt and managed to spread the little glob into a huge stain roughly the size of a dinner plate. The cheap napkin also disintegrated, mixing tiny paper balls into the greasy, orange spot. Now she was not only discouraged, she was humiliated too. She turned to Mac. "I'm a total mess."

"Yes, you are," he agreed. "You'll probably have to throw that shirt away. Not that it's a huge loss. It's too big for you and looks like something my grandmother would wear."

She was surprised by his comments but felt too low to defend herself. "Yes, Cecelia already told me I look terrible."

His eyebrows shot up. "I know that's not true. Cecelia's a very good judge of beauty."

Presley wondered again if there was something between Mac and Cecelia. He certainly seemed to have a high opinion of her.

"She said I look like Clark Kent." Presley expected him to laugh, but he nodded thoughtfully.

"I can see that, hiding behind a lousy disguise."

She was starting to get angry, which was an improvement over hopelessly discouraged. "There's a difference between *hiding* and just not being interested in your appearance."

"Yes, yes there is," he agreed.

She sat up a little straighter and turned to face him. She noted that although he'd been out working in the hot sun, he looked as handsome as ever. "What is that supposed to mean?"

"People who don't care about their appearance wear shabby clothes." He glanced down at his faded towing T-shirt and frayed jeans. "Their hair is a mess." He pushed at the clump of auburn hair that had fallen, as usual, over his eyes. "But your hair is always fixed, pulled back in a style you think is unattractive. Your clothes don't fit right, but they're clean and tidy." He held his nose up in the air and sniffed. "You don't wear makeup, but you take the time to put on perfume. To me that says it's all an act, a disguise. Maybe even a mask."

She swallowed hard. He was dangerously close to the truth. "So you're calling me Clark Kent too?"

"Yes. But I've got to tell you, Presley, it's not working. Your inner beauty still shines through."

That was the moment she started to love Mac McIntyre.

* * *

Mac pulled into the parking lot in front of Aunt Violet's law firm. He left the truck running but put it in neutral and set the emergency brake. Then he opened his door and climbed down before beckoning for her to slide over. This time when she reached down for his hand, he caught her around the waist and set her gently on the cracked asphalt.

Then he moved his hands up to her shoulders and let them rest there.

"So, is seven o'clock tonight good for you?"

She was having trouble concentrating on anything besides the gentle weight of his warm hands on her shoulders. But she managed to ask, "Is seven o'clock good for what?"

"For our date tonight," he said. "We've got to sell this romantic rumor."

For the first time since her aunt's car stopped, she was able to laugh at the ridiculous situation. "We don't have to sell Miss Eugenia's story."

"Yes we do, or you'll have Junior Mobley right back over here trying to get a date."

"Mac, you're still married."

"Just a legal technicality," he said. "And I'm not asking for a lifetime of devotion, just dinner and maybe a movie."

Presley lifted an eyebrow. "A movie too?"

"We'll have to go to Albany since there isn't a theater here," he told her. "And a date to Albany is several degrees more serious than a local one. So after tonight you should be safe from Junior."

She smiled. "Seven o'clock will be fine. But I'm paying my own way." Brave words, considering her dwindling cash.

"You can try," he said, clearly a challenge. Then he leaned down and kissed her cheek. "You might want to change that shirt, though."

She smirked at him, and he laughed. Moving aside, Presley watched him swing up into the cab.

"Seven o'clock," he repeated.

She squared her shoulders. "I'll be ready."

Then he drove off with her aunt's car strapped to the back of his truck.

All was quiet when Presley opened the door to her aunt's house. She walked into the kitchen, where Aunt Violet was reading a law journal.

"You made it home!"

Presley sat down across from her. "I'm sorry about your car."

"Well, it's certainly not your fault!"

"I'm beginning to wonder." Presley sighed.

"Mac said he'd take it to a repair shop in town. They don't work on Astons, but they do work on Hondas. It will be running in no time."

Presley felt like she should offer to pay for the repairs but didn't have the resources without going further into Dr. Khan's money. And all of that was going to have to be repaid at some point.

Aunt Violet said that she had a couple coming in for an appointment at five o'clock. "The divorce consultation I had to reschedule from yesterday. It's a local couple, and I'd like you to sit in."

Presley nodded. "As long as we're through by seven. Mac is determined to convince everyone in Haggerty that we're really dating to keep Junior Mobley from bothering me. So we're going to dinner and a movie tonight."

"I'll make sure we're through in time for your date," Aunt Violet promised. Then she closed her magazine. "I realized after you left with Loralee that we haven't discussed salary yet." She pushed a white envelope with Presley's name written on it across the table.

Presley pushed the envelope back to her aunt. "You don't have to pay me. Any work I do can just be counted toward rent."

Her aunt laughed. "I would never charge you rent, and you will certainly be paid as an employee of my law firm. I can't match what you earned in Ohio, but I can do five hundred dollars a week to start. Once we increase our client base, I'll raise your salary."

"That's too much!" Presley objected. It was a quarter of what she made when she worked for Sorenson and Lowe, but based on what she'd seen of Aunt Violet's practice, she probably didn't even bring in five hundred dollars a week.

"It's not too much." Her aunt had that firm tone in her voice again. She pushed the envelope back to Presley. "This is your first week's pay. I gave you cash since you don't have a local checking account yet."

"But it's only Thursday," Presley pointed out. "And I've only worked two days—if you could call what I've been doing *work*."

"I like to pay on Thursdays," Aunt Violet claimed. "And consider the extra for this week a signing bonus."

Presley really needed the money, but she didn't want to take advantage of her aunt. "I don't know how long I can stay. I mean, I might not be able to take over your practice so you can retire. If I try to get a license in Georgia—"

Her aunt held up a hand to stop her. "I'm not asking for any kind of a commitment. We'll take it week by week. Or day by day if you'd prefer. Then *every* day will be payday."

Presley smiled. "Week to week is fine. And thank you."

Aunt Violet seemed pleased. "Well, good. And now that you have some spending money, why don't you go over and let Cecelia give you a haircut—or maybe a full makeover. She doesn't have any appointments this afternoon, so I know she'd be glad for the business. Then you'll look your best for your date tonight with Mac."

"It's not a real date," she cautioned, as much for herself as for Aunt Violet.

"But you still want to look nice," her aunt replied. "And I hope you're planning to change your shirt."

* * *

The beauty salon was much nicer than Presley had expected. It was a shabby-chic style with lots of old mirrors and empty picture frames on the walls. The floors were a practical laminate but made to look like well-worn hardwood. The counters and sinks were marble, and the furnishings looked expensive.

Cecelia was sitting in one of the leather stylist's chairs with her feet propped up, watching television. "What in the world happened to you?" she demanded.

Presley plopped down in the chair beside Cecelia. "I borrowed Aunt Violet's car to take Loralee home. On the way back, it stalled out on me. So I sat for an hour in the hot Georgia sun. Mac picked me up and towed the car. I ate a chili dog—and the bun, even though it was full of carbs—because I was starving. And in the process I spilled chili sauce all over my shirt."

Cecelia threw her head back and laughed. "And I was feeling sorry for myself because I haven't had a customer all afternoon!"

Presley looked down at the stain on her shirt. "Now that I've let this set in, I don't know if I can get it out."

"No big loss there. I'd just throw it away if I were you."

"That's what Mac said."

Cecelia nodded. "Smart boy."

Presley decided that she should find out once and for all whether Cecelia and Mac had a mutual attraction, but she wasn't sure how to phrase the question. "Are you and Mac . . . I mean does he, or do you . . ." her voice trailed off in embarrassed confusion.

"Mac and *me*?" Cecelia cried. "Heavens no! Why did you think that?"

Presley felt silly and relieved. "I don't know. It just seemed like there was some kind of connection between the two of you. And now that the whole town thinks I'm dating Mac, I just didn't want it to be awkward."

"Mac's a good guy," Cecelia said. "We're friends, and if some chemistry had developed between us, I wouldn't have minded. But it didn't, and now you're here."

"Mac and I aren't really dating," Presley was quick to clarify.

"Hmm," Cecelia responded. "We'll see about that. Now, please tell me you're in here for the works!"

* * *

Presley left Cecelia's salon two hours later and two hundred dollars poorer, but she felt like a woman resurrected. Her hair was several inches shorter, just brushing her shoulders, and layered so that it framed her face. Her fingernails and toenails were painted a demure pink. She had allowed Cecelia to do a facial but had insisted that she use a light hand when applying makeup.

Her final purchase had been from the "Boutique Corner" in the back, where Cecelia kept a very limited selection of women's clothing. Presley had picked out a white cotton blouse that was cinched at the waist and edged with crocheted lace. It was feminine and made her feel almost like a Southern belle.

When Presley walked into her aunt's house, she saw that their five o'clock appointment had arrived early. Aunt Violet was ushering clients into her office. Presley got a folding chair from the lobby and pulled it into the only remaining space—basically the doorway.

The couple seated in the chairs by Aunt Violet's desk appeared to be in their early thirties. Both looked uncomfortable, but the husband seemed particularly ill at ease. First Aunt Violet got the introductions out of the way. "Presley, this is Mike and Donna Beus. Mike and Donna, this is my new associate, Presley DeGraff. She brings a wide range of skills and experience to my law practice."

Mike Beus just nodded politely, but Donna pointed a finger at Presley. "Aren't you Mac McIntyre's new girlfriend?"

"Uh, well, yes," Presley answered awkwardly.

"I figured you must be," Donna said. "I mean, how many Presleys can there be in Haggerty?"

"Are you representing both Mr. and Mrs. Beus?" Presley asked her aunt, changing the subject.

"For the time being, yes," Aunt Violet said.

"I'm sorry we're early," Donna apologized. "I told Mike we didn't need to leave until four forty-five, but he insisted that we leave at four thirty. He never listens to me."

"It's fine," Aunt Violet said. "As it turns out I didn't have an appointment before yours, so we can start now. Donna, why don't you begin?"

Since this was their second meeting with Aunt Violet, Presley was expecting Mrs. Beus to address the division of assets or custody arrangements, but instead she began a long list of grievances against her husband. These complaints ranged from frivolous—like his failure to take out the garbage—to more serious, like a series of overly friendly text messages to a coworker. Aunt Violet finally cut Donna off after she nearly came to tears because she claimed her husband had purposely weed-eaten her rose bushes.

Mr. Beus's list was shorter, and he didn't seem emotional about any of them. It was obvious to Presley that he hadn't been invested in the marriage for some time, and she had a nagging suspicion that he did, indeed, weed-eat his wife's roses on purpose.

By the time he finished mumbling his complaints, Presley was thoroughly confused. "Excuse me," she interrupted. "Before we go any further with this discussion, shouldn't we consult the family court calendar and schedule a date for your divorce hearing?"

Both Mike and Donna looked at her with varying degrees of horror.

"But Miss Violet said we needed to take it slow," Mike told her.

"She said we could come every week and talk about our issues," Donna added. "She said lots of times her clients don't even want a divorce anymore after they've met with her."

So this wasn't a complicated divorce that was taking a long time to work out; it was a non-divorce with unlimited consultations. Presley looked at her aunt, "You're providing them with marriage counseling?"

Aunt Violet shrugged. "We're just working on communication skills for now."

Presley rubbed her temple where a headache was forming. For the next forty minutes, she sat and listened while Aunt Violet led the Beuses through their list of complaints against each other. Some grievances were stricken from the agenda by mutual consent. Others were resolved immediately, and some were tabled until the next week. When the couple left, they seemed happier and more relaxed.

After Presley shoved the door closed, she turned back to her aunt. "I've got some experience with counseling, and you did a good job with them."

Aunt Violet seemed pleased. "I hope they're benefitting from the meetings. And I'm sorry that I didn't explain the situation to you before they came. I intended to, but they got here early."

"I wish I'd known," Presley said. "I'll make sure to go over each case with you well in advance from now on."

"They really should be going to a trained marriage counselor, but most people can't afford that and there's a stigma attached. So by letting them come here, I work around both."

"And you make twenty-five dollars," Presley teased.

"Pretty soon I'll be rich." Her aunt gave her a quick hug. "And may I just say you look fabulous!"

"Thanks." Presley reached up to touch her now shorter hair. "Letting Cecelia remake me was fun. And she foolishly offered to let me use her car if I need transportation before yours gets out of the shop."

The phone on the desk rang, and Aunt Violet reached over to answer it. After a short exchange, she extended the phone toward Presley. "It's the mayor, and he'd like to talk to you."

With some trepidation, Presley put the phone to her ear. "This is Presley DeGraff," she said in her most professional tone.

"Hello, Miss DeGraff! Welcome to Haggerty!"

"Thank you." She kept her voice carefully reserved.

"I'd like to meet with you for a few minutes tomorrow morning. Could you come to my office at about ten o'clock?"

"I believe so, but let me check my calendar." Presley covered the receiver and looked at her aunt. "What do you think?" she whispered. "Should I meet with the villain in our imminent domain case?"

"It can't hurt to talk to him," Aunt Violet whispered back.

Presley returned the phone to her ear. "Mr. Mayor, I'll be at your office tomorrow morning at ten."

"Great!" he sounded more thrilled than seemed requisite. "I'll see you then."

She hung up the phone and faced her aunt. "He probably thinks I'm a silly city girl that can be easily pushed around."

"Let him keep that notion," Aunt Violet suggested. "That way his guard will be down."

Presley nodded in agreement. "I've gotten several responses from the feelers I put out about imminent domain. I think we have a good chance. I'm going to call tomorrow and request a hearing."

"I wouldn't mention that to the mayor," Aunt Violet advised. "That will certainly bring his guard up."

CHAPTER THIRTEEN

Mac arrived at precisely seven o'clock. He was wearing jeans and a blue towing T-shirt that reflected the color of his eyes. His hair was neatly combed away from his face, although Presley knew it would be flopped onto his forehead before the night was over.

"Don't you look nice," Mac complimented when he saw her.

"Cecelia gets all the credit."

He helped her up into the truck. "She had a lot to work with."

Presley stood on the runner and turned to face him. "No more Clark Kent."

"No, tonight I'm looking straight at Superman. Or Super Girl."

"I believe the politically correct term would be Super Person," she said primly.

"Goodness knows I want to be politically correct," he told her with a smile.

He took her to a Brazilian place for dinner. "The food is great here," he said as they followed the waiter to their seats. "And they serve a lot of meats and vegetables, so you can easily avoid carbs."

She appreciated his thoughtfulness and enjoyed the food. There was a fairly complicated system for signaling the roving servers, so Presley let Mac handle that.

After dinner they went to the movies. It was a sappy romance, and Mac made fun of it from beginning to end. As they were walking out of the theater, he asked, "If I say I'm morally opposed to sentimental girly movies, does that mean I never have to go to one again?"

She shook her head. "That only works with violent contact sports. Girly movies never hurt anyone."

"If my brain wasn't numb, I might argue with you on that."

It was really late by the time they got back in to Haggerty, so Mac suggested that they should skip their nightly run around the football field.

"You don't have to run if you're too tired," she said. "And weak. And lazy."

He sighed. "I can't back down from a serious challenge like that."

She laughed. "That's what I was counting on."

"I've got shorts on under my jeans," he said. "I don't guess you're that prepared?"

"No," she said. "You'll have to take me home to change."

It was really late by the time they arrived at the football stadium.

"I don't see your hateful old coach," Presley whispered.

"That may be the only good thing about coming to run at this ridiculous hour."

They stretched and ran and then lay down on the grass in the end zone to catch their breath.

Staring up at the night sky, she asked, "If you could play football again, would you?"

He considered this for a minute. "You mean if my ex and the potential for lawsuits didn't exist?"

"Yes."

"No, I don't want to play professional football again. I'm too old and too jaded. It wouldn't be fun anymore. But if I could, I would coach football."

She rolled over so she could look at his profile. "High school?"

He nodded. "That would be my dream."

"I'm morally opposed to your dream."

"Football is not as bad as you think, at least not on the high school level. But you don't need to worry about that ending our friendship. There's no high school in Georgia that would hire me as a coach."

"Why? You had one bad game, but you know a lot about football."

"But I blew it, and they can't forget it."

"What happened to you in that game?" she asked. "I looked at the statistics, and you always played much better than you did that night."

He dragged his eyes up to meet hers. "Do you think I cheated?"

"No, but I think there's more to the story."

He exhaled audibly and turned back to the sky. "I have dyslexia. It's not severe, but one of my symptoms is occasional double-vision when I'm under extreme stress."

"Like kicking field goals in the Super Bowl?"

Mac dismissed this with a shake of his head. "I was used to that kind of stress. But that afternoon, while I was in the locker room waiting for the game to start, my wife came in and told me she was in love with someone else. She was pregnant with his baby, and she wanted a divorce."

"Oh, Mac," Presley whispered.

"It was the worst moment of my life, and while my thoughts and emotions were all in this horrible turmoil, I had to go out and play in the Super Bowl. I couldn't concentrate on anything for more than a second. And when I looked at the ball, I saw two. And three times I kicked the wrong one."

"Why didn't you just tell the coach you couldn't do it? Surely he had a substitute he could put in."

"I talked to the coach after the second miss, but our backup wasn't very good and had no big game experience. So the coach told me it was the Super Bowl and I needed to pull myself together."

"After the game, when people were accusing you of cheating, you could have told everyone about the dyslexia."

"I had hidden it from my coaches and teammates all those years. I figured if I tried to tell them, either they wouldn't believe me or they'd be even more mad that I didn't tell them in the first place. It was a no-win situation."

"What about your wife? You should have made her share the blame."

"I didn't want her kid to read that on the Internet one day. So I just kept it to myself and let the world think she left me because I was a loser."

"Sometimes being a Southern gentleman stinks," Presley said softly.

He nodded.

"Well, at least it's over."

"It will never be over," he said. "Every day I have to deal with the regret and the guilt and the anger." Finally he turned to look at her. "Be honest. If you'd known all this before, would you have wanted Miss Eugenia to make up a love rumor about you dating someone else?"

She smiled. "No, there's nobody I'd rather fake-date than you."

They were very close to each other, and for a second she thought he was going to kiss her. She wasn't sure she was ready for that, but she was pretty sure she couldn't move away.

Then a malevolent voice shattered the night and ruined the mood. "McIntyre! Get off of my grass!"

Mac stood and then pulled her to her feet. "It looks like our luck has run out."

"I won't even pretend to be surprised," she muttered as they walked side by side to his truck. "You don't have to worry about me repeating any of the things you told me tonight. I'll consider it lawyer-client privilege."

He smiled. "Do I need to give you a dollar for a retainer?"

She shook her head. "That probably is Aunt Violet's normal rate, but I still owe you for a tow, so I'll count that."

"It's a deal." He opened the door to his truck. "And that's just what I need—another lawyer."

During the drive home, she told Mac about the meeting scheduled with Mayor Witherspoon the next day. "It would be unethical for me to tell you any specifics, but basically he's trying to force some people to sell land to him at a cheap price so he can make millions."

"Mayor Witherspoon is doing that? He's always been nice to me."

"That's just because you don't have any land that he wants."

"I sure don't have anything of value," Mac tried to joke, but he couldn't quite pull it off. He parked in front of the law office and helped her down.

"I know the mayor is going to try to intimidate me."

"Take your gun," Mac advised.

"That's illegal."

"Well then, show no fear."

He kissed her on the forehead this time. She wondered if it was going to be her ear next as she watched him climb up into his truck and drive away.

* * *

On Friday morning Eugenia was making chicken soup for a neighbor with the flu when Mark Iverson came over.

"Do you want some breakfast?" she offered.

"No thanks. I stopped by the store last night for milk, so I fixed myself a bowl of cereal." He glanced over at George Ann, who was staring aimlessly out the window. "No improvement?"

Eugenia shook her head. "I've got to get a jigsaw puzzle. Violet Newberry always has one out on her kitchen table, and that's the only thing that seems to interest George Ann now. She's been staying at Violet's some each day, but I don't want to take advantage."

He raised an eyebrow. "Since when?"

"Very funny."

"Well, you're going to have to make some kind of decision about her soon. If she decided to run out into the road, you wouldn't be able to stop her."

"I know," Eugenia couldn't disagree. "I was waiting to see if the medication the doctor gave her would help, but it doesn't seem to be making a difference. Violet is compiling a list of nursing homes." She shuddered.

"They aren't all bad."

"Wait until you're our age, and see if you still think that." She took a deep breath and changed the subject. "What are Kate and the kids doing?"

"Shopping for Easter clothes today; they have an egg hunt tomorrow."

"That reminds me about the eggs the children dyed right before they left. I'd advise you to find them and put them in your outside garbage can. Count the ones you find, and if you don't have forty-eight, keep looking."

Mark nodded. "I'll do that. I wanted to tell you I ran those names through the FBI database, looking for info about Irma Heinrich. I came up with immigration records for her parents. And Irma did have a Dougherty County arrest in 1930 for public indecency, but there were no details listed."

"Which might just mean that she dressed a little too skimpily one night and someone in authority objected," Eugenia said. "Or maybe she was hanging around bars in Albany and misbehaving with men."

"The only other thing I've got is the complete autopsy report. The hole in the back of her head has specific dimensions." He pulled a picture from his shirt pocket and showed her. "It's got squared edges and some little serrations, so if we did find the murder weapon, it could be possible to match it up with the injuries."

"I'll ask Loralee where they put the Heinrichs' stuff after they died. Maybe the murder weapon is out there in a shed, just waiting for us to find it."

* * *

On Friday morning Presley put on a black suit in an effort to look lawyer-ish for her meeting with the mayor. Like the rest of her thrift store purchases, it was a little frumpy, and as she reviewed her appearance in the bathroom mirror, she made a promise to herself to start buying clothes again. Her financial situation didn't allow for a new wardrobe all at once, but she could buy one item every Thursday when she got paid. It felt like she was investing in the future, and Presley smiled encouragingly at her reflection.

After a quick breakfast shake, she worked on her imminent domain case for an hour. She lined up a couple of expert witnesses to come and testify at the hearing. She acknowledged to herself that the experts might be overkill, but she wanted to make a show of force and prove that she was not a lawyer to be taken lightly.

Then she sat in while Aunt Violet drafted a will.

At nine thirty she picked up her now completely dry—if a little stiff—Dooney and Bourke handbag and headed for the front door. She waved at Aunt Violet, who was finished with the will but not with the client. Shoving her way out the door, Presley walked over to Cecelia's to borrow yet another car.

The beautician shook her head when Presley walked in. "Girl, where do you buy your clothes? That suit looks like it walked right out of *That 70s Show*."

Presley made a face. "I know I need to improve my wardrobe, but that's something I'll have to do a little at a time."

"Well, your meeting with the mayor is today, and you don't look like a force to be reckoned with. Come here." She waved a hand toward the Boutique Corner. "I'm going to loan you a couple of things to update your appearance."

Cecelia made her take off the black suit jacket and put on a shiny gold tank top. Then Cecelia allowed her to put the jacket back on but told her not to button it up. Finally Cecelia added a red scarf thing that made Presley feel like a whiplash victim.

"You don't think this is a little much?" she asked, holding her chin up to avoid contact with her fabric neck brace.

Cecelia laughed. "There's no such thing as too much."

Presley sighed. "Then give me your keys unless you've changed your mind about loaning me your car."

"I haven't changed my mind, but I did drive Edison's old Volvo today instead of my Porsche. I hope you won't take it personally, but you are kind of a car jinx."

"Who could blame you?" Presley accepted the car keys. "Don't be surprised if I call in a few minutes and say it's being towed."

Cecelia narrowed her eyes. "I'm starting to think that's your way of flirting with Mac."

"Yes, I've got the 'hot and sweaty damsel in distress' act down pat." Presley tried to sound flip and casual but knew she'd failed when she saw a spark of interest in Cecelia's eyes.

"Violet says the two of you go to the football stadium every night. What's that all about? I thought Mac was done with football."

"I don't know if he'll ever be 'done' with it—emotionally at least. He loves the game even though it basically ruined his life."

"With a little help from that trashy ex-wife of his."

Presley nodded in vague agreement. "He'd coach at the high school if he could, but he said they'd never hire him."

"People around here aren't much on second chances." Cecelia frowned. "So every night you run with Mac and talk about football?"

"We run around the track so I can burn off the carbs that seem unavoidable in Haggerty. Then we sit on the grass and talk—about football, among other things. His old coach yells at us every night, but we do it anyway."

"Good for you!" Cecelia directed her toward the door. "Now keep that rebellious attitude while you go stand up to the mayor."

* * *

At ten o'clock, Presley was ushered into the mayor's office. It was nice without being fancy—about what she'd expected. The man himself, however, was nothing like she had imagined. She'd seen him on television briefly, but in person he looked much younger and not nearly so pompous. Today he was wearing jeans and a polo shirt. Compared to his casual attire, Presley felt overdressed, especially with the neck wrap thing.

Mayor Witherspoon stood and invited her in. Then, rather than return to his own chair around the desk, he sat beside her. It was a perception trick, and even though she recognized it, she found it compelling. He was sending off the message: *We're equals. I respect you. We can work this out.*

After some small talk about the skeleton in Aunt Violet's backyard and how glad he was that they didn't have a serial killer in Haggerty, he moved on to the situation with the Perkins family. He presented his case well. He said that the deal for the new subdivision would benefit not only him but the town as a whole.

It would provide jobs to local contractors and plumbers and electricians. It would increase tax revenue, which would translate into better schools and libraries and other public services. He was so persuasive that if she hadn't been prepared for a snow job, she might have believed him.

The mayor made it sound like four little acres were so insignificant, even though it was almost a third of the Perkins' holdings. He mentioned that the Perkins family had always been poor and what a privilege it was to ease their burdens by offering them above market value for the acres in question.

He paused here, obviously expecting her to fill the gap with praise.

Instead Presley said, "Did you offer them above *current* market value or market value when the four acres are a part of a huge subdivision with street access?"

He looked surprised—and not in a good way. But he recovered quickly. "Current market value, of course. Trying to predict future value would be like writing fiction."

"So you have no estimated value for the property after the four acres are added?"

He looked away. "I'd have to check with my business manager."

"Well, when you do that, we can compare the two and determine what a fair price would be for the land you want. I'm not saying the Perkins will sell, but at least we'll come up with a reasonable price to offer them."

"We don't need to wait. I've made a reasonable offer, and you should encourage your clients to accept it—for their own good and for the good of the community. I don't want to have to impose imminent domain. That would be my last resort."

"For the good of the community."

He nodded. "Right."

"How much do you stand to make?"

He blinked. "I beg your pardon?"

"How much will you make personally from the deal, the good of the community aside? One million? Two? Ten?"

"That is an inappropriate question."

"I don't see why. You've mentioned my clients' financial situation; why can't we discuss yours?"

He stood. "This meeting is at an end." He walked over and opened the door for her.

With the briefest nod in his direction, she sailed out of his office with her neck scarf flying proudly behind her.

* * *

Presley replayed the conversation in her mind during the drive to her aunt's house. She thought she'd been just the right combination of tough and ladylike. The mayor hadn't backed down, but he was now on notice that the Perkins weren't defenseless anymore.

Once she got home, Presley changed into jeans and a T-shirt so she could return both Cecelia's car keys and the Boutique Corner clothing at the same time.

Cecelia wanted to hear about her meeting, so she accompanied Presley back to Aunt Violet's kitchen. There Presley reported everything as accurately as possible, using direct quotes when she could. Then she described her plans for the hearing. "I think we have a really good chance of winning," she concluded.

"Morning, ladies!" Miss Eugenia called as she walked into the kitchen with her little dog and Miss George Ann. "I hope you don't mind that we let ourselves in."

"You're always welcome," Aunt Violet assured her.

Miss Eugenia turned to Presley. "What do you have a good chance of winning?"

"It's just a case we're working on," Aunt Violet answered. "What brings you here?"

"Well, for one thing George Ann needed a puzzle." Miss Eugenia settled the other woman in front of the partially completed Eiffel Tower. "And I also wanted to tell you what Mark Iverson found out from the FBI database."

"We're all ears," Aunt Violet told her.

Miss Eugenia addressed her avid audience. "Irma was arrested once in Dougherty County for public indecency. That could mean a lot of things but possibly supports the rumors that Irma was making loose with men at the bars in Albany. The hole on the back of her head had unique shape—square with serrated edges. Mark said if we could find the murder weapon, the forensics people in Albany could probably match it to the wound."

"How in the world would we find a murder weapon used almost a hundred years ago?" Presley asked.

"In most places that would be impossible," Miss Eugenia conceded. "But you've seen the way things are at Orchid Cove. I doubt that Loralee has ever thrown anything away. All the Armstrongs' stuff is sacred to her."

Presley nodded slowly. "That's true."

Encouraged, Miss Eugenia continued, "If Irma was killed in a moment of rage, the murder weapon was probably something handy like a farm instrument, and since it was during the Depression, when equipment was expensive and scarce, whoever killed her would have wiped the blood off and put it right back with the other tools."

"But a hundred years . . . ," Aunt Violet said.

Cecelia was frowning. "So let's assume that by some miracle we're able to come up with a hammer or something with a square, serrated head. Will the lab in Albany be able to get traces of blood off it? DNA? Fingerprints?"

Miss Eugenia shook her head. "Probably not, and there are no records to match to anyway—for Irma or her father."

"It all seems like a waste of time to me," Cecelia said.

"We can at least look around," Presley insisted. "I need to go visit Loralee this afternoon anyway—if Cecelia will loan me her car again."

The beautician shrugged. "I like to live dangerously."

Miss Eugenia turned to Aunt Violet. "I'm sorry to change the subject, but I'm concerned about George Ann's finances. I'm getting e-mails and phone calls about cashing out or re-investing or selling things off. We're going to have to have a meeting soon to go over everything and make some decisions."

Aunt Violet nodded. "We'll schedule a meeting for next week. Just let me know what day is best for you."

"I declare, I had no idea being rich could be so much trouble," Miss Eugenia said.

Cecelia laughed. "It's almost as much trouble as being poor."

"It's a huge responsibility," Miss Eugenia told them. "I want to use the money to help people, but I don't want it to be wasted. I want to maintain some control, so I'm leery of the big charity organizations."

"You should start your own," Presley suggested. "It can't be that hard since there are thousands of nonprofits."

"I could help you," Aunt Violet said.

"Me too," Cecelia seemed interested. "I could even contribute."

"You could name it after George Ann or her grandfather," Aunt Violet suggested.

Miss Eugenia nodded. "George Ann would like that." She stood and collected her dog. "We'll talk about this more next week. Right now I've got to go. Come on, George Ann."

Miss George Ann was reluctant to leave the Eiffel Tower, so Aunt Violet offered to send a few puzzles home with them. "I've got plenty," she said as she took three of the puzzle boxes from a closet near the bathroom.

"I'll carry those for you," Presley offered. She walked them to the door and put the puzzles in Miss Eugenia's trunk.

She had just returned to the kitchen when Mac called from the front door. "Can I come in?"

"Of course you can!" Aunt Violet hollered back.

"You car is fixed," Mac told Aunt Violet when he came through the kitchen door. "It was just some loose wires, so they didn't even charge you."

Presley felt greatly relieved.

"But you might want to be careful who you allow to drive it from now on." This with a wink at Presley.

"I'll have you know I've managed to drive Cecelia's car into town and back today without incident," Presley informed him.

"That may be a new record for you," Mac teased. Then he looked around. "No doughnuts?"

"Sorry," Cecelia said. "They were out at the Kwik Mart when I went by today."

Mac opened the refrigerator and took out an apple. "That's probably a good thing. It will force me to eat healthy." He walked back to the table and sat beside Presley. "How did it go with the mayor?"

"Good. I'd tell you the whole story now, but Aunt Violet and Cecelia have already heard it."

"We don't mind," Aunt Violet assured her. "Tell Mac."

Presley had just completed her summary for the second time when Wyatt walked in. "Knock, knock."

"Too late to knock," Cecelia pointed out. "You're already inside."

"Ah, Cecelia, ever the stickler for facts," he replied.

"What brings you here?" Mac asked.

Presley thought that Aunt Violet looked vaguely uncomfortable, but before she could react, Wyatt answered, "I'm here to let Miss Violet know that the Perkins versus Witherspoon case is settled."

At first Presley was just confused. "Settled?" she repeated. "How could it be settled? The hearing date isn't until next week."

"There won't be a hearing," Wyatt said. "The Perkins signed a contract thirty minutes ago. I got them a good price per unit and made Witherspoon take the whole fifteen acres and the dilapidated house."

"But they didn't want to sell."

"They did once I explained that they were each going to get over a hundred thousand dollars." He flashed her a smile.

"That was my case," she said softly. "It was unethical for you to make a deal for my clients without my permission."

"I'm a lot of things, but unethical isn't one of them," Wyatt told her. "You're not even licensed in the state of Georgia, so when you say 'my case,' you actually mean 'your aunt's case.'"

Presley nodded curtly.

"Did the Perkins give your aunt a retainer?" Wyatt pressed.

Presley looked at her aunt.

"No," Aunt Violet said.

"Then they weren't even *her* clients." He had a look in his eyes very similar to Aunt Violet's. And in that instant Presley knew. They had worked together against her.

"Besides, I did you a favor," Wyatt continued. "It's settled to everyone's satisfaction."

"Especially the mayor's," Presley said bitterly. "I had expert witnesses lined up. I think I could have won."

"But what if you didn't?" Wyatt demanded. "Then the Perkins would have nothing. This isn't a game, Miss DeGraff from Columbus, Ohio. It's real people with real lives. And unlike you, we're planning to stay here."

Mac stood. "Hey, watch how you talk to Presley."

Wyatt laughed. "What are you going to do? Beat me up? You'll come out on the worst end of that deal—as usual." He waved toward Mac's bruises in various stages of discoloration.

In that moment Presley hated Wyatt Abernathy, and she wasn't too pleased with Mac either. "I don't need anyone to fight my battles for me," she snapped at Mac. Then she turned her full wrath on Wyatt. "If you hadn't stolen my clients, I could have gotten them twice as much money. I knew that a settlement would eventually take place, but I wanted it to be from a position of strength. You robbed those people! Did the mayor split the savings with you?"

Wyatt flinched as if she had slapped him. "I didn't even charge them a fee for my services," he said quietly. "Here's what you don't understand, Presley. You could have made a big stand at the hearing, brought in expert witnesses, and impressed everyone with your legal prowess. The Perkins might have gotten twice as much initially. But then a year from now, when you're back in Ohio working for a fancy law firm, the mayor might decide to condemn this place and put your aunt out of business."

"He could do that?" Presley whispered.

"Of course he could," Wyatt snapped back. "He's the mayor. And he'd get even with the Perkins too. Maybe one of them would mysteriously lose their job and the other would have a frivolous lawsuit filed against them. In both cases, financial ruin would be the likely result, and the mayor would have his revenge. Of course, you wouldn't be here to see it."

Presley stared at him. She hadn't considered any of that—except that a year from now she wouldn't be in Haggerty.

"Your intentions were good," Aunt Violet said with sympathy in her eyes. "But I'm afraid in this case Wyatt is right. The Perkins' land isn't valuable to anyone except the mayor. This way it works out best for everyone."

Mac said, "Except Presley."

Wyatt turned to her. "I'm sorry, but I had to do what I thought was in the best interest of the client." He nodded to everyone else and left with a grim expression on his face.

"Well," Cecelia said after he was gone. "I'd better get back over to my salon just in case someone decides to drop in and pay for my valuable services."

Presley waited until the back door closed behind Cecelia and then faced her aunt. "Why didn't you just tell me?"

"I was afraid you wouldn't listen. You were so focused on winning the case."

Presley felt lost and alone in a way she hadn't since she'd come to Haggerty. She stood. "Well, I guess I'll go check on Loralee. If you'll trust me with your car again?"

Aunt Violet nodded, looking miserable.

But Mac said, "There's no need to borrow your aunt's car. I'll take you."

Aunt Violet seemed to perk up a little. "That's a great idea. Presley has a lead on her skeleton case. Maybe you could help her look for the murder weapon while you're at Loralee's. And that way we won't have to worry about whatever car she's driving breaking down."

Presley ignored the joke and her aunt. She turned and walked through the house to the parking lot. Mac joined her a minute later. She watched while he unloaded Aunt Violet's car. Then she climbed into the cab, intending to sulk all the way to Loralee's.

But Mac wouldn't let her. "You've got to let it go," he said when he swung in under the wheel. "They did what they thought was right."

She looked over at him. "Do you think what they did was right?"

"I'm not a lawyer; I don't *know* what was right. But I think you agree with what they did, just not their methods."

Her shoulders sagged. "I guess that's true. And maybe they had to do it all behind my back. I was pretty determined about taking the mayor to court."

He grinned. "Don't feel too bad. Maybe the mayor will try to swindle someone else soon and you'll get another chance to hold his feet to the flames of justice."

She couldn't help but give him a little smile.

"So what kind of murder weapon will I be looking for in Loralee's sweltering barn while you visit with her in an air conditioned house?"

Her smile widened. "Based on the hole in the skull, it's probably some kind of hammer or other farming tool that has a square head and serrated edges."

"Wow, a hammer in a barn. If that doesn't sound like a needle in a haystack. And what if, by some miracle, I find it?"

"We'll turn it over to the police. Unless you think Wyatt's right. Maybe I need to quit meddling in things here in Haggerty. It's not my home, and I'm not invested like the rest of you."

"I almost never think Wyatt is right," Mac told her. "And he has no concept of compromise. He wants it his way."

"So Wyatt's the bad cousin?"

"Well, there are a lot of people who would argue that I have that distinction," Mac said. "The only thing everyone agrees on is that Patrick is the good one."

Presley looked out the windshield. "I feel worse about Aunt Violet than I do Wyatt. She must have called and told him about the whole thing. There's no other reason that he would have been involved."

He nodded. "Probably."

"She betrayed me."

"She did what she thought was right for her clients. And she thought it was best for you too—for all those reasons Wyatt named."

Presley stared straight ahead.

"She's been awfully good to you since you got here. Maybe you could forgive her, just this once."

Presley cut her eyes over at him. "Are you sure you're not a lawyer because your negotiating skills are top notch."

He laughed. "No, I'm just a dumb repo guy who gets beat up on nearly every job."

Presley considered her options and finally settled on, "You're not *dumb*."

He laughed again.

CHAPTER FOURTEEN

This time when Presley knocked on the door to the little cottage, Versie wasn't there, so Loralee answered herself. She was pleasant but not animated.

"Are you feeling okay?" Presley asked.

Loralee nodded. "I'm fine. Of course, I might not wake up tomorrow. That's the way it is for us old people."

"Do you mind if I dig through your barn?" Mac asked her. "Presley's looking for a hammer with a square head and serrated edges."

Loralee turned curious eyes to her.

"Irma's murder weapon," Presley explained. "Based on the hole in her skull, that's what we think we're looking for."

Loralee nodded. "If we have any tools from the Heinrichs' house, they'll be in the barn."

Mac winked. "Well, I'll just go out and see what I can find."

Loralee offered Presley a glass of water, which she declined. They settled on the couch, and Presley said, "I was hoping you'd continue your story about Blanche and DuPont."

Loralee frowned. "Do you remember where we were?"

"You'd spent the winter at Orchid Cove for the first time," Presley prompted.

"Oh, yes." She leaned back and closed her eyes. "Well, in the spring of that next year, I walked to the house as I did every morning and found old Mrs. Monroe there and the household in an uproar. Miss Blanche was crying, and Mr. DuPont was pacing, a sure sign he was upset. When Mrs. Monroe saw me, she said that, having ignored her doctor's orders, Miss Blanche was going to have another baby. Rounding on Mr. DuPont, she added, 'Even though we all know that another pregnancy might kill her.'

"Mr. DuPont went pale as a ghost, and I felt sorry for him. I figured the best thing was to separate them, so I took Mrs. Monroe into the kitchen. I listened while she railed against Mr. DuPont and questioned Miss Blanche's sanity. After two cups of tea and a piece of pecan pie, she was a little calmer. I told her, 'You can't blame them too much. They love each other, and they love Eloise. It's natural that they would want another baby.'

"I'll never forget the look on her face when she answered me. Through clenched teeth she said, 'If he really loved her, he wouldn't risk her life.' That bothered me because I'd never doubted Mr. DuPont's love for Miss Blanche. She was his whole world. If Mrs. Monroe was right and his love wasn't as strong as it seemed, well, then I couldn't be sure of anything. Does that make sense?"

Presley nodded. "Unfortunately it makes perfect sense."

"Mrs. Monroe pulled a handkerchief out of her pocket and wept. She was just so worried about Miss Blanche. I told her I had a feeling everything was going to be okay, and for some reason she seemed comforted by that.

"When she had stopped crying, I took her back to the bedroom. She sat on the bed and pulled Miss Blanche into her arms and rocked her like a baby. Then I understood how Mrs. Monroe felt. Her love for Miss Blanche was unselfish, and she wanted Mr. DuPont to feel the same. But only a mother can love that way. She was expecting more of him than he could give."

"So she forgave them?" Presley asked.

"Not in so many words, but she quit giving Mr. DuPont death looks. Over the next few days, I realized that with Mrs. Monroe there, I didn't have as much to do. So I told Mr. DuPont I'd just stay at the cottage some—cleaning and doing repairs—until Mrs. Monroe went back home. He was so distracted I wasn't even sure he heard until he said he'd send the Heinrichs' boy over to help me."

"For the next few weeks, I did my best to rid this cottage of all signs that my father had ever lived here. I planted my own garden, and the Heinrich boy, Peter, came, just as Mr. DuPont had promised. He brought me food and a couple of chickens and a wagon load of wood. He said Mr. DuPont told him to build a coop for the chickens and put a new roof on the cottage. So he went straight to work. Once the chickens were cooped, he climbed up on the roof and started pulling off the rotten shingles.

"He was a shy boy, and his English wasn't good, so getting him to talk was like pulling teeth. But I'd sit on an overturned bucket and ask him questions. To be polite he had to answer, and so over time he got used to me and his English got better.

"I still visited at the big house once a week. Miss Blanche seemed happy, knitting baby booties and receiving visitors since everyone in the county wanted to wish her well. Mrs. Monroe was always fussing and made sure she got plenty of rest. I'll admit, after a visit there I was glad I could go back to my little cottage for some peace and quiet. Mr. DuPont wasn't so lucky. He had to stay, and to cope he started drinking beer behind the barn again.

"When Peter finished my roof, he replaced the broken panes in the windows and painted. I tended my garden and took care of my chickens. I missed not being at Miss Blanche's house as much, but I enjoyed having a life of my own. Eventually Peter ran out of projects, but he still came by regularly. He'd help me in the garden or just sit and talk."

"He liked you!" Presley guessed.

"I liked him too. And he needed to practice his English. And we were both lonely. We talked briefly about getting married, but I was still young and Hitler was starting to cause trouble over in Europe. As the son of immigrant parents, he was very patriotic. Since he spoke German fluently, he thought he could help. So he joined the army. He was sent to France as a consultant and was killed before the United States ever even entered the war."

"I'm sorry."

She sighed. "Me too."

They were quiet for a few minutes, and then Presley asked, "Miss Blanche had her baby then?"

Loralee nodded. "She went into early labor, and they didn't have time to make it to the hospital in Albany. So Miss Blanche's baby boy came here at Orchid Cove. They named him Liam." Loralee's voice became extra dreamy. "And, oh, was he a sweet baby!"

"So you started helping Blanche full-time again?"

"Yes. With two babies around, I figured there was enough work for me and Mrs. Monroe."

"How long did you help them?"

"Always," she replied. "Miss Blanche struggled with the asthma for the rest of her life. Mr. DuPont tried to get her to move to Arizona, where the air is dry and easier to breathe, but she wouldn't go. One time I asked her why, and she said Mr. DuPont couldn't be separated from Orchid Cove. She said if they moved to Arizona, it would be him that died. She lived to see all her grandsons born and then died when she was forty-nine years old."

"So young," Presley said softly.

"I was with her until she took her last strangled breath," Loralee related solemnly. "Mrs. Monroe was long gone by then, but I felt her with me during those final days. Mr. DuPont couldn't stand to hear Miss Blanche struggle, and sometimes he'd have to leave the room."

Presley's opinion of DuPont took a nosedive. "Did he hide behind the barn and drink beer?"

Loralee shrugged. "Sometimes. But I didn't judge him. It's hard to watch someone you love suffer. I didn't love her more than he did, I just loved her differently. I could stand to do things and see things that he couldn't. I'd think about Mrs. Monroe that day we found out Liam was on the way, holding Miss Blanche in her arms like a baby, and I'd think to myself, I've got to do what her mama would if she was here. So I bathed her and combed her hair and made sure that a fresh flower was pinned to her gown every morning. When she'd gasp for air, I'd bring in big pots of steaming water and rub menthol cream on her chest. I'd sing her soothing songs about Jesus and heaven."

"She was lucky to have you."

"We were lucky to have each other," she said simply.

"So what happened to DuPont after she died?"

"He was lost without her. Liam and his family moved into the big house in Albany, and Mr. DuPont stayed out here. His grandsons took turns coming to visit him—bringing supplies, cutting firewood, and keeping him company. He lingered six long years after she died, but he was never really alive once she was gone. They're buried in Albany, so I never visit their graves. I believe their spirits live on here, in this place they loved."

"And the grandsons who chopped wood for DuPont and brought him supplies?" Presley asked. "They were Mac and Wyatt and Patrick's grandfathers?"

She nodded. "And the three cousins all look like DuPont in one way or another."

It was an awkward question and none of Presley's business, but she had to ask. "Did the Armstrongs ever pay you for all those years of service?"

"I didn't have a regular salary, but they took care of my needs my whole life. Mr. DuPont paid for my father's funeral and deeded this cottage and an acre of land to me. And Eloise and Liam both left their shares of Orchid Cove to me when they died."

"So you own it all?"

She nodded.

"That's as it should be." Presley smiled. "Since you love it the most."

"And when I die it will go to Patrick and Wyatt."

Presley instantly felt indignation in Mac's behalf. "But Mac loves it more than they do!"

Loralee looked startled. "I can't leave a share to Mac, or his ex-wife might get it. The other boys will divide it up equally once that's all settled. Mac won't get left out."

There was a knock on the door, and then Mac let himself in. His cheeks were red, and his longish hair was damp with perspiration.

"No luck," he announced. "No square-topped bloody hammer, no smoking gun, no Colonel Mustard in the dining room with a lead pipe. I'm afraid that was a wild goose chase."

"We knew it was a long shot, but I felt like we should try," Presley said.

"Are you done here?" Mac asked.

"Yes, Loralee just finished Blanche and DuPont's story."

He glanced at Loralee, who was still staring out the window. "The end is always difficult," she said. "Even after all these years."

"I can tell how much you loved them, and I appreciate you telling me their story."

Loralee gave her a wan smile.

"It's time for us to go now," Presley said. "Thank you for letting us come visit."

"And dig through your barn," Mac added.

Loralee stood and patted his arm. "You're welcome to dig through it anytime."

As Loralee walked them to the door, Presley reminded her about Easter dinner on Sunday. "Aunt Violet taught me how to make cornbread, and I plan to pay close attention when she makes the dressing."

Loralee nodded. "Violet does make the best dressing."

Mac held the gate open for Presley as they moved away from the cottage. "I thought we might stop by the old house before we go. I need to take some measurements so I'll know how much lumber to buy."

"Fine with me."

So they walked along the dappled path from Loralee's cottage to Blanche's house side by side. He showed her points of interest along the way. "That's the tree Wyatt pushed me out of when I was ten, and I ended up with my arm in a cast."

"Stupid Wyatt," she said.

He pointed to several beach ball–sized rocks arranged in a sloppy semicircle. "That's where Patrick used to make us play church."

"Spiritual even as a child?"

"Oh, yes. He could preach for hours." Suddenly he took her hand and pulled her off the path. She was too busy dealing with the sensations of his strong fingers wrapped around her own to notice where they were going until they had arrived.

Growing along the bank of the creek was a little patch of wild orchids. "There are two age-old traditions associated with bringing a pretty girl to Orchid Cove," he said solemnly. "The first is to give her a flower." He reached down, plucked a blossom in full bloom, and handed it to her.

Presley remembered what happened when DuPont first brought Blanche to this spot. So she waited breathlessly for the second step.

"But the second tradition is the best." He leaned in close, put his hands on her shoulders, and pushed her straight back into the gurgling creek.

Presley plunged below the surface of the waist-deep water momentarily. She came up seconds later, sputtering and furious. But before she could lash out, Mac threw himself into the creek beside her.

"Are you insane?" she demanded.

"I've been called worse." He wrapped his arms around her. "Hold on, and let the current carry us."

Since she was already soaked to the skin, there didn't seem to be any real reason to refuse. So she relaxed in his arms, and they floated for a while. The water was cool, and the sun was hot. It was a nice combination.

"This floating means we're going to have to walk all the way back to your truck, right?"

He replied with his eyes closed. "Yeah, but it will be worth it."

A few minutes later they bumped to a stop along the rocky creek bottom.

"The creek is only about a foot deep for the next mile or so," he told her. Sitting cross-legged in the middle of the shallow water, wet hair plastered against his head, he should have looked ridiculous. But as she took in his blue eyes, the damp freckled nose, and the straight white teeth, she found it hard to fill her lungs. He was breathtaking.

She pushed a clump of her own light blonde, recently styled and formerly combed hair from her face. Her sodden jeans were so heavy, she was afraid they'd fall off if she tried to stand. And she'd lost a shoe.

"So, wasn't it great?" he asked.

"It was pretty great." She stuck her bare foot up out of the water. "Hopping all the way back might not be."

"I'll carry you on my back," he promised. Then without any explanation or warning, he lunged headfirst into the foaming water. He splashed back to the surface with a triumphant grin on his face and her shoe in his hand. "Got it!" he yelled unnecessarily.

She accepted the shoe and with significant effort was finally able to get it back on her foot. He stood and held out a hand to help her up. She gave him one hand and kept the other on the waistband of her jeans.

They sloshed together to the creek bank, holding on to each other for support. Once they made it to the path, it felt natural to continue holding hands. They walked in companionable silence, leaving a trail of creek water in their wake.

"So do you like it here?" Mac asked finally.

She looked up at him in surprise. "Who wouldn't?"

He squeezed her fingers gently in wordless approval.

When they reached Blanche's falling-down house, Mac pointed to the front steps. "Why don't you sit there and dry out while I take my measurements?"

She studied the termite-ridden wood for a few seconds and then narrowed her eyes. "Is that tradition number three—let your friend fall through rotten stairs?"

He laughed. "There is no tradition number three."

They heard a noise from the back of the house and exchanged a startled look.

"Stay here," he whispered.

"Yeah, right." She moved to his side and matched him step for step as he went to investigate. When they reached the back of the house, they saw a small form with long white hair coming up from the cellar.

"Loralee?" Mac called out.

The old woman turned, and Presley saw that she was holding a large hammer in her hand. The handle was wooden, and the head was cube-shaped with little spikes resembling the teeth of a saw along the edges. Presley knew immediately what it was and she could tell by Mac's stiff posture that he did too.

Presley took a step closer. "That's the hammer that killed Irma Heinrich."

Loralee didn't try to be coy. "We used it to break up small rocks in the garden. When you described it, I remembered seeing it, but I wasn't sure I could find it. After you left, I thought of the cellar. That's where we kept all the gardening equipment during the winter. So I decided to come see if it was here." She extended the hammer toward Mac. "And it was."

He accepted the hammer with two fingers. "I guess there's not any forensic evidence on here, but I'll try to handle it carefully just in case." He found a scrap of fabric and wrapped the hammer in it.

Loralee watched him with sad eyes. When she felt Presley's gaze, she shrugged. "I've always thought of the planting tools as good things. It's hard to accept that this was used to kill Irma."

"I understand," Presley said.

"What will happen now?"

"We'll give the hammer to the FBI, and they'll confirm that it's a match," Presley told her. "After that, I don't know. There's no one to arrest or prosecute. But Irma deserves some closure to the short and sad story of her life."

Loralee nodded. Then she looked at Presley more closely. "You're soaking wet. Did you fall in the creek?" Her eyes moved to Mac. "*Both* of you?"

"Tradition number two," Mac said.

Loralee's eyes widened. "Really?"

"You need to rethink the order of the traditions," Presley suggested. "When you pushed me in the creek, I lost the flower you gave me during tradition number one."

"By definition 'tradition' means you have to do something the same way it's been done in the past. If you change it, it's not a tradition anymore."

"That's nonsense," Loralee told Presley. "Every generation has made up their own silly traditions. The only one that has stayed the same since Mr. DuPont showed the wild orchids to Miss Blanche is that you only bring special girls."

Presley's heart fluttered, and she kept her eyes averted. She wasn't sure if she was ready to be anyone's special girl. Not yet.

"Okay," Mac said, and Presley could tell Loralee had embarrassed him. "We've got to go. Let me walk you back to your house."

"I don't need an escort," Loralee scoffed. "I rode my scooter over here, and I'll ride it back."

They watched her drive slowly down the path for a few minutes and then walked to the road where Mac had left his tow truck.

They climbed into the cab, and Mac put the hammer wrapped in threadbare fabric on the seat between them. Once they were on the road, he turned to her. "What Loralee said about special girls . . ."

Presley laughed and hoped she didn't sound as nervous as she felt. "Loralee is a hundred years old, and all she wants to talk about is people who have been dead for decades. I don't take everything she says seriously."

He winked. "That's wise, but in this particular case?"

She watched him, waiting.

"Loralee is exactly right. I've never shown the orchid patch to a girl before."

CHAPTER FIFTEEN

Aunt Violet was baking pies for Easter dinner when Mac brought Presley home. He put his nose in the air and sniffed deeply. "It smells wonderful in here!"

"Thank you, Mac." Aunt Violet's face was flushed with the effort of baking. "I like to get my pies done early. That frees the oven up on Sunday for the things that can't be made in advance."

"We've got something to show you." Presley placed the hammer, still wrapped in the faded fabric, on the table.

Aunt Violet pulled back the old material and stared. "Is that what I think it is?"

Presley nodded. "Loralee found it in the cellar at Blanche Armstrong's house. I don't know what to do with it. I guess I should call Miss Eugenia."

"I think that would be a good idea," Aunt Violet agreed. "The sooner we get it out of here, the better."

Presley placed the call and explained the situation to Miss Eugenia. After a short conversation, she hung up and reported, "She said she'll check with Mark Iverson and call us back. They waited in nervous silence for almost ten minutes. Presley worked on the Eiffel Tower, Mac drummed his fingers on the table, and Aunt Violet continued her baking. Finally Miss Eugenia called back. Presley put her phone on speaker so everyone could hear.

"Mark is on his way over there to get the hammer," she said. "He doesn't want anyone to touch it if they haven't already. Once he takes possession, he'll send it to Atlanta and notify the local authorities as a courtesy."

"Thanks," Presley said and ended the call.

"I'll go watch for him," Mac offered.

He returned a few minutes later with a tall man who looked exactly like an FBI agent. The man's brown hair was trimmed short, he was wearing a dark suit and tie, and his expression was serious.

After the agent had been introduced to Presley, he pointed at the fabric bundle on the table. "Is that it?"

Presley nodded.

"Who found it?"

"Loralee Puckett," Mac said.

"Why did she move it?" Agent Iverson looked unhappy about this.

Mac explained the circumstances and apologized for the error. "You're welcome to search the cellar if you'd like," he offered.

Agent Iverson nodded. "I'll let you know about that, but in the future if you find anything you think is evidence in a crime, leave it where you found it and call the authorities."

"I'll pass that information on to Loralee," Mac promised. He didn't smile, but Presley heard the humor in his voice.

Agent Iverson gave Mac a long look. Then he handed them each a card.

After Agent Iverson left with the hammer, Aunt Violet asked, "What does the discovery of the murder weapon mean?"

"Probably nothing," Mac expressed his opinion. "Everybody on the place had access to the hammer, so technically they're all suspects."

"The fact that the murder weapon was a garden tool kept on the property does seem to eliminate an outsider," Presley said. "So it probably wasn't one of the men she supposedly associated with at the Albany bars."

"I think her father is still the most likely suspect," Mac said.

"We'll probably never know exactly what happened." Presley regretted this but was realistic enough to acknowledge it. "At least we've done what we could."

Aunt Violet put a couple of pies into the oven and walked over to the table. "Now, enough talk of murder and hammers and dead teenage girls. What would you young people like for dinner?"

"Let's do something easy," Mac suggested. "We could get delivery from Pizza Palace."

Presley started to laugh.

"Why is that funny?" he demanded.

"The Pizza Palace was one of the first things I saw when I got to Haggerty, and I promised myself I would never eat anything from there. I don't know why I had such a negative first reaction. Maybe it's because it's called a palace and it's a trailer."

Mac said, "There's a Mexican restaurant in Albany that's two school buses stuck together."

"And I wouldn't want to eat there either."

Mac sighed. "Okay, I guess I'm driving to Albany for Pizza Hut."

Aunt Violet beamed at him. "Justifus McIntire, you are a keeper."

"Miss Violet Newberry, you are the only person on this planet who can get away with calling me that without starting a fistfight."

* * *

Presley helped Aunt Violet with pies while Mac went to get pizzas. When he returned they decided to eat outside since the evening was so mild. Mac got the card table from the basement, and Presley dragged out kitchen chairs. All the commotion drew Cecelia's attention as she was locking up her beauty salon for the night.

"Are y'all having a party without me?" she asked with a hand on one of her slim hips.

"It's just dinner," Aunt Violet clarified. "But you're welcome to join us. It's from Pizza Hut because Presley can't eat food prepared in a trailer or a bus."

"And it's delicious," Presley said with her mouth full.

Cecelia took a piece of ham and pineapple from the box on top. "I won't stay, but I'll take one for the road."

Cecelia had taken one step toward the front of the building when Brother Patrick arrived. He walked out of the shadows by the old video store and startled a little squeal from Cecelia.

"Why are you sneaking around in the dark?" she demanded.

Brother Patrick ran his fingers through his dark hair in a weary gesture. "I declined at least ten dinner invitations tonight, and I have to sneak around so that none of those people realize I wasn't really busy."

Presley frowned. "Why did you tell them all you were busy instead of eating with one of them?"

"Because if I eat with one family, the other nine will have their feelings hurt."

"Well, that's just silly," Presley proclaimed.

"But it's true," Brother Patrick assured her. He took a step closer to the table. "I'm starving. Can I have some pizza?" Then he glanced up. "As long as you'll all swear not to tell a soul that I was here."

Presley laughed, and Cecelia rolled her eyes. The preacher put a slice of pepperoni on a paper plate.

"That pizza is imported all the way from Albany," Mac told him.

"Because Presley has something against school buses," Cecelia added.

Presley didn't even try to fix this gross distortion of her original remark.

Aunt Violet insisted that everyone sit down. "Cecelia, you take that chair. Brother Patrick, you sit right there beside her. Mac, will you get one more chair from the kitchen? Presley, over here."

Once everyone was settled to her aunt's satisfaction, Presley addressed the preacher. "Brother Patrick, if you don't mind my asking, why do so many people want you to eat dinner with them?"

"It's kind of a status symbol," Brother Patrick responded. "The preacher can only eat at so many places a week, which makes whoever he chooses feel special."

"Also some people think that having the preacher come to your house for dinner makes your family more spiritual," Aunt Violet contributed.

Mac reached for another piece of pizza. "But mostly it's because all the mothers want him to marry their daughters."

Presley thought Mac was teasing but realized he wasn't when her aunt pursued the topic. "It's unusual for a Baptist preacher to be single," Aunt Violet pointed out. "So finding Brother Patrick a wife has become sort of a contest."

"Yep, our Brother Patrick is a rarity," Mac said with a smile.

Aunt Violet ignored this. "Mothers want the best for their children, and they associate preachers with trustworthiness, faithfulness, holiness. So a preacher should make a perfect husband."

"First of all, there's no such thing as a perfect husband," Brother Patrick began. "And secondly, I don't want anyone to *help* me find a wife."

"You are entitled to a private life, even if you're a minster," Presley said.

Mac laughed. "In Haggerty no one can expect to have privacy, especially not the preacher."

"Once Brother Patrick gets married, I think the ladies in town will take less interest in him," Aunt Violet predicted.

"But I don't know how anyone expects me to get married when I'm constantly under surveillance and any choice I make will be analyzed and critiqued and disapproved of by everyone."

"Except for the lucky girl's relatives." Mac seemed to be enjoying his cousin's dilemma, and Presley sent him a cross look. He grinned back.

"It takes a very special person to be a preacher's wife," Aunt Violet said. "I think Blanche would have been a good one since she was so hard-working and kindhearted. But DuPont hated church and organized religion in general."

Mac looked at his cousin. "And Loralee says you're the most like DuPont of us all. Oh, the irony!"

Brother Patrick ignored this and spoke directly to Aunt Violet. "I agree that it takes a special woman to be a preacher's wife, but the traits I'm looking for may not be the ones you'd think. I want a wife who can love me and support my calling to serve the Lord."

"What about playing the piano, motivational speaking, and beauty?" Mac asked.

Patrick smiled. "Those additional attributes would be a bonus."

Cecelia was uncharacteristically quiet during this discussion. She also didn't eat a bite of pizza, almost as if she'd lost her appetite. Presley made a mental note to ask her later if everything was okay.

"So Loralee finished telling Presley *The Story* today," Mac announced. "Or at least, she finished telling it to her for the *first* time today."

"What did you think?" Brother Patrick asked.

"Well," Presley began slowly. "I don't know exactly how I feel about the story or the Armstrongs. Loralee worships Blanche, but in the story she seemed kind of helpless, always needing her mother or Loralee or DuPont to take care of her. And DuPont loved her but not enough to take her to Arizona, where she could breathe. And he was always slipping out to drink beer behind the barn when there was a crisis."

"Your confusion stems from the fact that this was only your initial introduction to the Blanche and DuPont story," Mac explained. "Loralee gets you hooked by telling you the basics, but she leaves out details that would slow the story down. She'll fill those in later."

Presley was surprised to hear that there was more. "What kind of details?"

"Like that Blanche and DuPont singlehandedly provided medical care for this entire area during the Depression and almost never got paid for their services," Brother Patrick said. "She was also instrumental in making sure that poor children living in tent communities had access to public education."

"And that they fed hundreds of people with their homegrown vegetables and generosity," Aunt Violet added. "Blanche would get up every morning and start a pot of beans and a pan of cornbread for drifters that would come by during the day begging for something to eat."

"She didn't just feed the drifters," Brother Patrick clarified, "she *planned* to feed them. Do you see the difference?"

Presley nodded. "I think I do."

"Blanche was the definition of Christian kindness, and she deserved all of Loralee's devotion," Aunt Violet concluded.

"Well, I'll be looking forward to future installments of the story then," Presley said. "There is one thing that confused me. Why do the three cousins have different last names?"

Mac explained, "DuPont and Blanche had three grandsons. Then each of those boys had a daughter, and they were our mothers. So we're Armstrongs on our mothers' side."

"It seems a shame that the Armstrong name itself didn't survive," Presley said.

"Thanks to Loralee, the Armstrong family lore will never die," Mac assured her. "We'll be telling those stories for generations to come."

They were quiet for a few minutes, some people thinking about Blanche and DuPont, others just eating their pizza. Finally Cecelia broke the silence.

"One of my customers told me today that Coach Phil accepted a head coaching job over at a big high school in Macon."

"Really?" Brother Patrick confirmed.

"You're kidding, right?" Mac asked.

"No, I'm completely serious," Cecelia assured them.

The cousins exchanged identically baffled looks.

Mac shook his head. "I wonder why a big school in Macon would want old Phil?"

"And why he'd be willing to change schools so late in his career," Brother Patrick added.

Cecelia shrugged. "Maybe the money was too good to refuse. Or the prestige was irresistible."

Presley met Cecelia's eye, and the other woman looked away quickly. It was a small thing, but Presley wondered if it was possible that Cecelia had something to do with the coach's job change.

Mac turned to Presley. "You've been yelled at personally by Coach Phil on several occasions now. Does he look like someone who cares about money or prestige?"

She chuckled. "He must care about something because he's moving to Macon!"

Mac opened a new bottle of water and took a long sip. "That's a better mystery than your hundred-year-old skeleton. You and Miss Eugenia should try to figure it out."

Presley shook her head. "There is a limit to the number of mysteries I can solve at once, and I can't make myself care about any football coach, especially Hateful Phil."

"Phil and his reasons don't matter," Cecelia said. "The interesting part of all this is that Haggerty High will be looking for a new head football coach."

Now Presley was sure. Cecelia *was* involved in this. She had used her money to help Mac help himself. It was so quiet that Presley felt sure they could hear her heart beating.

Finally Cecelia said, "You should apply, Mac."

He turned to Cecelia and forced a laugh, but there was pain in his eyes. "If the school board only had two choices for the new football coach, me and the devil himself, they'd pick the devil."

"It can't hurt to try," she said.

"Oh, yes, it can," he replied softly. "Anyway, look who is talking."

Cecelia turned away. "I was just passing on some information I heard at my salon. If you don't want to use it for your benefit, that's your choice."

Presley looked between the two of them. "What's going on?"

"Nothing," Mac said, although that obviously wasn't true. "Some people just like to dish out advice they won't take themselves."

Brother Patrick stood up as if this was his cue. "Okay, well, I think it's time for me to go. Thank you for the pizza and the . . . interesting conversation. And remember, you never saw me."

After the preacher left, they cleared away the pizza boxes and paper plates. Then Cecelia said she needed to go home. She made a point of walking past Mac on her way to her car.

"No hard feelings?" she asked him.

He shook his head. "Naw."

"But really, Mac, you should try. What have you got to lose?" Then she sashayed off into the darkness.

Mac watched her walk away and then turned to Presley with forced enthusiasm. "So, are you ready to run?"

She nodded. "I am."

"I know it sounds crazy," he prefaced his next remarks, "but I need to go home and shower before we run. These damp clothes are already chafing me, and if I run like this, I'll probably need skin grafts on my thighs."

She laughed. "I wouldn't mind a shower myself. I keep thinking of the microorganisms from the creek that might be crawling around on me."

He made a face. "That settles it. We're both taking showers, and I'll be back to get you in about thirty minutes."

* * *

They drove toward the school with the brightly lit football stadium drawing them in like a beacon.

"I don't see your old coach," Presley said softly as they walked from the tow truck to the track. "I guess he's already packing up for Macon."

"I guess," Mac replied.

They ran their laps, and then, since they had free rein of the field, he took her out to the middle and demonstrated unlikely kicking techniques. The more he made her laugh, the harder he tried.

Finally exhausted they lay on their backs on the fifty-yard line and looked up at stars. After a few minutes, he said, "I wonder if it's symbolic that we're lying here with half of the field on either side of us."

"And that would be symbolic of what?"

"Life," he explained. "We have the past on one side of us and the future on the other." He demonstrated this by flopping each arm in turn, one for the past and one for the future. "And we're in the middle."

"I'm twenty-five," she pointed out. "If this is the middle of my life, I'll only live to be fifty."

"I said it was symbolic, give me a little creative license here."

She laughed. "Okay."

"Now where was I?"

"You were comparing a football field with life and thinking about how we're in the middle."

He nodded. "Oh, yeah. It's kind of like when you're kicking a field goal. You can't worry about the yards behind you and how far you've come and how hard it was to get where you are. Whatever got you there doesn't matter anymore. You just have to focus straight ahead at those goal posts, give it all you've got, and try to put the ball right in the middle."

"Unless you see two footballs, and then you've got a choice to make."

He rolled over and looked at her. "You don't get symbolism, do you?"

She smiled. "Maybe you should just spell it out for me."

"We're here, together, now." He twirled a finger between them.

She nodded. "I'm following you so far."

"We both have painful things in our past. You lost your parents, and I think there's more . . ."

She started to speak, but he held up a hand to stop her. "I don't want specifics. It would just bog down my epiphany. But I sense hesitancy in you, like you're afraid to commit to now because of things in the past. You were taught not to show fear, but I think you feel it. And I'm the same way. Failing once was terrible, and until tonight the thought of risking it again was, well, unthinkable."

She nodded.

"But when Cecelia was harping on and on about the coaching job, I realized that it's like a field goal."

"Apparently everything is."

He ignored this. "If you line the ball up and kick as hard as you can, you might not make it. But if you never kick at all, you're definitely not going to make it. We'll never forget the past and what got us here, but we can't focus on it. We have to focus on the future and give that our best shot."

She was quiet for a few minutes, and her eyes welled up with unshed tears.

Finally he said, "Do I need to simplify it a little more for you?"

She smiled. "No, I got it this time, and I think that it's almost profound. Imagine what someone who didn't hate football would think."

He reached out and wiped a tear from her cheek.

"I want to focus on the future, but you're right—I am still afraid of the past," she told him. "To change that, I'm going to have to face some things, and I don't know if I'm ready yet."

"There's no rush," he assured her. "We can hang out on the fifty-yard line as long as you want. But just remember the goal posts aren't that far away."

* * *

That night when she was in her room, snuggled under the covers, with the air conditioner on high, she thought about Mac's football analogy. *You've got no chance of making a field goal if you don't kick the ball.*

She'd thought that nothing could be worth what it would take to be free of Tate. But now, for the first time, she wondered if she'd been wrong. A future in Haggerty with Aunt Violet and Mac might not be possible, but she'd never know for sure until she tried.

These pleasant thoughts were interrupted by an insistent ring from her phone. Since Moon was the only person who had her number, she answered it quickly. "Is everything okay?"

"Everything's fine here," he said. "How about with you?"

She laughed. "You really want to know?"

"Sure," he said. "I'm on my dinner break, and I got an hour to kill."

Without using any names, she told him about the Clecklers and Aunt Violet and her charitable legal practice.

"Why can't I find a lawyer like that?" Moon muttered.

When she told him about Loralee, he was skeptical.

"She's really a hundred years old?"

"She is," Presley confirmed. "And she knows everything about what happened in this area during the Depression. Then there are the three cousins. One is a lawyer, one is a football player, and one is a preacher."

"Which one do you like the best?"

This question caught Presley by surprise. "I, well, I like them all."

He was quiet for a second, and then he said, "Calamity Jane, you need to be careful about getting too attached to that place. When your lawyer gets wise to us, you'll have to leave, and there won't be time for good-bye kisses."

"I know," she said, although for a little while she had allowed herself to forget.

"Your head knows, but I'm not so sure about your heart," he replied. "But it's not a maybe, it's a fact. Simu-Lady will be found out eventually. And then he'll come looking for you."

Presley felt foolish for allowing herself to bond with Haggerty and its residents. "Maybe I should leave now."

"Naw," he disagreed. "You're safe there and happy. What you need to do is find a good lawyer and get them to start working on your case. That way you'll be ready when the search starts."

"You're right, Moon. That's what I'll do."

"Good night," he said. "And sleep with one eye open."

CHAPTER SIXTEEN

On Saturday morning when Presley came downstairs, her mood was subdued. She was determined to remember the seriousness of her real life and resist the way Haggerty had of numbing her mind to danger.

She walked into the kitchen and found that Easter preparations were in full swing. Aunt Violet had finished her pies the night before and had now moved on to vegetables. The counters were covered with dishes in various stages of completion.

Aunt Violet looked up when Presley walked in. "Good morning!" she greeted.

"Good morning to you." Presley surveyed the works in progress. "What can I do to help?"

Aunt Violet pointed to a wreath that was resting on top of the Eiffel Tower puzzle. Made out of multicolored tulle, it looked like a huge pastel loofah.

"Can you go hang that on the front door? Otherwise people will think we don't love the Lord."

A few days ago Presley would have expressed disbelief over such a statement, but after a little time in Haggerty, she knew this could be true. So she picked up the wreath and examined it. "This isn't much to compare with the Cleckler's Easter display," she murmured. "You don't have any huge plastic bunnies in the basement?"

Aunt Violet laughed. "No, but we can go to the after-Easter sales on Monday and get some. That way we'll be ready for next year."

Presley smiled as she carried the wreath to the front of the house.

Cecelia pulled up to her beauty salon while Presley was trying to hang the wreath on the door. She climbed out and walked over wearing skin-tight, hot-pink pants and a clingy shirt that had what looked like cotton balls sewn all over it. On anyone else the ensemble would have been a disaster. On Cecelia it looked divine.

"Is this straight?" Presley asked.

Cecelia tilted her head. "It doesn't really matter. That thing is so awful. I told Violet to throw it away last year."

Presley laughed. "We're going to the after-Easter sales on Monday to get some decorations for next year."

"Next year, huh?" Cecelia's tone was speculative. "It sounds like you're planning ahead."

"I'm trying. Mac is too. I think he might apply for that coaching job."

Cecelia shifted her weight from one sparkly high-heeled shoe to the other. "He should."

"And if he doesn't get this one, he can apply other places, even in other states. Goodness knows they play stupid football everywhere."

This earned her a ghost of a smile.

Presley stopped trying to adjust the hideous wreath and gave Cecelia her full attention. "Are you okay?"

"Sure, why do you ask?"

"I don't know." Presley tried to pinpoint exactly what had been bothering her about Cecelia. "Last night when we were eating pizza you just seemed so quiet."

"Yeah, discussing all the women who want to marry Preacher Pat isn't my favorite subject."

Presley's mouth fell open as understanding dawned. "You're in love with Brother Patrick!"

"Shhhh!" Cecelia hissed, stepping closer in obvious alarm. "Do you want to get him fired and me run out of town on a rail?"

"He loves you too?!" Presley realized, but she whispered this revelation.

Cecelia lifted a shoulder in an elegant shrug. "Yeah, for all the good it does us."

"No wonder he's having trouble finding a wife among all the girls in town. He's already found the one he wants."

"Patrick can't marry me," she said flatly. "It would be professional suicide."

Suddenly Mac's words from the night before made sense. "You encouraged Mac to go after his dream. Why won't you do the same?"

"My dream isn't in question here," she said.

"What if Brother Patrick decides to give *his* dream up?"

"He's already offered, but I can't let him do that. You've seen how he is. It's like his great-great-grandmother Blanche has been reincarnated. He's all about service and sacrifice and helping others. If he couldn't be a preacher, he'd be miserable."

Presley frowned. "Do you want him to stop preaching?"

"Of course not," Cecelia replied.

"So it's just the Haggerty Baptist Church you are opposed to?"

"They hate me."

"Brother Patrick can find another church in another town," Presley said. "Then you can be his loving, helping, stylish wife, and everyone will be happy."

Cecelia smirked. "And all that wisdom coming from somebody who can't even hang an Easter wreath straight." She reached over and adjusted the ball of tulle.

Presley saw no noticeable improvement but decided to let the wreath criticism slide. "I mean it, Cecelia. You shouldn't sell yourself short, and you shouldn't give up on love."

"Well, thanks for the unsolicited advice," Cecelia quipped. "Now I'd better get to work."

"If you get bored, come over," Presley called after her. "Aunt Violet's going to show me how to make dressing."

Cecelia gave her a little wave of acknowledgment and walked on to her salon.

Presley reached for the doorknob and then stopped. "Cecelia?"

The other woman turned back. "Yes."

"The lawyers who helped you defend your husband's estate in court, would you recommend them?"

"Sure," she replied. "But they're expensive. If you've got a legal problem, you should ask your aunt or Wyatt."

"I'm not sure I need to talk to anyone, but if I do I might want someone more neutral."

Cecelia nodded. "Well, if you decide you need a neutral lawyer, let me know, and I'll set up an appointment."

* * *

It turned out that making dressing was a chaotic process that involved a huge pot, several large bowls, two food choppers, and all the available counter space. Presley followed her aunt's instructions—boiling a hen, chopping onions and celery, crumbling cornbread, beating eggs, melting butter—but completely lost track of amounts and the order ingredients were introduced to the batter.

"I'll never remember all this," she told her aunt when they put the pan of dressing into the oven.

"Not this time," Aunt Violet agreed. "But you'll learn, and one day it will be second nature."

Presley had her doubts, but she kept them to herself.

Mac arrived a little while later with Loralee and the world's largest ham.

"I hope this will be enough to feed us all," he teased as he put it on the table.

"I hope it will fit in my oven," Aunt Violet said without the hint of a smile.

Presley was alarmed, but Mac shrugged. "If not, we can always get Patrick to bake it in one of the industrial-sized ovens at the church."

"I guess that's true," Aunt Violet agreed. She turned away from the huge piece of meat on her counter and greeted Loralee. "You look a little pale. Have you been feeling okay?"

"As well as any hundred-year-old woman can expect to feel," Loralee replied. "I'm just thankful when I wake up in the morning." She walked over to the table and went to work on the Eiffel Tower.

Presley sat down across from Loralee. "I made my first batch of dressing, with Aunt Violet's help."

Loralee looked up from the puzzle. "You sure made a mess."

"But the dressing smells good," Mac added with a smile.

Presley laughed. "I guess that means I need to start cleaning."

Aunt Violet asked, "Mac have you eaten breakfast?"

He shook his head. "I was planning to steal another one of your apples."

"You're welcome to my apples," she assured him, "but I need someone to taste-test the pies I made yesterday, and I thought you might volunteer."

Mac stood straight and declared, "You know what they say, it's a tough job but somebody's got to do it!"

Cecelia walked in a few minutes later carrying doughnuts. She looked at Mac's plate full of pie in dismay. "I was afraid you'd starve to death if I didn't bring these, but I see that's not likely."

He grinned at her. "I'll take a few of those too—for energy."

She shook her head in mock disgust. "You give a whole new meaning to *blood sugar*." She opened the doughnut box and watched while he selected three.

Miss Eugenia was the next to arrive, all alone this time.

"Where are your buddies?" Presley asked.

"Lady is at the groomer, and George Ann is trying out a nursing home. If it looks like a good fit, she'll move in permanently on Monday."

"I know that will be a relief," Aunt Violet said.

"It will be," Miss Eugenia agreed. "But I've kind of gotten used to her shadowing me around."

Aunt Violet nodded. "As long as she's not herself, she's pleasant company."

"And she's good at puzzles," Loralee pointed out.

"Did Mark send the hammer to Atlanta?" Presley asked.

Miss Eugenia helped herself to one of Cecelia's doughnuts and nodded. "He had to go to Atlanta early this morning to catch a flight back to Salt Lake, so he took it personally. He's going to surprise Kate and the kids for Easter, which means I'm alone again."

Aunt Violet patted her hand. "Soon they will be home to stay."

Miss Eugenia made a face. "Unfortunately Polly and Annabelle will also be back soon. It's too bad I can't pick and choose the people I want to stay away."

"Oh, Eugenia, you don't mean that!" Aunt Violet said in despair. "Now tell us about George Ann's retirement home."

Miss Eugenia was happy to comply. "It's very nice and not too far away. I talked to Brother Patrick and the president of George Ann's Sunday School class. They promised they'd make sure she receives regular visits. And if she shows improvement at any time in the future, the doctor said she might be able to leave."

"That sounds encouraging," Aunt Violet said as they heard a knock on the front door.

Cecelia and Mac both volunteered to go answer it.

"So is it going to be me or you?" he asked.

She waved for him to go. "You need the exercise to work off some of that pie."

Mac winked at Presley and then walked toward the front of the house.

"Probably someone wanting to draw up a will right before Easter," Aunt Violet predicted.

"I hope it's someone wanting their hair fixed," Cecelia said. "Otherwise I'll be over here all day because I don't have a single appointment."

Mac returned to the kitchen, and the pallor of his skin was Presley's first indication that something was wrong. He'd gone pale, causing the freckles on his nose to be more noticeable. And he wasn't smiling.

Then she saw that Brother Patrick and Deputy Cade Burrell from the sheriff's department were right behind him. They also looked grim.

"What's happened," Aunt Violet said weakly.

"Is it something to do with the skeleton?" Miss Eugenia asked.

Brother Patrick shook his head. "No."

Deputy Burrell stepped forward. "I'm sorry, Miss DeGraff, but my wife is a news reporter. After she met you the other night, she did some digging, and she found out some things about your life in Columbus. She's preparing a series of special reports on you that will air in small segments every day next week. I would stop her if I could, but . . ." His voice trailed off in misery. "Some advance notice is the best I can do."

Everyone sat in shocked silence for a few seconds. Then Aunt Violet reached across the table and took Presley's hand. "Why don't you go into my office and talk to Cade in privacy," she suggested.

Presley felt surprisingly calm. She looked around the room at the worried, compassionate faces and shook her head. "I don't want to keep secrets from all of you anymore. We can talk here."

"Mac," Aunt Violet said, "will you call Wyatt and tell him to drop whatever he's doing and come immediately? I have a feeling we're going to need advice from a savvy, world-wise lawyer who does more than wills and simple divorces." As Mac pulled out his phone, she turned to their most recent arrivals. "Everyone take a seat. You'll make Presley nervous if you hover."

Cecelia leaned close. "I guess this is why you thought you might need a neutral lawyer?"

Presley nodded. "I still might, but we'll see what Aunt Violet and Wyatt have to say."

Mac ended his short conversation and told them, "Wyatt's on the way."

"Good," Cecelia said. "The suspense is killing me."

Mac shot her an annoyed look and sat down on one side of Presley. Brother Patrick took the other side, and Cade took the chair in front of her.

"If it's any consolation, I'm probably going to lose my job," the deputy said. "And I've moved to my parents' house."

"That doesn't make me feel better at all," Presley told him. "If the sheriff fires you over something your wife did, tell him you're going to sue. Aunt Violet will represent you for a ridiculously low fee. And move back in with your wife. I don't want my problems to come between the two of you."

"I feel like I can't trust her," he said. "Like she's putting what's best for her in front of what is best for you and me and everyone else."

"Then get some counseling," Presley advised. "But don't give up, at least not so easily." She glanced pointedly at Cecelia.

The beautician rolled her eyes. "Don't get her started on love advice."

While they waited for Wyatt, Aunt Violet made coffee. Cecelia called the Kwik Mart and asked them to deliver more doughnuts. Mac sat quietly beside Presley, his arm snug against hers in a silent show of solidarity.

Finally Wyatt rushed in wearing tennis clothes and carrying two boxes of doughnuts. He looked ridiculous in the short shorts, but nobody was in the mood to make fun of him. "I met a kid from the Kwik Mart on the way in. You owe me twenty dollars plus tip," he told Cecelia. "This better be good." He put the doughnuts in the middle of the table and took the only empty seat. "I was just about to win my match."

Presley cleared her throat and leaned forward, leaving the warmth of Mac's arm behind. This was something she had to do alone. "I appreciate you leaving your tennis game to come. In fact, I appreciate all of you—for your support here today and the friendship you've extended to me since I arrived in Haggerty. The first thing I need to say is that I came here under false pretenses. I apologize for misleading all of you."

She paused for a deep breath and then continued. "It's hard to know where to begin, and I'm not a good storyteller like Loralee." She glanced at the little old woman, who was watching her with sad eyes. "I guess I have to start with my childhood." She told them about her privileged youth, about traveling around Europe with doting, wealthy parents, and about her unusual but comprehensive education at the hands of international tutors. "The only bad thing about always being with adoring parents was that I didn't know I was ugly until I started college."

There were gasps all around, and she could see that they were each about to object. She pointed at her face. "This is not the face I was born with. This is the creation of an extremely talented plastic surgeon. It's like a mask. It's not the real me."

"Explain, please," Cecelia prompted.

"My face was misshapen," Presley continued. "I'm sure you'll see the pictures on Monday when the television segments start, but I want you to understand that I didn't feel ugly—not until college.

That's when I experienced prejudice and cruelty for the first time. I asked my parents if anything could be done about it, and they said they'd consulted with several surgeons when I was a baby. The consensus was that my face might not be fixable and that in order to try, I would have to endure several painful surgeries. They decided that the chance at improvement wasn't worth the risk and pain, but they would support me if I felt differently.

"I wanted to try the surgeries, but with college and then law school, I never had time to take months off. Then I got the job at Sorenson and Lowe, where I was tucked away in a little office and had no contact with the public. In the evenings, I went with my parents to restaurants and concerts and plays. My life was full and happy, and facial surgery didn't seem so important anymore. Then my parents died in a car crash, and my whole world fell apart."

Aunt Violet patted her hand again. "Bless your heart."

Presley forced herself to go on. "For a few weeks, I was nearly paralyzed by grief and loneliness. Without my parents there to shield me from the unpleasant things, I felt exposed and defenseless. Everything terrified me. I only left the house to go to work. I let lawyers and accountants handle all the financial decisions.

"It was during this time Aunt Violet suggested I move down here." She paused to smile at her aunt. "And if I'd accepted her invitation, I never would have met Tate Sheridan." She looked around at the group and said, "I know I'm dragging this out."

"It's okay," Aunt Violet assured her. "Take your time."

After another deep breath, she began again. "Tate was from a good family, fresh out of law school, and passably handsome—the kind of guy who never had any interest in me. Most of my research requests were sent through e-mail, but he came to my office to get help with trial research. I should have been suspicious when he showed up to ask personally, but I was naïve and stupid and, well, I'm getting ahead of myself.

"Tate was charming and friendly. He didn't give me false compliments, but he could always find something nice to say, like that my suit was a pretty color. For a couple of weeks, he spent hours in my office every day, working on his case. He'd order sandwiches at lunchtime so we could work through. As the trial dragged on, he started coming over to my house at night so we could prepare for the next day. Gradually I shared my worries and concerns with him about money and investments and taxes. He offered to help, and I was so appreciative. A few months later, he left Sorenson and Lowe to work for me. To make things easier, I gave him my power of attorney."

"Of course you did," Wyatt muttered.

Deputy Burrell cursed under his breath.

"He moved into my father's old office at a downtown professional building I owned and started managing my assets. The original plan was to keep the other lawyers and accountants that had worked for years with my father, but Tate found fault with them one by one, and soon they'd all been replaced by strangers.

"Then I started getting urgent calls about Tate's financial decisions. He was recklessly liquidating assets, selling property below market value and trading in blue-chip stocks at a loss, but whenever I asked him about something, he had what seemed like a reasonable explanation. Then I got word that he had put my parents' home on the market without even asking me. I was ready to fire him and maybe even sue him. But when I charged into his office that day, he dropped down on one knee and asked me to marry him. Of course I said yes."

She put a hand over her mouth briefly. "I'm sorry. This is just so humiliating."

"He is a con artist," Wyatt said. "You have nothing to be ashamed of. They're experts at tricking people."

For some reason Wyatt's opinion actually mattered on this particular subject, so his words steadied her.

"He claimed that selling the house was part of his proposal plan. He wanted us to start our lives together in a place of our own. He'd purchased a penthouse apartment in downtown Columbus and hired a decorator to supervise a complete renovation. He said he wanted me to be involved in that process, and I was excited to plan the wedding." She stared at her hands. "So I quit my job at Sorenson and Lowe."

"He cut you off from everyone who could help or advise you," Aunt Violet said softly.

"Yes, but it didn't seem that way at the time. I felt like he was pulling me closer to him. I was so involved in planning the wedding and decorating the apartment that I just didn't pay attention to what was going on around me. I didn't listen to people I *knew* I could trust. I chose him over everyone and everything.

"Then, on the day before our wedding, I stopped by the office to show him some gifts we'd received. I overheard him talking to some of the staff he had hired. He was bragging about all the money he'd stolen from me. He told them it was a huge personal sacrifice to have to marry a"—she struggled for the courage to say it—"a horse-faced girl like me. But he said the money was worth it." She reached up and touched her cheek. "It was the first time in a long time that I'd thought about my face. He'd convinced me that it didn't matter."

"What mattered to him was your money," Wyatt said curtly. "You could have been Miss America, and it wouldn't have changed things."

"Anyway, he saw me standing there and realized I'd heard everything. The really crazy thing is that if he'd apologized and given me some stupid excuse, I probably would have forgiven him. But instead he laughed. Then he said a lot of other horrible things while those people he was paying with *my* money watched.

"I realize now that he was trying to push me over the edge, and he did. Something snapped inside me, and I ran. I felt worthless and unlovable. I drove to the spot where my parents died, and I tried to kill myself by running my car off the road. Of course, I couldn't even do that right. But I did manage to total my car and break several bones in my face, including my oversized jaw bone.

"Fortunately for me, the doctors at the hospital where I was taken really cared. They called in a plastic surgeon, who also cared. Over the next few months, he fixed my face, while a series of doctors and therapists healed my broken psyche. Because of the suicide attempt, I had to stay in a mental hospital after my wounds were healed. And during all this time, Tate continued to manage my estate."

Wyatt grimaced. "With your power of attorney."

She nodded. "When I was healthy enough to care, I tried to revoke the power of attorney and fire Tate, but he'd had a judge declare me incompetent. That meant I couldn't get rid of him without a court hearing. My psychiatrist had agreed to testify, and we felt confident that the judge would rule in my favor.

"But then Tate came to visit me. He claimed that he'd sold my mother's jewelry, burned all our family photos, and filed a malpractice suit against my psychiatrist. He was trying to get a violent reaction out of me, and he did. I scratched his face, and now he had proof that I was a danger not only to myself but to others. So I forgot about the competency hearing and started planning an escape."

"How did you get away?" Mac whispered.

She told them about Simu-Lady and the nursing students and Moon. Then she glanced at Deputy Burrell. "That basically makes me a fugitive."

"I'm not going to arrest you," Cade said. "Someone else might, but not me."

Presley felt some of the tension ease out of her shoulders. "Anyway, once I was out, I purchased some clothes and a couple of suitcases at a thrift store, and drove to Georgia."

"The thrift store explains a lot about your wardrobe," Cecelia remarked.

Presley ignored her. "Tate didn't know about the Aston, which is the only reason it hadn't been sold. And you all know the rest of the story. It quit on me in front of the Cleckler's house."

"How long before the Sheridan guy figures out you're gone?" Cade Burrell asked.

Presley shrugged. "If he hasn't figured it out by Monday, he'll know as soon as your wife's series begins."

"What do you think he'll do?"

"He's got my money, so it's possible he'll just let me go," she said. "But then he'd have to worry that I'd get enough courage to fight him. I think he'll try to have me put back in a mental institution."

"You'll have to leave Haggerty," Aunt Violet said softly.

"That's why you couldn't commit to a future here," Wyatt added.

Presley nodded once to confirm both questions.

"Anyone can see you're not crazy," Miss Eugenia scoffed.

"The records tell another story. I tried to kill myself, and I scratched Tate."

"That was in the past," Mac pointed out. "We can get a doctor to say you're mentally healthy now."

"And Sheridan can hire two doctors to say she's not," Wyatt informed him. "Presley's situation is very precarious."

"Maybe he'll leave you alone if you don't try to revoke the power of attorney," Cecelia said.

Miss Eugenia shook her head. "You can't live that way—always afraid someone is going to knock on your door and cart you off to a mental hospital."

Presley shrugged. "If I try to fight him, I'll lose. He still holds all the cards—and he has all the money."

"I have money," Cecelia said. "I'll help you."

Tears stung Presley's eyes, but she shook her head. "Thanks, but Wyatt's right. Even with money, I don't stand a chance in a fair fight."

"Then we won't play fair." Aunt Violet had that firm look again.

Miss Eugenia raised an eyebrow. "Maybe we can beat him at his own game?"

Aunt Violet nodded. "We'll have to cut off his access to Presley's funds."

"The power of attorney is the key," Wyatt said. "Without that he can't control Presley."

"So how do we get the power of attorney away from him?" Presley asked.

"We could burn his office," Mac suggested.

"Mac!" Miss Eugenia cried. "Don't say things like that in front of a deputy sheriff!" She turned to Cade Burrell. "Will you step outside please?"

"You don't need to worry about me, Miss Eugenia," the deputy assured her. "I'm about to get fired anyway."

That did seem to alleviate Miss Eugenia's concerns.

"What if someone called him and said they had tons of money and didn't know how to invest it," Cecelia said, thinking out loud.

Wyatt nodded encouragingly. "A situation similar to the one Presley was in when he marked her?"

"Exactly," Cecelia confirmed. "We could tell the FBI how this guy operates. Then we could set him up, with them listening in. When he asks for an unlimited power of attorney, they can start an investigation. Maybe they would revoke all powers of attorney he holds, at least temporarily, while they investigate."

"I like that," Wyatt said. "It's simple yet crippling."

"It separates Sheridan from the money and the power," Cade Burrell also approved, "without specifically involving Presley."

Wyatt frowned. "But since he operates on a fairly small scale and within the state of Ohio, we might not be able to coax the FBI into investigating him."

"Mark Iverson will help us," Miss Eugenia said. "As an FBI agent, he should be able to get cooperation from the officials in Ohio."

Aunt Violet nodded. "They can get a search warrant, look through his records, and use the evidence they find against him. And we can quietly bow out."

"Whoever calls Sheridan will have to be legit though," Deputy Burrell said. "He's a rat, so he knows what one smells like. He'll check it out and won't even call back unless it's for real."

"Maybe the person who calls him could be an ex-pro football player," Mac said.

Wyatt shook his head. "You don't have any money, and it wouldn't take him five seconds to find that out."

"What about an attractive young widow with millions she inherited from her deceased husband," Cecelia proposed.

"I like that better," Wyatt said. "Your assets are all a matter of recent public record, so he could confirm your wealthy status quickly."

Brother Patrick spoke for the first time. "I'd prefer to keep Cecelia out of this."

"I'm a big girl, Preacher Pat," Cecelia said softly. "You don't have to look out for me."

He reached across the table and took her hand in his. "I want to."

Miss Eugenia looked between the two of them speculatively. Then she turned her attention back to the others around the table.

"No, it should be an elderly woman who has recently been given responsibility for the huge estate of a friend. She knows nothing about how to handle the investments, what to keep or what to sell. She can't be bothered with it since it's not her money anyway. She wants to find someone who will assume complete control. Maybe she could even mention liquidating all the assets and forming a nonprofit for charity."

Wyatt laughed out loud. "You are one smart woman! There's not a con man alive who could resist that!"

Miss Eugenia was obviously pleased by this praise. "George Ann's holdings and the fact that I have her power of attorney should both be easy for Mr. Sheridan to confirm."

Aunt Violet nodded. "He'll be too greedy to be cautious, and that's how we'll get him."

"And as a bonus, by branching out into Georgia, he's crossing state lines and giving the FBI clear jurisdiction," Wyatt added with a smile.

Presley said. "I love it."

Deputy Burrell stood and stretched. "Personally I liked the idea of burning down his office, but I'll go along with whatever."

* * *

It had been an intense hour, so they decided to take a break. When they reconvened, Aunt Violet apologized for not sitting down at the table with the others.

"I'll be right here, and I'll be paying attention, but I've got to get these side dishes done or my Easter feast tomorrow will be a disaster."

Cecelia and Presley offered to help, but Aunt Violet wouldn't hear of it. "You two need to concentrate. I can handle this."

Presley was too emotionally drained to argue, so she returned to her seat. Cecelia ignored Aunt Violet's instructions and started peeling sweet potatoes. And Loralee, who had been quiet during all of Presley's revelations, got up and started washing dishes.

"I would help you, Violet, if I wasn't the star of this show," Miss Eugenia called out.

Aunt Violet laughed. "Yes, you concentrate on your acting role."

Miss Eugenia put her phone on speaker and called Mark Iverson in Utah.

"This better be important," he said when he answered. "You just dragged me away from an Easter egg hunt."

"I'm sorry," she said, although she didn't sound remorseful. "But this is a matter of life and death."

"You haven't found any more skeletons, have you?"

"No, but I almost wish that was our problem. Dealing with dead people is much easier." She went on to tell him the whole story. Mark asked the occasional question, but mostly he let her talk. Presley and the others put in details when necessary.

When she was finished with their plan to wrest Presley's power of attorney from her unscrupulous ex-fiancée, Mark sighed. "That might work. I'll open an investigation on Tate Sheridan from here and change my return plane ticket to stop over in Ohio tomorrow afternoon. That way I can be at the attorney general's office first thing on Monday morning."

"That's perfect!" Miss Eugenia was all smiles. "I'll be practicing my helpless old lady routine."

"It will take some serious acting to convince anyone that you're helpless," Mark said.

"I'm going to take that as a compliment. Now get back to the Easter egg hunt and kiss your children for me!"

Once this call was completed, Wyatt got a legal pad from Aunt Violet's office and started to write. "Let's set up our time line for Monday. We'll want Miss Eugenia to call Sheridan early, and hopefully he will try to swindle her."

"But we have to give Mark time to explain the situation to the attorney general in Ohio and get his cooperation," Aunt Violet pointed out.

They decided on nine o'clock Eastern time. Presley felt Mac's eyes on her, and she smiled at him.

"Hopefully he'll call right back," Wyatt said. "But we'll have to be prepared for the possibility that he won't."

"This could take several days or even weeks," Presley cautioned.

Mac sighed. "And if Hannah-Leigh runs her exposé on Monday, she'll ruin the whole thing."

Everyone looked at Cade. He raised his hands like he was surrendering. "Hey, if I could stop her, we wouldn't be here right now."

"You're sure there's nothing you haven't tried?" Wyatt demanded impatiently.

"Short of tying her up?" Cade looked discouraged. "She said it's gone too far to stop now. The station has already reserved air time; it would ruin the whole newscast all week if she pulls her piece now."

"I say we tie her up," Mac said. He wasn't smiling.

"We could give her something else to use for her special report time," Loralee suggested softly from her position by the sink.

Wyatt looked up, a little startled by her comment. "What?"

"We can tell her about the new evidence in the skeleton murder case," Loralee explained. "She can do a weeklong special report on that instead of her report on Presley. I'll even let her interview me since I'm the closest thing there is to a witness. I'll give her lots of background information. I can show her Miss Blanche's house and the spot where the Heinrichs lived. I might even be able to come up with a picture of Irma."

Cade Burrell looked like he'd just been saved from a fate worse than death. "I think she'd go for that!"

"Will it be enough to fill up a weeklong special report?" Cecelia sounded skeptical.

"I never run out of stories about Miss Blanche and Mr. DuPont," Loralee assured her.

"And that is no joke," Mac confirmed.

"It's going to be a lot of trouble for Hannah-Leigh to change the report for next week," Cecelia pointed out. "We're going to have to make it worth her while. What else have we got?"

"She can run her special on Presley the following week," Loralee said.

Wyatt nodded. "So she's getting two weeks of special reports instead of one."

"I don't see how she can refuse," Aunt Violet said.

Cade suddenly looked uncomfortable. "I hate to say this, since she *is* my wife, but the problem isn't getting her to agree to this, it's getting her to keep her word."

Aunt Violet considered this for a few seconds. Then she addressed Wyatt. "If we have her sign a contract and she breaks it, can we have her arrested?"

He nodded. "It might not stick, but we could get her picked up for breach of contract."

Aunt Violet turned to Cade. "Get your wife over here. We'll meet with her in my office. Wyatt and I will handle the negotiations so we can be sure we've crossed every *t* and dotted every *i*. Because if she messes this up, she's going to jail."

"If she messes this up, I'll arrest her myself," Cade promised.

"So Presley is safe here?" Aunt Violet wanted to know.

Wyatt nodded. "Tate still thinks she's in the hospital. By the time Hannah-Leigh's special report airs, we hope to have the power of attorney revoked. If not, we'll move Presley somewhere else."

"That's it then?" Cecelia asked. "That's all we can do until Monday?"

"There's one more thing," Brother Patrick made a rare comment. "Whether this personal information about Presley comes out next week or the week after, it's going to come out. We know that the people in Haggerty are basically good, but we also know that gossip can be a problem here."

"Do we ever know that," Cecelia muttered.

"To minimize the negative effects, I'm going to go home and rewrite my entire Easter sermon." He turned to look directly at Presley. "I know it was hard to tell us your painful story, but I think in the long run the telling of it will change your life for the better."

Presley nodded. "I hope so."

"You have friends now," Brother Patrick told her. "And we want all of Haggerty to see that. So, as a show of support for Presley, I want every one of you to attend services at the Baptist church tomorrow."

"I can be there," Miss Eugenia said.

"I usually go to the Baptist church in Midway," Cade said. "But I guess I can come to Haggerty tomorrow."

"Of course I'll be there," Aunt Violet added. "Presley and I will pick up Loralee."

"I was going to get Loralee," Mac said. "And Presley."

"Well, I can't climb up in your tow truck," Aunt Violet reminded him.

"Cecelia, why don't you come by here and pick up Miss Violet?" Brother Patrick suggested. His eyes were locked with hers.

"That's asking a lot," Cecelia said.

"I won't be too much trouble, dear," Aunt Violet promised. "I can lift my own oxygen tank."

Cecelia smiled tremulously. "I didn't mean you, Violet. I am happy to give you and your oxygen tank a ride anywhere. I meant it will take a lot for me to walk into that church, where I know I'm not welcome."

Aunt Violet's cheeks turned pink. "Oh, yes, I see."

"But will you do it for Presley?" Brother Patrick pressed. "Will you help me stop gossip from hurting someone else?"

Presley was about to let Cecelia off the hook, but Mac put a hand on her arm. She glanced at him, and he shook his head ever so slightly. Mac didn't want her to interfere. This was apparently some kind of showdown between Brother Patrick and Cecelia. So she settled back to see who would win.

Finally Cecelia said, "My gosh! Since apparently Presley's eternal happiness is resting on my shoulders, I'll go." Her eyes still held Brother Patrick's.

"Thank you," he said.

There were tears shining in Cecelia's eyes, and she didn't seem like a woman who cried easily. Presley knew this concession was huge. And she knew Cecelia wasn't making it for her.

"Everyone can sit on my row," Loralee said, taking the attention away from Cecelia and Brother Patrick. "We can fill it up, just like the old days."

* * *

After Aunt Violet and Wyatt strong-armed Hannah-Leigh Burrell into signing an agreement for two weeklong special reports, the crowd began to disperse. Cade left with his wife, Miss Eugenia went to pick up Lady at the groomer, and Wyatt took Loralee home on his way back to the country club, where he hoped to play more tennis.

Aunt Violet made sandwiches for lunch, and then Brother Patrick left to do his prayer rounds at the hospitals. Cecelia, Mac, and Presley alternately helped Aunt Violet with her side dishes and watched a Julie Andrews marathon on TV.

Brother Patrick came back for dinner, openly this time. Presley wondered if this was Cecelia's reward for agreeing to attend church the next day. After the meal everyone helped clean up. Then they stacked casserole dishes in the refrigerator.

When all the preparations for Easter dinner were complete, Cecelia rubbed her back and said she was headed home.

"I've got to go pick out my flooziest outfit for tomorrow. I want to give the good people of Haggerty what they expect." She said this a little louder than necessary for Brother Patrick's benefit.

If he heard her, he gave no indication.

"I know the Lord will be happy to see you there," Aunt Violet told her. "No matter what you wear."

"I'll walk you out," Brother Patrick said to Cecelia, and they moved toward the door.

After they were gone, Mac turned to Presley. "Are you ready to run?"

"I don't know if I'm ready," she hedged, "but if I'm going to eat some of Aunt Violet's pies tomorrow, I've got to run."

"Why don't you come with us?" Mac invited her aunt. "I'll carry your oxygen tank."

Aunt Violet laughed. "Mac, you're a mess." She followed them out of the kitchen and turned off the lights. "You two have fun. I'm going to bed."

* * *

Presley and Mac ran their usual number of laps around the track and then stretched out on the thick grass. When Mac had his breathing under control, he said, "I know that was terrible for you today, but I'm glad you got it all out."

"It was terrible," she agreed. "I guess I'm glad it's out—if for no other reason than because that means I don't have to tell it again."

"The people in town aren't really as bad as Cecelia makes it sound," he said. "We have our share of gossips, but we have our share of good Christian people too. When Hannah-Leigh does her breaking news or whatever, I think you'll get a lot of support."

"Especially after everyone sees how many friends I have at church tomorrow."

Mac laughed. "I think that was Patrick's way of making sure Cecelia would be there."

"I think so too."

They were quiet for a few minutes, and then Mac said, "Presley?"

"Yes."

"You were always beautiful."

She turned to face him. "Mac, you haven't seen the pictures of me before . . ."

He shook his head. "Your parents could see it, and so can I. Even without this masterpiece of a face." He pressed a kiss to the tip of her nose. Then he stood and pulled her up. "Let's get you home. I have a feeling tomorrow is going to be a big day."

* * *

Just before bed, Presley checked in with Moon, as usual, but she didn't tell him any of their plans to trap Tate. It seemed like the fewer people who knew about it, the better. He reported that Simu-Lady was still impersonating her with the help of Dr. Khan and the nursing students.

"In fact, Dr. Khan said he's afraid the students are getting too attached to the mannequin and might need counseling when this is all over," Moon told her.

"You're kidding."

"Yeah," Moon admitted. "But they're real dedicated to the pretend you."

"I wish I could thank them."

He laughed. "Yeah, well, if you're going to do that you might as well call up that nasty lawyer of yours and just tell him the whole plan."

She sighed. "I'll call you tomorrow, Moon."

"I'm counting on it, Calamity."

CHAPTER SEVENTEEN

Presley was nervous as she got ready for church the next morning. She was used to the threat from Tate, so she knew that wasn't responsible for her anxiety. Maybe it was because she'd never attended church in Haggerty before. Maybe it was because she would be facing people who knew she had been stupid and crazy in the past. Or maybe it was because she was afraid Cecelia was going to back out on her promise to attend and disappoint both Brother Patrick and the Lord.

Presley only had one dress, a black-and-white print that had been purchased, like all her other clothes, at the thrift store. It wasn't a typical Easter dress, but combined with the black suit jacket she'd worn to meet the mayor, the look was okay. Then she styled her hair and applied some makeup. No more Clark Kent.

"Don't you look beautiful?" Aunt Violet said when she saw Presley. Her aunt was sitting in the living room, wearing black slacks and a pastel purple blouse.

"Thanks. You look very nice yourself," Presley replied as she smoothed the fabric of her dress.

Aunt Violet gestured toward the large window. "I'm watching for Cecelia."

"You don't think she'll be a no-show, do you?"

"Cecelia will come get me," Aunt Violet seemed certain. "That's why Brother Patrick made the assignment. He knew she wouldn't want me to miss church on Easter. Now whether *she'll* attend—that's another question."

Through the living room window, Presley saw Mac's truck pull into the parking lot. "Well, here's my ride. See you at church."

Presley twisted and shoved her way out of the front door. Then she waited on the sidewalk while Mac jumped down. He was wearing a gray suit with a crisp white shirt and a pink tie. His auburn hair was neatly combed, for the moment, and shone in the morning sunlight.

"Hello!" he greeted as he trotted up to her. "You're the cutest Easter Bunny I've seen so far today!"

"Don't ever call me a bunny again."

He threw his head back and laughed uproariously.

"Nice suit," she told him as he led the way to the passenger side of his tow truck.

He glanced down and pulled at his tie. "I hope it looks good because it's uncomfortable as heck. Cecelia gave me the tie, and I thought it was a little much. It's like I'm trying to advertise for cancer or something."

"If your tie makes somebody want to donate to cancer research, then that's a good thing." She grabbed his hand and vaulted herself into the seat. The air conditioning was going full blast, and she turned her face gratefully toward it.

When Mac climbed in behind the wheel, she said, "This climate is brutal. It's only nine thirty in the morning, and it's already ninety degrees outside."

He shrugged. "If you think it's hot now, wait until August."

Haggerty in August was something she hoped she would see, despite the heat. Their eyes met, and she smiled at him. "Let's hurry and get Loralee before she melts."

* * *

Loralee was standing under a shade tree near the path that led to Orchid Cove. She was wearing a loose floral dress that was several decades old. Her long, wild hair was pulled into a demure ponytail and tied with a ribbon at the back of her neck. And there was a lone white orchid pinned to her chest in honor of Blanche Armstrong. She looked like an ancient teenager—stuck in a time that had left her behind.

Mac parked the truck and jumped down to the road. He tucked Loralee's arm through his and escorted her to the passenger door as if she were the Queen of England. When he pulled the door open, Presley slid into the middle seat. Mac scooped Loralee into his arms and lifted her up. Then he stepped onto the truck's runner and placed her gently onto the seat.

"You look beautiful," Presley told her. "Like a spring bouquet."

"You look nice too," Loralee returned.

As Mac settled beneath the wheel, he took in Presley's close proximity and wiggled his eyebrows. "Well, isn't this cozy."

Presley pointed toward the road. "You'd better hurry or we'll be late. And it's going to be hard enough to walk into a new church if we're on time."

"This is the last time you'll ever have to walk in for the first time," Mac responded.

She gave him a bland look. "I'll cling to that."

He laughed again.

* * *

Mac parked his truck in a field across the street from the church to avoid blocking in other cars. He lifted Loralee out first. Then he reached up for Presley. She expected him to take her hand as usual, but instead he grasped her around the waist and swung her down. The result was somewhere between thrilling and terrifying.

"You could have dropped me!" she scolded breathlessly.

"But I didn't," he pointed out.

Then with a lady on each arm, he headed for the church, where the front doors were propped open in welcome. Planters full of Easter lilies were strategically placed around the vestibule for optimum effect.

Inside the sanctuary, soft organ music floated on the air while sunlight streamed through the stained-glass windows. Mac continued to walk, passing many rows with open seats. Loralee leaned around him and whispered to Presley, "My row is near the front."

Presley nodded in acknowledgement and kept walking. She saw several people she knew, like the Clecklers and Miss Raye from the

Piggly Wiggly. And Coach Phil. Mac nodded politely to everyone as they moved down the aisle.

Finally they reached their destination, a row with a little brass placard that said simply *Puckett*.

"Mr. DuPont bought this pew," Loralee said softly. "When they built the church, you could buy one for a hundred dollars, which was a fortune back then."

"I thought DuPont didn't like churches and religion."

"It was mostly preachers he objected to, I think, but it's true that he didn't attend church often. Miss Blanche convinced him to buy a pew. It was a way of raising money to build the church, each pew didn't really cost a hundred dollars."

Presley nodded to indicate that the concept of fundraising was familiar to her.

Loralee reached out and rubbed the little nameplate. "Mr. DuPont wanted to put *Armstrong* on his bench, but Miss Blanche said it should be my name since the Pucketts came to Orchid Cove first."

"And DuPont always did what Blanche told him to?"

Loralee considered this. "Most of the time he did."

They moved to the middle of the row and then sat down on the velvet-covered pew. Presley turned her head slightly so she could watch the entrance. Miss Eugenia came in and made her way toward them, but progress was slow since she had to stop and talk to people.

Cade and his wife were holding hands when they arrived at the sanctuary doors.

"Maybe there's still hope for that marriage," Mac whispered.

As the Burrells reached the Puckett row, they heard Hannah-Leigh mutter, "I still don't understand why we had to come to church here today." They settled on the far end of the row.

Presley shrugged. "So much for wedded bliss."

Loralee perched herself on the edge of the pew cushion. Her rapt eyes were looking toward the front, obviously waiting for Brother Patrick. Miss Eugenia finally made it to the Puckett row and had just settled beside Loralee when Wyatt walked in with a woman hanging on his arm. Her dress bordered on floozy and definitely qualified as skimpy.

"Heaven help us!" Miss Eugenia whispered.

"It looks like Wyatt brought a date he picked up at a bar," Mac said.

Presley studied the girl for a few seconds. "What was he thinking?"

"You never know about Wyatt," his cousin said thoughtfully. "He might be thumbing his nose at propriety. Or he might be making sure that someone besides Cecelia gets a share of the negative attention today."

Presley's mouth fell open in surprise. "If that's true, I may be forced to like him."

When Wyatt reached them, he introduced his companion as Diana.

She corrected him. "It's Dana."

She was older than Presley had originally thought and had a hard look to her. Now Presley wondered if, in addition to picking her up at a bar, money might have exchanged hands when this church "date" was arranged. The odd couple scooted down the row and settled between the Burrells and Loralee.

A few minutes before ten o'clock, a piano joined the organ, and their combined music crescendoed to a teeth-jarring decibel. Then the choir, wearing bright-blue robes, stood and began to sing. Presley had nearly given herself whiplash, checking the sanctuary doors so often to see if Aunt Violet and Cecelia had arrived. By the time the choir finished their first hymn, she had given up hope.

And then she heard the sound of wheels rolling smoothly on the wooden floor. She turned to see Aunt Violet coming down the aisle as quickly as an old woman on oxygen could manage. Cecelia was walking at a more leisurely—almost reluctant—pace right behind.

Presley studied Cecelia as she approached. She was unquestionably beautiful and could probably carry off any outfit. Presley had seen evidence of that in the short time she'd been associated with the beautician. But today the woman was truly spectacular in a melon-colored dress that fell demurely to her knees. The scooped neckline was edged with a feminine ruffle, and her tiny waist was cinched by a black belt. The outfit was anchored by black open-toed heels and black hoop earrings that were sassy without being trashy. Her makeup was understated, and she'd allowed her long golden hair to hang casually down her back.

"She could easily have just stepped off the fashion runway," Presley whispered.

"Easily," Mac agreed.

Aunt Violet and Cecelia were still making steady progress toward the Puckett bench when Brother Patrick stepped up to the podium. He had been handsome in regular clothes, but today, in his white robes, he looked angelic. Presley heard Loralee sigh and had to control an urge to do the same.

When Cecelia saw him, she faltered, and for a split second it was as if they were the only two people in the sanctuary. Then she regained her composure and covered the remaining distance in a couple of long strides. It wasn't until she slipped into the pew that Presley could see she was shaking.

"You made it," Presley said softly. "And you don't look floozy at all."

"I lost my nerve," Cecelia claimed.

"I don't believe that for a second."

Brother Patrick began the service with a welcome. His eyes scanned the congregation. He smiled at everyone as if he were personally glad to see them. "It's always good to be here with you, but it's especially sweet on this day that we celebrate the Resurrection of our Lord."

After a prayer, Brother Patrick directed everyone's attention to the choir, and they sang several hymns. When he returned to the podium, Brother Patrick said that he'd been praying hard to know what he should say and he had finally realized that he was supposed to speak about rocks. This earned him several good-natured chuckles.

"The first rock I want to talk about is found in John chapter 8. It's the one Jesus could have thrown at the woman caught in adultery, but Jesus chose to forgive the woman instead. May we all be like Jesus—loving and accepting and forgiving!" His voice rose a little for emphasis. The congregation was spellbound.

"The second rock is found in Psalm 62:2. 'He only is my rock and my salvation.' We cannot look to other people or material possessions to give us peace and happiness in this life. We have to turn to the Savior, who heals all wounds."

Murmurs of approval were heard around.

"And the last rock is found in Mark chapter 16. I want you to think about what it was like in Jerusalem for believers such as us on that first Resurrection day so long ago. For years those people had followed Jesus and listened to Him and loved Him. He had told them He was the resurrection, the truth, and the life. Yet they had seen Him hang on the cross and die. It must have been with heavy hearts that they approached the tomb to anoint His body and prepare Him for final burial.

"It must have seemed to them that evil had conquered good. It must have seemed that all hope was gone. As they walked, they discussed how to move the huge rock that would block their access to Jesus. And then there was that moment, that glorious moment, when they saw the tomb."

Brother Patrick looked up toward the ceiling. Presley noted that most of the congregation looked up too—except Cecelia. She kept her eyes on Brother Patrick.

"The rock had been moved away!" he called out in triumph. "He that was dead lived again! Hope was not gone!"

Brother Patrick returned his gaze to the congregation. "Friends, it is like that for us. In our lives we have huge stones that must be moved. We worry about how this will be accomplished, forgetting that He has the power to move anything—including our rocks. We think we're trapped and alone, with no hope, but if we will let Jesus in, we can be like those true believers on Resurrection morning. We can look up and see that the rock is gone and nothing blocks us from our Lord!"

After this rousing conclusion, the lights went out for a few seconds. Then a spotlight came on, illuminating only the choir in their bright-blue robes. As they sang “Amazing Grace,” Presley saw many people pressing tissues to their eyes.

Amazing grace how sweet the sound
That saved a wretch like me!
I once was lost but now am found,
Was blind but now I see.

’Twas grace that taught my heart to fear,
And grace my fears relieved;
How precious did that grace appear
The hour I first believed!

The Lord has promised good to me,
His word my hope secures;
He will my shield and portion be
As long as life endures.

Through many dangers, toils, and snares
I have already come;
’Tis grace hath brought me safe thus far,
And grace will lead me home.

Then the spotlight was turned off, and they were plunged into darkness again. The spotlight returned, this time aimed at Brother Patrick, who was standing in the midst of the choir. All in white against the backdrop of the blue choir, he looked like the resurrected Christ ascending into heaven.

And then he began to sing “The Old Rugged Cross” in a rich tenor voice with no musical accompaniment.

On a hill far away stood an old rugged cross,
The emblem of suff’ring and shame;
And I love that old cross where the Dearest and Best
For a world of lost sinners was slain.

Refrain:
So I’ll cherish the old rugged cross,
Till my trophies at last I lay down;

I will cling to the old rugged cross,
And exchange it someday for a crown.

Oh, that old rugged cross, so despised by the world,
Has a wondrous attraction for me;
For the dear Lamb of God left His glory above
To bear it to dark Calvary.

Refrain

In that old rugged cross, stained with blood so divine,
A wondrous beauty I see,
For 'twas on that old cross Jesus suffered and died,
To pardon and sanctify me.

Refrain

To the old rugged cross I will ever be true;
Its shame and reproach gladly bear;
Then He'll call me someday to my home far away,
Where His glory forever I'll share.

Refrain

When he finished there couldn't have been a dry eye in the room. Presley fumbled in her handbag for a tissue as Brother Patrick returned to the podium.

"This is a special day," he told them all. "I am going to remember the rocks we've talked about today. I will not throw stones of judgment at my brothers and sisters. I will remember that Jesus is my rock and my salvation, and therefore I will not be shaken! And I will not be separated from happiness by manmade rocks. I will allow the Lord to move those rocks for me!"

Presley was expecting another light show and more music, but instead Brother Patrick stepped away from the podium and walked down into the congregation. When he reached the Puckett row, he dropped to one knee in front of Cecelia, his white robes billowing around him like a cloud.

As the entire congregation watched in shocked silence, he held out a hand to Cecelia. Trembling like a leaf, she took it. Then he looked into her eyes and said, "Cecelia Moore, will you do me the honor of becoming my wife?"

There was murmuring all around the sanctuary, but Cecelia kept her focus on Brother Patrick. She seemed paralyzed, and Presley began to wonder if she was physically capable of a response.

Finally Cecelia managed a nod. Brother Patrick bestowed an angelic smile on her. Then he stood and returned to the podium.

"There you have it, friends. Cecelia Moore has agreed to be my wife. You're all witnesses, and you'll all be invited to celebrate with us once we've had time to plan the wedding."

You could have heard a pin drop inside the church.

Brother Patrick continued, "Happy Easter, everyone. Now let us pray!" Then he bowed his head and closed the service.

When he finished praying, the organ and piano blended in perfect harmony while the choir sang the final hymn. As they sang Brother Patrick left the podium. He walked down the aisle, pausing just long enough to collect Cecelia from the Puckett pew. Then they walked together out of the church and into the warm Georgia sunshine.

* * *

When the choir number ended, the piano accompaniment stopped and the organist continued on alone with a sedate postlude. People all around were starting to get up and gather in little groups to talk.

Mac looked at Presley. "Well, I thought that went well."

Presley rolled her eyes. "So what do we do now?"

"We get up and walk out," he said. "Smiling like nothing out of the ordinary just happened."

Wyatt checked his watch. "And we need to hurry. I've got to get Darla back to work."

"Dana," the girl said in a bored voice.

Miss Eugenia made eye contact with Presley. "Heaven help us," she said again.

Fighting near-hysterical laughter, Presley asked, "What if the gossips attack us?"

"I'll lead the way," Aunt Violet offered. "With this oxygen tank, I clear a pretty good path. Then the rest of you come behind me."

"Stay in a tight cluster," Wyatt advised. "If anyone gets separated, there could be a feeding frenzy."

Mac looked over at the Burrells. "We'll understand if you want to leave separately to minimize your association with us."

Cade smiled. "That's okay. We'll bring up the rear since I have a gun."

On the way out of the church, Presley clutched Mac's hand and kept a smile on her face while avoiding eye contact with everyone.

Just as they reached the door, Kitty Cleckler tried to break into their protective cluster, but Hannah-Leigh derailed her by asking if she could come over later for another TV interview about the skeleton murder.

"I'll be glad to tell you anything," Miss Kitty agreed, her whole body quivering with happy anticipation.

"Please wait for me at your house," Hannah-Leigh requested. "It might be a while before I can get free."

* * *

They drove in a caravan to Aunt Violet's house. Mac led in his tow truck, while Cade brought up the rear with his sheriff's department car. But once they had all arrived, Cade and Hannah-Leigh declined the invitation to lunch.

"We've got to go to her parents' house." Cade hooked a finger toward his wife.

"And then I've got to go interview Kitty Cleckler," Hannah-Leigh added with a roll of her eyes.

"We appreciate your sacrifice in our behalf," Aunt Violet told her.

"It's no sacrifice," the reporter said. "Miss Kitty always provides for some entertaining air time."

Cade waved. "I'll see you all tomorrow. Unless you need me sooner—then just call."

Mac nodded. "We'll be fine. And thanks."

Wyatt rolled down the window of his Mercedes. "I'm going to go drop Deidra off, and then I'll be back."

"Dana," Presley corrected.

Wyatt nodded vaguely and raised his window.

"Do you think when he says 'drop her off' he means on a street corner?" Mac asked.

Miss Eugenia had just one response to this possibility. "Heaven help us."

When they walked inside Aunt Violet's house, it smelled like baked ham. Brother Patrick and Cecelia were sitting on the living room couch. There were tearstains on her cheeks, and his arm was across her shoulders. His white preacher's robe was folded carefully on the couch beside them.

"I just got a call from Merle Boone," Brother Patrick said. "They've called an emergency meeting of the deacon's board this afternoon. I'll be notified of their decision once it's reached."

"What decision?" Miss Eugenia demanded. "Is it against your contract to marry someone?"

Brother Patrick shook his head. "No, but there is a clause in my contract they can use to fire me. It says something like, 'If the pastor and the congregation find themselves on separate spiritual paths, the pastor can be released from his contract by a unanimous vote of the deacon's board.'"

Aunt Violet shook her head. "You never should have signed that."

Brother Patrick shrugged. "It's too late now."

Cecelia looked out at the group. "I begged him not to do it, but he wouldn't listen. Now he's thrown his life calling away."

"The Lord will have other uses for me," Brother Patrick comforted her. "And we can accept any call that comes together."

Cecelia rested her head against his chest.

* * *

Everyone worked together to put the Easter meal on the table. The mood was a little subdued—everyone knowing that Patrick was about to lose his job—but the food was good. After the meal, Eugenia excused herself to go check on Lady. Aunt Violet tried to send leftovers home with her, but she refused.

Everyone else sat around, waiting for the phone to ring.

Finally, at almost five o'clock, Brother Patrick's cell phone rang. They all watched tensely as he answered it. The preacher's side of the conversation was short, just a few, "Yes, sirs." Then Brother Patrick put his phone down and faced his friends.

"They voted to retain me," he said in wonder. "And they've extended my contract for five additional years, without the separate spiritual paths clause."

Everyone cheered except Cecelia. She started crying again. This time tears of joy. "I never cry," she sobbed. "I don't know what's wrong with me!"

Aunt Violet smiled. "It's called love, dear."

"Now let's eat again!" Wyatt suggested. "I just got my appetite back!"

* * *

On the way to the football stadium that night, Mac asked Presley if she minded taking a small detour. "That depends," she replied, "on what kind of detour you're talking about."

"I just needed to tell Miss Eugenia something."

She nodded. "Miss Eugenia doesn't bother me. Now if you'd wanted to visit the Clecklers . . ."

"Nobody *wants* to visit the Clecklers," Mac assured her.

Miss Eugenia didn't seem surprised when she answered the knock on her back door and found them standing there. She picked up Lady to prevent an escape and then invited them inside.

Once they were settled around the kitchen table, Mac said, "I believe we owe you a debt of gratitude."

Presley's eyes widened, since she had no knowledge of this debt.

"You don't owe me anything," Miss Eugenia said. "I did what any Christian-minded woman with control over millions of dollars would do."

Presley looked back and forth between them. "What are you two talking about?"

"Miss Eugenia bribed the deacon's board into letting Patrick keep his job."

Presley gasped in surprise. "Of course, it all makes sense. You're the only one who left Aunt Violet's house before he got the call—unless you count Wyatt's hooker date."

"Heaven help us." Miss Eugenia shook her head.

"So?" Mac prompted. "How did you do it?"

"This stays here, just between us?" she clarified.

They both nodded.

"Well, after I left Violet's house, I went to the Baptist church and sat outside the pastor's office, waiting for all the deacons to get there. Thank goodness someone had left several bags of Easter candy for Brother Patrick, or I might have starved to death."

"So you sat there and ate Patrick's candy, and then the deacons arrived?" Mac ran through the events up to this point in the story.

"Correct," Miss Eugenia confirmed. "When they got there, I told them I wanted to address the board before they made any decisions they would regret."

"And how did they take that from a Mormon-Methodist?"

"Pretty well since I decided to take a page from Tate Sheridan's playbook," she said. "I told them I'm George Ann's executor and beneficiary and I hold her power of attorney."

Mac grinned. "So they let you into their inner sanctum?"

"Well, they let me into Brother Patrick's office, where I offered them a deal. If they kept Brother Patrick—and gave him a five-year extension with no stipulations—I'd use some of George Ann's money to pay off the building fund balance they're always whining about."

"Isn't that a lot of money?" Mac asked.

Miss Eugenia scoffed at this question. "George Ann has plenty, and I had to make them a deal they couldn't afford to refuse. Oh, and I also said they had to get the ladies' auxiliary to help Cecelia plan a lovely church wedding."

"And they took the deal?" Presley asked.

Miss Eugenia nodded. "They only had to pray about it for two minutes."

Mac laughed. "You're a genius."

"But, please," Presley began, "never compare yourself to Tate again."

* * *

After their run that night, Mac said they needed to talk about something serious. It had been a stressful day already, and Presley wasn't sure she could take anything too serious, but she nodded anyway.

"We have this plan set up for tomorrow with Miss Eugenia and the FBI and the Attorney General in Ohio . . ."

Presley nodded. "Hopefully it will work, and by this time tomorrow, Tate will be out of my life for the foreseeable future."

"What if it doesn't work?"

This was a possibility Presley really hadn't allowed herself to consider. But now he was forcing her to. She shrugged. "I guess I'll go to a mental institution until you and Aunt Violet can get me out."

He shook his head. "That's the one option I'm not willing to consider. Lots of money often brings out the worst in people. If you're in a hospital, defenseless"—he paused for a quick shudder—"they could drug you or even kill you and there would be nothing we could do. So, I figure if this plan doesn't work, I'll go to Columbus, beat Sheridan half to death, and tear that power of attorney up personally."

Presley paused a minute or so to give the impression that she was seriously considering this plan. Then she said, "What's backup option two? I've seen what happens when you get into a fight."

CHAPTER EIGHTEEN

On Monday morning at eight o'clock, Presley, Mac, and Aunt Violet rode together in the Honda to Miss Eugenia's house. Wyatt met them there. Everyone was a little nervous except the star of the show. Miss Eugenia seemed to be in her element.

At eight thirty they used Wyatt's cell phone to FaceTime with Mark Iverson. He was at the attorney general's office and said the people there had been very cooperative. "At the first sign of coercion, they'll get a warrant for Sheridan's financial records."

"I'll do my best to be coerced," Miss Eugenia said. "Now I need to hang up so I can get in the zone before my call."

Mark chuckled. "Wyatt will be transmitting and recording all interactions with Sheridan?"

"I will," the lawyer promised.

"Okay then, good luck."

After that call ended, Wyatt and Aunt Violet talked to Miss Eugenia for a few minutes. "One thing I want to point out is that, while you don't have to be completely honest, we want to stay as close to the truth as possible."

"We don't want to make it look like entrapment," Aunt Violet clarified.

"Even though it is," Presley added. "Not that I care."

Wyatt disagreed. "It's not entrapment because we never intend to use any information collected here in court. All the evidence will be collected when Sheridan's records are seized. Our little demonstration is just something to encourage the attorney general to investigate."

Presley waited until Miss Eugenia was not being given instructions and then went over to thank her. "I worry about you getting involved with Tate. He is ruthless and cruel and—"

"I won't be in any danger," Miss Eugenia said. "Mark will make sure he never knows that my call had anything to do with his arrest. Since I won't be an actual client yet, I won't be part of the investigation—"

"I know," Presley interrupted. "But you're still going to trouble for me, and I appreciate it."

Miss Eugenia smiled. "You're welcome. That's what friends are for."

Presley returned to where Mac was standing, her mind in turmoil. She didn't like the idea of people taking risks for her, but she did like the idea of having friends.

As the clock approached nine, Wyatt asked everyone to stand back from the table where Miss Eugenia would be sitting. "Turn all cell phones off, and you'll need to be absolutely silent. If you need to cough, even if you need to breathe heavily, go into another room."

Everyone nodded.

"What about Lady?" Presley asked. "Should we put her upstairs or something?"

Wyatt shook his head. "A barking dog is just part of Miss Eugenia's normal environment, but multiple cell phones ringing at the same time isn't."

He turned back to Miss Eugenia. "Miss Violet and I will be sitting here to advise you. If you have a question, write it down." He pointed to the legal pad. "If we need to tell you something, we'll write it also. There can't be any stray conversation. If Sheridan gets suspicious, then the whole thing is ruined. He'll take his files and be on a plane out of the country before the attorney general can get there."

They waited until seven minutes after nine to make the call seem more random. Then Miss Eugenia dialed the number Wyatt had written on the legal pad. The call was answered by a receptionist, who said Mr. Sheridan couldn't be reached and suggested that Miss Eugenia leave a message.

"It's very urgent," she told the receptionist. "I've just been given control of a friend's estate. It's very large, and people are calling me about taxes and reinvesting dividends, and I just don't know what to do. I found Mr. Sheridan's name on the Internet, and I was hoping he could help me. But if you think it's going to be a long time before he can talk, I can try someone else . . ."

That did it. "I'm sure Mr. Sheridan would love to talk to you," the receptionist said in a more friendly tone. "I'll interrupt his meeting and have him call you right back."

Miss Eugenia hung up the phone and then smiled at the others. "That was easy."

"He hasn't called back yet," Wyatt pointed out

And then the phone rang.

"Hello, Mrs. Atkins." Tate's smooth voice made Presley cringe.

"Oh, thank you so much for returning my call!" Miss Eugenia said loudly. "There's some static on the line. Can you hear me?"

"The connection sounds fine," Tate assured her. Presley could almost picture him moving the phone away from his ear. "My receptionist said you've been given control of a large estate and need help with the investments."

"Oh, I see from your address that you're in Ohio," Miss Eugenia continued. "I'm all the way down here in Georgia, so if you don't take clients from other parts of the country, maybe you can recommend someone."

"Why don't you tell me your situation, and we'll go from there."

Wyatt gave Miss Eugenia a thumbs-up. Things were going well so far.

"I have a friend, George Ann Simmons, who recently had to go to a nursing home. She doesn't have any family, so she made me her executor and her beneficiary. She also gave me a power of attorney, whatever that means. She has so much property, so many stocks and bonds. It's a huge responsibility, and I'm just not up to it. I'm eighty-three years old myself. I could die before George Ann does."

"I'm sorry to hear about your friend. It does sound like a big responsibility, and I'm sure I can help you."

Presley's heart pounded. They had him hooked.

Miss Eugenia was saying, "It's terrible to watch someone you know go downhill like this. My husband died a few years back, and we were never blessed with children so I'm pretty lonely. George Ann used to be somebody I could talk to." Miss Eugenia paused for a split second to roll her eyes. "Now she's lost her mind, and all she wants to do is put together jigsaw puzzles all day."

"Terrible," Tate commiserated.

"I was hoping you would come here and meet with me. I know it's an inconvenience, but I couldn't come to Ohio. I'm terrified of airplanes." This was a crucial part of the plan. They didn't want Tate to actually accept the invitation to visit Haggerty, so Miss Eugenia had to make the prospect sound even worse than it would actually be.

"I could introduce you to the folks here. George Ann owns all kinds of property—old houses, little farms, stuff like that. We would probably have to spend several days driving around to see it all. Then you can decide if we should keep it or sell it. We can look through all the bank statements and letters about her mutual accounts and stock funds and—"

Tate interrupted her at this point. "I'd love to come down to Haggerty and meet you sometime," he said. "But the first step will be for me to get a current valuation of all Miss Simmons's holdings."

"I have a statement her accountant prepared at the end of last month," Miss Eugenia said. "Will that do?"

"That will be perfect," Tate said. "Can you fax that to me?"

"I'll have to go to the library," Miss Eugenia said. "But, yes, I can do that. What's your fax number?"

Tate recited it from memory.

"Okay, I'll take care of that right now. You'll let me know when you get it?"

"I will," Tate promised.

Presley could almost hear the avarice in his voice.

***

Eugenia took a few deep breaths after ending the call with Tate Sheridan. It seemed like everything had gone well, but she still felt anxious and tense.

"That was great!" Wyatt praised her.

"He's interested," Presley said. "I can tell by the tone of his voice.

"And once he sees George Ann's assets, he'll be foaming at the mouth," Violet predicted.

"Well, good." Eugenia was relieved. "Now I've got to take this financial report to the library."

Wyatt drove her the three blocks to the library and went inside with her while she sent the fax. Once she had confirmation that it had gone through, they returned to her house.

When she walked into the kitchen, she told the others, "Well, that's taken care of. So now we wait."

Five minutes later the receptionist from Sheridan's office called to say that the requested faxes had been received. "Mr. Sheridan is reviewing them now. Once he's done he'll be in touch with you."

And then they were back to waiting. But not for long. Tate called fifteen minutes later and told Eugenia he'd be more than happy to take her on as a client.

"I've faxed some paperwork to the library," Sheridan continued. "Go ahead and sign it all and have it notarized there. Then fax me a copy, and overnight the originals. That way I can get started immediately."

"And what kind of papers did you send for me to sign?"

"It's just some legal stuff giving me permission to make investment changes as I see fit," Tate told her. "Once you give me your power of attorney, I'll start working on getting Miss Simmons declared incompetent."

"I'm not sure George Ann is incompetent," Eugenia said carefully. "Is that step necessary?"

"Incompetent is just a legal term." Sheridan's tone was silky, inspiring confidence. "It just means that I can handle things without bothering either of you."

"Oh, I see," Eugenia replied. "When are you coming here?"

"Soon!" he promised. "I'll check my calendar and see when I can work in a trip down South."

Everyone was excited when Eugenia hung up the phone.

Wyatt was smiling. "You showed the attorney general just what Sheridan does, how he takes advantage of people. The part about incompetence was pure genius!"

"Was it enough?" Eugenia still felt uncertain.

"You did the best you could," Violet assured her. "Now we'll have to wait and see."

Wyatt went back to the library to pick up the paperwork. While he was gone, Eugenia offered pound cake, but everyone was too nervous to eat.

When Wyatt returned he reported, "I have the paperwork, and while I was there, I faxed it all to the attorney general's office in Ohio."

"Won't Tate get suspicious when my paperwork doesn't arrive?" Eugenia asked.

"He won't have time to get suspicious before the police show up with warrants to seize his records. Mark will let us know when that happens."

It was almost eleven when Mark finally called. Everyone watched Wyatt and knew before he turned to address them that the news was not good.

"When the police arrived to serve the warrant, Sheridan was gone." Wyatt's voice was hollow. "The office was locked up, and no employees were present. It looked like he left in a hurry, and we're assuming he took all sensitive documents with him. Apparently somebody tipped him off."

"Are they going to try to find him?" Presley whispered. Her normally pale skin was almost translucent, and she swayed a little.

Mac put out a hand to steady her but kept his eyes on Wyatt.

"No." Wyatt shook his head. "They left messages at all his contact numbers. If he doesn't respond, they can go after him just for not giving them an opportunity to serve the search warrant—but not today. And probably not ever."

"Can't they get him on evading arrest?" Mac's disappointment was obvious.

"They weren't going to arrest him," Wyatt said. "He just evaded a search. And Mark said the Ohio Attorney General was never really big on going after Sheridan anyway. He's well-connected, well-liked; there are no complaints against him—not even from Presley. Her investments haven't done all that well under his management, but that might have been true even if she'd used someone else. The market's been bad. The attorney general just went along with this as a favor to the FBI."

"We didn't really care about getting any charges to stick," Violet said. "We just needed to have that power of attorney revoked."

Wyatt ran his fingers through his hair. "Well, my guess is that Sheridan has the power of attorney with him and will continue to profit from Presley's assets in a new location."

"We have no other options then?" Eugenia asked.

Wyatt shrugged. "Not unless Presley wants to bring charges against Sheridan for mismanagement. And fight the incompetency ruling."

Presley shivered and shook her head. "That won't work. Maybe I could make a deal with him—agree to sign over all my assets permanently. Then he'd have no need for my power of attorney, and maybe he'd leave me alone."

"You wouldn't be offering him anything he doesn't already have," Violet said. "And he doesn't seem like the kind of person who will give up power if he doesn't have to."

Presley looked devastated. "That's it then. I'll just have to leave and hide somewhere."

"He doesn't know you're here," Mac said. "We have until next week when the special reports start on Channel 3."

Presley shook her head. "I can't risk it. Anyone who helps me is in danger too."

"We're not going to give up," Eugenia said firmly. "And you're not going anywhere. Mark will be home this evening, and we'll figure out another plan. Tate Sheridan has to have an Achilles' heel. We'll find it, and then we'll get him."

Presley's expression wasn't exactly hopeful, but she looked a little less desolate.

Violet stood. "Okay, well, I guess we can go home for now. When Mark gets here, we'll reassemble and discuss options."

CHAPTER NINETEEN

After the others left, Eugenia sat at her kitchen table, feeling responsible for the plan's failure. She went over every word she'd said, looking for something that could have tipped Tate Sheridan off.

Finally she turned to Lady and asked, "Do you think it was my fault?"

The little dog rubbed her head against Eugenia's leg in a show of loyalty.

Eugenia sighed. "Well, it's just a shame."

She was trying to decide what to do next when the phone rang. Assuming it was Annabelle, she answered with a curt, "What?"

"Mrs. Atkins?" Tate Sheridan's surprised voice came through the receiver.

Eugenia's heart pounded as she pulled Wyatt's legal pad in front of her. Then she slipped back into character. "Mr. Tate! Did you get my faxes?"

There was a nervous little laugh. "Uh, no, as it turned out, I had to leave my office before the faxes came through. My calendar opened up, so I'm actually headed south right now. I thought I might take you up on your invitation."

Eugenia processed this quickly. "You're coming to Haggerty?"

The laugh again. "Yes, I should be there about seven o'clock tonight. I thought we could meet for dinner. Tomorrow we can tour the area and check out Miss Simmons's properties."

"Why, I just can't believe it." That was certainly true.

"The Columbus market is kind of saturated with investment counselors, and after talking to you, I got an idea. There are bound to be people just like you all across the country, so I might open a branch of my business specifically geared to elderly people—like yourself and your friend Miss Simmons—who need advice on how to maximize assets for their heirs."

"Is that a nice way of saying for people who are about to die?"

"Oh no!" His laugh was more genuine this time, and she could see how Presley was pulled in by him. He knew how to turn on the charm.

"I declare, I just can't tell you how excited I am!" This, too, was mostly true. "It will be like having a real celebrity visit. And if you want to meet old people, Haggerty is the place. Our median age is about seventy-five."

"Are you kidding?"

"Yes," she admitted. "But it's still got to be well above the national average." Her mind was racing, trying to think of a way to turn this to Presley's advantage. Then an idea started to form. "In fact, why don't I put together a little dinner party tonight—for people who might make good potential clients?"

"I hate for you to go to any trouble."

"Nonsense!" Eugenia insisted, making notes on the legal pad. "I have another rich friend who lives in a beautiful house on the edge of town. I think it would be the perfect place for us to have a casual dinner gathering. I'll make sure she's available, and then I'll call you back with the address."

They exchanged polite good-byes, and Eugenia hung up the phone. She turned to Lady and smiled. "Well, it looks like we're back in business."

* * *

Eugenia's first phone call was to Mark Iverson. She caught him just as he was about to board his plane. After he heard the news, he was less enthusiastic than she'd hoped.

"I don't see how Sheridan's presence in Haggerty can possibly be a good thing," he told her.

"It's good because where Tate is, Presley's power of attorney is also sure to be," she explained. "I'm going to ask Cecelia to have a little dinner party at her place. Even somebody used to luxury will be wowed by that house. We'll keep him there talking about all this money he could invest, until you can get there. Then you can search his car. Hopefully you'll find something really incriminating so you can throw him in jail. But if all you find is Presley's power of attorney, that's good enough."

"The Ohio search warrant won't do us any good in Haggerty," Mark explained. "I might be able to convince a judge in Georgia to issue one, but not from an airplane. That would have to wait until tomorrow. So unless Sheridan voluntarily allows me to search his car tonight . . ."

"Hmmm," Eugenia said. "I'll think of something. Just come to Cecelia's house as soon as your plane arrives."

"This Sheridan guy might be dangerous. You need to call Winston and keep him with you at all times until I get there."

"I'm not scared of Tate Sheridan," Eugenia scoffed. "And if Winston is there, he'll give the whole thing away."

"Miss Eugenia." Mark's tone was uncompromising.

"Okay," she relented. "I'll call Winston."

"And I'll get to Cecelia's as fast as I can. Now I've got a plane to catch."

Eugenia ended the call and then looked at Lady. "I promised Mark I'd call Winston." And so she did. "How are you?" she asked him when he answered.

"I'm fine," the police chief replied. "What's going on?"

"Not much," she said. "I just thought I'd call."

"Well, if you don't need me, I'd better get back to work."

"I can't think of anything I need," she told him. "I'll see you later."

Eugenia hung up the phone feeling proud of herself. Then she saw Lady's reproving look. "I had no choice. How am I supposed to con the conman with Winston hanging around?"

* * *

Presley had been pacing in her room for almost an hour. Every time she thought she had settled on a course of action, she would change her mind. There was no good choice, and she was having trouble picking between the bad ones. Then her aunt called from the bottom of the steps.

"I just need a little time alone to think," she responded as patiently as she could.

"Well, Miss Eugenia is here," Aunt Violet told her. "She says she has some good news."

Presley tried to keep her expectations low as she hurried down the stairs.

"Come, have a seat," Miss Eugenia invited when Presley walked into the kitchen, as if it were her house instead of Aunt Violet's. "The others should be here any minute."

Presley sat down reluctantly. "The others?"

"The Armstrong cousins and Cecelia," Miss Eugenia said. "I called them before I left my house and told them it was a 911 emergency."

Now Presley was alarmed. "What happened?"

"Tate Sheridan is on his way to Haggerty!" Miss Eugenia announced.

Presley rested her head on her arms. "I think I'm going to faint."

* * *

By the time the others arrived, Miss Eugenia had assured Presley that Tate didn't know she was in Haggerty. Furthermore, she insisted that his impending arrival should be considered a good thing.

"So what's the plan?" Wyatt asked. "I assume you have one since you called us all here."

"Of course I have a plan," Miss Eugenia said. "It's a simple one, since we don't have much time."

Aunt Violet nodded. "I think that's wise."

"All we really care about is getting Presley's power of attorney away from Tate Sheridan, right?" Miss Eugenia continued.

Differing opinions were expressed around the table, and finally Miss Eugenia held up her hand to stop the discussion. "I know it would be wonderful if we could get him put in a federal penitentiary, but that goal is a little too lofty. Once we take care of Presley, it will be up to Mark and the FBI to pursue things further."

"So how are we going to get the power of attorney?" Presley asked, trying not to get her hopes up too high again.

"I'm going to ask Cecelia to throw a simple dinner party tonight around seven o'clock at that ostentatious house of hers," Miss Eugenia said. She turned to speak directly to Cecelia. "Once Sheridan sees it, you won't have to prove that you're rich."

Cecelia nodded, conceding this at least.

"I hate this plan already," Brother Patrick said.

"Bear with me," Miss Eugenia requested.

Brother Patrick still looked skeptical, but Miss Eugenia pressed on. "I'll be there, of course, and Violet will attend as Cecelia's lawyer. I wish Annabelle could come, since she's rich and loves to brag about it, but she's not flying back from Charlotte until Wednesday. So this group will have to do."

"What about Patrick and Wyatt and me?" Mac asked.

"I want the gathering to be completely nonthreatening," Miss Eugenia told him. "So you boys will be positioned around the edge of the patio—out of sight but close enough to help if there's a problem."

"What about me?" Presley asked.

"Tate certainly can't see you! You'll stand near Mac."

"We all want to help Presley," Brother Patrick said. "But I can't agree to anything that will put Cecelia in danger."

"She won't be in danger," Miss Eugenia insisted. "She'll be as safe as she is right now."

"I'm not worried about my safety," Cecelia said. "I have a gun, and there's a metal detector built into the front door, so if Tate has one, we can take it away."

"I still don't see how all this is going to get Presley's power of attorney back." Wyatt sounded irritable.

"Cecelia will tell Tate that she wants to create a charitable foundation with all of Edison's millions," Miss Eugenia explained.

"Okay," Cecelia said. "What's the next part of the plan?"

"You'll play up the fact that you're getting remarried and you want to simplify your life. You could even mention that you think the people of Haggerty would accept you better if you weren't so rich."

"I don't know if I can make myself say that," Cecelia interrupted. "The people of Haggerty will never accept me, and I sure wouldn't spend millions in a futile attempt to win their approval."

"Okay, just say you want to start a new life with Patrick and that Edison's money will be in the way, so you've decided to put it in a trust. You don't have any experience with setting up a charitable fund, so you're looking for someone to take it from the beginning. He'd set it up, make the investments, file the required forms, everything. All you'd want to see would be an occasional statement."

"Millions of dollars and very little oversight," Presley said. "I don't see how he could refuse."

"To sweeten the deal, I'll tell him that I'd like to contribute George Ann's assets to the fund," Miss Eugenia said. "It will be a gradual thing until she dies, but he would have control over two huge portfolios that nobody cares about."

"Okay, there's no question that he'll jump at the chance to manage that fund," Mac said. "I'm almost tempted myself, and I'm not a crook. But how does that get us Presley's power of attorney?"

Miss Eugenia smiled. "Cecelia will tell him that because this is so big, for at least the first year or so, she wants him to work on her fund exclusively. She'll tell him he has to cancel contracts with all other clients and somehow casually throw in that she wants all powers of attorney revoked as well—so she'll know her charity has his undivided attention."

"Won't the mention of power of attorney make him suspicious?" Wyatt asked.

"Maybe not," Miss Eugenia said. "I'm hoping that whoever tipped him off in Ohio didn't know it was Presley's power of attorney we were after."

Brother Patrick raised an eyebrow. "And if you're wrong and he realizes that it's a scam the minute powers of attorney are mentioned?"

Miss Eugenia shrugged. "Then we'll burn his car."

* * *

Eventually the plan was approved with varying degrees of enthusiasm.

Cecelia stood and said, "I'd better get home and break the news to my housekeeper that we're having company for dinner."

"I'll come too," Patrick said. "To provide moral support."

She smiled, and they walked out hand in hand.

Wyatt said he had to go back to his office and actually work for a few hours.

"Just be at Cecelia's by six thirty so you'll be in place before Tate arrives," Miss Eugenia requested.

After Wyatt left, Mac said he should go too. Presley walked him to the front door.

"Hopefully this will work tonight, one way or another," he said when they were alone.

"The only way I'll have confidence in that is if somebody has plenty of extra gasoline and some matches," Presley muttered.

Mac smiled. "I don't think it will come to that."

She rubbed her hands up and down her arms. "I hate the thought of Tate being here," she admitted. "It's like he's contaminating my safe space."

"I'm glad he's coming," Mac said with rare seriousness. "It's like a dream come true to get that lowlife on our turf." Then his expression softened. "And I'm really glad you consider Haggerty your safe space."

* * *

Presley and Aunt Violet left for Cecelia's house at six o'clock that evening. Aunt Violet was wearing the same black slacks and purple blouse she had worn to church the previous day. Presley was wearing jeans and the white cotton lacy shirt she'd bought from Cecelia. It was about a ten-minute drive out to the house Edison Moore had built on a ten-acre estate—just barely inside the Haggerty city limits so he would have the benefit of police and fire protection.

Presley was expecting something like Tara from *Gone with the Wind*, but the house Cecelia had inherited from her elderly husband was very modern. With dramatic rooflines and a flawless blend of stacked stone, brick, and wrought iron, it was a lot like Cecelia herself—almost too pretty to be real.

"This place is stunning," Presley told her aunt as they drove through the security gate.

"Edison was an architect, and this was his dream house," Aunt Violet said. "His final masterpiece."

Cecelia met them at the door. "I gave the housekeeper the night off," she said. "I thought it would be better if we didn't have witnesses, just in case we have to kill this Sheridan guy."

"Cecelia!" Aunt Violet objected. "You shouldn't joke about things like that."

Cecelia shrugged and then offered to give Presley a brief tour. As they walked through the amazing house, she accepted all Presley's compliments in Edison's behalf. Then she led the way out to the back patio, which had several levels and bordered a natural stone pool that was beyond spectacular.

"The food is set up here," Cecelia pointed to a white iron table with several chairs close to the house. "It's just sandwiches and salads and fruits. I decided self-service was the way to go."

"Perfect," Aunt Violet assured her.

Miss Eugenia arrived next with Wyatt and Patrick. The preacher went directly to his fiancée, and their fingers laced together in a simple gesture of affection.

When Mac walked up, Presley gave him a little wave. He winked back.

Then Miss Eugenia announced, "I just got a call from Tate. He's in Albany and will be here in about ten minutes."

Presley's heart pounded as Miss Eugenia stationed them out of sight on opposite sides of the patio.

"You should be able to hear most of what's said without being visible," Miss Eugenia told them.

Presley stood close to Mac, grateful Tate wouldn't be able to see her.

"Are you okay?" he asked.

"I'll be better when this is over." She watched through a bare spot in the hedge as the others settled themselves near the food table. To anyone who didn't know better, it looked like a group of friends gathered to share a simple meal.

Eight minutes later they heard the sound of a car with a loud engine approaching. Presley's stomach lurched. Mac put a steadying hand on her arm.

They watched as Cecelia went into the house to greet their guest. A few minutes later, she returned with Tate by her side. He looked about the same as he had the last time Presley saw him, sans the scratches on his cheek. He walked around introducing himself to the other dinner guests. He was handsome, charming, and oh-so-happy to be there.

Presley noted that Tate was holding a small briefcase just big enough for a laptop and some files. She wondered if it contained the powers of attorney that allowed him to steal money from stupid girls. She looked up at Mac. "If it's in there, burning his car won't do any good."

"Then we'll burn the briefcase," Mac assured her with confidence.

Presley nodded but didn't see how that could be accomplished without Tate knowing she was behind this. And the thought of having him as a lifetime enemy made her blood run cold.

While they watched from the hedges, the evening went just as Miss Eugenia had choreographed it. The party guests helped themselves to the food Cecelia's housekeeper had prepared. Then they shared some casual small talk. As Miss Eugenia and Aunt Violet took turns asking questions and suddenly changing subjects, Presley realized there was method to their conversational madness. They were keeping Tate off balance, requiring him to think constantly and consider each response so thoroughly that he had no time to analyze the circumstances and maybe see things for what they really were.

Presley watched as Tate crossed one leg over the other, bringing the tassels on his expensive Italian leather loafers to her eye level. She found that she was less bothered by the fact that those expensive shoes had been probably purchased with her father's hard-earned dollars than she was by the fact that he was now trying to swindle her friends.

Finally the meal was over, and Miss Eugenia introduced the subject of a massive charitable foundation combining assets from Cecelia and George Ann Simmons. As Miss Eugenia and Cecelia discussed the scope of the project, Tate's foot began to swing with barely contained excitement. Each half-arc sent the fancy tassels bouncing.

"I think it should be called the Simmons Foundation," Miss Eugenia said. "In honor of George Ann's family."

"I want to name it after Blanche Armstrong," Cecelia disagreed, "with at least a nod to Edison. Maybe we could call it the Armstrong and Simmons Foundation and put Edison's company logo behind the name."

"Or we could put his logo on one side, an orchid for Blanche on the other, and Simmons Foundation in the middle."

Tate swung his head back and forth between them, looking for the chance to chime in with a worthwhile suggestion. The briefcase on the stone patio taunted Presley. Just a few feet away but still completely out of reach.

Finally they allowed Tate to direct them into a discussion of the specific assets involved. He already had Miss George Ann's evaluation and requested one from Cecelia. Presley saw the thick stack of papers pass from Cecelia's hand to Tate's. She stooped a little so she could see the look on his face as he scanned the impressive list. When he looked back up, it was as if the others had disappeared. Cecelia was the only person who mattered to Tate now.

"What percentage of your portfolio are you planning to put into the foundation?" Tate asked.

Cecelia smiled and said, "All of it."

"All of it?" Tate's astonishment was obvious.

"Even this house. Like I said, I want to start fresh."

"That is an amazingly generous gesture." Tate actually sounded emotional, no doubt moved by the thought of all the money he was about to steal.

"I guess we'll have to meet with some lawyers and draw up a document to govern the foundation?" Cecelia made it sound like this would be a huge inconvenience.

"Yes," Tate agreed. "But we can get the ball rolling as soon as I have a signed power of attorney. I can draw that up tonight, and we can meet again in the morning."

Cecelia pursed her lips. "Do we have to wait until tomorrow? I have a wireless printer. Can't you print the paperwork now?"

Tate looked surprised but pleased. "Well, sure."

"I just want this settled," she told him. "You don't have to print out everything tonight, but if we can at least print out the things I need to sign, you can get that ball rolling."

Presley saw Tate smile, and her heart hurt a little. Not because she still loved him but because she knew it wasn't genuine.

"In fact, I don't even need your printer," he was saying, "I have a portable one I can hook up to my laptop since we'll only be printing a few signature sheets tonight." Tate opened his briefcase and removed a laptop and a portable printer. Aunt Violet cleared some space on the table for him set it up.

Soon it was humming away, printing page after page of documents intended to separate Cecelia from her inheritance.

Once the printer was silent, Cecelia said, "I was advised by Miss Violet"—she waved vaguely toward the woman in question—"to have the foundation managed by a group of people instead of putting so much power and responsibility into the hands of just one man. But I trust Miss Eugenia, and she says you come highly recommended."

Presley could almost feel the tension emanating from Tate as he said, "I'll hire other lawyers and accountants and investment specialists to work for the foundation, of course, but I've found that it's best to have just one decision-maker."

Cecelia considered this for a few seconds and then nodded. "I agree. But I do have one condition. If I'm going to trust you with everything I own, I want you to give this foundation your full attention."

Tate relaxed and emitted a breathy laugh. "Oh, of course."

"No, I mean your *full* attention," Cecelia reiterated. "I don't want you to work for anyone but me—that includes Miss Eugenia for now." She looked over at the other woman and apologized. "You can add Miss George Ann's estate later, but in this important initial stage, I want to be Tate's only client."

"I can't make too many decisions yet anyway," Miss Eugenia said. "So that's fine."

Cecelia turned back to Tate. "That means you need to contact all your former clients and resign immediately."

"I don't have a problem with that," he said. "I'll do it first thing in the morning. I've worked closely with some of them for a while, and it's going to be quite a blow."

"I'm sure," Cecelia murmured.

Aunt Violet said, "But I can't allow my client to sign all those papers," she pointed at the stack he'd printed, "until we have that assurance."

Tate shifted in his chair, a sign that he was annoyed.

Cecelia said, "I just wish there was something you could do tonight, to reassure me and my lawyer that you aren't planning to hold on to any of your old clients."

The words hung in the thick Georgia night air for a few seconds. Presley didn't dare even breathe. And then Tate took the bait.

"What if I revoked the powers of attorney I have for my other clients now, right here in front of you?" he suggested like the fool they'd played him for. "Then you could be sure I was severing all ties with other clients."

Cecelia bestowed a gorgeous smile on him. "I love that idea. We'll have a little power of attorney ceremony." Then she frowned. "But surely you don't have those documents with you."

Tate went back to his briefcase and removed a file. "I keep important documents like that with me at all times." He placed the folder beside the stack of papers waiting for Cecelia's signature.

She walked over and fingered through the documents in the file. Then she glanced back at Tate.

"Only five?" she said. "I thought you would have more clients than that."

In that instant Presley knew her power of attorney was not one of the five. There would have been no reason for Cecelia to make this comment if the document was there. Her heart sunk as Tate responded.

"My business is more about quality than quantity," he claimed.

Cecelia tapped the file with a beautifully manicured fingernail. Then she said, "I have to be able to trust you, Tate. So I'm going to have Miss Violet check in the morning. If there is one single, itty-bitty power of attorney in your name that you didn't revoke tonight, the deal is off. I'll find someone else to create and manage this foundation."

His laugh seemed a little forced this time. "My goodness, I didn't know you had such a serious side."

She laughed too. "I'm not often serious. Only when it comes to trust issues."

He walked over to his briefcase. "I think I gave you all of the powers of attorney, but let me double-check. I'd hate for a misfiled piece of paper to keep us from this joint opportunity." He made a show of going through his briefcase again.

Mac and Presley exchanged a glance. They returned their attention to Tate just as he pulled a single piece of paper triumphantly from his briefcase.

"There's one more! Thank goodness you had me check. I'd forgotten about this one because it's inactive. The client is institutionalized, so I don't keep it with the others."

Presley started to tremble, and Mac put his hands on her shoulders.

Aunt Violet said, "You'll need to write *revoke* on each one. Cecelia and Miss Eugenia can sign as witnesses, and I'll notarize them."

This took a few minutes, but finally all the forms were revoked and signed. Aunt Violet picked them up and held them protectively against her chest. "I'll file them for you," she told Tate. "Since you're going to have your hands full with this new venture."

He thanked her but didn't sound particularly appreciative. "Now on to the other forms." He might as well have rubbed his hands together in the universal sign for greed.

Cecelia slowly and methodically read and then signed each form. Miss Eugenia witnessed her signature, and Aunt Violet notarized it.

Presley checked her watch. It was after eight o'clock. "I wonder when Mark Iverson is going to get here?" she mouthed to Mac.

He shrugged.

"We can't let Tate leave with those papers Cecelia is signing," Presley whispered. "It's too big a risk."

He nodded that he understood.

Finally the signing was complete. Tate put the documents into his briefcase and packed up his laptop. Now that the end was in sight, he seemed anxious to go. Miss Eugenia and Aunt Violet tried some stalling tactics, but Tate kept moving slowly and steadily toward the French doors that separated the fabulous patio from the even more fabulous house.

"We have to do something," Presley whispered more urgently this time.

Mac chewed his lip for a few seconds, and then he said, "I have an idea. Follow behind them and stay out of sight."

She watched as he trotted around the side of the house toward the front. Once he was gone, Presley returned her attention to the small group on the patio. Tate was passing through the French doors into Cecelia's house. Presley hung back, careful to stay hidden from his view as she followed them. She waited in the kitchen until he'd passed through the foyer, and then in the hallway while he walked out the front door. She had just gotten close enough to peer around the doorframe when she heard Tate call out.

"Hey!" he yelled. "That's my car!"

Presley looked outside. In the fading light, she saw that Mac had an expensive-looking car on the lift of his tow truck. She put her hand over her mouth to keep from laughing.

Tate charged down to the circular drive and demanded, "What do you think you're doing?"

Mac gave him the most disdainful look. "I'm a repo guy, and I'm towing this car. Apparently you're behind on your payments."

"That's ridiculous!" Tate spewed. Then he turned to his hostesses, who were standing a few feet away. "There's some kind of mistake! I don't even make payments on this car. I paid cash."

Cecelia, Aunt Violet, and Miss Eugenia stared at him without comment.

Tate turned back to Mac. "Get my car down off your truck right now!"

Mac held out a scrap of paper with a portion of the golden arches showing along the side. Written in what was obviously in his own handwriting on what was obviously part of an old McDonalds bag was an order to tow in a car with Tate's Ohio license plate number. Mac pointed at the scrap of paper. "It says right here that I'm supposed to tow this car."

Tate's face turned red. "Let me see that!"

Mac held it just out of his reach. "Sorry, I can't let you have my tow order."

"That is not a tow order!" Tate looked apoplectic. "That is a piece of garbage with preschool scribble on it! You can't tow my car based on that."

Mac ignored the insult. "Watch me."

Presley threw caution to the wind and rushed outside. Hoping it was too dark for Tate to recognize her, she moved up to stand beside Aunt Violet.

She arrived just as Tate grabbed Mac by the arm.

Mac said, "You'd better let go of me."

"Not until you agree to get my car off your tow truck."

In answer to this challenge, Mac swung with his right fist and caught Tate in the nose. Tate's head snapped back, and Presley hoped he would fall, but instead he came back with a right hook that connected with Mac's jaw, and Mac was the one who went down.

Presley started toward him, and then she felt a restraining hand on her arm. It was Wyatt. "Stay here," he said softly.

Patrick ran past them and took up the boxing match with Tate.

"You've got to stop this," Presley told Wyatt.

Wyatt shook his head. "If I try to stop it, I might distract Patrick and give Sheridan an advantage. It's better to just let them go—unless it looks like our side is going to lose. Then I'll get involved."

Presley groaned in frustration and turned back to see Patrick take a punch to the stomach that staggered him. While Patrick was bent over, Tate came back with a cheap shot. This enraged Mac, who lunged himself from his prone position into Tate's legs, and soon the two of them were rolling around on Cecelia's manicured lawn, punching and gouging.

Presley pulled free of Wyatt and took a step toward them, but before she'd gone more than a couple of feet, a shot rang out. They all turned to see Cecelia holding a small revolver over her head.

"That's it," she said. "Get up, both of you."

Mac released his hold on Tate and managed to get into a kneeling position. Tate sat up slowly. Presley relaxed, thankful it was over.

Cecelia lowered the gun and frowned at Tate. "I'm appalled."

Tate spread his hands. "It's not my fault! He was trying to steal my car."

Cecelia shook her head. "There were a dozen things you could have done, like call the police, rather than start a fistfight. I'm afraid I'm going to have to rethink this whole thing. I don't see how I can possibly trust someone who has such poor judgment."

Tate pointed at Mac. "You should be yelling at him."

"We can talk more tomorrow," Cecelia said. "But I've got to admit, my confidence is shaken. I want my power of attorney back until you can reassure me."

Presley watched warily as Tate stood and dusted a few blades of grass from his expensive suit. He leaned down and reached for his briefcase, but at the last moment, he grabbed Cecelia's hand instead and pulled the gun from her grasp. He pushed her roughly to the ground and pointed the gun at the group.

"I don't know what's going on here," he said, "but something is definitely wrong. We've got people materializing from nowhere, trying to steal my car and starting fights. A few minutes ago you couldn't wait for me to take care of your money, and now because I defended myself against a car thief, you're reconsidering." He shook his head. "I knew this was too good to be true, but I couldn't resist. I had to see for myself, just in case."

Presley and the others remained silent. She could feel the tension surrounding them. They all wanted to stop Tate, but mostly they wanted to prevent injury—or worse.

He waved the gun at Miss Eugenia. "You, pick up my briefcase and hand it to me."

She did as he asked, but when she held it out to him, instead of taking the briefcase, he grabbed her arm and pulled her against him. He put one arm across her neck and pointed the gun right at her head. Miss Eugenia was a brave woman, but there was fear in her eyes.

"Now, maybe we can make some progress here." Tate turned to Mac. "You, get my car off your tow truck."

Mac hesitated for just a second before walking over and lowering the lift. Once the car was back on the driveway, Tate took a few steps toward it, dragging Miss Eugenia along with him.

"You," he pointed at Aunt Violet, "get my briefcase and put it in the car. Backseat—other side!"

Aunt Violet pulled her oxygen tank along as she retrieved the briefcase. Then she walked around the car, opened the back door, and put the briefcase inside.

"Now get back over there by the others," Tate commanded.

Aunt Violet did as he'd instructed.

He gave Cecelia a smirk. "I think you're right. I'm not the man to run your foundation. I'm just not into *charity* work. I ran into some trouble in Ohio, so I've already made plans to leave the country. I had hoped to pad my retirement funds with this little opportunity. At least my detour to Georgia won't be a complete waste of time. Because tomorrow morning, as soon as the banks open, you're going to wire ten million dollars to an offshore account. I'll text you with the information."

"I don't have that kind of cash available," Cecelia tried.

"Oh, you'll figure out a way," Tate told her. "Because if you don't, your friend here dies." He pressed the gun more tightly against Miss Eugenia's temple.

It had to hurt, but elderly woman remained stoic.

"I can't hang around here, obviously," Tate said. "So I'll dump her somewhere—bound and gagged, of course. Once I get the money, I'll tell you where."

Then he lifted the gun and brought the handle down on Miss Eugenia's head with a quick, hard gesture. Miss Eugenia's eyes fluttered and closed. Then she collapsed against Tate. He staggered slightly under her weight. "I should have picked a lighter hostage," he muttered as he dragged her over to his car and stuffed her inside.

Presley knew the men were looking for an opportunity to rush him, but Tate was careful to keep the car between him and the others.

"I don't want to hurt her," he said, "and I won't as long as the money is in my account tomorrow."

Presley saw the look in his eyes and heard the tone of his voice; she knew he was lying. If they let him leave, he would kill Miss Eugenia without a qualm.

"We have to stop him," Presley whispered earnestly. The cousins nodded in grim unison. As Tate walked around the car to the driver's side door, the men took a simultaneous step forward.

Tate smirked. "Don't try to be heroes. You'll just get the old woman killed."

"You don't have enough bullets to kill us all," Mac pointed out.

"No, but I can get one or two of you. I think I'll aim at Cecelia first. She's tall enough to make a good target. Or maybe I'll shoot the little blonde or the old lawyer with the oxygen. So many choices," Tate taunted. "And I've definitely got enough bullets to shoot one of them."

Reluctantly the cousins fell back.

Presley felt responsibility for this whole disaster. She had to find a way to rescue Miss Eugenia without anyone getting hurt. So far Tate hadn't recognized her, and she wondered if she could use that against him somehow.

He inched closer to the driver's door. His fingers clasped the door handle, and she knew time was running out. So she stepped forward into a circle of light created by a decorative outdoor lantern. She didn't really have a plan, but Tate was her problem and she wasn't going to let anyone else get hurt trying to help her.

"Tate!" she said. "Tate, it's me, Presley!"

This had the desired effect. His head whipped around toward her, and he stared in astonishment. "That's impossible," he whispered. "You're in the mental hospital. You have an incurable disease."

Behind him she saw a movement so slight that, under other circumstances, she might have thought it was her imagination. But

Mac tensed, and she knew he had seen something too. Help was near. She just had to keep Tate distracted for a few seconds.

She took a step toward him, keeping his attention. "No, I escaped."

He ignored this announcement, still fascinated by her altered appearance. "They told me the plastic surgeon had repaired your face, but I wouldn't have thought this much improvement was possible. You actually look normal now!"

She didn't respond.

"If I'd known they could make you look this good, I might have married you after all." He gave an ironic laugh. "But instead you're *legally* incompetent!"

She stood there and accepted the verbal abuse without flinching. His words no longer had the power to hurt her.

"So I guess this was all about getting your money back," he went on. "But I've got a newsflash for you, it was a waste of time. It's all gone!"

"I don't care about the money," Presley told him. "But you've got to let Miss Eugenia go."

Tate laughed. "The old woman is the least of your worries." He pointed the gun at Presley and cocked it. "I've been dreaming about this for a long time."

And then it was as if the whole area exploded into motion. Cecelia picked up Aunt Violet's oxygen tank and threw it at Tate. He ducked, so the tank missed him and shattered his windshield instead. Cecelia then pushed Aunt Violet down and tackled Presley as the cousins rushed Tate in unison. He hesitated just a moment, presumably trying to decide which man to shoot first. In that split second of uncertainty, Mark Iverson was able to get an arm around Tate's neck from behind. He shoved Tate's arm up as he pulled the con man backward. The one shot Tate got off sent a bullet harmlessly into the starry sky.

A short scuffle ensued. Presley heard a bone crack as Wyatt wrenched the gun from Tate's hand. Tate started screaming. Mark ignored him and yanked the arm with the damaged hand behind Tate's back.

Then Mac stepped up and hit Tate solidly in the stomach. As Tate doubled over, Mac looked back at Presley. “He had that coming.”

“That and more,” she agreed.

CHAPTER TWENTY

PRESLEY SAT BESIDE MAC AND Wyatt on Cecelia's front porch and surveyed the surreal scene before them. Several police and sheriff department vehicles were parked helter-skelter on the lush grass. Some still had lights flashing; some still had doors open. Law enforcement personnel were milling around, talking in low tones.

Two ambulances were parked on the driveway. In one, Aunt Violet was receiving oxygen until a replacement tank could be delivered. Miss Eugenia was in the other one. According to Mark Iverson she was conscious now, but they were going to take her to the hospital as a precaution.

Tate was handcuffed and sitting in the backseat of a police car with an officer on either side. Tate's damaged car had been reloaded onto Mac's tow truck, this time with a real work order provided by the Haggerty Police Department. Tate looked cowed and in pain. Presley wished Wyatt had broken Tate's other wrist too.

Cecelia and Brother Patrick were standing a few feet away, answering questions for Chief Jones. A fine layer of broken windshield glass glittered in the lantern light on the driveway under their feet. Mark Iverson joined them, and the interview ended. Then Agent Iverson and Chief Jones turned and walked toward the front porch.

When Wyatt saw them approaching, he whispered, "My standard advice in situations like this is to decline comment based on the fact that anything you say might incriminate you."

Presley raised an eyebrow. "You're frequently in situations like this?"

"Not personally," he qualified his remark.

Mark stopped a few feet in front of them with Winston at his side. "I can't believe all you sensible people allowed Miss Eugenia to talk you into this." The FBI agent waved at the chaos behind him. "It's a miracle you weren't all killed."

"What we planned was very simple and didn't involve firearms," Presley explained. "This happened"—she pointed at the front yard—"because Tate is a psychopath."

"Even a simple meeting with Sheridan was dangerous," Winston insisted. "You shouldn't have attempted it without police support."

"I told Miss Eugenia that on the phone," Mark said. "I made her promise to call you and have you here when Sheridan arrived."

"She called me all right," the chief said, "but she didn't tell me about this little scam you all were planning."

"We got Presley's power of attorney," Cecelia pointed out as she and Patrick joined the group.

"And no one got killed," Patrick added. "So I'd say it was a success."

"It could have been a disaster," Chief Jones growled.

"And before tonight you didn't have any evidence against Tate Sheridan. Now you can charge him with attempted murder, assault and battery, attempted kidnapping"—Wyatt itemized using his fingers—"public nuisance, disturbing the peace—"

Mark nodded. "I get it. Thanks to all of you, we can throw the book at him."

Wyatt looked pleased. "Exactly."

"And nobody got hurt," Mac pointed out. "Except Sheridan, and we're not sorry about that."

"Apparently you haven't looked in the mirror," Mark said wryly. "You or Brother Patrick. Although Wyatt seems fine."

"I fight with my mind," Wyatt claimed. "Instead of exchanging punches with that lunatic, I made a tiny hole in his gas tank so when he left he wouldn't get far." He pointed at his head. "Brains always win over brawn."

"I'll hold him while you hit him," Patrick offered to Mac.

Mac grinned. "It's tempting, but I'd probably miss."

Both his cousins laughed.

Mark shook his head in exasperation. "Everybody go home. We'll sort this out tomorrow and get your statements."

"We really are sorry for the trouble we caused," Presley said earnestly. "We never intended for things to go this far."

"Oh, I know who the ringleader is," Winston said. "And if she wasn't in an ambulance right now, I'd seriously consider locking her up for the night just to teach her a lesson."

A deputy came over and told Presley that Miss Eugenia was calling for her. "Hurry," he encouraged. "They're about to take her to the hospital in Albany."

Presley and Mac trotted over to the ambulance. Miss Eugenia looked fine except for the gauze bandage wrapped around her head. She waved Presley forward with a weak hand gesture. "Come closer," she whispered.

Alarmed, Presley propelled herself into the back of the ambulance. Then she leaned down to hear what Miss Eugenia wanted to tell her.

Miss Eugenia's eyes opened, and her expression was more amused than pained. "I'm okay," she said softly. "The only reason I'm letting them take me to the hospital is because Mark and Winston are so mad at me."

"Winston is threatening jail time," Presley confirmed.

Miss Eugenia chuckled. "Thank heavens I've got good lawyers."

"And cheap ones," Presley added with a smile. Then her expression sobered. "I hope you don't get in trouble for this. But I really appreciate all you did. And I can't begin to tell you how it feels, knowing I'm free of Tate forever."

"You're welcome," Miss Eugenia said. "Now I need a favor."

Presley nodded. "Anything."

"Will you go by my house and take Lady to my neighbor, Miss Polly? She lives two houses down, right next to the Iversons. I don't know how long I'm going to have to pretend to be hurt, and I don't want Lady to be alone all night."

"We'll make sure Lady is taken care of," Presley promised.

Miss Eugenia nodded. "And if Winston asks how I am . . ."

Presley laughed softly. "I'll tell him you were talking nonsense."

The older woman sighed. "He'll definitely believe that."

* * *

Once the police cars and ambulances were gone, Presley turned to her fellow-conspirators. "How I can ever thank you?"

"I know how you can thank *me*," Mac said. "I'll take a hug!"

Amid whoops of laughter, she wrapped her arms around him, and they held each other for a few seconds. "Your poor face," she said. "And Brother Patrick looks even worse."

Mac grinned. "Now *that's* a first!"

"On a serious note," Wyatt said to Presley, "since the power of attorney has been revoked, you're responsible for your own assets. You need to find out what kind of shape your finances are in, and please, don't sign away control again."

"I won't!" Presley promised him.

Wyatt put his hands together in prayerful supplication. "Thank you!"

Presley laughed at herself along with the others. Then she said, "Wyatt, could you take Aunt Violet home? Mac and I have to do a favor for Miss Eugenia—who is incoherent if anyone asks."

"It would be an honor," Wyatt assured her. He collected Aunt Violet and her brand new oxygen tank and led them to his SUV.

Presley held out a hand to Mac. "Now let's go see about Lady."

* * *

Once they had the little dog settled with Miss Polly Kirby, Presley and Mack went to the football stadium and ran several laps around the track. When they were finished, they walked out to the middle of the football field.

"So," Mac said breathlessly, "how does it feel to be free?"

Presley spun in circles on the fifty-yard line with her arms and hands spread wide open. "It feels wonderful."

"I feel a little free myself," he told her.

She stopped spinning and grabbed his damp T-shirt with both hands to steady herself. "Free?"

He nodded. "My divorce became final at five o'clock today."

She drew him closer. "But how?"

"I gave my ex-wife most of our assets, but she doesn't have claim on my future earnings," he said. "That felt right finally. She can keep the past, but I want control of my future. Of course, the vengeful woman still insisted that I sign an affidavit swearing I will never play football professionally again."

Tears filled Presley's eyes. "I'm sad for you even though I *hate* football."

He laughed and then winced, putting a hand to his wounded mouth. "You don't have to be sad for me, but you might want to give football a chance."

Her head was still spinning. "Why?"

"Because I decided to apply for the coaching job at Haggerty High School."

"Oh, Mac, you got the job?"

He shook his head. "No. They gave it to the coach at a Class A high school over in Rock Creek about an hour away."

"I'm so sorry."

"I'm not. Because I got his job at Rock Creek High."

Presley screamed and wrapped her arms around his neck.

His laughing face got closer and closer until finally his lips were pressed gently to hers. "I don't want to hurt your split lip," she murmured.

"It will be worth the pain," he insisted.

Their first real kiss was sweet and soft and salty and very gentle—to accommodate his wounded mouth.

"I don't know why I keep crying," she told him when the kiss ended. "I'm happier than I've been in, well, maybe forever!"

"Happy tears," he said and wiped them away with his finger. "I know it's a little early to say this since I've only officially been a single man for a few hours, but I think I'm in love with you."

"It might be a little early for me too, since until a few hours ago I was a fugitive from the law and certified as crazy," she replied. "But I'm pretty sure I love you too."

"It won't be easy for us," he cautioned. "We both bring baggage to our new relationship."

"Your vengeful ex-wife."

"Your psychotic ex-fiancé," he added. "And some people still think I threw that football game."

"Some people still think I'm crazy."

"We'll get married like Patrick and Cecelia," he whispered.

"But there's no rush."

He nodded. "I want to enjoy every step of our journey together." He turned so they were both facing the far end zone. Wrapping his arms around her waist, he said, "We're going to give the future our best shot—together."

She leaned back against him and stared at the starry sky, framed by the distant goal posts. "I have a really good feeling about this field goal, symbolically speaking."

He laughed. "Me too."

Then his phone started ringing. He ignored it, but the ringing continued insistently for several minutes.

Finally she said, "You've got to answer it, Mac."

Reluctantly he pulled out his phone. "It's Wyatt," he said as he pressed Accept.

Presley could hear Wyatt's strident tone but couldn't understand the words he was yelling.

The conversation was short, and when it ended, Mac said, "Loralee's on TV with Hannah-Leigh Burrell doing her first special report segment."

Presley nodded, wondering how that could possibly have upset Wyatt so much.

Mac continued, "And she just announced to the entire Channel 3 viewing audience that she killed Irma Heinrich eighty-four years ago."

CHAPTER TWENTY-ONE

CADE BURRELL WAS WAITING FOR Mac and Presley when they rushed into the television station. He led them back to a conference room. Sheriff Bonham was standing right inside the door. Wyatt was staring out the window. Brother Patrick and Cecelia were sitting close to each other, looking miserable. Loralee was in a huge leather desk chair at the end of the table. She seemed small and a little scared.

She smiled when she saw them. "I always wondered how it felt to be arrested," she said. "It's nothing like the way it looks on TV."

Presley knelt down in front of the old woman and took her hand. "Why did you tell Hannah-Leigh that you killed Irma?"

Mac leaned down so he was also in her line of sight. "Were you trying to make the story interesting to protect Presley? Because you didn't need to. Everything is okay with her."

"I confessed because I killed her," Loralee replied simply. "I've carried that secret for eighty years. Since I might not wake up tomorrow, I wanted to get it off my chest. And while I was telling the story to Hannah-Leigh, I decided to let everyone know."

Cade cursed softly, and the sheriff said, "She's obviously senile."

"She's not," Mac disagreed.

"Prove it," Sheriff Bonham demanded. "She just confessed to a murder that happened over eighty years ago! If that's not crazy, I don't know what is!"

Wyatt walked over and spoke to Mac. "We don't want to say too much on the subject of sanity. We may need to use that as a defense later on."

"A defense?" Presley cried. "Surely no one believes this! It's not actually going to trial?"

"We've been put in an impossible situation!" the sheriff defended himself. "She confessed to *murder*! On television. With hundreds of people watching."

"The DA might decide not to prosecute," Wyatt said. "Since there's no evidence linking her to the crime—besides her confession—and because of her age. But the sheriff had to arrest her, so our first step is to get her out on bail. Your aunt's working on that now."

"Bail?" Presley turned on Sheriff Bonham and Cade. "Are you kidding me? She's obviously not a danger to anyone. And since she's never been farther than Albany in her entire hundred-year life, she can't be considered a flight risk."

The sheriff shrugged. "There are rules, Ms. DeGraff. I can't just ignore them when it suits me. Hopefully the judge will see things your way and let her go home."

Presley looked at Wyatt, who said, "We decided your aunt could play the sympathy card more effectively. So she's going to try that first. If the judge doesn't buy it, I'll step in and apply as much pressure as is necessary to get Loralee released. But that will be a last resort. Like I told you before, we have to live here."

Presley nodded. Aunt Violet was tougher than she looked and well-respected in the community. And no judge would want to put a hundred-year-old woman behind bars. So if the judge *could* be persuaded, Aunt Violet would do it. If not, Wyatt could use the threat of legal action and bad publicity to get Loralee home. Presley put a hand to her head. She knew this wasn't her fault, but she still felt responsible.

"It's going to be okay," Mac assured her. "For all the reasons you named. Loralee is no danger, and she's not a flight risk. The judge will send her home."

Aunt Violet came in a few minutes later, dragging her oxygen tank behind her and looking every bit her age. "The judge has released Loralee into my custody," she said wearily. "Let's get out of here before he changes his mind."

* * *

Driving back to Haggerty, Mac and Presley tried to make sense of what had happened.

"Even assuming that Loralee did kill Irma—which I seriously doubt—confessing makes no sense," Presley said. "Unless she really is senile."

"She's not," Mac insisted. "She has a little confusion sometimes, and she's always been kind of childlike, but she's not senile. I don't mind if Wyatt says that to get the charges dropped, but between you and me, she's not."

Presley nodded. "That's what I think too. She has done some odd things lately, like retrieving the murder weapon." She looked over at him. "I don't believe she was planning to give it to us. When I described that hammer, she knew exactly where it was and didn't tell us on purpose. She waited until she thought we were gone, and then she went to get it. She was probably planning to destroy it."

"Or put it someplace where it couldn't incriminate anyone."

"The only way confessing makes sense is if she's trying to protect someone."

"There are only two people who were alive when the murder took place that she'd risk murder charges for," he said grimly.

Presley sighed. "Blanche and DuPont."

"We've got to tell your aunt and the sheriff," Mac said. "We can get this straightened out tonight."

Presley stared out the windshield at the night sky for a few minutes. Then she shook her head. "Loralee loves Blanche and DuPont more than her own life. She's chosen to protect their memories. It's not our place to take that away from her."

"Even if one of them is a murderer?"

"Even then." Presley felt strongly about this. "Irma has been dead for almost a century."

"But if they decide to try Loralee for murder?"

"If it comes to that, we'll have to re-evaluate our position. But for now, I think she's safe. So let's let her keep Blanche and DuPont safe too."

* * *

Presley knew that Tate's arrest would be public knowledge soon, so once she got to her bedroom, she called Moon to let him know. When she finished her report, he cursed under his breath.

"Do you want me to come there?" he asked. "In case there's more trouble?"

"No," Presley declined the offer. "Tate's in jail, and I have friends here."

There was a brief pause, and then he said, "You have friends in Columbus too."

"I know," she replied gently. "I owe my life to you and Dr. Khan."

"Don't forget the nursing students and Simu-Lady."

She laughed. "No, I can't forget any of you."

"But you're staying there, aren't you?"

"Yes," she said. "I think I've found a cowboy I can ride off into the sunset with. But once everything is settled, I'll come back to Columbus for a visit."

"You promise?" He sounded a little melancholy.

"I promise. And Moon?"

"Yes?"

"I hope it won't happen, but if you ever find yourself in need of a good cheap lawyer, I know where you can find one."

He laughed. "I'll keep that in mind. Good-bye, Calamity Jane."

"Good-bye, Moon."

* * *

On Tuesday Presley called the accountant who had handled her father's accounts for years and asked him to check into the state of her finances. He called back an hour later with the news that her parents' estate was worth roughly half of its estimated value before Tate Sheridan took control.

Half was twice what she'd expected, so Presley was momentarily encouraged.

The accountant continued, "We know he was illegally transferring funds to his own accounts, so it's possible that some of that money might also be returned to you."

This was even better.

But then the accountant gave her the bad news. "However, I can pretty much guarantee that there will be lawsuits. Several of your father's companies were sold, and people lost their jobs and their pensions. When they find out there was evidence of fiduciary malfeasance, they'll want their money."

"How bad could it be?"

"Catastrophic," he said. "One lawsuit leads to another, and, well, you'll want to talk to an attorney, but my advice would be to put all remaining assets from your parents' estate—including anything that might be recovered in the future—into a trust. These funds would be used for any claims or lawsuits. And when the money's gone, they can still sue you personally, but if you don't have any assets . . ."

So being poor did have some advantages. "Thank you for this information."

"I wish I had better news," he said. "If there's anything else I can do for you, I'd consider it an honor. Your father was a good man."

Presley swallowed hard to control her emotions. Then she said, "Actually, I do need a favor, if you don't mind. A friend loaned me money recently, and I need to pay him back. If I wire the money to you, along with the name and address, can you arrange to have a check delivered to him?"

"I will be happy to."

Presley felt like another huge weight had been lifted off her shoulders. Soon she'd be as light as Blanche Armstrong's buttermilk biscuits, floating in the air.

After her phone call, she went in and talked to Aunt Violet. She described her money situation, and her aunt agreed that a trust would be a good way of doing the right thing and protecting herself.

"We'll probably want to get Wyatt to handle that, though. He's better at the tricky stuff."

"I feel terrible about the companies Tate destroyed and the lives that were adversely affected. Up until now I was looking at this as my personal tragedy. Now I realize that a lot of people have suffered because of my poor judgment. I'm going to try my best to right wrongs, and I can't hold anything back. So I'm going to have to sell the Aston." Just saying the words made her heart hurt. "It's worth a great deal, and as for my memories, well, I get to keep those."

Her aunt smiled. "You *have* learned a lot through this process."

Presley smiled back, and the pain in her heart eased a little. "I'll have my accountant contact Mac and arrange for the car to be transferred to Columbus."

Aunt Violet nodded. "On another topic, I've filed an injunction to stop Channel 3 News from airing any more special report segments that involve either you or Loralee since you're both part of ongoing criminal investigations. Then I warned Hannah-Leigh and her employers that we are considering a law suit against them for allowing an old woman to incriminate herself on television. She'll be lucky if she keeps her job, and she definitely won't be doing more exposés anytime soon."

"That's a relief," Presley said. "I know all this about Tate will get out eventually, but I'd rather it be a slow trickle instead of a public announcement."

There was a knock on the front door, and Aunt Violet checked her watch. "That will be someone arriving for the meeting Wyatt called for this morning."

"And what is the purpose for this meeting?" Presley asked.

"I'd rather let him explain," Aunt Violet replied.

Presley walked to the front of the house and opened the door to admit Wyatt. "You don't look like you got much sleep," she observed.

"I didn't," he said. "I spent all night preparing for a possible legal battle in Loralee's behalf. There isn't much in the way of precedence for hundred-year-old murderers."

Presley smiled, although she could tell he wasn't joking. She left the door open a crack for the others who would be joining them and then followed Wyatt into the kitchen.

Once everyone had arrived and settled around Aunt Violet's kitchen table with a box of doughnuts to fortify them, Wyatt said, "I talked to the district attorney this morning, and he has no plans to prosecute Loralee. He isn't dismissing the charges, but he'll just drag things out until nature takes its course."

"In other words, he'll make sure Loralee is dead before her case comes up for trial?" Aunt Violet asked.

He nodded. "And I heard from the FBI forensics lab in Atlanta. They're finished with Irma Heinrich's remains and want to know what to do with them. I figured we couldn't put them back in Miss Violet's backyard, so . . ."

"We could bury her in our family section at the Rose Lawn Cemetery," Brother Patrick suggested. "There are plenty of plots available, and since she used to work for DuPont and Blanche, that seems appropriate."

"Appropriate?" Wyatt scoffed. "She was murdered, and we all know the only sensible reason Loralee would confess to it was if she thinks either DuPont or Blanche killed the girl."

No one could argue with his logic.

After a minute Presley said, "Even if that's true, I think Irma should be buried in the Armstrong section. It's a little something Blanche and DuPont can do for her now."

Wyatt sighed. "Okay, I'll agree on one condition. She gets buried by the state with no funeral or special sermon or orchid plants by her headstone. If Hannah-Leigh gets an idea that there's more to this story, she'll be off and running again. And this time Loralee could end up in jail."

"It doesn't seem right just to throw Irma in the ground with no funeral," Cecelia said.

"Again," Presley added.

"State funerals can be presided over by a member of the clergy," Brother Patrick told them. "I won't go myself," he promised Wyatt, "but I'll arrange for someone I trust to do it."

"I can be satisfied with that," Presley said.

Wyatt smirked at Presley and then looked between her and Mac. "So you're staying here with your aunt?"

"Yes," she confirmed. "I'll start studying for the Georgia Bar, get licensed, and gradually take over Aunt Violet's unprofitable law practice so she can retire."

"I don't know if I want to retire," Aunt Violet replied. "But I'm anxious to have a law partner."

"And while we're talking about employment," Mac said, "I'd like to announce that I have a new job." He smiled at Presley. "Starting on July 1, I'll be coaching the Rock Creek Panthers."

"That is great news," Aunt Violet said.

"I guess we'll all have to become Panther fans," Wyatt added.

"What are their school colors?" Cecelia asked with a frown. "I hope they aren't something garish."

Presley laughed. "Like there's a color that wouldn't look beautiful on you."

Cecelia acknowledged this compliment with a little shrug. "Some colors look more beautiful than others."

"It's just a Class A school," Mac told them modestly. "Certainly not the big time."

"It's a chance to do what you love," Brother Patrick corrected. "That's as big as it gets."

"While we're talking family business," Mac said, "I'm going to get serious about the old Armstrong house this summer. I hope to have it ready to live in by the end of the year. So I'd like to buy your shares."

Wyatt looked at Brother Patrick. "What would you say the value of that house is?"

"I'd say nothing," he responded.

"So if you divide nothing three ways and separate out our two shares, how much would Mac have to pay us to buy it?"

Brother Patrick pretended to think hard. "Math was never my strongest subject, but I think the total would be . . . like maybe, nothing?"

"I know you're worried because it cost me every dime I own to get free of my ex-wife," Mac said. "But I'll be earning a salary from the coaching job, and I can still do repos on the side. So I can afford to pay you, and I want to be fair."

"We want to be fair too," Brother Patrick said. "And the only value that house has is the sentimental kind. It's going to cost a fortune to fix it up, and it probably still won't be worth anything."

"I try to steer clear of losing propositions," Wyatt said. "So I'll be happy to gift you that headache."

"Thanks," Mac's voice shook a little. "It means more than you know."

Brother Patrick smiled. "I guess this would be a good time to tell you all that I resigned my position at the Haggerty Baptist Church today."

Wyatt frowned. "Why? I thought they gave you a good deal."

"They did," Brother Patrick confirmed. "But I know their hearts aren't in it, and Cecelia will never be comfortable there."

"They don't deserve either of you," Presley said with feeling.

"So are you going to find a new church?" Aunt Violet asked.

Wyatt gave them a sly look. "Or are you going to take Edison Moore's money and become international jetsetters?"

"That's a possibility we hadn't considered," Cecelia said. "But maybe we should."

Patrick rolled his eyes. "The first thing we're going to do is get married—on Saturday at Loralee's cottage."

"Assuming she isn't in jail by then," Wyatt quipped.

"I think I can guarantee that won't happen," Aunt Violet said. "But Saturday is so soon. That doesn't give us much time to plan."

"Or your face much time to heal," Presley added.

"I think all those bruises make Patrick look even more handsome," Cecelia claimed. "And we want to keep the wedding simple."

"Mark Iverson, the FBI agent, is also a Mormon bishop. I've asked him to marry us, and he agreed."

Aunt Violet laughed. "Oh, you just had to get one last dig in at the Baptists, didn't you?"

Cecelia smiled. "That was my idea."

"We'll be there," Mac promised.

"And we'll help with the wedding," Presley added.

"We appreciate that," Brother Patrick said. "Since we don't have to rush into a new preaching job—"

"And since I only have like five customers," Cecelia put in.

Patrick continued, "We're tossing around the idea of really starting a charitable foundation like the one we made up to lure in Tate Sheridan."

Cecelia smiled at him. "Some of the stuff I told Tate is true. We really do want to make our own way in the world, and we'd like to put Edison's money to good use."

"What kind of charity will it be?" Presley was intrigued.

"Something for needy kids," Cecelia said. "Like ones with facial deformities who can't afford surgery."

Tears sprung to Presley's eyes. "If I have any money left over after people get through suing me, I'd like to contribute."

Mac said, "Maybe you could help kids with dyslexia too. I don't have any money to give, but I could come forward with my story and help publicize the problem and the foundation."

"And when people understand what happened, they might quit accusing you of throwing that game," Wyatt said hopefully.

Mac shrugged. "Maybe, but that's not the most important thing to me."

"I don't have any money either," Aunt Violet said. "But I could provide free legal services."

"Why not?" Presley laughed. "She does for everyone else!"

* * *

Tuesday afternoon, Miss Eugenia came over to visit Aunt Violet and Presley. Lady was in with her, but Miss George Ann was not.

"Are you okay?" Aunt Violet asked. "I was afraid you might have a concussion."

Miss Eugenia rubbed the back of her head. "I'm fine, but don't tell Mark or Winston. I'm still trying to keep them sympathetic so they won't fuss at me."

"That whole thing was terribly reckless," Aunt Violet said.

Miss Eugenia shrugged. "All's well that ends well."

"It's the things that don't end well that worry me," Aunt Violet replied.

Miss Eugenia waved this aside. "I'm tired of talking about Tate Sheridan. I actually came here to verify a rumor. I just heard that Brother Patrick has resigned!"

"That might be the only true thing being discussed in Haggerty today," Aunt Violet told her.

"At least you won't have to give the Baptist church all that money for their building fund," Presley said. Then she covered her mouth, belatedly realizing she had promised not to mention this to anyone.

"It's okay," her aunt reassured her. "As George Ann's lawyer, I had to be informed about the well-meaning, if unethical, arrangement Eugenia made with the deacons at the Haggerty Baptist Church."

Presley was relieved but still embarrassed.

Miss Eugenia said, "I'll honor my promise about the building fund. After all, the deacons board did keep their part of the bargain, and goodness knows George Ann can afford it. I also heard that Patrick and Cecelia really are starting a nonprofit foundation to help needy children."

"Well," Aunt Violet said, "now we know *two* true things are being discussed."

"I'll be looking for places to put George Ann's money, so I'd like to learn more about their charity," Miss Eugenia said. "And I'd like to see how they go about it. If I outlive George Ann, I'll probably set something like that up for her assets when she dies."

"You could combine your assets and make one foundation!" Aunt Violet said. "Won't it be hilarious if you and Cecelia end up doing exactly what you told Tate you were going to do?"

"It would be kind of poetic justice," Miss Eugenia agreed.

"So is George Ann still at the nursing home?" Presley asked.

"Yes, she's happy there—as long as I keep her supplied with jigsaw puzzles."

"Did you hear that Patrick and Cecelia are getting married on Saturday out at Orchid Cove?"

Miss Eugenia raised an eyebrow. "That I did not hear. But I'd like to help."

"They want to keep it simple," Aunt Violet warned.

Miss Eugenia scoffed. "That's what everybody says, but it never happens."

* * *

Presley wasn't sure whether the wedding plans were always destined to become something other than simple or whether Miss Eugenia's involvement sent things in a more complicated direction. But the little wedding in Loralee's front yard quickly became a catered affair for two hundred guests.

The Haggerty Baptist Church, anxious to show that there were no hard feelings between them and their former pastor, provided tables and tablecloths. Miss Eugenia borrowed antique crystal vases from all the old folks in town and filled them with flowers from her backyard. And chairs were borrowed from the Haggerty Mortuary.

Cecelia was determined to have an authentic vintage wedding gown that would fit her nearly six-foot frame. She finally found a woman in New Orleans with a tall Creole ancestor who had a dress she was willing to sell. So Cecelia took off for New Orleans, and all the wedding tasks fell to Presley.

Mac was also commandeered. He received endless assignments from Miss Eugenia relating to the venue. He cut grass and trimmed trees. She even asked if he had time to build a cute little bridge across the creek, but he assured her he had neither the time nor the skills for a project of that magnitude.

Mac spent Thursday building a fence around the old house to keep anyone from wandering too close and getting hurt. On Friday he arranged port-a-toilets behind a line of trees while Presley folded napkins and ironed tablecloths and filled little tulle bags with birdseed. Their only peaceful time came at night when they ran around the track at the football stadium and talked about their future.

But on Saturday morning all the effort seemed worthwhile as Cecelia—wearing her incredible vintage gown of slightly yellowed silk and carrying a bouquet of white orchids—walked down the brick walkway in Loralee's front yard toward the rose arbor that arched across the top of the gate. Patrick waited for her there, dressed in a black tuxedo. He wore an orchid on his lapel in honor of his great-great-grandmother Blanche. And most of the bruises on his face had faded to a muted yellow.

Mark Iverson performed the simple ceremony. His daughter, Emily, was the flower girl and his son, Charles, was the ring bearer.

Presley was the maid of honor. Mac and Wyatt shared best man duties.

After the ceremony, the guests walked through the woods to Orchid Cove and ate at the wooden tables and benches that had been re-created to resemble parties held in the old days. The menu had been carefully chosen by Loralee, who had watched those parties from high in the trees. Some guests even took off their shoes and waded in the creek.

Presley was at Miss Eugenia's beck and call and had nearly run herself ragged when Loralee came up beside her.

"Could you take me home?" the elderly woman asked softly. "It's been a busy day, and I'm tired."

"I'd be happy to," Presley assured her. "Just let me tell Mac." She found him lifeguarding by the creek.

"Miss Eugenia says a child can drown in an inch of water, so I can't leave this spot until the guests take their unsupervised children and go home."

Presley laughed. "I guess it's best to put safety first."

"I guess it is when you can assign someone else to stand out in the ninety-degree heat," he muttered.

"I wish I could help you, but Loralee's tired. I'm going to take her back to her cabin."

He nodded and reached out to save a child from falling. "I've already caught him twice," Mac said as he put the child on his feet.

"Keep up the good work." She waved and then hurried off to the side of the house where Loralee was waiting.

Loralee rode her scooter up the path while Presley trotted along beside her back to the cottage. The front yard with its rows of chairs now slightly askew looked deserted and a little sad.

Despite her claims of fatigue, Loralee took a tour around the yard, telling Presley the history of each plant. Finally she stopped by the door and looked up at the house. "It's hard to believe that this cottage has been in this exact same spot for more than a hundred years. People have come and gone, but the cottage is still here."

Presley politely agreed that it was amazing.

Loralee sighed. "Well, I guess we'll go in now." But she looked back out at the yard again as if she hated to leave it behind. "I never know when I'll see it for the last time," she explained. "A hundred years is a long time to love a place."

Presley smiled. "Yes, it is."

Inside the house it was cool and quiet. Loralee stretched out on the bed and motioned for Presley to sit in the chair beside her.

Once Presley was seated, Loralee curled onto her side and gazed out the window. "There's something I need to tell you," she said without taking her eyes from the view outside.

Presley felt a prickling of trepidation.

"Two things, actually," Loralee corrected herself. "One is an apology, and one is a burden."

Presley had to control the urge to groan. Surely she had enough burdens already—her parents' death, Tate's betrayal, the loss of her inheritance . . .

But Loralee was already pressing on. "I'll start with the apology. Part of the story I told you about Miss Blanche and Mr. DuPont was a lie. I'm sorry."

Loralee seemed very upset by this admission, and Presley was quick to reassure her. "It's okay. I don't have to know every detail of their lives."

"You have to know this one. That's the burden. I've carried it for eighty-four years. Now you'll carry it."

Presley was becoming alarmed. "What kind of burden? What are you talking about?"

"To explain, I have to go back to the part of the story when Miss Blanche was expecting a baby for the second time."

Against her better judgment, Presley nodded.

"Miss Blanche seemed so much healthier than she did with Eloise. She got fat and her cheeks turned pink. She sang as we worked together." Loralee smiled slightly at the memory. "She was so looking forward to the new baby. That's all she talked about. And then one day, for no reason, she started cramping. There wasn't time to send for the doctor in Albany."

"She lost her baby?" Presley guessed.

"Yes. And then the grief triggered an asthma attack. It was the worst one she'd ever had, and for a while I thought we were going to lose her. I did everything I could, but my love and my care didn't seem to be enough. It's terrible not to be enough."

Presley just nodded again.

"Then one night a couple of days after the miscarriage, I was sitting in the kitchen, and there was a knock on the back door. I opened it to find Peter Heinrich standing on the step with a little bundle in his arms. I heard a strange mewling sound, and then Peter pulled the cloth back to show me a tiny face."

"A baby?"

Loralee nodded. "Irma's. She didn't even know who the father was. He said his mother had sent the baby to Miss Blanche to replace the one she'd lost."

"Irma agreed to that?"

"No," Loralee said. "But I didn't know that at the time. I found out later when she came and tried to take the baby back."

Presley couldn't control a whimper.

"I know it sounds harsh, but in those days, babies born out of wedlock suffered and so did the girls that had them. Mrs. Heinrich really was trying to do what was best for them both."

Presley couldn't make herself speak.

After a few minutes, Loralee continued. "For the baby's sake, we needed everyone to believe that he was Miss Blanche's natural child. Miss Blanche had been expecting, and now she had a baby. All we had to do was pretend like he came early."

"And promise to keep the secret of his birth for the rest of your life."

"Yes," Loralee acknowledged. "Mr. DuPont made up a false birth certificate. They introduced Eloise to her little brother. Miss Blanche perked up. The baby thrived. The Heinrichs got to see him often. Everyone agreed that it was the perfect solution. Everyone except Irma."

Presley felt suddenly weary. "So who killed her?"

"Peter," Loralee said softly. "He didn't mean to; he was just trying to stop her from taking the baby. She was too far ahead of him, and he knew she'd make it into the house before he could get to her. The gardening tools were on the ground beside the flowerbed. He just grabbed the first thing his hand touched and threw it at her. I saw the whole thing, and I've relived it in my mind at least a million times. If he had grabbed something besides that heavy hammer with those sharp edges. If he'd missed her or hit her in the arm or the leg instead of the head, she might not even have been badly hurt. But . . ." Loralee exhaled heavily. "It was all over in a few minutes. I helped him bury her. Then I hid the hammer in the cellar."

"And Blanche got to keep Irma's baby." Presley couldn't help feeling a little bitter about it all.

Loralee nodded. "I believe Liam saved Miss Blanche's life. *He* was enough."

They sat lost in sad thoughts until Presley broke the silence. "I can't figure out why you said you killed Irma. I thought it was because either Blanche or DuPont was the guilty party. But you must have known that there wasn't enough evidence to prove who killed Irma. So there was no need to protect any of them."

"I wasn't trying to protect Irma's killer," Loralee said.

"Then who?"

"My boys," she whispered. "Blanche's legacy."

And then it all became clear. The cousins—Mac, Wyatt, and Patrick. They were all descendents of Liam, not Eloise. If anyone figured out that Irma was Liam's biological mother, they'd realize that the Armstrongs of Orchid Cove had all been dead for a long time.

Loralee said, "When you got the idea that Irma might have been pregnant, I wanted to send the investigation in another direction. The boys are proud of their family history. I didn't want anyone to take that away from them."

"So it was a distraction tactic," Presley realized. "If everyone was concentrating on you, they weren't looking more closely at Irma and possibly learning about her baby in the process."

Loralee nodded. "It was wrong, but I had to do it."

"To protect the lie you agreed to eighty-four years ago."

"Yes."

"And why are you telling me?"

"In case there's ever a reason that someone would need to know the truth, a medical reason or something. I can't live much longer, and that's why I had to tell you. So someone would know."

Presley turned so she could look out the window and see the view that had been Loralee's for a hundred years. "At least I don't have to wonder what happened to Irma," she muttered. "That's what I get for having a curious nature."

Loralee laughed softly. "I think Miss Blanche would have liked you."

* * *

By the time Mac came to get Presley, Loralee was asleep.

He smiled fondly at the old woman. "She's had a big day."

Presley stood and stretched. "She certainly has."

"Versie will be here soon," he whispered to keep from waking Loralee.

"Let's go outside. Patrick and Cecelia are about to leave, and I know you want to throw birdseed at them."

* * *

It only took an hour to remove all signs that a wedding had taken place at Orchid Cove. The funeral home had collected their chairs, the Baptist church had loaded up their tables, the crystal vases were returned to their owners, and the caterer packed away all the clear glass dishes in crates.

The bride and groom, still dressed in their wedding finery, were standing near the clearing where Cecelia's Porsche was parked. Bedraggled, sunburned wedding guests were lined up, ready to pummel the newlyweds with birdseed.

Mac and Presley took up positions at the end of the line. A horn blew, indicating that the couple could make a run for the car. They dashed between the lines of birdseed-throwers. Cecelia tossed her bouquet of orchids to Presley just as she got in under the wheel.

"Hey, that's not fair!" Kitty Cleckler complained.

Presley ignored this and waved good-bye with the orchids pressed to her chest.

Once the Porsche was out of sight, Mac took Presley's hand and pulled her toward his tow truck. "Now let's get out of here."

* * *

After they ran that night, Presley and Mac discussed their own wedding and ways it would be different and similar to Patrick and Cecelia's. Then they went over plans for the house they would restore. Mac was doing most of the talking, and finally he asked if she wasn't feeling well.

"I'm tired," she told him. "It was a long day."

"But a good one," he said. "I'm happy for Patrick and Cecelia."

"At first I thought *you* liked her," Presley admitted.

"Naw," he said with a smile. "Cecelia always had eyes only for Patrick. And me, well, I was just waiting for you to get here."

CHAPTER TWENTY-TWO

On Sunday morning Presley woke up to the sound of someone knocking on the front door. She groaned and looked at her phone. It wasn't even six o'clock yet. She burrowed her head in the pillow and tried to go back to sleep. But her aunt's voice calling up the stairs put an end to that attempt.

She dragged herself out of bed and walked down to the living room. Her aunt was standing there with Wyatt. Their expressions were solemn, and Presley's heart started to pound. "What is it?" she whispered.

Wyatt stepped forward and put a hand on her shoulder. "I'm sorry, Presley. Loralee didn't wake up this morning."

* * *

It was a small group that gathered that funeral morning at the Rose Lawn Cemetery near Albany, Georgia. The sun shone brightly, but the temperature was mild. A canopy covered the waiting grave to minimize its harsh significance.

The casket was made of natural pine. Aunt Violet said it cost "the earth," but Cecelia insisted on it and paid for it. She said Loralee spent her life surrounded by trees, and she would want the trees to be with her in death as well.

Loralee had on the floral print dress she'd worn to Brother Patrick's Easter sermon. A white orchid in full bloom was pinned to her chest with an antique broach. A picture of Blanche and DuPont Armstrong had been placed in her folded hands.

Darnell and Junior Mobley of the Haggerty Mortuary had set up chairs for the few family members and friends who had been invited to attend. Then they stood at a respectful distance, prepared to offer assistance as needed. Junior blushed every time he saw Presley, and he seemed nervous around Mac. Apparently he didn't know about Mac's lack of success when it came to fighting.

When it was time for the service to begin, Mac and Wyatt sat in chairs on either side of the casket. Patrick stood between them and addressed the gathering.

"Loralee was preceded in death by all of her contemporaries. Her life was full of service and love. From an early age, she was at one with nature, which kept her close to God. She was optimistic and cheerful, even when facing death. And while we know that she didn't wake up here on earth last Sunday morning, I assure you that she did wake up and that she is in a much better place.

"She is with Jesus and with her precious Blanche and DuPont and Eloise and Liam. She's had the chance to meet her mother and has probably made peace with her daddy because we all know Loralee was never one to hold a grudge. Surely she's found Peter, who died fighting for his new country. I like to think that they'll be eternal sweethearts. I'm glad that she is finally at rest. And I know that she will always be with us. We are who we are because of her. She requested that I sing this song, and I ask for your prayers that I can do this last thing for Loralee."

He bowed his head briefly then raised it and sang "Whispering Hope." His voice seemed to fill the cemetery and rise up into the sky above.

Soft as the voice of an angel,
Breathing a lesson unheard,
Hope with a gentle persuasion
Whispers her comforting word:
Wait till the darkness is over,
Wait till the tempest is done,
Hope for the sunshine tomorrow,
After the shower is gone.

Refrain:

Whispering hope, oh how welcome thy voice,
Making my heart in its sorrow rejoice.

If, in the dusk of the twilight,
Dim be the region afar,
Will not the deepening darkness
Brighten the glimmering star?
Then when the night is upon us,
Why should the heart sink away?
When the dark midnight is over,
Watch for the breaking of day.

Refrain

Hope, as an anchor so steadfast,
Rends the dark veil for the soul,
Whither the Master has entered,
Robbing the grave of its goal.
Come then, O come, glad fruition,
Come to my sad weary heart;
Come, O Thou blest hope of glory,
Never, O never depart.

Refrain

When the song was over, Brother Patrick asked everyone to bow their heads for the prayer, but Presley kept her eyes open. She looked at the two fresh graves. The women were buried at almost the same time although they died eighty-four years apart. Irma had died too young, and Loralee had lived too long. And now Presley felt a kinship with both of them. In their own way, they each gave life to Liam. And from him came the three cousins. She loved their boys, and she was the keeper of their secrets.

She looked at Patrick with his head bowed in prayer. Wyatt was looking off into the distance, probably thinking about a big case at work or a girl he wanted to date. Then her eyes moved to Mac, who had come to mean everything to her. His head was bowed too, in respect if not exactly reverence. The sunlight shone on his auburn hair, and she could see golden highlights—maybe a gift from the German ancestry he didn't even know he had.

He felt her gaze on him and looked up long enough to wink. Then he squeezed his eyes closed again.

After the service was over, the guests paid their respects to the cousins, and gradually everyone headed to Aunt Violet's house, where a brunch was being provided by the Haggerty Baptist Church Women's Auxiliary.

Mac told his cousins that he and Presley wanted to stay for a while. Once everyone was gone, the couple stood back and watched while the grave was filled. Presley thought it would be a sad moment when the dirt started to cover the beautiful wooden coffin. But Patrick had painted the picture of Loralee in heaven so well that she didn't even briefly consider this spot the old woman's true final resting place.

When the Mobleys and the cemetery workers were gone, Mac and Presley stood by the grave in peace.

Earlier Presley had made up her mind to tell Mac the truth. She felt like it was a bad idea to begin what she hoped would be a lifelong relationship with a lie between them. But as she stood there beside the freshly turned earth on Loralee's grave, she wavered. Clutching his hand she asked, "How do you feel about secrets?"

"It depends on what kind of secret," he replied. "We established that first day you came to Haggerty that girls are entitled to a few. So as long as it doesn't hurt anyone . . ." He shrugged. "I'm okay with a secret or two."

He had made the decision for her then. She would keep Loralee's secret—at least for now.

Holding her fingers tightly, he said, "It seems funny to stand here in front of the people who started it all—DuPont, Blanche, even Loralee. They were a lot like us. They didn't have much of anything when they began their lives together."

"Except Orchid Cove," she said.

He nodded. "They had their struggles and problems, but they loved each other and they loved Orchid Cove. So they were happy."

"Yes," she agreed. "And we'll be happy too, no matter what struggles we face."

He turned and pulled her into his arms. "Does this mean you'll come to all the football games at Rock Creek High School?"

She hung her head. "Yes. Even though that proves I have no moral fiber. I really am opposed to all violent sports—especially football—yet I'll be in the stands every Friday night this fall, screaming like a banshee. How can you love me now that you know I've abandoned my principles so easily?"

"I'll love you forever, no matter what."

She frowned. "Do you mind putting that in writing?"

"I don't mind at all. You'll have a legally binding agreement when we sign our marriage license. Is there anything else you want while I'm in this magnanimous mood?"

"I want you to stop repossessing things so you won't get beat up continuously. And I guess you'd better teach me about football so I don't scream for the wrong team."

"I will happily agree to both conditions—if you'll give me a kiss."

She looked around. "Right here in front of all your dead relatives?"

"Right here," he confirmed.

She moved into his arms. "I guess they can't complain if they're offended."

"Soon they will be your relatives too." He pressed his lips to hers. "And I'm sure none of them want to complain about that." He gave her another quick kiss.

Then they walked away from the Amrstrong section of the cemetery with their hands clasped together and their hearts set on the future.

ABOUT THE AUTHOR

BETSY BRANNON GREEN CURRENTLY LIVES in Bessemer, Alabama (a suburb of Birmingham). She has been married to her husband, Butch, for thirty-six wonderful years. They have eight children, two daughters-in-law, three sons-in-law, and sixteen grandchildren. She is currently the Gospel Doctrine teacher in the Ensley Branch. She loves to read, when she can find the time, and enjoys sporting events—especially if they involve her children or grandchildren. Although born in Salt Lake City, Betsy has spent most of her life in the South. Her life and her writing have been strongly influenced by the town of Headland, Alabama, and the many generous, gracious people who live there, especially her ninety-six-year-old grandmother, Grace Vann Brannon. Her first book, *Hearts in Hiding*, was published in 2001. *Puzzle Pieces* is her twentieth LDS fiction novel.